SAINTS AND SINNERS

Contact info: authoralyssagreen@gmail.com

Cover Design | Book Design and Typesetting: Green Spark Publishing
Conceptual Editor: Kasey LeAlma
Line Editor: Lana Staux
Copy Editor: Natalia Leigh, Enchanted Ink Publishing
Proofreader: Brittany Riley
Character Art: TL Combs

ISBN: 978-1-963126-12-9 (E-book)
ISBN: 978-1-963126-13-6 (Paperback)
ISBN: 978-1-963126-15-0 (Hardback)
ISBN: 978-1-963126-16-7 (Barnes and Noble Paperback)
ISBN: 978-1-963126-17-4 (Barnes and Noble Hardback)

First Edition: February 2026
Published by Green Spark Publishing
Thank you for the support of the author's rights.

Printed in the United States of America

SAINTS AND SINNERS

Alyssa Green

For everyone who has religious trauma.

CONTENT WARNING

This story contains themes and content that may be upsetting or triggering for some readers. Please be advised that the following sensitive topics are depicted:

- **Religious Guilt:** Characters struggle with their faith and question long-held beliefs and religious doctrine.
- **Sexual Content:** Explicit descriptions of intimacy and sex, and discussions of sexuality, including within a religious context.
- **Infidelity:** References to emotional betrayal and temptation within relationships.
- **Alcohol Abuse:** A character copes with trauma by engaging in nonviolent, excessive drinking.
- **Grief and Loss:** A character grapples with the aftermath of a loved one's tragic death.
- **Emotional Manipulation:** Emotional tension between characters, including moments of manipulation related to faith and relationships.
- **Judgment from Religious Community:** Characters face judgment and exclusion due to their personal beliefs.
- **Suicide Attempt/Self-Harm Ideation:** Includes a detailed scene of being found after a suicide attempt, and there are multiple references to a character's history of self-harm.

Please take care while reading and step away if these topics become overwhelming. Your mental and emotional well-being are important.

AUTHOR'S NOTE

Writing this story has been part of my own journey with religious trauma and healing—a slow, messy process of unlearning and questioning the doctrines and expectations that I once accepted without hesitation. Somewhere along the way, I discovered that faith and freedom don't have to be opposites. It's possible to honor beliefs without feeling confined by them, and this story is my tribute to that balance. It's for anyone who has felt caught between devotion and self-discovery—between tradition and the pull to live authentically.

Of course, this is also a love story—a spicy one—between a priest and a nun who find themselves on that same fragile line between faith and desire. Thank you for stepping into Damian and Claire's world and sharing in their journey.

—Alyssa Green

The fluorescent lights of the emergency room cast harsh shadows across the waiting area as I paced back and forth, my footsteps echoing against the linoleum floor. My girlfriend, Claire, sat hunched in one of the plastic chairs, her face pale, fingers tangled in the rosary beads she always carried. She'd been at my house studying when we got the call about my brother. Now, every few seconds, her eyes would dart between me and the clock mounted high on the sterile white wall—11:11 p.m.

It was spring break; Rico and I had come home from college. I'd promised to be his designated driver. Had sworn that I'd pick his drunk ass up, no questions asked, whenever he texted. But I'd gotten lost in Claire, in the honeyed taste of her lips and the sensation of her fingertips tracing patterns on my skin as we lay tangled on my parents' couch. Time had slipped away, my phone buried somewhere beneath the cushions, forgotten in a haze of desire. My brother had texted—once, twice, three times.

Rico is—was—destined to become a priest.

The memory of his last text clawed at my chest like an angry demon. The words were seared into my brain with excruciating clarity.

RICO

It's cool. Don't worry about it.

Four simple words that would haunt me for the rest of my life. I could picture him typing them, his familiar half smile on his face, shaking his head at his little brother's unreliability.

Rico had started walking home on a stretch of road with no sidewalk. Just a narrow shoulder barely illuminated by the occasional streetlight. The driver didn't even bother to stop, leaving him bloody, broken, and alone in the darkness. Some faceless coward who couldn't be bothered to face what they'd done. A truck driver had spotted him on the side of the road minutes later. Thank God they'd stopped and called an ambulance. At least my brother hadn't died alone in a ditch because of my irresponsibility.

"Dami—" My mother's voice cracked as she grabbed my arm, halting my pacing. Her fingers dug into my skin with desperate strength, her wedding ring cold against my flesh. "Everything's going to be okay, right?"

I tried to speak—to offer some comfort—but my throat closed up. Antiseptic burned my nostrils and mixed with the icy regret in my chest.

"He was laughing just this morning," Mom said, her voice distant. "Sitting at the breakfast table, talking about going to seminary school, stealing your bacon like he always does. He was so excited to lead people to the faith . . ." She pressed her hand to her mouth.

Dad stood by the window, his reflection a ghost in the darkness. He hadn't moved since they'd wheeled Rico through those doors. "Another broken promise, Damian," he muttered.

He was right. I'd broken countless promises in my young life.

The double doors at the end of the hall swung open. A man in blue scrubs approached us, his tan face grave. My stomach dropped. I recognized that look. Had seen enough medical shows to know what it meant. *No. Please, God, no.*

"Mr. and Mrs. Bellucci?" he asked, his voice gentle, dark circles rimming his eyes. "I'm Dr. Martinez. I've been tending to your son."

My mother let go of my arm and stepped toward him, her own rosary beads clacking together as she moved. Dad only turned, leaning back against the window, his face a mask of stone.

"Our son?" Mom's voice quivered. "How is he? Can we see him?"

The doctor glanced at each of us in turn, his expression softening with practiced sympathy. He pulled over a nearby chair, the metal legs scraping against the polished floor, and sat, his shoulders drooping. With an open palm, he gestured to the empty row of seats. "Please," he said quietly.

My father moved first, his normally confident stride reduced to mechanical steps. He guided my mother with a trembling hand at the small of her back. She lowered herself with painful slowness, her knuckles white as she clutched her purse in her lap. The vinyl seat creaked under Dad's weight as he settled beside her, his spine rigid, jaw working silently.

That small gesture—the doctor wanting them to sit—made my legs go weak. My stomach hollowed out like a grave. I remained standing for a heartbeat too long, unable to make my body cooperate.

Bad news is always delivered sitting down.

With numb limbs, I finally fell into the chair beside my mother, the plastic cold and unyielding beneath me. Claire slumped into the seat next to me.

Dr. Martinez began, "When Enrico was brought in, he had sustained massive trauma from the impact. We took him straight to surgery and did what we could." He paused, allowing the words to sink in.

Stop speaking in the past tense.

"The damage was . . ." he hesitated.

"But he's okay?" Mom asked, her grip on Dad's hand tightening. "He's strong, my Rico. He's always been so strong."

The surgeon's eyes filled with genuine sympathy. "I'm so very sorry. But the injuries were too severe. Your son didn't make it."

I watched the exact moment my mother's world shattered—the way her face crumpled and her shoulders slumped. For a split second, the world was absolutely silent, like the universe itself was holding its breath.

"No," she wailed, clawing at my dad's shirt. "Not my baby. Not my Rico."

He held my mom, his own tears falling. Claire sat frozen, silent tears streaming down her face. She focused on the doctor, as if staring hard enough might make him take back those words.

"Dad?" I pleaded, my voice breaking. He didn't respond. Didn't blink.

Dr. Martinez was still talking, something about arrangements and paperwork, but his words faded into white noise. All I could focus on was my mother's grief-stricken sobs and my father's deafening stoicism.

Mom continued to weep in Dad's arms, her pain so raw and visceral it made my own heart splinter.

"Dad, please," I tried again, desperate for him to say anything. But he remained frozen, locked in whatever private hell he'd retreated to.

In that hospital waiting room, isolation crushed me. My chest caved inward, each breath burning through constricted lungs as reality sank in.

Rico is gone. My brother is gone.

Claire reached for my hand, but I pulled away. I couldn't look at her—couldn't bear to see my own raw anguish mirrored in her eyes. Not when I'd broken the promise for her.

THE WALK FROM RICO'S GRAVE TO SAINT ANTHONY'S WAS MUSCLE MEMORY, A path I'd taken daily for the past three months since his funeral. Each step was weighted with the hope that somehow it would lead me to answers. To peace. To anything that might fill this emptiness. The God I'd grown up believing in—the one Rico had taught me about during late-night talks about destiny and purpose—seemed to have vanished the night we lost him.

The church stood silent and dark against the evening sky, its stained glass windows dulled by the fading light. I slipped inside, the heavy wooden door groaning shut behind me. Incense drifted through the sanctuary from evening Mass. In front of the tabernacle on the right of the altar, candles flickered, casting eerie shadows on the stone walls.

I hadn't planned to come here tonight. After another dinner spent watching Mom push food around her plate, tears streaming down her face, while Dad retreated to his study without a word, I couldn't stay in that house. I couldn't breathe in the suffocating silence that had replaced my brother's presence.

Where was God when Rico needed Him?

What kind of loving Father would let this happen?

What kind of brother forgets his promises?

If I had just paid attention to my phone, he'd still be alive.

My steps echoed in the vast quiet of the church as I made my way down the center aisle. The crucifix loomed above the altar, towering and still—its presence unwavering. Christ's gaze seemed to follow me, his face etched in pain, expressing a grief that couldn't be put into words.

I reached the front pew and sank to my knees, the hard wooden bench pressing against my shins. My fingers curled tight around the edge of the pew rail in front of me, knuckles blanching. I bowed my head, praying for Him to tell me what to do.

The silence surrounded me, heavy and unyielding. No burning bush. Nothing.

"What should I do, Lord?" I asked, voice echoing back to me from the dim sanctuary. "Rico was the one meant for this life, not me. He was the faithful one, the worthy one."

What would Mom and Dad want me to do? Should I hunt down the driver who stole my brother's future? Sacrifice my own? I would gladly take his place if I could.

"Give me something," I demanded, anger seeping into my prayer. "Anything."

The crucifix stared back, unmoved by my desperation, while Rico's absence screamed louder than any answer God might have offered. Rico had talked about seminary school the morning before he died. His eyes had lit up as he explained how serving God meant helping others find their faith.

Claire had been trying to call ever since. But I'd let it go to voicemail, like I had for weeks now. How could I talk to her when I could barely speak to my own family? How could I explain that every time I looked at her, I saw everything Rico would never have—no future, love, just the confines of a coffin? How could I deserve those things when my carelessness had robbed him of them all? How could I have been such an idiot and miss his messages?

I pulled out my phone, scrolling to my saved voicemails. My thumb hovered over Rico's name. I hadn't listened to it since the night before the funeral, but somehow, pressing play felt like the closest thing to prayer I could manage right now.

"Hey, Dami." Rico's voice filled the emptiness, vibrant and alive. "Just checking if we're still on for Mass this Sunday? Father Collins mentioned they need more altar servers, and I told him my pain-in-the-ass brother might be interested." His laugh echoed through the sanctuary. "I know you've been kinda distant about church stuff lately, but . . . I don't know. There's something about faith that brings me peace. Like I'm part of a bigger purpose, you know? Maybe you'd feel it too if you gave it a chance." A pause. "Anyway, call me back. Love you, bro."

The message ended, but I kept the phone pressed to my ear, like I might hear more if I listened hard enough. I pressed play again.

I tilted my gaze to Jesus on the cross. "Mom doesn't talk anymore. She's transformed into a shell of who she used to be. Dad might as well be gone too. It's like they lost both of us. But I'm still here, walking around like a ghost they don't want to see."

I closed my eyes, memories flooding my mind: Rico and me as kids playing in the backyard. Him teaching me to throw a baseball, patient even when my aim sucked. The pride in his voice when he told everyone at church that his little brother was going to UC Berkeley.

"I should've been there . . ." A sob caught in my throat. I hadn't cried since the funeral, but in the empty church, all the buried grief and anger I'd been holding back came rushing forward. "What am I supposed to do?" I whispered, tears streaming down my face.

A beam of moonlight broke through one of the stained glass panes, casting vivid colors across the altar. The light shifted and danced, almost as if it were reaching for me.

In that moment, the tightness in my chest eased, replaced by warmth. It wasn't happiness—I wasn't sure I'd ever feel that again—but it was . . . purpose. Direction.

"Is this what You want from me?" I asked, my voice steadier now.

Priesthood? A life dedicated to God, to His people, to service. To offer Him more than my own pain. A life without the things I'd wanted, the career I'd dreamed of, the future I'd planned with Claire. A sacrifice to balance what my mistake had cost Rico.

My penance.

"If I give my life to You, would it help? Will Mom smile again? Will Dad *see* me? Will You forgive me for what I've done?"

I stared at the flickering candles in front of the tabernacle, watching the flames stretch and bend. My hands clenched the wood in front of me. Pain shot through me, grounding. Comforting.

What did I expect? If I knelt here long enough, I'd feel a change? That this anchor weighing on me, drowning me, would somehow release me?

"Make it more than anger and regret," I said, wiping my tears away with the hem of my tee. "Make it atonement."

Moonlight shifted again, and for a brief moment, the colored light seemed to wrap around me like an embrace. Like benediction. Like acceptance of my offer.

"Fine. I'll do it. I'll give *You* everything. My dreams. My heart. All of it. Just help me make this right."

I stayed there until the light faded, until my knees ached from the hard wood beneath them. And when I finally stood, my decision was made. Dedicate my life to finding a way to make all of this mean something, even though I was giving up my future with Claire and the person I could have been. Maybe this was how I could save what was left of my family. I would become a priest.

Maybe this is how I pay for my sins.

A WEEK AFTER MY REVELATION IN THE CHURCH, I FOUND MYSELF STANDING IN front of Claire's parents' house. The night pressed against me, a salt breeze carrying the bite of autumn and the scent of impending rain. My fingers tangled in my hair again, greasy from running my hands

THROUGH IT ALL EVENING WHILE I'D PACED MY ROOM, REHEARSING THIS moment until the words tasted like ash in my mouth.

My throat closed up. How many times had we sat in my truck, sharing glazed donuts and mapping out our lives? College. Marriage. The little craftsman with the blue door she'd circled in a magazine. Kids—two boys and a girl, she'd always said, her eyes lighting up when she talked about them. The memory rushed to the surface, so vivid I could almost hear her laugh, threatening to crack my resolve. But I couldn't falter—not when I'd finally gathered the courage to do what needed to be done.

Claire stood beneath the flickering streetlight, a thin cardigan pulled tight around her shoulders against the chill. Her gray eyes fixed on me—eyes that used to make me believe anything was possible. Now they just reminded me of everything I couldn't be for her.

Behind her, the house was dark and quiet, her parents already asleep. In a few minutes, their daughter's heart would be shattered, and they wouldn't know until morning.

She felt further away with each passing second, though she hadn't moved. Or maybe I was the one drifting, untethered since Rico's death and searching for a sanctuary I couldn't find. Not even in her. I couldn't keep pretending I was still the guy she'd fallen in love with. That guy died in the hospital waiting room with his brother, leaving behind this hollow shell who couldn't feel anything but pain and regret.

Part of me wanted to run. To get in my truck and drive until the ocean swallowed the sun. But I'd made my choice.

"I can't do this anymore." The words tumbled out before I could stop them. "I can't keep pretending I'm fine."

She blinked, her eyes widening, confusion clouding her face. She took a hesitant step toward me, her voice trembling. "What do you mean? I'm here for you. I've been here for you. We can work through this."

Her words should've been what I needed, should've given me hope, but all I felt was the pain I'd let consume me. I shook my head, my jaw tight, a coldness seeping into my voice even though my heart was breaking. "No. You can't fix this. I need to leave. Need to get away from all of this. Away from you."

She stepped back. "What're you saying, Dames?" Her voice cracked on my nickname, and deep inside, my chest splintered.

I closed my eyes for a brief second, fighting the urge to pull her close and take it all back. My hands trembled, and I shoved them into my pockets so she couldn't see. But I couldn't. I wouldn't. The force of my hurricane of emotions was too much. I couldn't stay. "I need something more. More than you. More than this life we've been talking about. I need a purpose."

Her breath hitched, tears welling in her eyes. "I thought that was our future," she said, her voice just above a whisper. "We were going to build a life together."

Her words hung in the silence between us. Each one constricted my chest until I could barely breathe. I dug my nails into my palms, focusing on the sharp sting instead of the sorrow on her face. The words I'd been fighting spilled out—not because they were true, but because it would make her finally let me go.

"I don't want that anymore." Bitterness coated every word. "I don't know who I am anymore, and I don't know if I ever did."

Claire flinched as if I'd slapped her. Her tears spilled down her cheeks, reflecting the harsh streetlight, and I hated myself in that moment more than I ever thought possible. Her shoulders slumped, the fight leaving her. She stared at me like she didn't recognize me either.

The breeze picked up, rustling the leaves in the trees lining the street. A car passed somewhere in the distance. But all I could hear was my broken heart pounding in my ears and the soft hitched sound of her crying.

She didn't say anything more. She didn't need to. The look in her beautiful eyes said it all—betrayal, hurt, confusion. It was a look I would never forget.

Without another word, I turned, opened the truck door, and got in. As I drove away, I glanced in the rearview mirror one last time. Claire was still standing on the sidewalk, staring after me, her face illuminated by the streetlight, one hand half raised like she was reaching for me.

I gripped the steering wheel so hard my knuckles turned white. I wanted to unsay the words, to slam on the brakes and run back to her. It was too late. I'd fucked up whatever was left between us. Permanently. But the priesthood was my only purpose.

Chapter One

DAMIAN

Eight Years Later

My routine had remained unchanged since my first day at Saint Anthony's. The darkness of early morning held its own kind of holiness. I'd been here since 5 a.m., a daily reminder of all those ancient leaders who sought God in the deserts while the rest of the world rested. These moments before dawn were sacred to me.

The stained glass was beginning to cast jeweled patterns across the altar as I knelt in the empty sanctuary. First, the Divine Office with its ancient rhythms, then my personal devotions, and finally, my time of unstructured prayer, where I simply knelt, waiting for God to speak. My morning prayers rose with the dust motes dancing in the colored light. Just God and me in the silence before the din of the world intruded with its endless needs and self-inflicted suffering.

"In Your light we see light," I whispered, the psalm settling in my chest, offering me comfort.

My fingers traced the worn wooden beads of the rosary Rico had given me for my sixteenth birthday. The smooth surface, polished by years of prayer, connected me to my brother in a way that transcended his absence. I wrapped the beads around my wrist as I stood, the gentle pressure a reassuring touch against my skin.

The sunrise had fully transformed the sanctuary, painting the walls and pews in vivid colors. The crucifix above the altar caught the light, shadows emphasizing Christ's agonized face. I studied it, as I did every morning, searching for some new understanding within those carved features.

I was content to belong here. Being Father Bellucci instead of just Damian, the lost boy seeking penance after his brother's death, was better than living without a purpose. The weight of the vestments was only a fraction of the weight of my vows. The rhythm of the liturgical calendar ordered my days with meaning. My parishioners—their trust, their faith, their reliance on my guidance—gave shape to a calling I'd never expected to have, but now I couldn't imagine my life without them.

And yet . . .

I stood and moved to the sacristy, my footsteps echoing against the stone floor as I approached the ornate cabinet where the sacred vessels were kept. *"In nomine Patris, et Filii, et Spiritus Sancti,"* I whispered, crossing myself before inserting the brass key. The cool metal against my fingertips grounded me in the solemn ritual that had been performed by thousands of priests before me.

Every movement, gesture, and preparation was prescribed by centuries of tradition. Each act connected me to the divine. I breathed in the lingering fragrance of frankincense and myrrh that clung to the air, mingling with the pure aroma of beeswax candles.

With reverent hands, I withdrew the chalice, holding it briefly at eye level in silent veneration before placing it upon the purificator. Next came the paten, the ciborium, and finally, the Roman Missal, which I positioned on its stand with careful precision. *"Domine, non sum dignus,"* I murmured, the ancient Latin flowing from my lips as naturally as breath.

I moved to prepare the altar for morning Mass, first laying the pristine corporal cloth in the center, aligning its edges with mathematical exactness. My fingers traced the intricate embroidered cross on the green chasuble as I lifted it from its drawer. *Tempus Ordinarium*—Ordinary Time in the liturgical calendar. There was nothing ordinary about the hollow space that sometimes opened inside me during private prayer—a void that neither the Liturgy of the Hours nor the Eucharistic sacrifice seemed able to fill.

As I vested, each garment became a silent prayer: The amice around my neck. *Lord, set the helmet of salvation on my head to fend off all the assaults of the devil.* The alb flowing to my feet. *Purify me, Lord, and cleanse my heart so that, washed in the Blood of the Lamb, I may enjoy eternal bliss.* The cincture at my waist. *Lord, gird me with the cincture of purity and extinguish my fleshly desires, that the virtue of continence and chastity may abide within me.* And finally, the stole and chasuble, transforming me from man to vessel—from Damian to Father Bellucci, servant to the servants of God.

Like a shadow at the periphery of my soul, the emptiness had no name. No clear shape. Impossible to see directly but undeniably there. I'd first noticed it about six months ago, during a men's retreat. While other priests spoke of profound spiritual experiences, I'd encountered only this unsettling sense of something missing, a note in the chord that should have been there but instead was muted.

"God is love, and His love is eternal," I reminded myself. My seminary professors had warned about the moments of spiritual dryness that came to even the most devout. "The saints themselves experienced the dark night of the soul."

I ran my fingers over the communion hosts, counting enough for the morning congregation. Wednesday Mass usually brought about thirty parishioners—mostly retirees and a few working people who made the effort to come before their day began. I knew their faces, their particular ways of receiving communion, and even the pews they preferred.

Serving them brought me joy. Real, genuine joy.

So, why does this hollow feeling persist?

"This isn't darkness," I murmured to myself, placing the wine and water cruets beside the chalice. "This is just . . . life."

Everything was technically correct but somehow missing the essence. Like speaking words in a language I'd studied for years while never having lived among its native speakers. Like reciting poetry without understanding the metaphors.

I shook my head, pushing the thoughts away. I didn't need to deepen the sensation by dwelling. Better to lose myself in the concrete needs of my parish. The mystery of this emptiness could wait.

"Good morning, Father," Mrs. Walker said, her cheerful voice breaking through my contemplation as she bustled in with fresh flowers. Her gray hair was neatly pinned back, and she carried white lilies that filled the air with heavy perfume. At seventy-eight, she moved with the energy of someone twenty years younger. Her faithfulness to her church duties was as reliable as the tides.

"Morning, Mrs. Walker." I smiled at her, grateful for the interruption of my circular thoughts. "Beautiful bouquet."

"From my garden," she said, arranging them in a vase near the altar. Her hands moved with practiced precision, placing each stem with artistic care. "The good Lord blessed me with a green thumb, though my knees aren't what they used to be for all that gardening."

I watched her work, admiring her dedication. Mrs. Walker had been widowed for fifteen years but never seemed to lose her joy. She lived alone in the small house she'd shared with her husband for forty years, tending her garden and serving the church with equal devotion.

What is her secret to finding such contentment?

"Before I forget to mention it," she continued, adjusting a lily that seemed determined to flop to one side, "Bishop Valenti called to say we're getting a new director of religious education tomorrow. A nun from the Sisters of Divine Light."

"Really?" I adjusted the missal, making sure the ribbons marked the correct readings for the day. "Did he say who they're sending?"

"Not by name. Just that she's young but highly qualified. Apparently, she grew up in this area." Mrs. Walker stepped back to examine her handiwork, nodding with satisfaction. "It'll be good to have that position filled properly. The temporary arrangements have been . . . less than ideal."

I nodded, a weight lifting from my chest. Another nun to work with wasn't exactly exciting news, but at least it would help distribute some of the administrative duties that had been piling up since Sister Josephine had retired six months ago. I'd been covering many of those responsibilities myself, stretching my days even thinner. It had gotten so busy that Mrs. Walker had volunteered some of her time to help.

"That's good news. The position's been vacant too long," I said, returning my attention to the altar preparations. "That role needs consistent leadership."

"Indeed, Father." Mrs. Walker gathered her empty basket, patting my arm as she passed. "The children deserve better than substitutes and temporary solutions. Speaking of which, little Tommy Rodriguez asked if you're still taking them for ice cream after tonight's youth group."

I smiled. "Tell him I haven't forgotten. But only if he brings his math homework to show me his progress."

She chuckled. "I'll pass that along." Halfway to the door, she paused. "Oh, and don't forget the parish council has moved tonight's meeting to seven instead of six thirty."

"Duly noted."

When Mrs. Walker finally left to prepare the lectionary, I continued setting up. Maybe a new staff member was exactly what this parish needed—fresh energy, new perspectives.

The sound of early arrivals filtered in from the vestibule: Mr. Lionel's distinctive cough, the tap of Mrs. Garcia's cane against the marble floor. I straightened the altar cloth one final time, making sure every fold fell perfectly. In a few minutes, I would stand before these faithful souls and lead them in the Mysteries of Our Faith. The thought filled me with both humility and dedication.

I moved through the last of my preparations, yet that persistent hollow feeling remained, like an essential part of me was just out of reach.

The morning light shifted from gold to the clear white of day. It illuminated the altar, the crucifix, the waiting pews. It all appeared so ordinary and yet so sacred at once. This paradox was at the heart of our faith—finding the divine in the mundane, the extraordinary within the routine.

"Lord, You are enough," I whispered, the words both affirmation and question. "Help me find contentment in Your presence alone."

The prayer felt simultaneously honest and incomplete, as if I was asking without knowing exactly what I needed. But wasn't that often how prayer worked? Bringing our confused longings to God and trusting Him to sort out what we truly required?

I headed to the back of the sanctuary and walked in procession to the altar. Minutes later, the sound of the opening hymn rose around me. I couldn't shake the feeling that whatever unnamed absence I'd been sensing lately was about to become clearer, though I had no idea why that thought suddenly crossed my mind.

"Yes, I know what plans I have in mind for you, Yahweh declares,
plans for peace, not for disaster, to give you a future and a hope."
—Jeremiah 29:11 (New Jerusalem Bible)

Chapter Two

CLAIRE

I t had been years since I'd seen Carmel, California—the place I'd grown up and where I'd been molded and broken in equal measure. The hum of the car's engine seemed louder than usual as I navigated the winding Pacific Coast Highway. I never imagined I'd return swathed in modest black and white, but sometimes God's GPS takes the most unexpected detours.

After all these years, it was still timeless. The coastline's azure hues stretched out to the horizon, the noontime sun framing it in golden rays and bathing the cliffs in warm light. Waves crashed beneath swooping seagulls like nothing in this corner of the world had changed.

Except for me. A walking existential crisis, now with religious gravitas.

My new assignment meant a change in routine. Morning prayers at 5 a.m. with the strict rhythm of devotions marking every hour. Lauds at dawn, Prime in early morning, Terce at midmorning, kneeling until my knees ached through the Divine Office seven times a day. Sext at noon, None in the afternoon, Vespers at sunset, and Compline before bed.

Sext at noon. I snorted. Someone in the early Church must've had an affinity for Afternoon Delight.

Saint Anthony's parish wasn't just going to be my new home; it was going to be a resurrection of my past. I thought I'd escaped all this small town represented—its narrow expectations, the relentless rules, and all those judgmental eyes. Never in a million years would I have expected to return wearing a veil. Once, I had hoped to wear a white one, not one of black meant to reflect a life of absolute devotion to God.

To be honest, becoming a nun hadn't exactly been my plan. If anyone had told twenty-one-year-old party-girl me that I'd one day take vows of celibacy and service, I would've laughed in their face. Before, my life had been about freedom. Exploring every boundary I could find and pushing it until it broke. And God knew I'd broken plenty. My parents had watched helplessly as I spiraled, their disappointed sighs a soundtrack to my rebellion. While my sister, Jasmine, had fought for acceptance in her own quiet way after coming out, I'd fought against everything—especially myself.

After years of living carelessly, chasing highs that never lasted, it happened. At twenty-five, the "call" came. It wasn't some booming voice from the heavens or a blinding light. It was whispers in my darkest moments.

I was twenty-one when my life started falling apart—after Damian lost his brother and abandoned me. But then Jasmine came home one night, tears streaming down her face after coming out to the parish priest.

"They won't let me take Communion anymore," she'd whispered. "Father Constantine said I need to 'pray away' my feelings for Tina."

My parents had just stood there, silent and uncertain, while the Church I'd grown up in wounded my sister in ways that left invisible scars.

That was the first time I reached for a blade, vowing to carry them for her.

I'd spent countless nights alone, and when everything else spun out of control, at least I was in control of the sharp sting that brought clarity and focus. I'd hoped the pain would anchor me, give shape to the demons swirling inside, and make sense of the screaming thoughts I couldn't quiet.

It wasn't peace. It was a punishment I could meter upon myself for not changing what seemed unchangeable to protect her. For not protecting love. For not being . . . enough.

The relief was fleeting, streaming down my thighs and leaving me emptier than before.

Then the police announced they were going to stop looking for Rico's murderer. Just like that. Case closed. Filed under "unsolved."

That was the night I'd lost all hope. In the hospital, slumped in a cold plastic chair, thigh bandaged, I'd met Sister Agnes. She didn't preach at me or try to save my soul. She just sat with me, hour after hour, throughout the endless night.

"God doesn't need you to be perfect," she'd said, her weathered hand covering mine. "He just needs you to be present."

Her calm certainty reached a part of me nothing else had touched. Where I'd found only emptiness in chaos, she'd found boundless meaning in surrender.

After that, I'd started volunteering at St. Catherine's shelter. Standing in the soup kitchen on Christmas Eve, ladling stew for people whose hope had long since vanished, I felt it—a wave of purpose washing over me, clear and powerful. For the first time, the endless noise in my head had quieted. This was where I needed to be . . . Helping others.

Mother Superior pulled me aside one evening. "You fight yourself with the same passion you could give to God," she'd said. "What if you directed all that fire toward something greater?"

Something greater. Like reform. I could make a difference in the Church for all these people.

I'd chosen to take temporary vows three years ago. A trial period. Time to discern whether this life was for me. The physical discipline of prayer—the kneeling, the genuflecting, the hours of contemplation—offered me a different way to inhabit my body. The scars on my thighs faded as my knees calloused. Now, in my final year, it would all come to a head. I was supposed to make a choice: take my perpetual vows and fully commit to being a nun or walk away.

The pressure had been building for months, like a shaken-up soda can ready to pop. Mother Superior, Sister Agnes, everyone expected me to continue wearing this habit, but the closer I got to the decision, the more uncertainty reared its ugly head.

Sister Agnes wrote to me monthly, her letters a gentle reminder of that night that had changed my entire life and the promise she saw in me that I sometimes still struggled to see in myself.

I'd be lying if I said I didn't think about what I'd be giving up. Not the obvious things—sex, intimacy, marriage—but an entire future I would never know.

Late at night, when the convent was quiet and it was just me, God, and my thoughts, I wondered if I was ready to close those doors . . . forever. Was the peace I'd found within structured walls and ancient rituals strong enough to sustain me for a lifetime? Or was I just trading one extreme for another—the wild rebellion of my youth for the strict discipline of religious life?

But there were things within the Church that needed to change. Namely, the outdated traditions that felt more like shackles than guidance. How they treated people like my sister, Jasmine.

They clung to the old, rigid beliefs about love, marriage, and sex. It was suffocating sometimes. How could a place that was supposed to embody love be so restrictive of it? I was looking forward to being the new director of religious education at Saint Anthony's parish school. Part of me—maybe the biggest part—had come back with a purpose that went beyond teaching.

I wanted to change things from the inside, to make sure no one else felt the rejection Jasmine had experienced in those very walls. To create a space where love, in all its forms, could be celebrated, not condemned. And yet, despite all the contradictions, I couldn't deny the way my heart settled when I was in prayer or teaching others about faith.

The bell tower rose against the horizon, its white stone almost glowing in the afternoon light. With its brick facade and large arched windows, the school building itself had a cozy academic feel.

With late August settling in, there was already that back-to-school energy in the air, that mix of anticipation and possibility that came with every new academic year. Soon the halls would be filled with the shuffle of students finding their way, slamming lockers, and nervous, angsty energy. A sense of eagerness flowed through me at the thought of stepping in front of a classroom again, breathing life into the stories of the saints and showing these kids that faith wasn't a series of rules, but that it could lift them up when the world got too heavy.

The parking lot of Saint Anthony's was built at the center of everything; the school, the church, the rectory, and the hall all surrounded it like a small interconnected village. It hadn't changed much since I was a kid walking past on my way to the beach.

I parked along the edge of the church's lot. The view opened up over the cliffside, and the land dropped steeply into the rolling blue waves below.

As soon as I opened the car door, the ocean breeze rushed to greet me. It carried the scent of seaweed and the faint briny tang of the tide, embracing me like an old friend, yet it also brought a bittersweet pang to my heart.

I let the door swing shut with a quiet thud. The wind lifted a few strands of hair from beneath my veil, and I didn't bother tucking them back. God made the wind too, right? The Almighty probably wasn't losing sleep over my slightly disheveled appearance.

This place had always been a refuge. A sanctuary in every sense of the word. It had a way of reminding me how small I was in the grand scheme of things. How my problems were just tiny droplets in God's vast ocean.

It felt good to be back. Different, but good. Every decision I'd made had led me here, to this moment in time.

I was about to head toward the church, and then I heard *him*—the one voice I'd *never* expected to hear.

"Claire? What are you doing here?"

No way. No way in hell. Every muscle in my body tensed. My stomach dropped like I'd missed a step going down stairs. I'd practiced confronting him in my head a thousand times, but still . . .

I turned slowly, heat creeping up my neck and spreading like wildfire across my cheeks. Low and behold, standing a few feet from me was my ex-boyfriend, Damian Bellucci. His black button-up shirt was crisp, tucked neatly into black slacks that looked like they'd been pressed that morning. The white clerical collar stood out sharply against his sun-kissed skin, a constant reminder of the God he represented.

Even as a priest, he remained annoyingly attractive. I tilted my head to the sky. *Seriously, God?*

My gaze traced the broad line of his shoulders, the way his rolled-up sleeves hugged the muscles of his arms. His dark tousled hair made me wonder if he bothered to tame it in the mornings. And Jesus, Mary, and Joseph, his face. Strong jaw, sharp enough to cut through the tension that had thickened between us. Emerald eyes—intense, like they could see into my soul if I let them.

No one should look *that* good in a clerical uniform. He was a picture-perfect priest, standing as if temptation had never once knocked on his door. Even now, with our history, my body recognized him, despite never having had sex with him. We'd done other things . . .

I pushed those dangerous thoughts away, disgust and desire warring in my chest. I was supposed to be above this. Beyond this.

My eyes narrowed. How had I missed this detail? How had no one told me that the *one* person I never wanted to see again was going to be *the* priest at my new home?

Damian stood in front of me like he owned the place, staring with those gorgeous green eyes that had once seen more of me than anyone in this universe. My jaw clenched, and I fought the urge to turn right back around, get in my car, and drive until I hit the ocean.

It'll be fine. Is this all part of His plan? Though lately, God's plans seemed designed specifically to test my resolve.

"I'm the new director of religious education." I gave him my best professional tone.

His eyebrows shot up, and a dark cloud seemed to pass over his face. "Excuse me?"

"Director of religious education," I repeated, drawing out each syllable like I was explaining calculus to a kindergartner. "You know, the position that involves actually teaching rather than just standing around looking holy. Shouldn't you know these things?"

"My God," he said, massaging the space between his eyes.

"Funny, He's mine too. Small world." I twirled the end of my veil around my finger, enjoying his discomfort perhaps a bit too much.

He shook his head, a muscle twitching in his jaw. "This isn't happening."

"Actually, it is. Physics and all that . . . We both exist in the same time and space. Quite the miracle, really."

Damian's shoulders hunched forward as if carrying an invisible weight. His voice dropped to a low rumble. "This arrangement won't work."

"And why's that? Afraid I'll outshine you in Bible study?" I arched an eyebrow, daring him to admit the real reason.

"Because," he muttered, staring at the ground before meeting my eyes with that smoldering intensity that always made my stomach flip. "It's not going to be good for anyone. You, me, this community."

"So, what you're really saying is *I'm* not good enough?" I placed a hand over my heart dramatically. "And here I thought my teaching credentials and theological training would count for more. But I guess your comfort level trumps all that."

"That's not what I mean," he growled, stepping closer, his voice barely above a whisper. "We"—he gestured his index finger between us—"have history."

I folded my arms over my chest. "You don't get to dictate whether or not I belong here, Father Grumpy."

"No way in the nine hells can we be here at the same time, Claire," he gritted out, his intensity dialed up to eleven.

"First of all, it's *Sister* Claire now, though I appreciate your commitment to casual blasphemy. Second, the nine hells isn't even Catholic doctrine—but I must say, your knowledge of Dungeons & Dragons cosmology is impressive for a man of the cloth."

His eyes flashed, and for a moment, I saw the Damian I remembered. The one who had left me. The one who'd broken my heart when he decided a future with me wasn't enough.

He crossed his arms, the fabric of his sleeves tightening over the hard curve of his biceps. "You're really going to stand there and argue about doctrine with me?"

"I don't know." I grinned. "Am I winning?"

"Look"—he sighed heavily, staring off into the distance like a moody hero from a Gothic novel—"this is about what's best for *my* parish."

"Your parish?" I clutched my invisible pearls. "I didn't realize God had transferred the deed to your name. How convenient. You think I can't handle the job because of our ancient history? Or is it just easier to blame the community than admit you're scared?"

His jaw tightened, a shadow passing over his features.

I adjusted my black veil with a flourish and shifted my weight to one leg. "This is about you. Your discomfort." I couldn't help it now. "God forbid you're forced to deal with a little awkwardness. Or that you have to work with someone who knows the *real* you."

"That's not fair."

"What's not fair is acting like this is your decision to make. I have a lot to offer this community, and I'm not going to let you scare me off because you're uncomfortable. Put on your big boy Roman collar and deal with it."

We stood in the parking lot, staring each other down. My heart was racing. Neither of us wanted to admit it, but the past was right between us. The words we never said hung in the ocean air.

He exhaled, his shoulders slumping like Atlas bearing the weight of the world. "You're right."

"What?" I blinked.

"It wouldn't be very fair to not give this a chance. So . . ." His voice was low, resigned. "Let's see what you got, *Sister* Claire."

I cocked an eyebrow and crossed my arms. "Is that a challenge, *Father*?"

Damian smirked. "Maybe."

With a conceding huff, I said, "Fine." It wasn't a truce, but I didn't want to stand there in the sun arguing with him anymore.

As much as I hated to admit it, I wasn't entirely sure I wanted to stay anyway. The careful walls I'd built around my heart were cracking, and I'd only been here five minutes. I'd been taught to know when to flee from temptation. But how was I supposed to run when the place I'd be running from was exactly where God called me to be?

I rolled my shoulders back and offered up a silent prayer. *All right, Big Guy, if this is your idea of a divine comedy, I hope you're enjoying the show. But a little help with the plot would be appreciated.*

Chapter Three

CLAIRE

After morning Mass, Mrs. Fontana approached. The gleaming silver crucifix she wore glinted against her finely pressed blouse. Her sensible heels clicked on the marble as she positioned herself directly in my path.

"Welcome back to Saint Anthony's, *Sister* Claire." Her sugary-sweet voice preceded the cold and assessing judgment framed by her expensive glasses. "It looks like we're becoming one of those progressive parishes."

I inhaled deeply, centering myself, and tried to ignore the heavy scent of her designer floral perfume cutting through the lingering incense from the service. I focused on the sunlight casting pools of ruby and sapphire across the vestibule floor, turning the stone into a kaleidoscope of color. It was much more beautiful than Mrs. Fontana's thinly veiled disapproval.

"Thank you, Mrs. Fontana." I kept my tone warm.

"I remember when you were younger. Always so . . . spirited." She made it sound like a sin. "Your mother must be relieved you've finally found some direction."

Heat crept up my neck. "My family's very supportive. Mom says

God must have a wonderful sense of humor, calling me to serve after all those years of me driving her to prayer."

Mrs. Fontana's lips twitched—not quite a smile, but maybe it was progress considering her smile rarely reached her eyes. Her gaze drifted toward Damian, who stood by the main doors speaking with parishioners, sunlight haloing his dark hair in a way that was completely unfair.

"Hmm." She glanced back, her gaze sharpening on me. "Father Bellucci has been a blessing to this parish. The best priest we've had since Father Martin retired. He's just so devoted to tradition, you know?" Her eyes narrowed with suspicion. "I hope you're not going to have a problem with such a nontraditional living arrangement."

The rosary beads wrapped around her wrist clicked softly as she adjusted her purse. Behind her, two older women watched our exchange with poorly disguised interest.

"Did you know he leads the Latin Mass once a month?" she continued. "It's beautiful, and he's so reverent about it. The old ways. The way the Church was meant to be."

I fought the urge to roll my eyes. Instead, I brightened my smile until my cheeks hurt. "Sounds wonderful. Although personally, I've always thought God understands all languages. Even teenage slang, which is practically its own dialect these days. Last week I learned what 'rizz' means. I'm practically fluent now."

Her rigid face remained unchanged. *Tough crowd.*

Mrs. Fontana had always appointed herself guardian of the respectability of Saint Anthony's. I could still remember her leading the charge against the youth group's more modern worship music when I was in high school, clutching her crucifix and citing it as *undignified.* And now she'd appointed herself guardian of Damian too.

"He baptized the Morales twins last Sunday," she added. "Such devotion in his pretty green eyes. I especially admire the *certainty* in his vocation."

My fingers found the cross at my neck, tracing its edges. "The parish is lucky to have him."

"You should know by now that we protect our own," she said, the statement carrying weight beyond its simple words. "This community raised him. Supported him after that tragedy with his brother."

The memory of Rico's funeral flashed through my mind—Damian's hollow eyes, the grief weighing on all of us. It wasn't fair that Rico's murderer was still out there living life. My throat tightened as I pushed away the thought.

"You remember that? Before you ran away?"

I left because my world was falling apart. I wanted to argue, but if I'd learned one thing from my time in the convent, it was to choose my battles wisely. And I'd rather not get on Mrs. Fontana's bad side. Though it seemed I was already there.

"I look forward to working with Father Bellucci," I said, keeping my voice neutral despite the way my heart hammered against my ribs. "We both want what's best for the parish. Variety is the spice of life, don't you think?"

Mrs. Fontana's perfectly penciled eyebrows rose. "Sure." Her lips pressed into a thin line that emphasized the delicate wrinkles around her mouth. "Just remember, *Sister*, he has important work here. A true calling. He carries on his brother's legacy." She leaned closer, her perfume almost suffocating in its intensity. "I'd hate to see anything distract him from that."

I shifted my weight to one leg, suddenly aware of how close she stood, how her eyes seemed to be searching mine—for weakness, perhaps, or evidence of thoughts unbecoming a nun.

"My only interest is to be of service to God and this community," I said, the words feeling simultaneously true and incomplete. "I hope to bring a little light where it's needed."

Before I could elaborate, she'd already turned, her skirt swishing around her ankles as she moved to join the line near Damian. The abrupt dismissal left me with the distinct feeling I'd been marked as a threat.

As she reached Damian, her entire demeanor transformed, softening, brightening. She took both his hands in hers. Patted his arm in a maternal way. He bent slightly to hear whatever she was saying. Her own private audience.

She glanced back at me once, her message clear: *He belongs to us. To this parish. To honor Rico's memory.*

"Bless your heart, Mrs. Fontana," I muttered, a phrase my Southern college roommate had taught me. It was the sweetest way to say, "You're being terrible right now."

The air was crisp as I walked out of the church and toward Saint Anthony's school, the soft hum of the ocean behind me offering a fleeting sense of calm. *Lord, grant me the grace to deal with the Mrs. Fontanas of the world without losing my sanity or my smile.* I crossed myself, my palms a little clammy. It was my first day in the role I'd been sent here for. I just hoped those shoes wouldn't be too large to fill—and that they'd be comfortable enough to outrun judgy parish matriarchs.

I stepped through the doors, the scent of wood polish and floor cleaner hitting me immediately. My footfalls echoed in the wide quiet hallway as I approached the administration office. The semester didn't start for another week, giving me time to settle in before the beautiful chaos of students arrived.

"Sister Claire?" a warm female voice called out from down the hall. I turned to see a tall woman in her late forties with neatly trimmed dark hair streaked with silver. She was dressed in a pale blue blazer and had an air of calm authority about her.

"That's me," I replied, nerves settling.

She extended her hand, her smile genuine. "It's been a long time. Welcome back to Saint Anthony's. God, look at you. Such a beauty."

"It's good to be back, Mrs. Omura," I said, shaking her hand.

"Please, call me Laura. You're not a student here anymore," she mused.

I'd have to get used to calling my former principal by her first name. "I'm excited to be back . . . Laura."

"I'm glad. We have full faculty meetings starting tomorrow, but I wanted to meet with you one-on-one before then," she said, her eyes twinkling with an understanding I hadn't expected. "Let me show you around. A lot has changed since you graduated."

Laura and I walked side by side down the hallway, the sunlight streaming through tall windows. My mind flickered back to my teenage self hurrying through these same corridors, sneaking glances at Damian between classes, both of us flush with first love. The walls that once held student artwork and bulletin boards now featured sleek Chromebook charging stations—a far cry from the single computer lab I remembered.

"We've grown quite a bit," Laura remarked, gesturing to the newly constructed STEM wing ahead. "Added six classrooms and finally updated the science lab. I still have nightmares about the time Alex Campbell accidentally created that foam explosion."

"Oh, Lord, I remember that." I giggled. "It reached the ceiling. Poor Mrs. Peterson nearly had a heart attack."

Each room we passed had its own personality, but they all featured whiteboards in place of the old chalkboards. Some rooms were meticulously organized with perfectly aligned desks, while others felt more lived-in, with well-loved paperbacks spilling from shelves.

Laura pointed out the prayer room they'd converted from an old storage space. The same closet Damian and I had used to steal quick kisses between periods had been transformed into a quiet sanctuary where students could find reflection between classes.

This building held decades of faith and learning within its brick walls, but it had evolved with the times. The slight mustiness of old textbooks mixed with the sharp scent of fresh paint from the summer updates. Walking these halls again, I could almost hear the echoes of my younger self's laughter, the whispered prayers, the dreams I'd held so close.

"We're starting a robotics program this fall," Laura added with pride. "Times change, but our mission stays the same. We're finding new ways to serve our community." Her words carried the weight of wisdom, reminding me that growth didn't mean leaving tradition behind. "What led you back to Saint Anthony's?" she asked, glancing at me with a curious smile.

I tucked a loose strand of hair into my black veil. "I think it's God's will that I'm here. I love teaching, but there's something about being in a community like this. It's purposeful. More connected."

Laura nodded. "Saint Anthony's is special in that way. It's not just a school, but an extension of the church. The heart of the community. Everyone's family here."

Back when I was a teenager, word traveled through Saint Anthony's faster than morning prayers. One whispered conversation after Mass could ignite a wildfire of speculation that wouldn't die down for weeks. The older ladies perched in their usual pews with rosaries in hand could weave entire scandals from a single raised eyebrow or absence from Sunday Mass. That particular brand of Catholic small-town drama was one thing I definitely hadn't missed.

She chuckled. "The kids will know all there is about you by the end of the week. What you like to eat, where you get your coffee, who your favorite saints are."

The image of children with their curious questions about my life amused me. "I'll have to prepare myself for that."

"You'll do fine," she said, nodding. "You seem like the kind of person they'll latch on to. Kind, approachable. They'll trust you in no time."

Her words struck me in a way I hadn't expected, like she had seen more in me than I had shown. "I hope so."

Laura glanced at me as we continued a slow pace down the hall. "You have teaching experience from before you joined the convent, right?"

"I taught at a public school for a few years."

"We've never been assigned a nun from your order, but I've heard concerns from the more traditional folk in the parish. Could you tell me why you joined and a little about the Sisters of Divine Light?" she asked.

What had she heard? And from whom? With a deep breath, I started, "Well . . . the Sisters drew me in because of their focus on education and community service. We're a newer order, established after Vatican II, emphasizing independence in our ministry. Unlike traditional congregations, we live within our parishes as well as convents. Our Mother Superior believes it helps us better serve our communities." I smoothed my black veil, a simpler version of the traditional habit that marked our more modern approach. "Plus, we get Wi-Fi and Netflix."

Laura studied me, smiling, her keen eyes softening. "One of the regular parishioners here said your order has a reputation for shaking things up. When they started allowing nuns to live independently, it caused quite the stir in more traditional circles." Her smile widened, a hint of admiration in her expression. "Having one of their sisters here at Saint Anthony's . . . Well, let's just say I have a feeling you'll bring exactly the kind of change we need."

My stomach tightened at her words. "As long as it doesn't involve too much controversy."

"Sometimes a little controversy is needed to push us closer to God." She winked. "Here's your classroom." She opened the door at the end of the hallway and gestured for me to step inside.

I stepped through the threshold, taking it all in. I could feel Laura watching me, assessing my reaction. The room had bright posters on the walls, a wide whiteboard at the front, and rows of desks neatly arranged. A blank slate, ready for whatever I could bring to it.

"You're right. This place has a certain energy," I murmured, glancing back at her.

"It does," she agreed. "And so do you."

I hesitated, then said, "I have to say, I didn't expect you to still be here. Thought you would've retired by now."

Laura's smile softened once more, and she crossed her arms, leaning casually against the doorframe. "I've been here for over twenty years now. Can't bring myself to resign just yet. I found a purpose here I didn't even know I was looking for."

"That sounds like my calling," I said, not bothering to hide the admiration in my voice.

"Don't get me wrong, it has its challenges, believe me," she said with a chuckle. "But I wouldn't trade it. This parish has shaped me as much as I've shaped it."

There was a profoundness about dedicating yourself to a community, to watching it grow and change over the years. Like a parent raising children.

"I'm glad you're here, Sister Claire," she said after a pause, her voice more serious.

"Me too," I said, the sincerity in her words a quiet affirmation.

"We're going to be working together a lot. If you ever need anything, whether it's help with lesson plans or someone to talk to, my door's always open," she said with a wink.

My lips tilted up. "I'll keep that in mind. Thank you."

THE FIRST WEEK PASSED IN A BLUR OF LESSON PLANS AND SETTLING IN. Usually, by five o'clock, I'd be skating back to the small cottage the parish had so kindly arranged for me. But today, a parent-teacher conference had run longer than expected. It was the first time meeting my students' parents. It had gone well enough. I inhaled deeply, hoping the peaceful evening breeze would settle my frazzled nerves.

When I stepped out of the two-story building, the sun was taking its final glorious plunge below the horizon, painting the sky in strokes of gold and magenta that would make even the most devoted ceiling artists jealous. I dropped my skateboard onto the pavement, the familiar thud bringing a smile to my face. As I pushed off across the parking lot, someone caught my eye. I glanced toward the rectory and stopped in my tracks, one foot still on the board.

Holy Mother of Divine Timing.

I recognized the figure cutting across the lot in long, purposeful strides, and sparks tingled my insides. Father Bellucci—Damian— was jogging toward the rectory wearing nothing but loose basketball shorts that clung to his hips and white running shoes. His build was different, more filled out, as though life had carved strength into every inch of him. Broad shoulders, solid arms. The effortless way he carried himself made him look like he was always in control.

Sweat glistened on his tanned skin, trickling down the ridges of his stomach. It was entirely too distracting for a man of the cloth. His dark hair framed a strong jawline. And Lord help me, those eyes. Green and intense, like they could see straight through my carefully constructed composure and right into the parts of me I was desperately trying to hide from myself.

I wasn't the only one who noticed. A couple of the moms still walking out of the school were practically drooling as they watched him run past. Their shameless gawking made me both irritated and relieved that I wasn't the only one struggling not to stare.

The warmth in my belly spread, working its way up to my cheeks. I needed to go anywhere but in his direction. *Time for a strategic retreat.* I kicked my board around and started skating the opposite way, even though it added an extra ten minutes to my route home.

I could use the practice anyway.

"Claire!" The voice pulled me from my thoughts. Jessica Reed, walking hand in hand with her daughter, flashed me a bright smile as she approached. "Or should I say Sister Claire now? Good to see you."

The memory of her lips on an intoxicated Damian tortured my mind. I pushed it away with a long exhale. She was in her late twenties now, but there was no mistaking her poise, the sway in her step that drew attention. Tall, with long, perfectly straight blond hair that always seemed to catch the light just right. She carried herself with confidence that bordered on intimidation. Her sharp blue eyes always assessing, calculating. And that bright practiced smile with just the right amount of charm and a hint of mischief underneath.

She was always so put together, even in casual clothes. Her skinny jeans and fitted blouse showed off her figure, paired with heels that clicked against the pavement. She knew exactly who she was and didn't care what anyone thought.

I stepped off my board, semithankful for the distraction. "Jessica, it's been years. Hello, Sadie."

The young girl gave me a polite greeting.

"I see you didn't let nunhood stop you from skating," Jessica said, her tone dripping with barely concealed judgment. "Admirable."

I smiled. "Jesus walked on water; I roll on concrete. We all have our gifts." I winked at Sadie, who giggled. "How have you been?"

Jessica adjusted her name-brand purse on her shoulder. "I've been well. I married Blake Fletcher. Bet you didn't expect that."

She'd had quite the crush on Damian, even while we were dating. "As long as you're happy." I looked at Sadie and asked, "How're you liking your classes?"

Jessica answered for her. "She's a little troublemaker, but she's enjoying it." She winked and then told Sadie to wait in the SUV. The young girl obeyed, already occupied by her phone.

A corner of my mouth rose. *The apple doesn't fall far from the tree.*

Jessica's gaze shifted behind me. "Speaking of trouble . . ."

I didn't have to turn around to know who she was looking at. Jessica's eyes tracked Damian's every step as he stretched in the driveway of the rectory, her lips curling into a smirk. "Too bad he decided to become a priest."

My pulse quickened. *Nothing to see here—just two women admiring God's handiwork.*

"No offense." She glanced at me before her eyes went back to Damian. "But he could bless me anytime."

I laughed, not sure what to say.

She shrugged. "It's a damn shame. Wouldn't you say?"

Another beat of silence passed as I pretended to be fascinated by a particularly interesting cloud.

Jessica elbowed me in the arm. "Come on, Claire. You weren't always a nun."

She was right about that. I grinned and said, "I mean, I did date him once upon a time. Let's just say his spiritual guidance was already well-developed." I waggled my eyebrows dramatically.

Crossing her arms, she nodded. "Touché."

I excused myself before the conversation could get any more awkward, hopping back onto my board with a cheerful wave. "Great seeing you. Tell Blake I said hi!" I skated down the sidewalk. The extra ten minutes was a divine intervention rather than an inconvenience.

The ride home didn't do much to clear my head. Even the rhythm of wheels on pavement and the rush of wind through my veil couldn't dislodge the image of Damian from my mind. The board's gentle sway beneath my feet just reminded me of the way he moved, all fluid grace and controlled power. When was the last time he'd stepped onto a board? I knew he'd stopped after Rico passed.

I couldn't help but laugh at the way my body had reacted to him. It may as well have been some kind of Pavlovian response to his mere existence. The salty air stung my cheeks, but it couldn't cool the heat spreading through me. If there was one thing Damian was good at, it was getting my body all riled up. Not even the satisfying rumble of urethane on concrete could ground me.

God, what are You doing? I glared up at the sky. *If this is a test of willpower, couldn't You have picked someone who looks less like they stepped off the cover of* Clergy Monthly: Hot Priest Edition?

When I reached my cottage, I could at least breathe again. The quaint Victorian-style house sat nestled between a couple oak trees, its whitewashed walls and green shutters looking like it had come straight out of a fairy-tale movie. The weathered porch creaked beneath my weight as I stepped up, and the scent of jasmine drifted in from the garden. If nothing else, at least I had this: a quiet retreat to hide away from the judgment of the world.

I kicked off my sneakers and set my skateboard next to the shoe rack in the tiny coat closet. I went straight to my bedroom, peeling off my habit and pulling on black bike shorts and a sports bra. After tying my shoulder-length hair into a ponytail, I slipped into my tennis shoes and hopped onto the stationary bike I'd set up by the window in my bedroom. I needed to work off some of this extra energy before my mind took me places I had no business going.

No way on God's green earth was I going to get myself off to the image of Father Bellucci's glistening chest. *I refuse.*

I could imagine that confession scenario clearly. *Forgive me, Father, for I have sinned by thinking about your rock-hard abs.*

I pedaled harder, the rhythmic churn of the bike helping clear my head. *Finally.*

Evening rolled around, and the sun dipped below the horizon, leaving a soft violet glow in the sky. I sat on the porch swing, a well-deserved glass of red wine in hand, watching as the stars began to poke through the twilight. The sound of the ocean in the distance was a steady hum, a comforting reminder that even with everything spiraling around me, some things were constant.

Besides being assigned to the same parish as my ex, this gig wasn't all that bad. Peaceful, even. *I can get used to this . . .* If I could just stop picturing Damian every time I closed my eyes.

Chapter Four

CLAIRE

Eight Years Ago

The red digits on my nightstand blinked 9:03 as I folded my clean laundry. I glanced again—9:04. Again, after putting it away—9:05. Each skip of time was like carrying my own personal cross. I checked my phone for the hundredth time, the brightness making me squint. Still nothing. I sighed, dropping it onto my fuzzy purple comforter.

"Come on, Big Guy. Just one text. Is that too much to ask?" I muttered to the ceiling, where Damian and I had arranged glow-in-the-dark stars to form our favorite constellations. The North Star stared back, mocking in its brightness.

A month had passed since Rico's accident, and ever since, Damian had been building a concrete wall of silence between us. I tried to call him one more time but got his voicemail. Again. The old recording sounded so normal compared to the hollow-eyed boy who'd been avoiding me since the funeral.

Tonight, that silence was unbearable. I couldn't just sit anymore. I puffed out my cheeks and tried a few of his friends, my foot tap-tap-

tapping against my bed frame until finally, one of them mentioned a party across town.

My stomach dropped faster than a roller coaster. *No. Not again.* He was out somewhere, drowning in the grief I should have been helping him navigate.

I snatched my keys from my cluttered desk, nearly knocking over a collection of mismatched photo frames—me and Damian at the beach, me and Jasmine making peace signs, our whole family at Christmas.

As I slipped out into the hallway, I whispered a quick prayer: "Just let him be okay. Please."

The golden glow of streetlights blurred past as I drove, my ancient Honda protesting every sharp turn. I glanced up through the windshield at the clear night sky, automatically searching for the North Star—our star. Before Rico's accident, we'd lie on the Cliff Overlook, fingers intertwined as we stared up at the constellations.

"By the light that guides us," Damian had whispered once, "I promise to always find my way back to you, no matter how lost I get."

I'd squeezed his hand, making my own promise. "By the light that guides us, I'll be your safe harbor."

Now those words felt like childhood promises written in the sand, where tides of grief washed them away before they had a chance to set. Still, I held on to them as I drove toward the party, hoping beyond hope that this time would be different. That maybe tonight, he'd actually let me back in.

When I pulled up to the house, bass pulsed through my car windows, making the little hula dancer on my dashboard shimmy with more enthusiasm than I felt. Crumpled red cups dotted the lawn like bizarre flowers. Drunken teenagers flitted between them like wayward butterflies. I shifted into park and took a deep breath, giving myself a quick once-over in the rearview mirror.

"You've got this, Claire Bear," I told my reflection, using my dad's old nickname. "Just find him, get him home safe, and save the lecture for tomorrow."

I pushed my way through the crowded house, wrinkling my nose at the scent of beer and smoke. My eyes scanned all the faces, searching for the one that always made my heart skip, even after all this time.

And then there he was.

Damian.

He was slumped against the wall, amber liquid sloshing in the bottle dangling from his fingers. His normally bright green eyes were glazed over—vacant, like someone had dimmed the lights inside him. But it was the flash of blond hair that made my stomach twist into a pretzel.

He wasn't alone.

Jessica Reed's manicured fingers threaded through his dark hair. Their lips pressed together. His arm curved around her waist, holding her so tightly that there wasn't space for even a whispered prayer between them.

I. Completely. Froze.

My world skewed sideways, like that time Damian had convinced me to try the Tilt-A-Whirl after eating cotton candy. My lungs forgot how to work, each breath catching somewhere in my throat. The bass from the speakers faded to a dull roar in my ears, everything tunneling down to that corner of the living room. His hands on her body. The lazy pleasured look on his face.

My nails dug into my palms. Heat crawled up my neck, prickling across my skin like sunburn. I opened my mouth, but the words dissolved on my tongue like communion wafers. My feet had turned to stone, rooting me. Made me watch my carefully constructed future crumble with each undulation of their mouths.

The boy who'd held my hand through Sunday Mass, who'd kissed me beneath the stars and promised me forever, was disappearing before my eyes.

Come on, Vergara, don't you dare cry here. Not with twenty pairs of eyes already watching this disaster unfold.

Salt burned behind my eyes as I bit the inside of my cheek until I tasted copper, forcing back the hot pressure building in my throat. My feet carried me through the crowd, shoulders bumping against mine as I navigated toward the exit. This was what I got for thinking I could be what he needed. For thinking I could save someone who clearly didn't want saving.

Stupid, stupid, stupid.

By the time I made it outside, the cool California air hit me like a much-needed slap to the face. My breaths came in shallow, ragged bursts. With trembling fingers, I fumbled with my keys, metal scraping against metal. I'd watched him self-destruct countless times since the funeral. Stayed up late praying he'd let me in. Made excuses to Jasmine for why he hadn't called.

Sliding into the driver's seat, I slammed the door shut, the sound echoing through the car like a gunshot. I gripped the steering wheel, the worn spots under my fingers offering no comfort tonight.

"God, I'm trying . . ." My voice cracked as I rested my forehead against the wheel. Tears streamed down my face, hot and relentless, smearing the little bit of mascara I'd bothered to apply.

You really thought you could love the grief out of him? Fix him with just patience and understanding? That's adorable, Claire.

The memory of last Sunday flickered through my mind. His head in my lap as we watched movies, fingers laced through mine. He'd whispered, "I don't know what I'd do without you."

"Well, apparently, the answer is 'make out with Jessica Reed,' " I said to no one, laughing through my tears at the absurdity of it all.

I could just hear what my *lola* would say: *Ay nako, Claire! Boys will always disappoint you. That's why all you need is Jesus and good girlfriends.* The thought of her no-nonsense wisdom made me smile, even as tears continued to fall.

Maybe if I'd been stronger, pushed harder, been enough . . . No. I shook my head, wiping roughly at my eyes. *No more maybes.*

"This isn't on you," I told myself firmly, starting the car with a determined twist of the key. "He's hurting, sure, but that doesn't give him permission to hurt you too."

My whole body shook with sobs I couldn't hold back anymore. I let them come, drowning out the image of his hand in Jessica's hair, his lips on hers, the hollow look in his eyes that said he was already gone.

Damian had chosen the bottle. Chosen Jessica freaking Reed. Chosen to sink into his grief rather than let me help pull him out.

Was any of it real? Or was I being the good Catholic girl who was the placeholder while he traversed into the depths of his hell?

I pulled away from the curb, tears blurring the streetlights into halos. I didn't know where I was going, but I knew I couldn't stay there another second.

"Start fresh tomorrow," I whispered to myself, finding comfort in the mantra my *lola* always used during hard times. "The sun will rise, and so will you."

I wouldn't think about tomorrow or the next day. Wouldn't think about how I'd face him knowing that his lips had been on someone else's.

After tonight, I wasn't sure there'd be anything left for me to save. Maybe there hadn't been for a while, and I'd just been too hardheaded —too hopeful—to see it.

But that was the thing about hope. Like a stubborn little seed, it had a way of taking root in the most unlikely places. Even in a heart that was broken.

Chapter Five

DAMIAN

Present Day

Youth group should have been the highlight of my week—the bright, questioning teenagers had always invigorated my ministry. These past three weeks, it had been an exercise in self-control. Two hours of watching Claire effortlessly connect with the kids in ways I never could despite years of trying.

"All right, everybody, circle up," I called over the chaos of thirty teenagers demolishing the last of the pizza. The church hall echoed with laughter, and the metal chairs scraped against linoleum as they reluctantly formed their usual prayer circle.

Claire entered through the side door, skateboard tucked under her arm, her habit replaced by jeans and a simple tee for our more casual youth activities. The energy in the room shifted as she walked in. Even the most disinterested kids straightened.

"Sorry I'm late," she said, sliding her board against the wall. "Principal Omura needed help with the fall festival plans."

"We're just getting started," I replied, forcing my tone to remain neutral despite the way my pulse quickened. Three weeks of working together, and I still couldn't look directly at her without feeling like I was staring at the sun.

She took her place in the circle, and I began our opening prayer, the words automatic after years of repetition. But my focus slipped as I watched Claire through lowered lashes. She had her eyes closed, lips moving silently along with the prayer we'd both known practically our whole lives, completely present.

During our discussions about service projects, Claire leaned forward in her chair. "What if we did a cleanup at the skate park downtown?"

Mia Foster, our resident rebel who rarely contributed, perked up. "When did you start skating, Sister Claire?"

"Twelve," Claire confirmed with a grin. "Though these days I'm more about cruising than tricks."

"What's your board setup?" Jason Rivera asked, intrigued.

Claire launched into specifics about her deck and trucks, and despite myself, I nodded along. When she mentioned switching to softer wheels for a smoother ride, I almost jumped in to debate the merits of 99A versus 85A durometer—a conversation Rico and I had had countless times. I stopped myself just before speaking. This wasn't about me or my memories. I was their priest, not their skating buddy.

"Father Damian used to skate too, right?" Michael Clayton asked, turning to me with unexpected interest.

My smile faltered. Claire's eyes met mine across the circle, a flicker of buried sorrow passing between us.

"A lifetime ago," I managed, clearing my throat. "My brother taught me."

"He was better than me," Claire added, her voice softening with memory. "Could land tricks I'd never even attempt."

The moment stretched between us, taut with history the teens couldn't possibly understand. I broke eye contact first, redirecting their attention to the upcoming food drive. But the damage was done. That brief connection had weakened my armor further.

The rest of the session passed in a blur of discussion and planning. I found myself watching Claire more than participating, mesmerized by how she'd mention a scripture passage and then immediately translate it into a language these kids actually understood. Where I quoted catechism, she shared stories. Where I offered theological explanations, she asked questions that made them think.

By the time we ended with closing prayer, half the group had already committed to her skate park idea. I wasn't surprised. Claire had always made people want to follow her into whatever adventure she proposed.

"Okay, who's on cleanup duty tonight?" I asked as the teens started dispersing.

Michael, Jason, and Elijah volunteered, already stacking chairs with the efficiency of routine.

Claire grabbed her skateboard, heading toward the door. "I'll be in the parking lot if anyone needs me," she called over her shoulder, the invitation clear in her voice.

I watched as several of the girls trailed after her, drawn by curiosity. Through the windows, I saw Claire demonstrating basic stances, her movements fluid and confident. The setting sun caught her hair as she laughed at something Emma said, the sound carrying through the open door.

"Father Damian?" Elijah's voice pulled me back to the task at hand. "Where does this tablecloth go again?"

I turned my attention to the remaining cleanup, directing the boys through our usual routine. We worked in companionable silence for a while, the distant sound of wheels on asphalt and teenage voices filtering in from outside.

"Father?" Michael said hesitantly as we wiped down the last

table. At sixteen, he was in that awkward stage between boy and man, all gangly limbs and uncertain confidence. "Can I ask you something?"

"Of course," I replied, sensing the seriousness in his tone.

Michael glanced toward Jason and Elijah, who were arguing over the proper way to stack the chairs. Satisfied they weren't listening, he lowered his voice. "There's this girl in my bio class. We've been friends since freshman year, but lately . . . I can't stop thinking about her differently."

My chest tightened. *Not this. Not tonight.*

"She's Catholic too," he continued, oblivious to my discomfort. "Really devoted. Like, she helps with adoration and everything. But I'm worried if I tell her how I feel, it'll ruin our friendship." He ran a hand through his dark hair. "How do you know when it's worth the risk?"

I set down the cleaning spray, buying myself a moment. Through the window, I could see Claire performing a perfect manual across the parking lot, balancing on her back wheels while the girls cheered her on.

"That's a tough one," I admitted, forcing my gaze back to Michael. "Friendship is precious. But sometimes . . ."

There are people who enter your life and redraw all your boundaries. People whose presence makes sacred promises feel like sandcastles against the tide. People who carve spaces in your heart that remain empty when they're gone.

Jason and Elijah finished their tasks and headed outside to join the fun, leaving me and Michael in the empty hall.

I cleared my throat. "Sometimes feelings like that don't just go away, no matter how hard you try to ignore them."

Michael nodded. "So, you think I should tell her?"

"I think," I said carefully, "that you need to be honest with yourself first. Ask yourself if what you're feeling is just attraction or if it's more. Real love isn't only about how someone makes you feel—it's about who you want to become when you're with them."

Like how Claire made me want to be more authentic and present. The way she was with these kids reminded me why I'd chosen to serve in the first place. How, even now, just having her nearby made me feel less alone.

"And if it is . . . deeper?" Michael asked.

Claire was showing Jason how to improve his stance on the board, her hand on his shoulder to steady him.

"Then you have to decide what matters more—protecting the friendship or being truthful with your feelings." I met his eyes directly. "Just be prepared for things to change either way."

Michael considered what I'd said, then offered a grateful smile. "Thanks, Father. That actually helps."

As we finished cleaning, my gaze kept drifting outside. Claire had progressed to showing off now, executing a perfect ollie that had the teens whooping in appreciation. The joy on her face was incandescent. No self-consciousness. Completely Claire.

The words came to me, unbidden. *Be truthful about your feelings.*

My reality was that every moment spent with Claire was eroding my defenses. Every smile. Each accidental touch. The shared glance across a room full of people who had no idea what had once existed between us. It all chipped away at the walls I'd so carefully constructed.

I watched as she high-fived Elijah. Her honeyed voice carried through the evening air, wrapping me in memories I couldn't escape.

God help me. I turned away from the window, because my strength was failing, and I wasn't sure how much longer I could pretend otherwise.

Night had fallen by the time I locked the hall. The parking lot was empty now, the teens and Claire long gone. The concrete still held ghost impressions of her wheels, invisible tracks I could almost see in the moonlight. My footsteps echoed across the asphalt as I made my way toward the church, drawn there by instinct rather than conscious decision. I needed guidance. I needed clarity. Most of all, I needed strength I didn't possess on my own.

Tuesday night confessions were usually quiet: a few regulars, the occasional tourist seeking absolution for weekend revelries. The scent of furniture polish filled the small space, a comfort I'd come to treasure.

The door on the other side of the built-in confessional creaked open. I straightened, adjusting my stole, the weight of the silk band familiar around my neck.

"Bless me, Father, for I have sinned." The voice was male, possibly middle-aged, slightly trembling. "It's been . . . God, I don't even know. Twenty years since my last confession?"

I leaned forward. "Welcome back. Our Lord rejoices when His children return to Him."

A heaviness filled the space. His breaths came uneven and strained. I'd heard many confessions in my short time as a priest, from venial to mortal sins and everything in between.

"I don't know if I can do this," the man murmured.

"Take your time," I encouraged, slipping into my pastoral role, which felt like a second skin most days. "Whatever burdens you carry, you don't have to bear them alone."

The man took a shuddering breath. "I killed someone."

My body went still. Years of training kept my voice even. "Continue."

"It was a long time ago. I was driving home from the bar. I'd had way too much to drink. Not falling-down drunk, but I shouldn't have been behind the wheel." His voice cracked. "It was dark. Raining. I didn't see him until it was too late."

My pulse quickened. His story prickled at my consciousness like a crown of thorns.

"I hit him, and I . . . I panicked. I didn't know what to do. Just kept driving. Left him there on the road." The man's breathing grew labored. "I saw in the paper that the hit-and-run victim had died."

The air in the booth grew thick, suffocating.

"I can't believe I'm saying these words out loud. I've lived with it for so long." The stranger's voice dropped to a whisper. "I took his life. The paper said his name was Enrico."

My world tilted sideways. I gripped the edge of the seat as blood thundered through my ears. *Rico. This is the man who killed my brother.* He'd left him bleeding on the side of the road while I was oblivious, forgetting my promise to pick him up because I was enraptured with Claire.

The seal of confession shackled my voice in every way. I couldn't react, demand answers, reach through the screen and grab this man by the throat. The confessional—this sacred space that had always brought me peace—had become my torture chamber.

Silence stretched between us, broken only by the man's ragged breaths.

I swallowed hard, forcing words past the tightness in my throat. "Why . . . Why are you confessing this now?"

"I buried my wife this morning. She had cancer." Another pause. "She made me promise to make things right. She was the only one who knew."

I closed my eyes. My nails dug into my palms. "And how do you plan to make things right?"

"I'm going to turn myself in," the man said. "But I needed this . . . I needed to confess first. To God. Before I face what's coming."

My mind raced. If this man turned himself in, the police would contact my family. I would learn his identity anyway. But for now, in this moment, I was bound by my sacred duty.

"What you did . . ." I began, struggling to separate the priest from the grieving brother. "You took a life. A precious life."

"I know." The man's voice was hollow.

"But God's mercy is greater than any sin, even this one." The words were glass in my throat, tearing their way out, but they were true. They had to be, or what was the point of any of it? "Contrition requires not just confession, but restitution. You must follow through. Turn yourself in. Face justice."

"I will. Tomorrow. I promise."

My hand trembled as I made the sign of the cross. "Through the ministry of the Church, may God give you pardon and peace, and I absolve you from your sins in the name of the Father, and of the Son, and of the Holy Spirit."

"Amen," the man whispered.

The wood creaked, the only sign that he'd stood.

"Wait," I said, forgetting myself. "Your penance—"

But the door had already opened and closed. The man was gone.

I sat frozen, collar damp with sweat. Waves of grief and rage crashed over me. The confessional walls closed in. Questions screamed through my mind, but the sacrament of reconciliation held me in silence.

I stumbled out into the empty sanctuary, falling to my knees before the altar. "Why?" I whispered, the word echoing in the sacred space. "Why now? Why like this?"

No answer came, only the distant sound of traffic and the constant tick of the old church clock. I stared up at Christ's suffering face on the crucifix above.

As a priest, I'd forgiven my brother's murderer out of pure obligation, but as a man . . .

"How am I supposed to forgive this?" I asked. "How am I supposed to celebrate Mass, counsel others, and speak of Your mercy when all I want is . . ."

I couldn't finish the thought. Admitting anything meant admitting to the rage burning through my veins.

Pulling my cell from my pocket, I entered the code, unlocking it. God, I wanted to tell Claire everything—about the man and his confession to leaving Rico broken on the road that rainy night. My fingers hovered over her contact in my phone. I wanted her to hold my hand like she had at the hospital while we'd waited for the news that would destroy my family. But it was too late. And the seal of confession bound me to silence with the force of sacred vows.

Moonlight filtered through the stained glass windows of the empty sanctuary. The altar was bathed in the soft glow of votive candles. I knelt before it, my body tense, hands clasped. I'd lingered long after evening prayers had ended. Long after the last parishioner had left. Long after I should have returned to the rectory.

But I couldn't leave. Not with the weight of the confession continuing to crush my chest like a vise. My brother's killer had sat mere inches from me just a few days ago, separated only by the thin screen of the confessional. I'd granted him absolution, even as rage and grief tore through me.

"I don't understand." My voice echoed in the emptiness after an hour ruminating on God's grand scheme in this. Since the confessional, my mind had raced with thoughts of Rico. Claire. My life before the accident. How much I wanted to tell her what that man had confessed. "Why now, with Rico's killer finally surfacing, did You send her back here? To test me? To punish me?"

The crucifix loomed above, silent and unmoving, Christ's suffering face illuminated by the flickering light of the sanctuary candle. I'd knelt here hundreds of times since taking my vows. Found comfort within these sacred walls. But tonight, peace eluded me.

"Three weeks. Three fucking weeks, and I can barely breathe when she's near." My voice cracked, the confession tearing from my throat. "I want—need—to tell her tonight. I want to hold her hands and tell her about the man."

I shifted my weight, my knees aching from hours pressed against the hard stone floor. The pain was grounding, a small penance for the thoughts I couldn't seem to control.

She was everywhere—in the hallways of the school, in the back pew at morning Mass, in the parish office filing paperwork. Her jasmine-and-ocean scent lingered throughout the air. Claire Vergara. *Sister* Claire now. We'd both given ourselves to God, made vows of celibacy and service. We should have been allies in faith, not . . . whatever this was that made my heart race and my collar tight.

"Give me strength," I prayed, desperation coloring each word. "Help me see her as a colleague. Another sister in Christ. Help me bear this confession alone as I've sworn to do."

But that was the problem, wasn't it? I'd never seen Claire as *just* anything. Even in the midst of my turmoil over Rico's killer. After all these years, my body remembered hers. The way she fit against me and the softness of her lips. The sound of her laughter under the stars. Those nights on the cliff, pointing out constellations, making promises I wouldn't keep.

An unbidden memory crashed over me: me and Claire at seventeen, in my car, parked at the overlook above the bay. Rain drummed against the roof, blurring the world outside into a watercolor of streetlights and shadows. The windows had fogged over, cocooning us in our own private universe.

"I don't think I'll ever get tired of being with you. Looking at you," she'd whispered, her fingers tracing the outline of my jaw with such tenderness it had made my chest ache.

I'd captured her hand, pressing my lips to her palm. "You see me differently than anyone else does."

"I see all of you, Damian Bellucci," she'd said, her gray eyes holding mine with that intense focus that always made me feel like I was the only person in her world. "The parts you show everyone else, and the parts you keep hidden."

"And you still want to stay?" I'd asked, vulnerability making my voice rougher than intended.

Instead of answering with words, she'd moved closer, straddling my lap in the driver's seat. The heat of her body against mine had sent electricity coursing through every nerve. When her lips met mine, it wasn't just a kiss—it was communion, confession, and absolution all at once.

We'd explored each other carefully that night with shaking hands and whispered permissions. Her skin under my fingertips had felt sacred, my touch drawing soft gasps that I swallowed with my mouth. Though we'd made our boundaries clear—saving that final intimacy—the way she'd arched against me and guided my hands to learn her body had created a connection deeper than anything physical alone.

"I feel like I've been looking for you my whole life," I'd confessed against her neck, breathing in her scent. "Like every prayer I've ever said was just me asking the universe to lead me to you."

She'd looked at me then, tucking my hair behind my ear, her eyes bright with emotion. "You talk to God about everything else," she'd murmured. "Do you talk to Him about us?"

"All the time," I'd admitted. "I ask Him how something that feels this right, this pure, could ever be wrong."

"And what does He say back?" The vulnerability in her question had made my heart constrict.

I'd pressed my forehead to hers, our breaths mingling. "That love like this—it's the closest thing to heaven we'll find on earth."

She'd kissed me again then, deeper. Her body melted into mine until I couldn't tell where I ended and she began. Our heartbeats had synced, our breathing falling into the same rhythm. A transcendent connection had passed between us, beyond lust and teenage hormones. In that fogged-up car, with rain creating a symphony around us, we'd shared a connection that felt eternal.

By the light that guides us, I promise to always find my way back to you, no matter how lost I get.

I'd been young and stupid and so fucking in love.

"I made a vow to You," I reminded God, and myself. "I chose all of this. This life. This duty." I swallowed hard, forcing the words out. "I chose You over her."

My ragged breathing broke the silence. Somewhere in the church, wood creaked as the old building settled, the sound startling in the stillness.

I closed my eyes, trying to focus on prayer. Scripture. On anything but the memory of Claire's eyes and the way she'd looked at me earlier when we were in youth group—guarded, distant. Like I was a stranger. It hurt more than I wanted to admit. Just as it hurt to know the truth about Rico's death and be unable to tell the one person who'd held me through that initial grief.

"What am I supposed to do?" I asked, resting my forehead on my folded hands. "Tell me what to do. How do I carry this burden alone? How do I look at her every day and not share this with her?"

My voice broke from the dual weight of my feelings for Claire and the confession's secret threatening to crush me.

No answer came. No divine revelation. No bolt of clarity.

Just the weight of my choices, the heaviness of my vows, and the growing certainty that seeing Claire every day while bearing this secret was going to break me if I didn't find a way to strengthen my resolve.

I reached into my pocket, retrieving my small wooden rosary.

"Hail Mary, full of grace . . ." I began, clinging to the learned words and letting them flow through me.

The repetition was soothing. A rhythm to follow when my mind wanted to wander back to gray eyes and soft lips or to the man's confession and how Claire would react when the news broke about Rico's killer. I moved through the decades, each prayer a step away from temptation and toward the certainty I'd once felt in my calling.

By the time I finished, pins and needles were shooting through my legs. How long had I been here? Hours at least. My back ached, my knees throbbed, and my throat was dry from whispered prayers.

And yet, despite the physical discomfort, a fragile calm settled over me. Not peace, exactly—I was too honest with myself to call it that—but a renewed determination.

I would be stronger. I had to be. For my congregation, my vows, and my soul.

For Claire.

Because the last thing I wanted was to make her life harder by burdening her with the weight of feelings that should have died years ago or reopening healing wounds with the truth about Rico. She had her own path now. Her own calling. I wouldn't disrespect that by letting whatever was stirring inside me show.

I pushed myself to my feet, wincing as blood rushed back into my legs, the pain sharp but clarifying. A reminder of the physical reality of this fragile vessel that housed my soul—a body I'd committed to keeping pure in service to God.

As my trembling fingers made the sign of the cross, I offered one final prayer.

"Help me to love her as You would have me love her—purely, selflessly, and without expectation or desire. Help me bear this secret with dignity, strength, and acceptance of Your divine plan."

I walked down the center aisle, each step steadier than the last. By tomorrow, I would finally face her with the composure a priest should have. I would be cordial but distant. Professional. Proper.

I would not think about the curve of her smile or the way her voice softened when she spoke to the children. I would not remember how it felt to hold her, taste her, or love her under skies so full of stars we felt like we were drowning in light.

Even after days of praying, the man's voice haunted me. *His name was Enrico.* The conversation still replayed in my mind like a horror film I couldn't turn off.

I have to be stronger than this.

As I pushed open the heavy church doors, the night air cool against my face, I steeled myself for what lay ahead—to uphold my vow.

I wouldn't tell a soul.

Chapter Six

DAMIAN

After twelve o'clock Mass, the church was almost empty except for a few stragglers offering final prayers. Mrs. Anderson had shown me the attendance numbers for the month, and they were alarmingly low. With dwindling attendance came dwindling donations, which meant less funding for outreach programs, building maintenance, and community services.

But it wasn't just about the money—each empty pew represented souls I wasn't reaching. People who might need spiritual guidance but weren't finding their way to God's house. How could I get more people into these seats? We hadn't had any big events or festivals lately.

Maybe the upcoming fall festival would spark interest, bring people together, and remind them that Saint Anthony was more than a Sunday obligation—it was the beating heart of the community. We needed it to be meaningful so that it would draw people back to their faith.

I made my way down the aisle of the sanctuary, mentally scrolling through my daily tasks. Two scheduled confessions—one with Mrs. Walker, who always needed extra time to unburden her soul. She would probably take one hour alone. Then counseling with David Conrad, a troubled sophomore who'd been acting out in his classes.

I still needed to dig through the storage room for Advent decorations, though that could probably wait. What really needed to get done was the stack of marriage prep paperwork gathering dust on my desk. Three engaged couples, all needing their Pre-Cana documents processed before Christmas. Rounding the corner near the side chapel, I nearly walked straight into Claire.

She froze, startled, clutching a stack of papers to her chest—flyers to put in the lobby, most likely. Her eyes darted up to meet mine, that familiar guarded look flashing across her beautiful face. My gaze caught on the delicate silver crucifix hanging from a matching thin chain around her neck.

"Sorry," I muttered but didn't move to let her pass.

Silence swelled in the space between us, thicker than the scent of the lingering incense. Her gray eyes shifted to a point over my shoulder, while I definitely did not study the contours of her face.

It amazed me how time had molded her features, softening some edges while sharpening others. She still had the same beauty, but there was a quiet strength in her face now. Gone was the carefree girl I'd loved all those years ago. In her place stood someone who had lived through her own battles and had come out the other side. She wasn't the Claire I'd once known . . . She was more layered, more complex, and somehow even more breathtaking.

Sunlight filtered through the stained glass, casting scattered patterns across the stone floor that resembled a constellation of stars. My teenage promise came crashing through my mind like a tidal wave.

By the light that guides us, I promise to always find my way back to you, no matter how lost I get.

The faint echo of a door closing somewhere in the church cut through the stillness.

Claire's lips pressed together as though she were biting back words.

My hands itched to move, but I kept them firmly at my sides. "How're classes going?" I asked, my voice sounding far too casual for the way my heart was pounding.

"Well. Thanks for asking, Father." Her tone was polite, but there was an undertone of wariness that made me think she'd rather be anywhere but here. She glanced past me, toward the door, as though planning her escape.

I forced my lips to curve up. "Good. I'm sure the kids love you. What do you think about Jessica's little girl? Sadie."

"She's . . . tenacious. Nothing I can't handle." Claire shifted on her feet, clearly eager to keep moving. "We've been going over various saints this week."

"Great." I inhaled deeply as the quiet consumed us. She was so distant. I didn't blame her. "Do you have a favorite? Saint, that is."

She tilted her head, and it was so goddamn adorable.

"Saint Dymphna," she said, then seemed to catch herself, as if she'd revealed more than intended. Her fingers moved unconsciously to touch the crucifix at her neck. "She's . . . the patron saint of mental health."

A shadow crossed her face, and I could see her weighing how much more to share. "I discovered her during a difficult time in college." Claire's voice grew softer. "Dymphna was young when she died, trying to help others who were suffering. There's a poignant honesty about her story. She didn't pretend her life, or the world, was perfect."

She looked up at me then, her eyes holding a vulnerability I hadn't seen since our teenage years. "I suppose I've always been drawn to saints who understood what it meant to feel broken. Who found God not in spite of their struggles, but through them."

Her admission floated there, fragile and unvarnished, pressing tight against my ribs. This was the Claire I remembered. The one who never shied away from difficult truths, even when they hurt.

Forcing myself back to the present, I thought of the promise I'd made in this sanctuary just the other night. *Cordial. Professional. Proper.*

Fuck, this is hard. Staying away and pretending like nothing had ever happened between us. Like I'd never tasted her lips. Like we'd never lain beneath the night sky making promises by the light of the North Star.

I wanted to tell her about the confession. It was on the tip of my tongue, burning there like a coal I couldn't swallow. Claire deserved to know that Rico's killer had finally come forward, that after eight years of wondering, of that unsolved case file gathering dust, there were finally answers.

But the seal of confession bound me tighter than any physical chain. Here I was, sworn to celibacy, fighting an attraction to a woman who'd taken similar vows, and the thing keeping us apart in this moment was duty.

As though remembering herself, she said quickly, "If you'll excuse me, I have work to do."

I nodded, clearing my throat. "Right. Of course."

She strode past me, her steps soft against the stone. Her silhouette disappeared into the dim light near the entrance. I fought the urge to run after her. To grab her arm and make her look at me instead of through me.

Cordial. Professional. Proper.

Claire wasn't just some test of faith. She was my first love, my first kiss, my first heartbreak. And now she was here, testing the limits of my self-control.

God, it killed me—the way she'd clutched those papers to her chest like it was a shield. We used to be so easygoing together, so natural. Could we get past the suffocating tension?

I raked a hand over my face, a poor attempt at grounding myself. The faint scent of incense filled my lungs, but instead of bringing peace, it just reminded me of all the prayers I'd whispered in the dark, begging God to help me forget her.

Maybe I need to right my wrongs with her. Tell her how sorry I am for what I put her through. Then maybe these feelings would leave me, and I could finally move on with my life.

But would she even want to hear my apologies? Eight years was a long time to nurse hurt, and the way she'd looked *through* me suggested she'd built walls I may never scale. I'd abandoned her when she needed me most. Chose my guilt over her love and made her feel like loving me had been a mistake.

And now here she was, having clearly reconstructed herself without me. Confident, strong, at peace.

At peace.

Maybe that was what scared me most. Not that she couldn't forgive me, but that she already had. That she'd moved so far beyond what we'd been that my guilt was just a relic of a past she'd already made peace with.

If not an apology, then that left one possible alternative: go to Bishop Valenti and request her reassignment.

Lord, give me courage. Actually, forget courage—give me a sign.

After that encounter with Claire, I returned to the rectory and found myself reaching for my phone and tapping in the number I still knew by heart despite how rarely I called.

Three rings later, the line connected.

"Damian, everything all right?" my father asked, voice gruff and distant.

"Fine, just checking in. How's Mom?"

"Same as always." His words were clipped. "She had a good day yesterday. Put flowers on Rico's grave."

I closed my eyes, pressing my fingers against my temple. "That's good." I wanted to ask if he'd heard anything from Detective Alvarez about Rico's case, but the words stuck in my throat.

Surely Alvarez would've called me if there were any developments. Right? What if he doesn't do it? What if my family doesn't get that closure? What should I do now that I know and he hasn't done it?

I cleared my throat. "You'll never guess who's back in town. Claire Vergara. She's the new director of religious education at the parish."

A pause. I could almost see him straightening in his chair, his jaw tightening.

"Claire, huh?" His tone softened. "Rico always liked her. Said she was good for you."

"Yeah, he did."

"Speaking of your brother," Dad continued, as if I hadn't spoken, "I found some of his seminary application materials when I was cleaning out the garage. His personal statement . . . You should read it sometime. The conviction he had, even then."

And just like that, Claire was forgotten, and Rico's ghost was summoned to stand between us, like always.

"I'd like that," I said, though I wasn't sure I would. Reading Rico's words about a calling he never got to answer might just break me.

"Your mother keeps asking if you'll say a special Mass for him this month."

Offering a Mass for my brother had become a habit after my ordination. "Of course."

"Good." Dad cleared his throat. "Well, I should go."

"Dad—" I started, not even sure what I wanted to say. That I missed them? That I was struggling? That seeing Claire again had unearthed a plethora of buried feelings and complications?

The confession came rushing to the forefront of my mind again, but I couldn't tell him about any of it. How I'd wanted to take justice into my own hands. How I'd wanted to deny him absolution.

"Take care, Dame." The line went dead.

I set the phone down, the rectory sitting room suddenly too quiet, too empty. Eight years later and I still couldn't have a real conversation with my own father. All he saw when he looked at me was the son who lived while Rico died. The son who took vows to honor a brother's memory.

I ran a hand over my face as Claire's gray eyes flashed through my mind. How they'd widened when she nearly collided with me in the church. The ghosts of my past were determined to haunt me, but unlike Rico, she was here. Real. Breathing the same air.

God help me . . .

Chapter Seven

DAMIAN

The following day, I jogged down the coastal trail, but my usual rhythm felt off. It had been two weeks since the man had come to confession—two weeks since he'd claimed responsibility for Rico's death and promised to turn himself in. I'd expected to hear something by now. A call from Detective Alvarez, an arrest in the news. The silence was eating at me worse than the original grief.

I passed the cliffs where tourists stopped for photos, then the small coffee shop that marked my usual turnaround point, but my mind kept circling back to that other weight I'd been carrying.

Maybe I need to right my wrongs with her. Tell her how sorry I am for what I put her through. Then maybe these frustrating and inconvenient feelings will leave me, and I can finally move on with my life.

When I neared Saint Anthony's parking lot, I found myself stopping. Not from curiosity this time, but from decision. The dried leaves skittered across the pavement, and the salty breeze carried the chill of fall off the ocean. I'd been a coward for eight years. Maybe it was time to stop running. The crisp wind whipped against my sweat-dampened skin. Maybe seeing her in her element would give me the courage to follow through on what I'd come here to do.

Wiping the sweat off my forehead with the hem of my cut-off shirt, I made my way up the worn stone steps and into the wide empty corridor. The students were in their first class of the morning.

My white running shoes squeaked against the freshly waxed floor. The scent of chalk dust and old books mixed with the sharp tang of pumpkin spice from the teachers' lounge. It brought back memories of my own days at Saint Anthony's.

I passed the front office, its glass window stacked with slips and manila folders, then down the main corridor, where faded trophy cases guided me along the walls. A flight of stairs branched toward the library and cafeteria, but I kept straight, following the stretch of hallway lined with classrooms. The crucifixes above each door glinted in the cold white light streaming from the ceiling fixtures.

At the far end, a sliver of light broke across the polished floor. The door to Claire's classroom was cracked. I slowed, drawn to it, and peered through the narrow slit.

One of the students, a girl with wide eyes, spotted me. I raised a finger to my lips, giving her a quick wink. She nodded, her mouth forming a small O, as if she'd caught on to a secret. She averted her gaze to focus on the lecture.

Claire moved gracefully around the front of the classroom. Her skateboard leaned against the side of her desk. *Is that the same one she had as a teenager?* That pink hibiscus sticker looked too new. A corner of my mouth rose. I was willing to bet it was still her favorite flower.

Some things never change.

Her honeyed voice carried through the space, warm and commanding enough to draw every student's attention. Beneath the sweetness was a husky edge, subtle but unmistakable as it seeped into the corners of the hallway.

"What makes Saint Joan of Arc so remarkable isn't just her military victories," Claire explained, gesturing to a projected image on the whiteboard. "It's that she followed her convictions even when everyone told her she was wrong. She heard voices—what she believed were divine messages—and trusted them completely, even when it led her to the stake."

She scanned the classroom of captivated faces. "The saints weren't perfect people." Her voice dropped slightly, creating an intimate atmosphere despite the classroom setting. "They were flawed, struggling humans who sometimes made terrible mistakes. Saint Augustine lived a wild life before his conversion. Saint Peter denied Christ three times. What made them saints wasn't their perfection—it was their willingness to keep trying. To follow what they believed was right, even when it was difficult."

A student raised her hand. "How do you know if you're hearing God or just making things up in your head?"

Claire smiled. "That's the question we all wrestle with, isn't it? Even the saints questioned themselves. True faith isn't found in absolute certainty—it's discovered in the courage to take the next step even when the path ahead is unclear."

Damn, she had no idea how close to home that hit.

I shouldn't be here. But I made no effort to move.

She had always been the type to talk with her hands, but not to a distracting degree. Her black sneakers were silent as she moved across the dark wood floor. The skirt that fell past her knees swayed with each step, modest yet still able to draw my attention. A black leather belt cinched her small waist, keeping the crisp white tunic in place beneath a fitted black vest. The silver cross around her neck glinted softly under the classroom lights. Her black veil covered the dark wavy hair I knew lay underneath, framing her face in a way that was elegant.

I forgot where I was, captivated by her natural islander beauty.

Claire glanced at one of the students, who'd asked a question. She was in her element. Compassionate, patient, and utterly in control. God, it made me want to be closer to her.

I came here with a purpose. But watching her like this . . . How could I interrupt this to dredge up the past?

I turned to leave, and my stomach dropped. Standing a few feet away, watching me with a knowing glint in her dark eyes, was Principal Omura.

I froze for a heartbeat as her gaze flickered between Claire's classroom door and me, an amused smile playing on her lips.

"Father Damian," she said, her voice sharp and sweet.

I nodded, forcing a tight smile. "Laura."

Before she could say anything else, I ducked out of the hallway toward the exit. My heart was racing by the time I stepped into the parking lot. *Fuck me.* I hoped to God no one else had seen me staring at *Sister* Claire.

I inhaled deeply, the cool ocean air doing little to calm the heat rising in my cheeks. I'd been stupid. Careless. Letting my guard down like that was dangerous. And it *had* to be the principal of the fucking school, of all people.

I heard footsteps behind me, and I knew Laura had followed. I turned to face her, dreading what I knew was coming. Sure enough, there she stood, her arms crossed, smile laced with mischief.

"Did something in Sister Claire's lecture catch your attention, Father?" Her gaze was far too perceptive for comfort.

I cleared my throat, rolling my shoulders back. "I was just making sure the kids weren't giving her a hard time. You know how they can be." It was partially true. When the hell had I become a man of half-truths? *Dammit, Claire.*

Laura's eyebrows rose; she wasn't buying it for a second. "Uh-huh." She shifted her weight to one leg. "You have nothing to worry about. The kids adore her. And I must say, quite a few of our single dads have taken an interest in parent-teacher conferences lately."

Hot possessiveness flared in my chest. The thought of other men watching Claire, admiring her—I clenched my jaw. "Really?"

Laura grinned and used a tone I hadn't heard since I'd graduated. "What the lips can't speak, the eyes confess, young man. And right now, yours are saying plenty."

"I don't know what you're talking about," I muttered, the lie bitter on my tongue.

"Of course you don't."

I crossed my arms. "Did she say anything about me?"

"Nothing I don't already know."

I was almost afraid to ask. "Meaning?"

"Listen, I may be an old crone now, but I can see a spark from a mile away," Laura said, tucking a strand of peppered hair behind her ear.

I tilted my head toward the clear blue sky and let out a breath. "There's no spark. There can't be. We dated in high school. That's it."

She stepped closer and lowered her voice as she said, "You may want to be more mindful of the lingering stares, then. Especially during Mass."

My cheeks warmed, but I said nothing and nodded, hoping that would end this conversation. She studied me for a moment longer, then finally turned away, leaving me standing in front of the rectory. My heart continued racing. I'd been seen. There was no denying it. But worse than that, I couldn't ignore this cursed pull. The conversation with Laura only confirmed what I already knew: I was fooling myself if I thought I could just ignore Claire's presence here.

And with Rico's case weighing on me, the silence from the detective, the guilt that never seemed to fade . . . I needed to face at least one of my failures. I couldn't fix what had happened to Rico, but maybe I could finally be honest with Claire about why I'd left her.

Principal Omura walked back toward the school, but it didn't stop my churning stomach. And if Laura had noticed, who else might start to?

I jogged into the rectory and made a sandwich for lunch. Turkey, cheese, and mustard. God, I missed my mother's lasagna—the way the house would fill with the scent of garlic and herbs on Sundays before Rico died. Now, quick meals alone had become the norm.

Afterward, I showered and managed to get a little bit of reading done, though the words barely registered. By the time five o'clock Mass rolled around, I was thankful for the distraction of familiar prayers and routine.

As soon as Mass ended and the quiet evening settled in at home, I couldn't shake the weight pressing on my chest. Rico's killer was still out there—at least as far as I knew. And Claire . . . I'd carried my guilt about her for eight years, telling myself it was better to stay away. But Laura's words echoed in my mind: *What the lips can't speak, the eyes confess.*

I was tired of carrying secrets. Tired of half-truths and avoidance. I couldn't tell Claire about the confession—that was sacred—but I could finally tell her why I'd really left. Why I'd broken both our hearts rather than risk failing her the way I'd failed Rico. I slipped on some tennis shoes and made the ten-minute walk toward her house, my heart hammering with each step.

With my hands in the pockets of my gray sweats, I stood in front of Claire's cottage on the uneven sidewalk. The structure looked foreign surrounded by all the clean lines and polished glass of the modern neighborhood. The weathered white paint had stood against the coastal winds for years, and the front porch sagged just enough to give it character. Jasmine lined the walkway, and old green shutters framed the windows. It suited her. Simple, beautiful, and stubbornly out of place in this quiet corner of the world.

I knew a few parishioners who lived nearby, so I needed to be careful.

The cool wind off the ocean bit at my skin, but it wasn't the chill that kept me from moving. It was a memory, pulling at me like a demon I couldn't escape.

I was sixteen, she was seventeen. Claire had been sitting beside me, her jaw tight, arms crossed. She had always done that when she was upset but wouldn't let herself break. We'd just had a petty argument about something that seemed monumental then but was ultimately trivial. It had left both of us in silence, neither wanting to be the first to apologize.

I didn't know what to say, so I'd chosen nothing. Just watched her as the quiet stretched between us, salt air clinging to our skin and the setting sun painting her profile in gold. That was when I saw it—a sparrow, small and unassuming. It hopped along the ground, pecking at the grass. The bird seemed oblivious to the two teenagers sitting there, worlds apart but side by side.

For a moment, I'd envied that damn sparrow. It seemed so at peace. Certain of itself, even though it was small and easily overlooked. The way it moved with purpose, surviving despite its fragility. That was when it hit me: Claire was like that too. She carried her wounds where no one could see them. Wasn't the type to make a fuss or shout about her pain. She just kept going. Suffered in silence. Found strength in being overlooked.

"You remind me of that sparrow," I'd said, my voice breaking through the tension like a ripple on still water.

She had looked up at me with guarded eyes. "A sparrow?" Her voice had been skeptical, almost amused.

I nodded, watching the bird hop closer to us. "Yeah. Quiet, but strong. Beautiful without trying to be." I paused, reaching for her hand. "Didn't Jesus say God notices every sparrow that falls? That's how I see you. Someone worth noticing. Worth caring about."

She'd stared at me. The corners of her mouth twitched. She wanted to smile but wasn't quite ready to give in. Her eyes had softened, as though my words had touched a part of her that rarely saw light.

We'd sat there for a while longer, the argument forgotten. She leaned into me, resting her head on my shoulder as I wrapped my arm around her. Everything had felt right again. Just us, the quiet, and that damn sparrow before it had flown off into the trees.

"My sparrow," I'd called her, from then on. The name had become my silent vow to protect the fragile strength I saw in her. But eight years and countless prayers later, I hesitated outside her cottage. Some vows, once broken, could never be renewed. And I'd shattered this one beyond repair when I walked out of her life.

The light inside cast a warm glow through the windows. Through the lace curtains, her silhouette moved around the living room. Slowly, I made my way up the three porch steps and stopped in front of the worn front door.

All I had to do was knock. But I hesitated. An old fear crept back in. What if I knocked, she opened the door, and she didn't want to hear an apology eight years too late?

I clenched my fists at my sides, forcing a breath from my lungs. She had always been the strong one. Maybe it was my turn to show some courage. I reached for the door, my knuckles hovering just inches from the wood.

Just do it, you fucking coward.

With my heart thundering against my ribs, I knocked three times. The door swung open, and all my carefully constructed walls crumbled. All the air rushed out of my lungs. She stood there in black shorts that showed off the curve of her hips and a sports bra that hugged her full breasts. Her dark hair was pulled into a ponytail, loose strands framing her face.

"What're you doing here, Father?" She crossed her arms, the title falling from her lips, a challenge. Like she knew exactly what it did to me, hearing her call me that while standing there, temptation at its finest.

I opened my mouth, the apology right there on my tongue. *I came to apologize. For how I left. For never explaining why.* But looking at her—seeing the guarded way she held herself, the careful distance she maintained—my courage fled. "Just wanted to check on you."

Her eyebrows rose slightly, and I caught what might have been disappointment flash across her face. "Check on me?"

"Yeah. You know, make sure you're settling in okay. The parish can be . . . a lot." The lie tasted bitter, but it was easier than the truth.

She leaned against the doorframe, studying me with those captivating gray eyes. "I thought we had an unspoken agreement to avoid each other."

"The Church taught me a great deal about silence," I said, running a hand through my hair. "But I don't know how to do that when it comes to you."

It wasn't the apology I'd planned, but it was more honest than my excuse about checking on her. Something flickered in her expression. Confusion, or was that fear?

She pushed off the doorframe. "You want to come in for a glass of wine?"

I should say no. But I followed her inside anyway, watching as she moved through her kitchen with the same grace she'd shown in her classroom. She'd always been comfortable in her own skin, a confidence that came from knowing exactly who she was, even if that person didn't fit neatly into a box.

"You like merlot?" She grabbed two glasses, the domestic normalcy of the moment making my chest constrict.

"Yeah." I sat at her kitchen island, trying not to think about how this felt both dangerous and right. Like confession and sin packaged in velvet and wrapped into one moment.

She poured generously and took a drink from her own glass. The Claire I'd known had barely touched alcohol.

"That kind of day?" I asked.

Her eyes narrowed. "No. I just love wine. It's one of my vices."

I lifted my glass with a smirk. "Hope that wasn't the reason you became a nun."

She laughed, but there was an edge to it. "No. Though it's certainly a perk." She took another drink, longer this time, and she stared at the liquid as though she was somewhere else. "I thought if I could earn my place in the Church, maybe I could help kids like the ones I teach now understand that God's love doesn't come with conditions. That acceptance isn't a sin." Her eyes snapped to me—back to the present—and she bit her bottom lip. "Shit. I probably shouldn't have said that."

My brows rose. The honesty in her voice caught me off guard. I knew something had happened when her sister, Jasmine, came out, but Claire had never given me the full details. Not that I'd given her the chance. Here she was, being vulnerable, sharing her struggles with faith and identity. The least I could do was return that honesty.

"Claire," I started, then stopped. The apology was right there again, but my throat felt tight. "You never liked wine when we were younger."

Coward. I'd deflected rather than face the conversation I'd come here to have.

A corner of her mouth lifted. "Yeah, well, things changed. I'm not so innocent anymore."

I nearly choked on my wine.

"You okay?" she asked, but I caught the knowing look in her eyes.

"Fine." I cleared my throat, searching for safer ground. "How're you liking being back in your old parish?"

She leaned a hip against the counter, and I took a moment to study her. She carried herself like someone who'd fought her own battles with faith and identity. Someone who might understand my own struggles more than I wanted to admit.

"I forgot how amazing this community can be. Although, I feel like I'm on Mrs. Fontana's shit list." For the first time in eight years, she smiled at me. The kind that reached her eyes and made my heart stutter. It wasn't just the alcohol warming my insides. It was the knowledge that we were more alike now than we'd ever been before.

"She can be territorial, but I'm sure she just needs to get to know you like I do," I said, swirling the crimson liquid in my tumbler.

"*Knew* me." Her gaze bored into me. "I'm not that girl anymore, Damian."

Of course she wasn't the same—eight years would change anyone. But I'd been trying to hold on to an image, the Claire I'd left behind rather than the woman she'd become, despite recognizing the differences firsthand since she'd arrived. "You're right. I'm sorry."

She studied me for a moment. "I had to figure out who I was without you." There was no accusation in her voice, just quiet sincerity. "Rebuild myself from scratch."

I gripped my glass tighter, guilt sinking deeper into my chest. I'd always been terrified of being unreliable with her—the way I'd been unreliable with Rico that night. So I'd made the ultimate unreliable choice: I'd left completely.

Claire tapped an index finger on her glass, the soft sound filling the silence between us. "I've come to the conclusion that doubt isn't the opposite of faith. It's part of it. It strengthens faith." Her eyes found mine again. "Jasmine taught me that. When the Church rejected her, she didn't lose her faith—she found a deeper, more honest version of it. One that didn't require her to deny who she was."

I inhaled a breath and then released it. There was liberation in hearing someone else voice the questions I'd been carrying alone. *Damn, I almost forgot how easy it is to talk to her, to listen to her.* She deserved to know about Rico's killer, but I had to uphold my vow. My voice was rougher than intended as I said, "Rico loved the Mass, but sometimes I stand at the altar and wonder if I'm worthy of this. My collar feels heavy some days."

Claire studied me, her head tilting in that adorable way I loved.

"Sounds like you're comparing yourself." She faced the sink and turned the knob on the faucet. Water sprayed everywhere as she squealed. "Holy shit. Cold."

I got up from the stool and rushed to her side. I didn't care that I was getting drenched in the process. Liquid splashing onto the tile echoed in the small space as I crouched down, reaching under the sink, and fumbled for the valve. My fingers slipped over the wet pipes, but I found it, twisting the metal until water stopped gushing.

I straightened, pushing back my now-wet hair.

Claire stepped back, her bare feet sliding on the slick floor. Pure instinct took over. My hand shot out and slipped around her waist, pulling her body against mine.

The moment her warmth seeped through my soaked clothes, guilt and desire warred inside me. This was exactly why priests weren't supposed to be alone with beautiful women.

Her wide eyes met mine, startled. My arm tightened around her waist, the scent of her hair, fresh and floral, filling the small space between us. Every breath felt sinful, every point of contact a betrayal.

Lord, I've led myself into temptation. But wasn't God also the one who created this spark between two people? Who designed our bodies to react this way? The questions I'd been wrestling with lately rose again, demanding answers.

Claire's breath hitched, and then, just as quickly, she untangled herself from me and stepped back. Her gaze roamed everywhere but at me.

"Thanks," she muttered, her voice a little too casual. The forced normalcy in her tone only highlighted how far from normal this was.

I nodded, my heart still pounding, water dripping from my sleeves, every drop judgment running down my skin. Yet my eyes wandered to her sports bra, where her hardened nipples poked through the thin material. I wanted to suck on them. Make her squirm as I flicked my tongue over them again and again. The thought came unbidden, shame burning hot in my chest. Here I was, a man of God, letting my base desires override the vows I'd sworn to uphold.

And I'm hard again. The physical evidence of my weakness pressed against my pants, mocking my attempts at self-control. I couldn't do this. The Bible said to avoid temptation, and an apology was never going to rid me of these thoughts and desires. I knew what I had to do.

"I'll have someone come fix that for you." I gestured to the faucet, desperate for something practical to focus on.

"Okay. Thanks." She dried herself off with a kitchen towel, then offered me one.

I needed a cold shower and about fifty Hail Marys. More than that, I needed to kneel in that confessional until this burning need for her was purged from my system. Except wasn't that what I had tried over and over already to no avail? "I'm good."

She flung the towel into the sink and walked me to the door. "Thanks for checking on me, I guess."

Years of seminary training and countless hours of prayer and meditation weren't enough to erase the familiarity of her body against mine. I was supposed to be a shepherd, a guide, a man above such primal desires, but my body's reaction to her told me I was failing . . . spectacularly.

"This isn't working, Claire." The words tasted like ash in my mouth. "We need to speak with the bishop ASAP about having you reassigned. For the sake of the parish." *For both our sakes.*

Her expression shifted, caution replacing the earlier warmth. "I thought we were doing okay. Some wet clothes too much for you to handle?"

" 'Okay' isn't enough. There's too much history between us."

Her eyes widened, hurt flashing across her face before her expression hardened. "What're you *really* afraid of, Damian?"

I'm afraid that what I want and what I've sworn to be can't exist in the same place.

She stared at me for a long moment, then gave a curt nod. "Fine. Do what you need to do."

I turned away, unable to bear the look in her eyes. Sprinting back to the church, I worked off this pent-up frustration and punished myself, each footfall matching the rhythm of my heart.

I managed to turn a ten-minute walk into a four-minute run. Crashing through the front door of the rectory, I flopped onto the cool floor and stared up at the dark ceiling. *God grant me strength.* But even as the words formed in my mind, I wondered if strength was what I needed. Maybe what I needed was understanding of myself, of these feelings, of what it truly meant to serve God while still being human.

But one thing was clear—Claire couldn't stay at Saint Anthony's.

"Stay awake, and pray not to be put to the test. The spirit is willing enough, but human nature is weak." —Matthew 26:41 (New Jerusalem Bible)

Chapter Eight

CLAIRE

The scratch of pencils on paper was the only sound in my classroom as my students worked through their quiz on the lives of the saints. Twenty-two seventh graders bent over their desks, brows furrowed in concentration.

I sat at my desk, pretending to grade yesterday's assignments. Staring at the same paragraph about Saint Teresa of Avila for the third time, my mind replayed every moment of Damian's visit the night before.

I clicked my red pen a few times. Emma Ramirez chewed on her pencil eraser as she stared at the paper in front of her. The poor girl had been struggling lately—her parents' divorce was taking its toll. At least someone's family drama had a clear resolution in sight, unlike the unholy mess I'd stepped into.

Damian had stood on my doorstep looking like a man with a mission, but had then given some flimsy excuse about "checking on me."

Right. Because Father Damian Bellucci is known for his spontaneous wellness checks at eight o'clock at night.

The wine had helped loosen my tongue last night, but it seemed to tie Damian's in knots. He'd been about to tell me something. Twice. But for some reason, he hadn't been able to get the words out. So typical. *Damian always runs when things get complicated.*

This isn't working, Claire. We need to speak with the bishop ASAP about having you reassigned.

His words still stung, even twelve hours later. *For the sake of the parish,* he'd said. More like for the sake of Father Damian's peace of mind. Well, I'd spent nearly a decade learning to advocate for myself and others who didn't fit the Church's neat little boxes. I wasn't about to let him ship me off. I doubted the bishop would want to do the paperwork.

Although, if I was being honest, Damian's discomfort wasn't exactly one-sided.

The moment his arm had wrapped around my waist when I'd slipped on the wet kitchen floor, every nerve ending in my body had come alive. Eight years, and my body had remembered his touch like it was yesterday. The way he'd looked at me afterward, desire and guilt warring in those green eyes . . . *Maybe that's what scared him.*

I glanced at the crucifix hanging above my whiteboard and sent up a silent prayer. *Well, Big Guy, I think I'm missing the point here. Some help would be great.*

The truth was, I understood why Damian was struggling. The physical attraction between us was undeniable, and for someone who'd built his entire identity around his vows, that had to be terrifying. But running away wasn't the answer. We were both adults committed to serving God. Surely we could figure out how to work in the same parish without destroying each other. Right?

My gaze drifted to the window, where morning sunlight streamed through the glass. Light had always been important to me—finding it in dark places, sharing it with others who needed it most.

That's what I'm meant to do here.

Justin Williams was fidgeting in the third row, clearly struggling with a question on his quiz. I caught his eye and gave him an encouraging nod. He'd been acting out lately, probably processing his own family issues. So many of these kids were carrying adult-sized worries on their young shoulders.

I looked down at the assignment I was supposed to be grading, finally focusing on the words. Carly Liu had written about Saint Joan of Arc: *She didn't let anyone tell her she couldn't do what God called her to do, even when it was scary and everyone thought she was wrong.*

Smart kid. Joan had confronted kings and bishops, armies and executioners, because she trusted what she heard in her heart more than what others told her was proper or possible.

The sharp ring of the bell startled me from my thoughts. Papers rustled as students gathered their belongings, the quiet meditation of test-taking dissolving into the familiar chaos of middle schoolers eager for freedom.

"Don't forget," I called over the noise. "Tomorrow we start our unit on saints who faced persecution. Think about what courage means to you."

Most of the students filed out quickly, but Emma Ramirez lingered, taking her time to organize her pencils and erase stray marks from her desk. I noticed the way she kept glancing toward the door, then back at her quiz.

"Take your time, Emma." I walked over to her desk. "How do you think you did?"

She handed me her paper with a small shrug. "Okay, I guess. Sister Claire? Can I ask you something?"

"Of course, sweetheart. What's on your mind?"

Emma fidgeted with the strap of her unicorn backpack. "It's about my parents. Divorce stuff." Her voice dropped to barely above a whisper. "Is it normal to feel mad at both of them? Like, sometimes I'm mad at my dad for leaving, but sometimes I'm mad at my mom for . . . I don't know, not trying harder?"

My heart squeezed. At twelve, Emma was trying to process emotions that challenged even adults. I knelt beside her desk, meeting her at eye level.

"What you're feeling is completely normal," I said. "Divorce is hard on everyone in the family, especially kids. It's okay to feel angry, or sad, or confused. It doesn't make you a bad person."

"But shouldn't I pick a side? My friends keep asking who I want to live with, like it's some kind of game."

"This isn't about sides, Em. Your parents' marriage didn't work out, but that doesn't mean either of them stopped loving you. Sometimes adults make decisions that hurt, but it doesn't mean those decisions are about you or because of you."

She nodded, some of the tension leaving her shoulders. "My mom's been really stressed about everything. She cries when she thinks I'm not looking."

"Your mom is going through a big change. It's natural for her to be emotional right now. But that's not your responsibility to fix, okay? Your job is to be twelve. Focus on school and friends and figuring out who you're becoming."

"That's what my uncle says too. He's been helping out more since Dad moved out." Emma shouldered her backpack, her face looking a bit brighter. "He said he'll be picking me up from school when Mom has to work late or has meetings with lawyers and stuff."

"That's nice of him to help your family."

"Yeah. He said he wants to make sure I'm doing okay with everything. He asks a lot of questions about school and stuff." Emma paused at the doorway. "Thanks for listening, Sister Claire. You always know what to say."

"Anytime, sweetheart. You can talk to me about anything, okay? And if things get too overwhelming at home, we have counselors who can help too."

After Emma left, I stood in the quiet empty classroom, our

conversation replaying in my mind. She was lucky to have family support during such a difficult time. It reminded me of how Jasmine had been my anchor when I was questioning everything about faith and identity. Having someone in your corner could make all the difference.

Which brought me back to my current situation. Maybe Damian felt alone. His position as priest meant he probably felt like he couldn't show weakness or uncertainty.

I gathered my things and locked my classroom door, my steps lighter than they'd been all morning. If Damian wanted to involve the bishop, fine. But he'd underestimated one crucial thing: I wasn't the same girl he'd walked away from.

Joan of Arc had faced down armies for what she believed in. I could certainly handle one stubborn priest and a bishop's meeting.

As I walked toward the parking lot, a shift happened inside me—not resignation or defeat, but determination. Whatever happened next, I wasn't going anywhere without a fight. This community, these kids, this calling I'd found . . . They were worth fighting for.

I climbed into my car and sat for a moment. Tomorrow would bring new challenges, new questions, new opportunities to make a difference. I'd face whatever came next the same way I'd faced everything else these past eight years—with courage and an unshakeable belief that faith always finds a way.

Chapter Nine

DAMIAN

An hour before morning Mass, I sat on the couch in the rectory with my head in my hands. The sun found its way through the gap in the curtains, reminding me that another day had started, whether I was ready or not.

So much for making things right with Claire. If this was a test sent by God Himself, I'd failed. How was I supposed to serve faithfully with Claire as a constant reminder of the life I'd given up?

This is for the best.

I couldn't work with her—not after everything we'd been through. Being near Claire had ignited desires I had no business feeling as Father Bellucci. The one person I'd never allowed myself to have was right in front of me, and all I could do was try to resist her gravitational pull.

The bishop had the power to fix this mess.

I stared at the wall, my pulse hammering in my ears. Then, like a bad movie on repeat, the memory hit me—Claire, standing in front of me, her voice cracking as she said, *We were going to build a life together.*

Her words had haunted me, even as I went through seminary

school. I couldn't remember most of the conversation, just that one line.

Honestly, at twenty years old, breaking up with her was one of the hardest decisions I'd ever made, like tearing away a piece of my soul.

My gaze drifted to the corner of the room, where Rico's old skateboard leaned against the wall, collecting dust. I didn't even know why I'd taken it when I moved out of my parents' house. It had been one of the few things I'd grabbed, along with some clothes and books.

Maybe I thought having a piece of him with me would help, but mostly it just sat there like a monument to my guilt. Every time I caught sight of it, I remembered how he'd tried to teach me patience, balance, how to get back up when I fell. But I'd failed him when it mattered most. How could I trust myself not to fail Claire as a friend?

I thought it would be easier to let her go rather than drag her to hell with me. I replayed those last moments in my mind—the pain in her gray eyes as I walked away.

After earning my bachelor's degree at Berkeley, I'd gone through four years of seminary school. And somehow, my first assignment landed me here at Saint Anthony's, the parish I'd grown up in, offering Mass to the same faces every morning. Some of my old classmates were parishioners. They'd come in, holding their kids' hands, or walking arm in arm with their spouses. The church had always been a sanctuary for my turmoil, a place where I could confront the demons swirling inside me, even as I grappled with the ache of losing *her*.

Part of me wondered if I'd made the right choice. I'd dreamed of marriage once, of waking up beside someone who knew me in all the ways no one else could. I had wanted kids, a boy, maybe two. A little girl. Someone to pass on my father's stories and my mother's recipes. I had wanted the kind of love that was built on more than Catholic doctrine and societal expectations.

I often thought about how much easier this calling would be if the Church allowed priests to marry. It wasn't as if the need for companionship and connection just vanished when I put on the collar. That desire was still there, buried deep but persistent.

God created us for love, didn't He?

Why should priests be denied that? I still believed the Church was good, but it was flawed. Like the rule about celibacy. God knew I loved sex—raw, hard, long nights of fucking. Mother of God, I missed it. The topic had come up in one of our clergy meetings but wasn't taken seriously. Then again, who was I to challenge ancient ingrained traditions?

I leaned back on the couch, staring up at the ceiling. Fuck, by simply being here, Claire was making me question my sanity. At least, that was what I wanted to believe. That she was the problem, my temptation, my weakness. It was easier to blame her than admit I'd been wrestling with these doubts long before she'd come back into my life.

If the bishop reassigned her, I could go back to ignoring these fractures in my certainty, back to serving the parish with quiet resignation, back to telling myself this emptiness was just part of my sacrifice.

After celebrating Mass that morning, I removed my chasuble, folding it before setting it aside. The short homily I'd given on Peter denying Christ still clung to me. It had been about how fear can make us betray the very thing we claim to love most.

I slipped my cell from the pocket of my black slacks. Bishop Valenti's secretary had left a voicemail confirming a same-day appointment for me and Claire. When I hung up the phone, I exhaled a slow breath, though the unease hadn't completely dissipated.

One step closer to remedying this mess.

Claire had been on my mind all fucking night. Admittedly, I hadn't stopped wondering what she thought of all this. Did she see this as divine providence? Some twist of fate? Chain crucifixes we were meant to untangle together? Dammit, there was a time when she'd have been the one I turned to for advice.

My chest tightened. Her opinion shouldn't matter anymore. Shaking my head, I pushed the thought away, but it lingered just out of reach, like the ghost of a prayer I wasn't ready to say.

I strode out of the sacristy and into the lobby of the church. Claire was standing in front of the bulletin board, reading the announcements. She was so cute squinting at one of the flyers. I'd told Mrs. Walker to make the font bigger.

"Ready?" I asked, cutting straight to the point.

She looked at me, tilting her head, her expression curious. "For?"

"A meeting with the bishop. He managed to squeeze us into his schedule today. Thank God," I said, already heading out the double doors.

Claire followed, her black sneakers scuffing the sidewalk. "You didn't waste any time, did you?"

We made it to the rectory driveway, where my burgundy truck was parked. I glanced at her as I climbed into the driver's seat. "The sooner we can resolve this, the better."

She slid into the passenger's seat and scowled at me, a flicker of the fire I remembered from high school lighting up her face. That look incited other memories. *Nope, not going there. What the hell is wrong with me?*

A picturesque blur of cliffs and ocean meant nothing as the silence between us thickened. The steady hum of the engine droned on, blending with the distant crash of waves, the coastal road twisting beneath us. Sunlight filtered through the window, casting fleeting patterns onto the dashboard.

What had she been up to in the time we'd been apart? Did she have boyfriends when she went off to college? Had she ever wondered about me? I gripped the steering wheel tighter with each second, my knuckles white against the black leather.

We should've taken separate vehicles. Every time she shifted next to me, I felt a spark of electricity crackle in the air. Even her breathing seemed amplified, filling the space in a way that had my nerves on edge, and yet . . . I couldn't break the silence.

Finally, we pulled up in front of the diocesan building, an unassuming beige structure tucked between a couple other government offices. Claire unbuckled and muttered, "Let's get this over with," as she stepped out of the truck.

The chancery had the same sterile feeling it always did: gray walls, wood-paneled doors, and the faint hum of an ancient air conditioner rattling in the corner. The scent of incense hung in the air, as if someone had tried to mask the stale undertone of paperwork and formality with a touch of holiness.

After checking in with the secretary, Claire and I walked over to the waiting area. My foot tapped against the marble floor, a soft echo in the otherwise quiet space. Every tick of the clock on the wall made my pulse jump, like we were waiting for more than just a meeting that would have Claire sent far away from me.

The silver-haired woman poked her head in and said, "Father Bellucci, Sister Vergara, the bishop will see you now."

I stood, smoothing out my black button-down and fixing my collar. I led the way to the bishop's office at the end of the hallway and could tell Claire was having trouble keeping up with my long strides. A corner of my mouth rose. *She's so fucking cute.*

Bishop Valenti was seated behind his oak desk when we finally entered. He was a broad man, maybe in his early sixties, his dark eyes sharp with just enough warmth to soften the lines on his face. He was known for pushing for change—trying to make things more inclusive within the diocese.

"Ah, Sister Claire, Father Damian, good to see you both," he greeted us, standing for a moment before gesturing for us to sit. "How are you settling in to your new parish, Sister?"

I shifted uncomfortably in the chair next to her.

Claire cleared her throat, her voice resolute, though I knew better. "That's actually why we're here, Your Excellency."

"Really?" The bishop's brow lifted as he clasped his hands on the desk. "What's the issue?"

Here we go.

I tried to keep my voice as neutral as possible. "We can't work together."

Claire glanced at me.

The bishop leaned back, crossing his arms. "But didn't Sister Vergara just get settled? What *exactly* is the problem?"

Damn it, why is this so hard? I swallowed hard, words sticking in my throat. "We dated in high school."

Claire rolled her eyes. "Eight years ago."

Like that would soften the blow.

Bishop Valenti's expression didn't change, though he shifted in his seat. "That's a long time, wouldn't you say?"

I nodded, avoiding Claire's gray gaze. "It is . . ."

"But," the bishop interjected, leaning forward now, his sharp eyes unwavering on the both of us, "I understand the complication here. And trust me, I don't take it lightly. As servants of God, your personal feelings must come second to your mission. You both took vows of service, of celibacy, and of devotion to His people. I expect you to honor them with the same seriousness that brought you to this life."

His words were an icy slap to the face. I held my tongue, waiting for him to finish.

"Saint Anthony's is a small parish, but the work there is vital. The community needs both of you. I won't pretend that working together will be easy, but it's not impossible. God often tests us in ways we don't expect. Consider this one of those tests."

Well, shit. My gut twisted.

The bishop's expression softened a fraction. "Now, I could talk to Mother Superior and request to have Sister Vergara reassigned, but that would be the easy way out. The Church doesn't shy away from challenges, and neither should you. Both of you are strong in your faith and your calling, and I expect you to act with professionalism and grace. You're here for the parish, not for yourselves."

There was a heavy pause, his words lingering in the air like the faint scent of incense filling the room. Claire and I exchanged a glance, her expression unreadable.

Bishop Valenti continued, "If either of you feels this assignment will compromise your ability to serve, speak now. But understand that avoiding difficult situations isn't what we're called to do. Sometimes, the best way to heal old wounds is to face them head-on."

The ball was in our court now. My hands clenched into fists, but I forced myself to breathe. I hated that he was right. Damn it, I hated it.

I finally broke the silence. "Thank you for your time, Your Excellency. We'll . . . make it work."

I could feel Claire's eyes on me; she was probably wondering if I'd lost my ever-loving mind. The irony wasn't lost on me—I'd spent years praying to forget her, and now God was forcing us together as some kind of divine test. If this was His idea of a lesson in fortitude, He could've been more subtle about it.

"Thank you, Your Excellency," she echoed, her voice tight.

Bishop Valenti blessed us both as we stood to leave, and we shuffled out of his office. I stuffed my hands into my pockets, trying to block out the chaos in my head.

Walking through the hallway lined with portraits of saints who'd faced their own trials, I wondered if the bishop had seen something I'd missed.

Maybe this wasn't about getting Claire reassigned at all. Maybe this was exactly what he meant about rising to the challenge—not running from it, but learning to navigate it with the faith and discipline that defined us both. The thought settled in my chest. A revelation. This was the sign I'd been praying for, wasn't it? Not the easy solution I'd wanted, but the difficult path that would truly test what I was made of.

"We'll make this work," Claire said quietly as we reached my truck, almost as if she was trying to convince herself.

I nodded, climbing into the driver's seat, but my response felt different now, less like resignation and more like determination. What I needed was a nice long run to clear my head.

Claire Vergara was here to stay, and fuck me if that didn't terrify and exhilarate me in equal measure.

"Blessed is anyone who perseveres when trials come. Such a person is of proven worth and will win the prize of life, the crown that the Lord has promised to those who love him." —James 1:12 (New Jerusalem Bible)

Chapter Ten

DAMIAN

A day after the meeting with Bishop Valenti, his words about *rising to the challenge* kept replaying in my head. I couldn't shake the feeling that I was missing a crucial puzzle piece, or maybe I was seeing it all too clearly—and that was what scared the shit out of me.

I needed to get out of Saint Anthony's, away from the walls that should have been comforting but instead seemed to be closing in on me, away from the possibility of running into Claire in every hallway and feeling that electric pull that made my collar feel like a noose.

I also needed to talk to someone who'd understand my situation —not as a man wrestling with desire, but as a priest wrestling with his vocation. The only person who could do that was Father Maximillian Sullivan, who was the priest of Saint Mark's in the neighboring city. We'd been through seminary together, survived the same grueling theology courses and late-night discussions about celibacy that had seemed so much easier to navigate in theory than in practice.

Max had always been the one with unwavering faith, the guy who never seemed to question whether he belonged behind the altar. If anyone could help me figure out whether I was losing my mind, it was him.

The drive to the city gave me time to think, to pray, to find some clarity in the rhythm of the road. It at least got me far enough away from Claire that I could breathe without catching her jasmine scent on the air.

I pulled into the small parking lot of one of my favorite authentic Italian restaurants, which just happened to be within walking distance of Saint Mark's Cathedral. The bell above Mangiamo's door chimed as I stepped inside, the familiar scent of garlic and marinara wrapping around me like a comforting hug. I caught my reflection in the window and barely recognized myself. *God, I look like shit.* Dark circles shadowed my eyes, and my usual neat appearance had begun to slip—shirt wrinkled, hair unkempt.

Max was already seated in our usual corner booth, his blond hair catching the afternoon light that streamed through the window. He was only two years older than me, but he carried himself with humble confidence I'd always envied.

He smiled, a knowing glint in his blue eyes that made my stomach sink. After all these years, he could still read me like one of his worn theology books. The same way he'd read me years ago when I'd rushed into seminary after university.

"You look like hell," he said by way of greeting.

I slid into the booth, reaching for a menu. An empty laugh escaped me, lacking any real humor. My voice was scratchy from another night of shitty sleep. My brother's killer's confession continued to haunt me, along with the way Claire had felt pressed against me in her kitchen. And then there was the bishop's lecture . . .

"I ordered our usual." Max's voice cut through the memory.

My gaze stayed on the menu as I muttered, "Mm-hmm." It was silent for a beat too long. I glanced up, and Max was studying me intently.

"It hasn't been that long since we've seen each other," he said.

It's been a few weeks. I set the laminated menu down. "Just tired. You know how it gets around the holidays."

"I call bullshit." He leaned back, crossing his arms.

"Max . . ."

"Don't 'Max' me. What's going on?"

Rosa approached our table and set our food down: his usual spaghetti and meatballs, my chicken parm—the closest thing I could find to Mom's cooking these days.

"Anything else I can get you boys?" Rosa asked, and then she stared at me for a heartbeat longer. "My God, Father Bellucci, you look like you've been dragged through purgatory and back."

Max's lips tilted up.

"Thank you, Rosa. I think we're good," I said, running a hand down my face.

"Okay, but I know when a man's carrying the weight of the world and then some." She walked away with her empty tray in hand.

"Talk to me." Max's tone was full of warning now, like he'd send God's wrath after me if I didn't confide in him.

I stared at my plate, the scent of garlic and cheese turning my stomach. The spire of Saint Mark's was visible through the restaurant's window, its shadow stretching across the street lot like an accusing finger.

I wanted to tell Max that I'd met the man who'd hit my brother, that Rico's killer had sat in my confessional and confessed his sins while I'd been bound by sacred law to absolve him. That secret was eating me alive, but somehow, it felt easier to carry than admitting what Claire was doing to me. At least with the confession, I knew my duty. With Claire . . . I didn't know shit. "You're going to think I'm pathetic."

Max grinned. "Come on, brother. I've heard a lot of confessions. Infidelity, drug addiction, porn addiction, food addiction."

He was right. If anyone could handle the mess I was about to confess, it was Max. But this felt different from the usual sins he heard. This was me, his friend, admitting that everything I'd built my life around was crumbling because of a woman I'd loved and lost a lifetime ago.

I inhaled, then blew it out. "It's a woman."

He didn't look at all surprised. "Who is she?"

I dropped my fork onto my plate, metal clinking against the thick ceramic. In five minutes, I managed to summarize who Claire had been and who she was now. Max just sat there, an unreadable look on his face. He had never been one to judge. I tapped my finger on the white tablecloth, waiting for him to speak.

He glanced out the window before meeting my gaze. "And you brought this to the bishop, right?"

I nodded. "He said we needed to 'rise to the challenge.' That the mission is bigger than us."

Max let out a breathy laugh.

"I'm glad you find this amusing." I couldn't help but grin.

His lips thinned. "So . . . how bad is it?"

Sitting back in my seat, I raked my hand through my hair. "She's fucking everywhere. Not just in my head, but in the whole damn parish. You should see how the kids light up when she walks into youth group. They practically fall over themselves to talk to her. And don't even get me started on that laugh of hers. It carries down the hallway, and I find myself walking in that direction without even meaning to. She brings this . . . energy to Saint Anthony's. The parents trust her, and I'm sitting there during staff meetings trying not to stare at the way she gestures when she gets excited about a new project. It's like watching the sun after years of rain. And I know— believe me, I fucking know—how wrong that is. But I can't turn it off."

A corner of Max's mouth rose as he stared at me. "Sounds like a certified infatuation to me." He continued, "You're human, Damian. Having these feelings doesn't make you a bad priest." Max's voice was gentle, but his eyes held a shadow of old pain.

I studied him, my hands clenched so tight my knuckles had turned white. "You don't get it. It's like she's rewired my entire soul. I used to wake up thinking about my homily; now I wake up wondering if she's watching the same sunrise. I made a promise to give God everything, but shit . . . What if she's not my weakness? What if she's exactly what He wanted me to find?"

Max was quiet for a long moment, pushing his meatballs around his plate.

Silence stretched between us, filled with the clatter of dishes and murmured conversations from other diners. Finally, he set his fork down. "There was someone once."

I caught the raw emotion in his voice.

"It was before I met you at seminary. Her name was Maria." His eyes grew distant, focusing on something or someone I couldn't see. "She used to come to Mass every Sunday, always at the same time. Beautiful voice, loved to sing in the choir." He swallowed hard. "I thought about quitting school and abandoning my vocation. Came damn close too."

I leaned forward, my food forgotten. "What happened?"

"Nothing. I chose to take my vows." He picked up his fork again but didn't eat. "She got married. Lives in Arizona. Has three kids now." The words carried the weight of years of wondering. "Do I still think about her sometimes? Sure. Do I wonder what might have been? Of course. But I made my choice, and I stick by it. Not because the Church's rules about celibacy make sense. Honestly, they don't. But because this is the path I chose."

"And you've never regretted it?"

His gaze met mine. "Regret implies I made the wrong choice. I made the right one for *me*. The question is, What's the right choice for you? Because I've got to tell you, I've never seen you look this tormented."

I pushed my plate away, my appetite completely gone. "When I'm with her"—I lowered my voice, leaning closer—"everything else disappears. But it's different now. Back then, we were just kids playing at forever." I traced the rim of my coffee cup, searching for the right words. "She sees the parts of me I've tried to bury."

"And that's what draws you to her?"

"She told me her favorite saint is Dymphna. That alone tells me she understands struggle in a way she couldn't have at nineteen." I let out a slow breath. "The other day, she talked about how doubt isn't the opposite of faith. That it's part of it. And fuck—it was like she'd reached inside my head and said the one thing I've been afraid to admit."

"That kind of connection is rare," Max said.

"When we were young, love was simple. Pure." I glanced out the window at the passersby. "Now she knows what it costs to choose a purpose bigger than yourself. To question that choice. To wonder . . ." I paused. "When I'm with her, I don't feel like I have to pretend to be this perfect vessel of faith. I can just exist."

"That's a lot to come to terms with, D." Max wiped his mouth with a napkin, then placed it on his empty plate.

"But it's not everything either, is it?" I ran a hand through my hair, tugging at the strands. "After Rico—" I stopped, throat tight. "I promised my life to God."

"Yes, you did. But vows taken for the wrong reasons aren't any more sacred than lies told with good intentions." Max's words sliced through my defenses like a blade.

I sat back, the leather booth creaking beneath me as memories flooded in. Rico's funeral, the way I'd fled to the Church, desperate for anything to numb the pain.

Outside, a car horn blared, making me flinch. The diner had filled up around us while we talked, the late-lunch crowd bringing with them a buzz of conversation and the clatter of silverware. But all I could hear was the truth in Max's words, echoing in my head like church bells.

"I should get back," I said, reaching for my wallet with an unsteady hand.

Max waved me off. "I've got this one." He caught my eye. "Just promise me something?"

"Okay."

"Don't make any decisions out of fear. Make sure it's what you truly believe is right." He paused, his next words barely above a whisper. "Sometimes the hardest part of faith is trusting that God's love is bigger than our rules."

I nodded, standing. "Thanks, Max."

He placed a heavy hand on my shoulder and squeezed. "Anytime, brother."

The drive back to Saint Anthony's felt longer than usual. Max's words echoed in my head, *Vows taken for the wrong reasons aren't any more sacred than lies told with good intentions.*

Those words felt less like a request for correction and more a plea for understanding. The afternoon sun caught the gold cross hanging from my rearview mirror, making it flash. What was that? A sign? A warning?

God, help me. I don't know what to do.

There was an unfamiliar sedan parked in the driveway of the rectory when I pulled up. Dark blue government plates—the kind of car that never brought good news. My stomach dropped before I even turned off the engine.

A man with dark hair and perpetually tired dark eyes got out of the driver's side, favoring his left leg as he straightened. I recognized that limp anywhere, a souvenir from a shooting three years back that had made the local papers. Detective Luis Alvarez. The man who'd been working Rico's case since day one and had called every few months for the first couple years with updates that led nowhere. The man who'd eventually stopped calling at all when the leads dried up.

"Detective Alvarez."

"Father Bellucci," he said, extending his hand. His grip was firm, weathered from years of shaking hands with grieving families and suspects who lied through their teeth. "Been a while."

I shook his hand, my heart racing against my ribs like it might break free. The confession from days ago crashed through my mind—*twenty years since his last confession. Fuck.* This was it. "What brings you here?"

"Is there somewhere we can talk?" His tone was careful, professional, but I caught the weight behind it. This wasn't a social visit.

I led him into the rectory, my legs wavering beneath me. The space suddenly felt too small, too quiet. I offered coffee that Alvarez declined with a shake of his head, and we sat in the small living room. Sunlight streamed through the windows, highlighting dust motes that danced in the air between us like tiny prayers I couldn't quite catch.

Alvarez settled into the worn armchair across from me, his weathered hands resting on his knees. "Nice place you got here. How long have you been at Saint Anthony's now?"

"About a year," I managed.

"Good parish. My mother-in-law used to attend Mass here before she moved to Sacramento." He glanced around the room, taking in the simple furnishings, the crucifix on the wall. "You settling in well? I imagine it's different from seminary life."

Small talk. Normal conversation. But I could see the tension in his shoulders, the way his fingers drummed against his leg. "It's been an adjustment, but the community's welcoming."

Alvarez nodded, then grew quiet for a moment. The casual mask slipped, and I saw the cop underneath—tired, carrying the weight of cases that never left him. "Father, I want to start by saying that I know this has been a long road for your family. Eight years without answers . . . I can't imagine what that's been like."

My chest tightened. *Here it comes.*

"I'm here because there's been a development in Rico's case."

I forced my expression to remain neutral, my hands clasped tightly in my lap to keep them from trembling. "After all this time?"

"He turned himself in. Thomas Mercer. Former high school chemistry teacher." Alvarez watched my face carefully. "Said he couldn't live with it anymore."

I had to look away, afraid my eyes might betray me. *Thomas Mercer.* The name burned into my mind.

"We checked his vehicle records. Found the car in a storage unit he's been paying for all these years. Paint samples match what we found on your brother's clothing." Alvarez leaned forward. "He's confessed to everything, Father. Driving under the influence. Leaving the scene. The whole thing."

I nodded, a strange sense of unreality washing over me. "Have you told my parents?"

"Called them right before coming here to set up a time to talk to them. Thought you might want to be with them when they process this."

"Yes. Thank you." The words felt mechanical, rehearsed.

Alvarez studied me, head tilted slightly. "You seem . . . I don't know. I expected more of a reaction. This is big news."

I met the detective's gaze, my jaw tight. "I'm a priest, Detective. I've learned to process grief differently." The half-truth was bitter on my tongue.

"Well, there's more. Mercer wants to meet with your family. Part of his attempt to make amends, he says."

I needed to confess first. To God. Before I face what's coming. His words from the confession echoed in my mind.

"I'll have to talk to my parents about that," I said carefully.

Alvarez nodded, standing. "Let's get going, then. If you don't have any prior engagements."

I had a few hours before I had to prep for evening Mass. "I have some time. The sooner we tell them, the better."

Moments later, I found myself in the passenger's seat of Alvarez's sedan. The faux leather seat squeaked beneath me each time I shifted. The car's interior smelled of stale coffee and the faint chemical sweetness of department-store air freshener. My gaze fell on the maple leaves, blazing oranges and reds, dancing across the sidewalk.

The detective was quiet, his nicotine-stained fingers drumming against the steering wheel, eyes fixed on the road ahead. I was grateful for that. I needed the silence.

Alvarez drove us through my childhood neighborhood, passing the old oak tree at the corner, its gnarled branches now half bare and scratching at a steel-gray sky. In the distance, I spotted the faded stop sign Rico and I used to race to when riding our bikes.

The house was the same: faded white brick, a porch with the swing my mom used to sit on every summer evening. But the warmth that used to radiate from this place was long gone. Now it was a shell, a house filled with ghosts that didn't know how to move on.

Mom's dahlias had bloomed, their velvety petals catching the wan afternoon light like drops of blood against the brown grass as we pulled up the driveway.

Dad opened the door before we could knock, his face strained with anticipation. He'd aged so much in the past eight years, hair completely silver now and shoulders stooped.

"Detective," he said with a curt nod before turning to me. "Damian."

We followed him inside, where Mom waited in the living room.

The TV was off, the house unnaturally quiet. She sat perched on the edge of the sofa, hands tightly clasped in her lap, looking too small in the space she'd once filled with laughter and warmth. It seemed she was having one of her good days. Since Rico died, she'd become a shell of the person she once was.

"Mr. and Mrs. Bellucci," Alvarez said, taking the seat across from her. "Thank you two for seeing me today."

I sat next to Mom, feeling her trembling as she reached for my hand. Her grip was cool and dry, fingers tight around mine.

"You've found something?" she asked, her voice steadier than I'd expected. "About Rico?"

"Yes, ma'am," Alvarez said gently. "We've identified the driver responsible for your son's death."

Dad made a noise between a gasp and a sob as he lowered himself into his armchair. Mom took his hand, her fingers intertwining with his.

"Who?" Dad asked, the single word weighted with eight years of waiting.

"Thomas Mercer," Alvarez replied. "Former high school chemistry teacher at Westridge. He turned himself in a few days ago."

"After all this time?" Mom's voice cracked slightly. "Why now?"

Alvarez elaborated about Mercer's confession, the evidence, the charges. I sat in silence, watching my parents absorb the information, looking for signs of the release I'd expected them to feel. But there was only quiet devastation, as if Rico had died all over again.

"He wants to arrange a meeting with you all," Alvarez finished. "To apologize in person."

"Apologize?" Dad's voice hardened. "He killed our son and ran. Left him on the road to die like some animal."

"I understand your anger, Mr. Bellucci—"

"No, you don't," Dad cut him off. "Unless you've buried a child, you don't understand anything."

"Leo," Mom said, placing her free hand on his arm. "Please."

The room fell silent except for the ticking of the old grandfather clock in the hallway—Rico's restoration project from high school. The memory blindsided me: him leaning over the workbench, brow furrowed in concentration, fingers moving with deliberate care over each tiny gear. *He spent months on that clock, determined to bring it back to life.*

Rico had always been about restoration, about fixing broken things. And here I was, eight years later, with the chance to meet the man who'd broken us all.

What would Rico do? I already knew that answer. My brother would have found a way to forgive, to understand, to turn this shit show into something meaningful. He'd always been better at that than me—better at seeing people's humanity even when they'd failed catastrophically.

"I'd like to meet with him," I said, surprising myself. "Alone."

Three pairs of eyes turned to me.

"I don't think that's wise," Dad started.

"I need to," I insisted. The pressure of my dual roles—son and priest—threatened to suffocate me. "As a priest, it's my job to seek understanding, to offer forgiveness . . ."

Dad's voice rose. "He doesn't deserve forgiveness."

"It's not about what he deserves." The words came from somewhere deep inside me. "It's about finally doing right by Rico. Doing what he would have done himself."

Mom studied my face, her eyes still sharp despite the years of grief. "There's more you're not telling us, Damian."

I looked away, that damn seal of confession crushing me from the inside out. "I just think I should be the one to do this."

The silence that followed was heavy with unasked questions. Finally, Mom squeezed my hand.

"If that's what you need to do, then you should do it." Her voice was quiet but firm.

Dad looked like he wanted to protest but remained silent.

"It's been eight years," she said, her eyes never leaving mine. "Eight years of waiting and anger. If Damian thinks this will help, then I trust him."

Dad slumped back in his chair. "Fine. But I don't want to meet him. Not yet. Maybe not ever."

"You don't have to," I assured him. "Either of you."

Alvarez watched the exchange with practiced patience. "I can arrange for you to visit Mercer at the county jail, Father Bellucci. Just let me know when."

After the detective left, the three of us sat in the quiet living room, the news settling around us like dust. Mom went to make tea—her answer to everything, even this. Dad stayed in his chair, his eyes distant.

"Your brother would've been thirty-one," Dad said suddenly.

"I know," I replied, the date already circled on my mental calendar, as it was every year.

"Sometimes I try to imagine what he'd be like now. What kind of priest he would've been. What kind of man." Dad's voice was soft, almost tender. "Better than me, I bet."

"Rico knew what he wanted," I said. "His calling was real."

"And yours?" The question hung in the air, more pointed than Dad had likely intended.

I hesitated, words catching in my throat. "I thought mine was too. Now I'm not so sure."

Dad's eyes, so like Rico's, studied me for a long moment. "That's why you want to meet this man, isn't it? To figure that out."

I nodded, unable to explain the full complexity of it all—the confession I couldn't discuss, the absolution I'd already granted, the impossible position of being both priest and victim.

"Just be careful, son," Dad said, reaching across to grip my shoulder. "Don't go looking for answers this man can't give you."

Later, as I prepared to leave via Uber, Mom held out a small package wrapped in tissue paper. "Rico's rosary," she said, her voice catching. "I think he'd want you to have it now."

"Mom, I can't take this."

"Take it, Dami," she insisted. "And remember—sometimes the most faithful thing you can do is follow your heart, not just your head."

I hugged her tightly, her shoulders frail beneath my hands. *When did she get so small?* She had her bad days, but there was still that fierce strength in her embrace that had held our family together through eight years of hell. The same arms that had rocked me through nightmares as a kid, that had held me the night we buried Rico, that had somehow found the courage to let me go when I'd announced I was becoming a priest.

On the ride back to the rectory, Rico's rosary burned like a coal in my pocket, every bump in the road making the beads shift against my leg, a constant reminder of the weight I was carrying.

Soon, I would come face-to-face with the man who had changed not just my life, but my parents' lives. Thomas Mercer had taken Rico from us, but in doing so, he'd also taken the version of me I might have been—the version who could have loved Claire openly. The Damian Bellucci who would have chosen a different life. But maybe it wasn't too late to find that version of myself again.

Chapter Eleven

CLAIRE

Evening Mass had just ended. Kneeling, I said a few short prayers before standing and heading toward the exit. I'd known Bishop Valenti wouldn't see my and Damian's romantic history as a valid excuse to reassign me. The irritation had been written all over the bishop's face. The paperwork involved, the bureaucratic hoops, and for what? An old high school relationship? I'd just have to accept that this was the will of God. My duties would keep me busy enough. If I was lucky, I'd only see Father Bellucci twice a day, maybe less. *Hopefully a lot less.* Though with my luck, he'd probably appear around every corner like a holy game of Whac-A-Mole.

I remembered when we were younger and used to share everything with each other—our hopes, fears, and frustrations with the world.

We'd been close to having sex, but we had never crossed that final line. We'd been waiting until marriage. For some undefined future. But it hadn't stopped me from wondering what it would've been like to have the length of him moving in and out of me.

God forgive me. I was wet thinking about it.

That was never going to happen now.

Part of me wished I hadn't opened the door, because now I was stuck with all of these forbidden thoughts. Truthfully, I didn't trust my feelings when it came to him.

The air held the warmth of the late-afternoon sun, but a cool breeze from the coast drifted in, carrying the scent of salt and eucalyptus as it brushed against my skin.

Damian and I walked out of the church together, our footsteps echoing softly on the worn stone steps. The last few stragglers from evening Mass murmured their goodbyes as they made their way to their cars in the parking lot, their voices a gentle hum mixed with the distant crash of waves. The fading light bathed Saint Anthony's in a soft glow that caught the edges of the stained glass windows, and for a fleeting moment, peace fell over me—the kind I used to find here as a teenager before my world fell apart.

I glanced at Damian, and an ache I knew too well twisted in my chest. There was a restlessness in his emerald eyes, discontentment that seemed to run deeper than his usual brooding.

The nun in me, which had been trained to comfort and counsel, wanted to reach out and ask him what was weighing so heavily on his heart. But lingering bitterness left me angry as hell at him, whispering that he was probably just wallowing in that martyrdom complex he'd perfected.

Let him be. You don't owe him comfort anymore.

Still, I couldn't quite silence the softer voice that remembered how his eyes used to light up when he laughed, or how different he looked now from the carefree boy who used to steal my breath with just a smile.

"See you tomorrow," I said, adjusting my bag on my shoulder, eager to part ways.

Damian's hands slid into his pockets, his expression calm. "Wait, I need to talk to you."

Before he could continue, a couple approached us, their footsteps quiet on the pavement.

What are their names again?

Tod and Sarah, parishioners who had been married for a decade. They looked exhausted, shoulders slumped as though they were carrying heavy weights on their backs. Sarah's eyes were red rimmed, and Tod kept his gaze fixed on his hands.

"Father Damian, Sister Claire," Sarah started. "We were hoping we could talk to you both. We don't . . . We don't know where else to turn."

I exchanged a quick glance with Damian, noting the urgency in her tone. "Of course. What can we do for you?"

Tod looked up, his face etched with pain. "We're thinking about separating. Actually, Sarah's already talked to a lawyer."

Sarah's breath hitched. "I moved my things into the guest room last week. We can't keep doing this to each other. Or to our kids."

My heart sank, and I motioned for them to sit on one of the benches near the church entrance. Damian followed, his quiet presence oddly reassuring despite the history between us. The sun was dipping lower, golden light softening the edges of everything.

"Tell us what's going on," I said, giving them my full attention.

Sarah's voice trembled. "It's just . . . It feels like we're strangers. Like we've forgotten how to talk without fighting. Every conversation turns into an argument about money, or the kids, or who forgot to do what."

Tod sighed. "We've hurt each other, Sister. Said things we can't take back. And now when I look at her . . ." He shook his head. "I don't know if she can ever forgive me for the things I've done. The trust I've broken."

"What kind of trust?" Damian asked gently.

"I had an emotional affair," Tod admitted, his voice cracking. "Nothing physical, but I was talking to someone else about things I should have been sharing with my wife. For months. Sarah found out three weeks ago."

Sarah wiped her eyes with the back of her hand. "How do you come back from that? How do you forgive someone who chose a stranger over you?"

Jesus. The words scraped the inside of my chest raw, and I had to swallow hard to keep from flinching.

"Forgiveness doesn't mean pretending the hurt never happened. It means choosing not to let that hurt define your future." I could feel Damian's gaze burning into me, but I kept my eyes on Sarah. "Sometimes we hold on to anger because it's the last connection we have to what we lost. But clinging to anger isn't the same as holding on to love. One keeps us trapped in the past, the other sets us free to honor what matters most."

Tod leaned forward. "But how do we even start over when everything feels broken?"

A beat of silence passed before Sarah spoke up, her voice hopeful. "Maybe what we need isn't just time for us, but time to connect with others in the same situation. Other couples who've been where we are. A retreat, maybe."

Damian raised an eyebrow, looking at her with interest. "A marriage retreat?"

"Yes," Sarah continued, her eyes brightening. "I've heard of other parishes doing them. Intensive weekends where couples can work through their issues with guidance. It might be our last chance before . . ."

It wasn't a bad suggestion. I glanced at Damian, surprised to find a glimmer of hope in his expression.

"That's a great idea," he said, his voice gaining strength. "It could be a weekend full of workshops, time for prayer, activities to help couples communicate better. To learn how to forgive and rebuild trust."

Tod nodded. "If other couples have made it through this, then maybe there's hope for us too."

The last sliver of sunlight dipped below the horizon, leaving behind streaks of purple and pink in the sky. The tension that usually crackled between me and Damian had softened, reshaped itself into . . . shared purpose.

"Let's do it," Damian said, his voice firm. "Let's give couples like you—like all of us struggling with forgiveness and trust—a chance to heal."

As the couple thanked us and walked away, hand in hand, I glanced at Damian. The sky was dark now, and the cool breeze did nothing to slow my pulse with him standing this close. I released a breath, trying to wrap my head around what had just happened.

Damian stood and started toward the rectory.

"Well, that escalated quickly," I muttered, half to myself, following him. "You do know we have to run this by Principal Omura, the bishop, and the admin team, right?"

Damian turned and gave me one of those half smirks that used to make my stomach flip when we were younger. It definitely didn't do that now. Nope. Not at all. "Come on, Sister Claire. You don't think they'll go for it?"

I stepped in front of him, my sudden movement making him stop before he nearly walked into me. His pupils dilated as his gaze dropped to my lips for a fraction of a second.

"I didn't say that. Don't start putting words in my mouth."

He raised an eyebrow, his green gaze sharp and unwavering as his chest rose and fell. "You didn't say no."

I scoffed, crossing my arms. "This is typical. Always making split-second decisions without thinking them through."

Damian's lips pressed into a thin line, the muscle in his jaw ticking as his eyes narrowed. His fingers flexed at his sides as if he were fighting an urge. "Forgive me for thinking about what's best for the parish. They brought up a great idea. This could help a lot of couples."

"And I agree with that," I shot back. "But we can't just jump into this without a plan. We need to think through logistics. Resources. Volunteers. Not to mention the time it'll take to organize. You can't just assume it'll fall into place."

Damian exhaled, clearly trying to rein in his irritation. "I'm not. I simply have faith. We can make it work. The parish needs this, and we're more than capable of pulling it off."

I stared at him, weighing his words, that frustration surfacing. This was how it always was with him. Bold, impulsive, always pushing forward without considering the fallout.

His expression suddenly shifted, a heaviness descending over his features. He looked away, swallowing hard.

"Back to what I was going to tell you." His voice dropped low, almost a whisper.

I tensed at his tone, my stomach immediately knotting. That wasn't his usual careful priest voice or even the frustrated tone he'd been using with me lately. This made my chest tight with dread. "What is it?"

Did something happen to his parents? Is he being transferred? Did Bishop Valenti say something about us working together? My mind started cycling through possibilities, each one worse than the last. The way he'd gone pale mixed with the careful choice of words—this was bad news. The kind that moved mountains.

He guided me back to the nearby bench and gestured for me to sit. "They found him, Claire. The driver who . . ." He paused, his voice hitching. "The man who hit Rico."

Reality tilted, stealing my breath. "What?" That single word came out choked.

"His name is Thomas Mercer. A chemistry teacher." Damian's hands trembled slightly. "He turned himself in a few weeks ago."

I felt like I'd been throat punched. Rico's easy smile and the way he'd ruffle Damian's hair just to annoy him flashed in my mind. "After all this time? Eight years and he just . . . decided to come forward now?"

"His wife died. Made him promise to make things right." Damian's jaw worked for a moment. "He wants to meet my family. Apologize to them, maybe."

I couldn't speak, tears burning my eyes. The wound I'd thought had scarred over was raw, bleeding again.

Eight fucking years. Eight years of wondering if Rico's killer was living his life without consequence while the rest of us tried to pick up the pieces. Eight years of that faceless monster haunting every prayer and moment while I'd wondered if there would ever be justice.

And now this stranger had the audacity to want to *meet* with them? To what? Apologize? Make himself feel better? Clear his conscience before he joined his dead wife?

How dare he. He'd waited until his own mortality stared him in the face before deciding our pain mattered. Thought a conversation could somehow balance the scales of what he'd taken from us—Rico's laugh, his terrible jokes, his dreams of becoming a priest. Even my and Damian's future. Everything could have been different if this coward had just stayed sober, stayed home, stayed the fuck away from that road that night.

Shit . . . He has me cursing. Forgive me, Lord.

A sob caught in my throat, and I pressed my fingers to my lips to keep it in.

"What're you going to do?" I managed, reaching for his hand without thinking.

He let me take it, his fingers warm against mine. "I'm going. Alone."

"Damian . . ." I squeezed his hand. "I could go with you if it'll help." The offer came automatically, from the place where we'd once been everything to each other.

He hesitated, conflict clear in his eyes. "I don't know if that's a good idea."

"Why?"

"Because I don't know what I'll do when I see him face-to-face," he admitted. "The things I might say. I don't want you to see that side of me."

I pulled my hand away, already missing his warmth. "Just think about it."

He nodded, his expression unreadable in the darkness. "I should go. Confessions in the morning."

I stood, too aware of how close we'd been. "Good night, Father Bellucci." With that, I started my walk home, but I could feel Damian's heated gaze on me.

"Good night, Sparrow."

I froze mid-step, my heart stuttering at the sound of that old nickname on his lips. *Sparrow.* It brought back memories of lazy afternoons, his hot breath whispering it against my ear.

I turned around slowly, my throat tight. "Don't. You don't get to call me that anymore."

But even as the words left my mouth, that thing that pumped blood through my body was melting.

Damn him.

After all this time, he could still unravel me with one word.

TWO DAYS AFTER OUR CONVERSATION WITH SARAH AND TOD, THE AUTUMN AIR carried enough chill to make recess comfortable. The clear, cloudless blue sky matched the cheerful energy of fourth graders racing around the playground. They were tiny rockets fueled by fruit snacks and freedom. I'd worn my favorite black sneakers today, perfect for the outdoor activities we'd planned for recess. Nothing like being prepared for playground warfare.

"Sister Claire, come play with us!" Sadie waved frantically from the makeshift kickball field, her ponytail bouncing with each jump.

"Yeah!" Lenny chimed in. "We need a pitcher."

I laughed, tucking a strand of hair back under my veil. "All right, all right. I'm coming."

The kids cheered as I jogged over, their excitement bubbling. I loved these pure, uncomplicated moments when the world narrowed to nothing more than a playground game and laughter—this was heaven on earth if you asked me.

"Sister Claire's the best pitcher!" Michaela announced to her teammates. "Nobody can hit her curveball."

"Is that so?" called out a voice I knew, and those cursed butterflies in my stomach started fluttering.

I turned to find Damian walking along the edge of the playground, his clerical collar and black button-down a stark contrast to the colorful playground equipment.

"Father D," several kids called out in unison. "Come play with us!"

I raised an eyebrow, schooling my expression into what I hoped resembled professional amusement rather than a mixture of attraction and irritation. "I'm sure Father Bellucci has very important priest business to handle. Holy water to bless, confessions to hear. Maybe some sacred brooding to catch up on."

Damian's green eyes locked with mine, that infuriating half smile playing on his lips. "Actually, I think I can spare a few minutes for kickball."

The children erupted in cheers, and before I could object, they'd ushered him toward home plate. *Great.* Just what I needed. Another opportunity to prove that whatever was between us never truly went away.

"Don't you dare hold back, Sister Claire," Damian called, taking his position.

I rolled the red rubber ball between my palms, feeling my competitive streak flare to life. "I wouldn't dream of depriving these children of a valuable lesson in humility, Father."

Standing at the makeshift home plate—a bright orange frisbee that looked ridiculous but served its purpose—he had the audacity to wink at me. Like we were still teenagers flirting on the beach instead of two people in religious habits surrounded by fourth graders who were about to witness their priest get absolutely demolished.

My eyes narrowed.

The kids fell quiet, watching with wide eyes as I wound up and delivered my first pitch. The ball rolled perfectly, curving just as it reached Damian. He swung his leg and missed completely, the ball sailing past him to smack against the backstop.

"Strike one," Lenny exclaimed.

Damian's brow furrowed in concentration as he repositioned himself. I bit back a smile, enjoying his obvious frustration a more than was appropriate. Some things never changed, and his competitive streak was definitely one of them.

"That was a warm-up," he muttered, loud enough for only me to hear.

My second pitch came faster, another curve that had Damian swinging and missing again. The kids on my team erupted in cheers while Damian's team groaned.

"Strike two!"

"Come on, Father!" Sadie called from the sidelines. "You can do it!"

Damian straightened, rolling his shoulders back. The playfulness had vanished from his expression, replaced by an intensity that made my stomach do kickflips. I'd seen that look before when we were teenagers and he refused to lose at anything, whether it was video games or debate team arguments.

I took a deep breath and delivered my third pitch, putting all I had into it. The ball rolled straight and fast toward him.

This time, Damian was ready. His leg connected with a solid *thwack*, sending the ball soaring over our heads and into the far reaches of the playground. The kids' mouths dropped open as they watched its arc. A perfect hit.

"Home run!" Damian's team screamed, jumping up and down.

Damian jogged around the makeshift bases, high-fiving every kid he passed. When he rounded third base, his eyes found mine again, that insufferable smirk in place. Despite my irritation at being shown up, I couldn't help but smile. This was the Damian I remembered. Playful. Someone who'd once spent an entire afternoon teaching me skateboard tricks so I could impress my friends.

The kids surrounded him as he touched home plate, clamoring for more high fives and fist bumps. After indulging them, he made his way over to me, stopping just close enough that the kids wouldn't get any wrong ideas about our proximity.

"Good game, Sister," he said, his voice dropping to that rough timbre that sent shivers down my spine.

I crossed my arms, feigning annoyance. "You got lucky, Father. The sun was in my eyes, the wind changed direction, Mercury is in retrograde—take your pick of excuses."

"Luck had nothing to do with it." His eyes sparkled with mischief, and he leaned a fraction closer. "I've always been good at handling your curves."

My cheeks warmed, but I managed to give him a good eye roll.

Before I could respond, he said, "This job suits you. You seem happy."

Taken aback by his sincerity, I fumbled for a response that

wouldn't reveal how much his words affected me. "These kids don't care about doctrine or rules. They care about whether God loves them. Whether they matter. Teaching them reminds me that's what it's all supposed to be about. Connection. Love. Not judgment."

His gaze dropped to my lips for just a heartbeat before he caught himself, taking a deliberate step backward, as if putting physical space between us was the only thing keeping him grounded. "I've been thinking about your offer," he murmured. "Regarding Thomas Mercer."

My pulse quickened at the mention of *him*. "And?"

"I set up a visit two weeks from now." His eyes searched mine, vulnerability bleeding through his composure.

I nodded, uncertain what to say.

"I'd like you to come with me. If your offer still stands."

"Of course it does," I answered without hesitation. "What changed your mind?"

Damian's gaze drifted to the children playing nearby, then back to me. "You knew Rico too. Loved him." He swallowed, his Adam's apple bobbing. "And I don't think I can face Thomas alone. Not without . . ." He trailed off, but I understood what he couldn't say.

"What time?" I asked, brushing my fingers against his arm.

"Pick you up at ten?"

I nodded, resisting the urge to reach for his hand. "Sounds good."

Relief softened his features. "Thank you, Claire." The way he said my name, without the formal "Sister," made my heart skip a beat.

"I should get back," he said, his voice returning to its normal volume. "Can't spend all day playing games, tempting as it might be."

I watched him walk away, his confident stride painfully familiar. The sun caught his dark hair, and for a moment, I was nineteen again, watching him walk across the school parking lot, waiting for him to turn around and wave.

And then he did. My lips curved up as I returned the gesture, trying not to give away the fact that my insides had liquified.

Movement near the school building caught my eye. Mrs. Fontana stood by the entrance, arms crossed, with a slight scowl on her face that could curdle milk at twenty paces. Her eyes darted between Damian's retreating figure and me, narrow and calculating.

My stomach dropped. How long had she been watching? That woman could win gold medals in surveillance if parish gossip ever became an Olympic sport.

"All right, everyone," I called, my voice a little too bright. "Time to head back inside. Line up, please!"

As I herded the children toward the building, I could feel Mrs. Fontana's eyes boring into my back. The comfortable autumn day suddenly chilled, the joy of the game evaporating under her scrutiny.

This was like dancing on holy eggshells—not just for me, but for Damian too. We needed to remember that in a parish this size, every glance was noted. Every smile catalogued. Shared laughs analyzed. Even our innocent kickball rivalry could become fodder for after-Mass coffee conversations.

I forced myself not to look back and check if Damian had turned to watch us go. Some things were better left unknown, especially when knowing only made the wanting worse.

Chapter Twelve

DAMIAN

It had been three days since I'd played kickball with Claire and the kids, and now I was sitting through the tail end of another admin meeting. Claire had sent her apologies—a last-minute parent conference that couldn't be rescheduled.

After dismissing the staff members, I stuffed folders into my backpack. Mrs. Fontana approached like a hawk circling prey, her silver hair shellacked to perfection.

"Father Damian." She beamed at me with too-white teeth. "Such a relief about that Thomas Mercer turning himself in, isn't it? Finally, justice for your poor brother."

I stiffened, trying to mask my reaction.

"Yes," I managed. "It's . . . been a long time coming."

"I saw his picture in the *Chronicle* this morning," she continued, studying my face. "Doesn't look like much of a man to me. A chemistry teacher, of all things. I suppose you can never tell who's capable of such horrible iniquities."

Of course. It was in the papers. "No, you can't," I agreed.

Claire's words from the other night echoed in my mind: *Sometimes we hold on to anger because it's the last connection we have to what we lost.*

She'd been talking about Sarah and Tod, but every word had cut straight through me.

How long had I been carrying this . . . whatever this was? Guilt, resentment, self-reproach? All because it was easier than looking too closely at my own part in what had happened? Easier than admitting that maybe forgiveness had to start with me?

Mrs. Fontana placed her hand on my arm. "I imagine this must be difficult for you and your family."

"We're handling it," I said, avoiding her probing gaze. What I couldn't tell her was how the confession had already torn me apart a week ago and how I'd carried the knowledge in silence while bound by sacred duty. Definitely couldn't say that Claire's wisdom about forgiveness had been haunting me.

"The Lord works in mysterious ways," she said with practiced sympathy. "Perhaps this is His way of giving your family closure before you embark on new endeavors."

"What do you mean?" I questioned, though I already knew where she was headed.

"The marriage retreat, of course," she replied, her smile sharpening. "Congratulations on securing the budget approval. I had my doubts, but you managed to convince the finance committee, you charmer."

"Thank you." I forced a smile, sensing this wasn't just about the retreat. "I think it'll be good for our community. We've been needing this sort of thing for a while now."

"Oh, I absolutely agree, Father." She clasped her hands together, the diamonds on her rings catching the light. "Marriage is a sacrament, after all. It deserves all the protection it can get in today's world." She glanced around the empty room before leaning closer, her floral perfume almost suffocating. "Speaking of, I wanted to discuss something with you."

Fuck. Here it comes. I shouldered my bag. "What's on your mind?"

"It's about you and Sister Claire heading this retreat together." Her voice dropped to a conspiratorial whisper I'd heard too many times from parishioners with *concerns*. "You'll be spending a significant amount of time with her."

My neck warmed beneath the white collar. "That's part of the job, Mrs. Fontana."

She patted my arm like I was still the altar boy she used to slip twenty-dollar bills to on Christmas. "I just wonder if it may be wise to have someone else present during these planning sessions when they begin."

"A chaperone?" I didn't bother hiding my irritation. Christ, I was a twenty-eight-year-old priest, not some hormone-driven teenager.

Mrs. Fontana's smile stayed fixed while her dark eyes turned to steel. "Not exactly. More of a third perspective. Mrs. Walker has excellent organizational skills. Or I'd be happy to assist myself."

The thought of Mrs. Fontana's watchful eyes during meetings with Claire made my guts bubble. "That won't be necessary," I said, smoothing out my black button-down. "Sister Claire and I are clergy. We're perfectly capable of maintaining professional boundaries."

I hope . . .

"I don't doubt your intentions, Father." She fiddled with the gold crucifix around her neck, a gesture that seemed more warning than piety. "But we must be mindful of appearances. This is a small parish. People notice things."

People like you, who have nothing better to do. I bit back the words. "I appreciate your concern, but I assure you there's nothing inappropriate with our working relationship. Adding unnecessary personnel would only complicate the planning process."

She studied me like she was trying to read my soul. "Very well. I trust your judgment, Father." She gathered her designer purse from the round oak table, another relic of her late husband's success. Her next words were carefully chosen. "Your brother would be proud of the man you've become. The way you've devoted yourself to God, just as he planned to do."

The mention of Rico hollowed me out, leaving me momentarily unmoored. "Thank you," I managed, though the words tasted sour.

"I'll be praying for the success of your retreat," Mrs. Fontana said, her smile returning. "And for you, Father. The path of righteousness isn't always easy to follow, is it?"

Making my way to the school, I loosened my collar, suddenly feeling like I was choking. Her message had been clear: She was watching us. And she wasn't the only one. I'd fought off her suggestion of a chaperone, but at what cost? Her radar was up, suspicions aroused before Claire and I had even started working together.

I hadn't realized our potential collaboration would be under such scrutiny. The last thing I needed was the parish gossips keeping tabs on every interaction between Sister Claire and me.

Twenty minutes later, I pulled open the door to Isaiah Wright's classroom. He paced back and forth, salt-and-pepper hair catching in the sunlight slanting through the windows—a rare break in his polished presentation. Claire was already here, perched on the edge of the teacher's desk. He'd asked the two of us to stop by to discuss a struggling student.

"Thank you both for coming on such short notice," Isaiah said by way of greeting. For a man who'd traded years of missionary work in Kenya for raising four kids with his wife in the suburbs, being a teacher—even for algebra—suited him well.

"We're happy to help," Claire said. Her expression remained concerned despite her black skirt rustling as she swung her legs. She smiled, and it drew my attention like starlight cutting through darkness.

I leaned against the wall. *Fuck. I need to focus.*

"Connor Ryan has been skipping classes," Isaiah said, running a hand through his graying hair. The motion set his wire-rimmed glasses askew on his nose. "His grades are slipping. He's withdrawn. Yesterday I caught him sitting alone in the chemistry lab during lunch, staring into space."

"Has he opened up to any of the other teachers?" Claire asked.

He shook his head. "I brought this to Principal Omura. She recommended both of you." He stopped pacing, eyes moving between us. "I think she's right. Connor would listen to you two. You'd probably relate better." Isaiah glanced at Claire. "He loves skateboarding."

So do I.

Claire and I looked at each other, sparks crackling between us for that brief moment.

"What makes you think we're the right people to help?" I asked.

Isaiah's lips curved in a knowing smile. "Because I've seen how well you two work together. You balance each other. Connor needs someone who can speak to both the structured and free-flowing sides of faith."

"What do you mean?" Claire asked, voice soft and curious.

"Father Bellucci's approach is through tradition and ritual. The established pathways. But you, Sister Vergara, seek Him in the spaces between. You encourage students not to hide their doubts but to explore them as part of their journey. You find God in the wrestling and uncertainty. In the moments when we admit we don't have all the answers." He gestured between us. "Together, you show there's more than one way to know God."

I shifted, hyperaware of Claire's presence. He wasn't wrong. Claire's relationship with God had always been different from mine. More intimate.

"God meets us where we are," she said. "Sometimes that's in Mass, or during everyday tasks." Her eyes met mine again. "Sometimes it's the people He puts in our path."

My heart stuttered. We weren't talking about Connor anymore.

Isaiah nodded, oblivious to the context of Claire's last sentence. "Exactly. So, will you help him?"

I pushed off the wall, needing to move, to burn some of the energy thrumming through me. "Of course we will."

Claire's head tilted in concentration, her fingers absently tracing the crucifix that hung low on her neck. We were supposed to be focusing on helping Connor, but all I could think about was how right Isaiah was. We *did* balance each other in ways that went far deeper than counseling styles.

"He should be waiting in administration now," Isaiah said, checking his watch. He thanked us both before Claire and I made our way out of his classroom, the scent of dry markers and teenage angst following us into the corridor.

I walked beside her down the wide hallway, drawn by that invisible thread that always seemed to pull us together. The rubber soles of my shoes squeaked against the freshly waxed floor. "Maybe it's not such a bad thing. How well we work together."

Her gaze kept straight ahead, but I caught the slight upturn of her lips. "No. Maybe not."

When we reached administration, Laura offered us her private office, stepping out to give us privacy. But Principal Omura's presence lingered in the potted peace lily by the window, the inspirational quotes arranged on the wall, and the faint scent of green tea from the cup she'd left cooling on her desk.

Dust motes danced in the amber sunbeams as I wondered if this was God's plan all along, bringing me and Claire together not just to help others, but to help each other find our way back to Him. Back to ourselves.

The room was quiet except for the gentle whir of the ancient wall clock and the muffled sounds of the secretary answering the phone in the outer office. Connor slouched in one of the wooden chairs across from us, the troubled fifteen-year-old refusing to meet our eyes. The scent of cigarette smoke clung to his rumpled uniform. Claire shifted, the leather of her seat creaking, and I could sense her concern matching my own.

"Mr. Wright says you've been skipping classes," I finally said, my voice gentle.

Connor scoffed, staring at his scuffed shoes. "What does he know?"

Claire leaned forward, gesturing to his skateboard propped against his chair. "How long have you been skating?"

Connor's head snapped up, surprise flickering across his face. "I don't know. A few years?"

"Someone I was close to used to live for it," Claire said with a soft smile, and I caught the quick glance she threw my way. "I spent so many afternoons watching him practice heelflips. That's what scraped up the side of your shoe, isn't it?"

"Yeah," Connor admitted, some of the tension leaving his shoulders. "Been trying to land it clean. The concrete by the storage building has a good spot, but . . ."

"But you're supposed to be in class," I finished, keeping my tone neutral. A sharp ache lodged behind my ribs at the memory of Rico teaching me to skate.

Connor's defiance crept back into his expression, but Claire jumped in again.

"My friend used to say skating cleared his head. Helped him deal with stuff when life got hard." Another brief silence. "Is there something in your life that's hard to deal with right now?"

The teenage boy picked at a loose thread on his uniform sleeve, the blue fabric fraying under his nervous fingers. "I don't know . . . Everything's fucked." His voice cracked. "My dad bailed on us last month. Just disappeared. Mom's breaking her back working doubles, and everyone keeps telling me to pray like that's gonna magically fix our life."

I remembered my own father's emotional absence after Rico died. The prescribed prayers and platitudes that never quite reached the heart of the pain.

"Prayer isn't a magic wand," I said. "It doesn't make the hurt disappear overnight."

Connor's brown eyes snapped to mine, surprised.

"God isn't fragile," Claire said, leaning forward. "He can handle your rage, your questions, your doubt. He'd rather have your raw honesty than polite lies."

"Aren't you supposed to feed me some bullshit about God's plan?" Connor asked, knuckles white as he gripped the arms of his chair.

"God's plan doesn't mean your pain doesn't matter," I said, meeting his eyes. "Jesus wasn't some serene robot. He lost His shit in the temple when He saw injustice. Sobbed when His friend died. Experienced abandonment on the cross. If the Son of God could feel that broken, why wouldn't you?"

"Faith isn't about pretending you're fine when your world's falling apart," Claire added, her voice carrying quiet steel. "It's about being honest enough to admit when you're drowning."

For the first time, Connor really looked at me, tears threatening to spill. "So, I don't have to pretend I'm not pissed off at God?"

"Not at all." I leaned forward, the leather of my chair squeaking. "But how we handle that anger? That's the choice we get to make. Skipping school, letting your grades slip? That's only hurting you in the end."

Connor swallowed hard, his Adam's apple bobbing. The wall clock ticked steadily behind us, marking each moment of silence. "I don't know what else to do."

"What if we found another way?" I suggested. "The Y has a

boxing program. Supervised, structured. A way to channel that energy somewhere productive."

Claire straightened. "And I could help you catch up on the homework you've missed. We could set up study sessions during lunch so you don't fall behind."

"You'd help me with that?" His voice was uncertain, like he wasn't used to people offering support without conditions.

"That's what we're here for," I said. "Not just to pray with you, but to guide you through this."

"We want to see you succeed. Not only in school, but in life," Claire added.

Connor wiped his eyes with his uniform sleeve. "Thanks, Father B. And . . . Sister Claire." He stood, shouldering his backpack and grabbing his skateboard. As his footsteps echoed down the empty hallway, a spark of joy settled in my chest.

This was ministry. Connecting with people. Offering practical help alongside spiritual guidance.

Claire's eyes met mine, understanding passing between us without words. The sunlight caught her face, making her gray eyes almost luminous. "That went better than I expected," she said.

My lips curved up, and I couldn't stop myself. "You're amazing."

Standing, she started for the door. "You're not so bad yourself, Father Damian." She stood in the threshold, arms folded over her chest.

I straightened and followed her out of the office and into the corridor toward her classroom. "We need to talk about the marriage retreat."

She glanced over her shoulder at me. "Sorry I couldn't make the meeting. Were you able to get it approved?"

I nodded. "They all love the idea. We have full support."

"That's awesome, Dames." She turned, strolling into her classroom and up to her desk, where she started gathering papers.

I froze in the doorway. *Dames.* She'd said it so casually, like no time had passed at all. Like we were still teenagers and she hadn't just called me by the nickname that used to make my heart skip.

She looked up from her papers, and I saw the moment she realized what she'd done. A flush crept up her neck. "Oh . . . I'm sorry, Father. I didn't—it just slipped."

But the damage was done. That one word had pulled me right back to being nineteen and stupidly in love. Standing in her classroom, watching her try to pretend it didn't matter, I wasn't sure I could act as if it meant nothing and go back to the careful distance we'd been maintaining.

The tension lingered between us for a moment before I exhaled. "Look, we're going to be working together. Maybe we should just accept that some old habits will surface?"

She nodded. "You're right. We're adults now. We can handle a few slips."

I crossed my arms, watching her. "Anyway, we should probably start the planning process."

"Okay, I can text you some ideas." She placed a thick folder into her leather messenger bag and then grabbed her skateboard from the side of the desk.

Following her back into the hallway, I said, "Actually, I was thinking we could meet. Go over it properly." I hesitated, then added, "Maybe dinner in the rectory? I'll cook. Ideas flow better in a less formal atmosphere."

She stopped, facing me, eyes wide. "I don't know if that's—"

"You wouldn't skip an opportunity to have a home-cooked meal, would you?" I teased.

"My cooking skills have improved drastically since high school, thank you very much." She started walking again, her nose upturned.

"How about Friday? Seven o'clock?" I asked, mentally crossing my fingers.

We reached the double doors, and I held my breath.

"Fine. Friday," she said.

She pushed off on her board, her fluid grace unchanged since we were teenagers. The sight of her gliding away brought back memories of countless afternoons watching her disappear down this same path. Back then, I was just a boy who loved a girl.

FRIDAY EVENING CAME AROUND, AND THE SCENT OF GARLIC AND RED PEPPER flakes filled the rectory kitchen as I stirred the arrabiata sauce, watching it bubble and thicken to the consistency Mom had taught me. The recipe was etched into my memory from countless Sunday afternoons spent in her kitchen—*more garlic, tesoro, and don't rush the onions.* But I'd added extra crushed red pepper, knowing Claire's love for heat. *The spicier the better*, she'd always said.

I tasted the sauce, adjusting the seasoning until it carried a perfect balance of heat and sweetness from the San Marzano tomatoes. The homemade gnocchi waited nearby, each hand-rolled piece ridged with the tines of a fork. It was Mom's signature dish, one that could coax a smile even on Dad's darkest days after Rico died.

The wooden spoon slipped from my grasp, and sauce splattered over the off-white tiles. "Shit." It had been a while since I'd cooked anything in this kitchen. I made quick work of cleaning up the mess with paper towels. *This isn't a date. Just a meeting between two colleagues.*

When Claire showed up, my breath caught. Gone was her usual habit. In its place, she wore loose lounge pants and a fitted off-the-shoulder sweater that revealed the elegant curve of her collarbone. Her black-framed glasses perched on her nose, making her softer, more approachable. More *her*. The sight of her so casual and unguarded sparked my entire body to life, including my cock. It was a good thing I'd opted for jeans.

"Hope the food's done. My stomach is eating itself." She stepped inside, hugging her tablet to her chest. Her gaze roamed the open space before landing on the table set with a steaming platter of food. She looked at me with appreciation in those soft gray eyes. "Gnocchi arrabiata?"

"My mom's recipe." I grinned, sending up a silent prayer for strength. "With an extra kick."

She stared at the place settings across from each other.

I studied her. "Is something wrong?" For a split second, I swore tears brimmed in her eyes, but she blinked before I could be sure.

She shook her head and sat down at the table. "Looks delicious, Father."

I grabbed the bottle of Cabernet Sauvignon from the counter, the dark glass cool against my palm. The corkscrew twisted with more force than necessary, the cork coming free with a satisfying pop that echoed. I filled each glass with burgundy liquid, rich and deep as the silence between us.

Setting the stemless wineglasses on the scarred wooden table, I caught her watching my hands—just for a second, but long enough to make heat crawl up my neck. The glasses clinked softly against the wood, the sound too intimate for what this was supposed to be: two colleagues having a work dinner. *Right. Who the hell am I kidding?*

"It's not the most expensive bottle. It was on sale if I'm being honest," I said.

Claire smiled, picking up her tumbler and swirling it before tasting it. "You didn't have to go through this much trouble."

I took my seat across from her, serving her before myself. "It's no trouble. This is for me as much as it's for you."

Her lips remained curved up. "Thanks." My heart sped up at the sincerity in her words. A mustard seed of hope planted itself in my chest. Maybe we *could* move forward. A chance we could be friends at the very least.

After we ate, we migrated to the living room couch and started planning. We agreed to hold the retreat on the second weekend in January, giving people enough time to settle into the new year.

The budget was next. Claire and I decided a big bake sale would be enough to raise the extra funds we needed. Then we started looking at nearby hotels that had conference rooms.

Claire sat next to me on the couch, legs tucked beneath her, like she always had in high school—comfortable, like she belonged in any space she took up. *My Sparrow.* Except stronger, tougher. And, fuck me, I was staring again.

We began discussing how we'd handle the couples attending, but I couldn't keep pretending I'd invited her here solely to plan the retreat. I needed to clear the air, finally face the damage I'd done all those years ago.

Claire pushed her glasses up the bridge of her nose and then jotted a note down on her tablet.

"Can we talk?"

She didn't look up. "We are talking."

I huffed, rolling my eyes. "Claire."

Her gray eyes flicked from the tablet screen to me. She let out a breath, turning it off. "What is it?"

Now that I had her attention, my mind decided to go blank. *How do I do this?*

"Well?" she asked impatiently.

I scooted closer, inhaling deeply before I said, "I think it's time for us to talk about how things ended."

Annoyance flickered in her eyes, but she didn't look away. She just waited, her expression guarded.

I rubbed the back of my neck. "The things I said were cruel and far from the truth."

She didn't respond, but her silence said it all, and I could always tell when her walls were going up. But I had to say my piece. "I wasn't in my right mind. After Rico's accident, I couldn't handle anything. And breaking up with you . . . I thought it would make things better for you."

Her eyes softened, but she stayed silent, shifting on the couch as if she was bracing for whatever came next.

"I hurt you," I admitted, the words leaden on my tongue. "And I can never take it back."

The room was too quiet, the air itself seeming to wait for her response. I stared at her, hoping for any sign that would indicate she understood. But her face remained unreadable, lips pressed into a thin line.

"Damian," she started, her voice low. "What do you expect me to say? That it's all okay because we were young and dumb? That I understand why you left me when I needed you most? I lost Rico too, you know. He was like a brother to me."

"No. I don't expect you to tell me it's okay. And it never dawned on me how close you two were. It's shitty of me to say, but I was too consumed in my own grief to notice." I swallowed, the knot in my chest tightening.

Her gaze dropped, fingers picking at the edge of the cushion. A bitter laugh escaped her. "Do you know how long it took me to put myself back together? How many nights I spent wondering what I did wrong?"

The pain in her voice sliced through my defenses, every word a judgment I'd earned. The walls she'd built, the scars I'd left. She had every right not to trust me—to keep her distance.

Eyes brimming with unshed tears lifted to me. "I really want us to be friends, Dames." She let out a long breath. "I know the Bible says to forgive seventy times seven, but I'm not Jesus. It's going to take time."

Her words festered between us, an open wound bleeding with memories neither of us could escape. In my heart, I made a silent vow. *I will never hurt you like that again. I'll spend every day proving myself to you.*

Words wouldn't be enough for her, and she deserved more than that. "I don't expect you to forgive me right away. Or ever. I just needed you to know how sorry I am. For all of it."

We sat in silence, the tension between us different now, raw and honest. It wasn't gone, but somehow, facing it head-on made it easier to breathe. Maybe even easier to heal. But as she sat there in her loungewear and those glasses, I felt that damn pull again—the one that had always been there, but stronger than ever now.

She shot up from the couch, holding her tablet to her chest. "I should go," she said, starting for the door.

"Wait, Sparrow." I stood and, in a few strides, slid in front of her, cutting her off.

Her breath hitched.

Neither of us moved.

The ticking clock on the wall may as well have been a beating drum in the silence hanging between us.

"I told you not to call me that," she whispered.

"Shit," I breathed. "I'm sorry." I wanted to reach for her. Pull her close and tell her all that had been going through my mind since she'd walked back into my life. All the questions. All the doubt. Everything.

She peered up at me, gray eyes searching mine. My heart pounded in my chest as I placed my hand on her shoulder. She didn't pull away. Instead, she stepped closer, until we were standing inches from each other.

Unable to resist, I whispered, "Can I hold you?" My hand slid down to her waist, feeling the warmth of her body through the fabric of her sweater. "Just . . . for a minute."

Her eyes closed, but she conceded with a nod. She placed her tablet on the coffee table.

I pulled her against me, wrapping my arms around her. Her head rested against me, and her chest steadily rose and fell against mine. Her body relaxed, like we fit together in ways that terrified and thrilled me. I cupped the back of her head, fingers threading through her wavy hair.

The tension in the air between us wasn't heavy anymore. It'd shifted, become like the quiet of an empty church just before dawn. Peaceful.

She slipped her arms around my waist. Her palms, warm through the thin T-shirt, rested against my back. The fabric rustled, her fingers spreading wide, as if she were trying to memorize the shape of me in the way I used to with the feeling of her hand in mine during Mass as teenagers. Her touch was gentle but certain. She was anchoring herself to this moment—to me—despite every reason we both had to let go.

For a second, I let myself believe that maybe this wasn't wrong. That the way my soul recognized hers across time and heartache and vows was sacred.

My throat constricted, and I pressed my chin to the top of her head, losing myself in her flowery scent. "You have no idea how much I've missed this."

The world outside these walls ceased to exist; there was only Claire, solid and real in my arms. Fear kept me from moving— breathing too deeply—certain that reality would come crashing back the moment I let her go. I wondered if she could feel the physical betrayal of every emotion I was trying to contain.

Claire pulled back enough to look up at me, her eyes full of an emotion I couldn't name. "We should pray," she said, but there was no guilt in her voice.

I nodded, understanding her intent. Not to ask forgiveness, but to share this moment with God and invite Him into *this*.

I pressed my forehead to hers.

Claire started first, her voice soft but assured. "Our Father, who art in heaven . . ."

I joined in. "Hallowed be Thy name . . ."

Our voices wove together in perfect harmony. The prayer acted as a bridge, connecting us not just to each other, but to our faith, to Him.

"Thy kingdom come, Thy will be done," we spoke in unison.

By the time we reached "deliver us from evil," tears were streaming down Claire's face, but she was smiling. I took her hand, our fingers intertwining as we finished the prayer.

"Amen," we whispered together.

We stood there, in my living room, surrounded by a serenity I hadn't felt in years. This was communion, as holy as any Mass I'd ever celebrated.

"I feel Him here," Claire murmured.

"Me too," I admitted. "Maybe He's always been here."

Claire seemed to remember herself. She cleared her throat softly, stepping back. "I should really go now." Her voice was gentle but firm as she gathered her tablet from the coffee table. "It's getting late, and we both have early mornings."

Before she made it to the door, I found myself stepping closer. "Wait."

She turned, those gray eyes questioning.

I lifted my hand, my thumb tracing the sign of the cross on her forehead with deliberate tenderness. "May the Lord bless you and keep you," I whispered, my voice rough. "May His face shine upon you and give you peace."

Without thinking, without permission, I leaned down and pressed my lips to her forehead where my thumb had been, a kiss so reverent it felt like prayer itself. She went perfectly still beneath my touch, her breath catching, but she didn't pull away.

When I finally stepped back, her eyes were wide.

"Good night, Father." She turned on her heel and walked away, her footsteps soft against the hardwood floor of the rectory. The sound of the front door closing behind her echoed through the empty hallway, final and somehow devastating.

I went to the window, unable to stop myself from watching as she made her way down the pathway and across the small patch of grass to the driveway where her car waited. The porch light cast her silhouette in warm yellow. She clutched her tablet against her chest, movements careful and deliberate. Her fingers fumbled with her keys for a moment—a nervous habit I remembered from high school—before unlocking the car door.

The engine turned over with a quiet hum, headlights cutting through the darkness as she backed out of the driveway. I stayed at the window, watching her taillights grow smaller and smaller until they disappeared around the bend, taking her back to her little cottage and leaving me alone with the lingering scent of her perfume while the weight of what I'd just done sank in.

I'd spent years believing that holiness meant denial, but holding Claire made that feel backward. What if our connection wasn't pulling me away from God, but bringing me closer?

Seminary had taught me that human desire was a distraction from the divine, but what if it was actually a pathway? The thought bloomed in my chest—dangerous, beautiful, and somehow more true than any homily I'd ever preached. For now, I wouldn't push for answers. This moment of clarity, however fleeting, was enough.

"Better two than one alone, since thus their work is really rewarding. If one should fall, the other helps him up; but what of the person with no one to help him up when he falls?" — *Ecclesiastes 4:9-10 (New Jerusalem Bible)*

Chapter Thirteen

CLAIRE

Sitting on the wooden porch swing, I closed my eyes and soaked up the early-morning rays. Warmth seeped through the ceramic mug in my hands, the scent of coffee grounding me in the present. I should've been at morning Mass, kneeling in the sanctuary, praying to my God. Instead, here I was, wrapped in an old throw blanket, my legs tucked beneath me.

The silence was heavier than usual, as if He knew I was avoiding something—or rather *someone*. The sunlight caught the edges of the trees swaying in the breeze, but the peace I sought in moments like these was nowhere to be found.

My phone buzzed with a text, briefly illuminating the screen.

LAURA

Happy Saturday, Sister Claire. Just wanted to let you know I left the permission forms for next week's field trip to San Carlos Mission on your desk. They need your signature before we can send them home with the students. Also, the bus company needs a final head count by tomorrow. Have a blessed day!

Letting out a slow breath, I set the phone back down without responding. The field trip—I'd almost forgotten. Another reason I couldn't hide away forever. My students were counting on me, and now I'd have to coordinate with Damian since he'd promised to help chaperone. Just what I needed: a whole day trapped on a bus with him.

I sipped my coffee, bitter and lukewarm now, willing myself to get my day started. But the squeezing in my chest told me I wasn't ready to face the sanctuary, the altar, or *him*.

What the hell happened last night? Dinner had been delicious, the wine he'd chosen, perfect, but the highlight of the night . . . Damian's arms had wrapped around me in a way that felt too intimate. Then there was the way I'd melted into him, like no time had passed at all. Like I hadn't chosen my current life. Like I wasn't angry at him anymore.

My fingers tightened around the coffee mug as I tried to make sense of it. *It's nothing more than physical attraction.*

God knew it had been a while since I'd been touched by a man. "Touch starved" were the words that came to mind. I hadn't realized it until last night, but my body had been aching for contact. Connection. Years of suppressing and pretending I didn't miss that simple warmth had all come crashing back the second Damian embraced me.

The sinner in me had hoped for things to escalate. That he'd take things further.

Nope. Not going there.

There was only one person who'd understand. I reached for my phone, my fingers hovering for a second before I hit call.

My beautiful sister, Jasmine, picked up after two rings, her face popping up on the screen. "Sister Claire? Gracing me with a call on this fine morning? Shouldn't you be feeding the poor?"

I forced a laugh, but it came out thin. "Is that what you think nuns do?"

She shrugged. "Call it an educated guess." Her smile faded as she studied me for a moment. "Everything okay, *ate*?"

My heart squeezed the way it always did when she used that word. The Filipino term for "big sister" had stuck since we were kids, a small reminder of our heritage, which had followed us throughout the years. Even when we'd fought, she never dropped that title. It was her way of saying I was still hers to worry about, no matter what I was wearing or what vows I'd taken.

I leaned back, tilting my gaze toward the old tongue-and-groove ceiling like it might give me answers. "I don't know."

"Uh-oh. Trouble in paradise?" she asked, her tone shifting.

I exhaled. "You remember Damian Bellucci, right?"

"Yeah, the asshole who broke your heart."

"Well, believe it or not, he's a priest now." I rubbed my forehead, trying to find the right words.

Her brow rose. "And how do you know that?"

"I've been assigned to his parish. Saint Anthony's. I'm the director of religious education." Lord have mercy, that was a mouthful.

Jasmine's lips curved up before she broke out into full-on laughter.

I rolled my eyes. "This isn't funny, Jaz."

When she finally calmed down, she said, "God clearly has a sense of humor."

"Or He's punishing me."

"He still hot?" she asked, a coy grin gracing her features.

"You don't even like men." I took another sip of my cold coffee.

"That doesn't mean I don't recognize hotness."

If anything, Damian's looks had only gotten better with time. *Damn him.* "Anyway. We've been working together, and last night we kinda sorta had a small moment of weakness." My voice caught, and I swallowed hard, trying to push past the lump in my throat.

Jasmine raised a sculpted brow. "Hate to break it to you, sis, but you two used to practically combust every time you looked at each other. What did you think would happen? That eight years and some holy water would magically cure you of wanting to jump his bones?"

I huffed. "It's just physical attraction. That's all it is. I'm not some lovesick teenager anymore. There's work for me to do here, kids to teach. I know why I'm at Saint Anthony's. But my body apparently didn't get the memo about moving on."

"Says who?" Jasmine asked, leaning closer to the camera. "Maybe your body's trying to tell you what your brain doesn't want to hear."

"It's telling me I'm human," I said, frustration bleeding into my voice. "Which is inconvenient as hell when I'm supposed to be deciding on perpetual vows. I know exactly what I want from this ministry—to help people, to show them God's love without all the judgment." I remembered the heartbreak he'd put me through. "I can't bring myself to forgive him. Not after everything. Does that make me a horrible person? A horrible nun?"

Jasmine's expression softened, the teasing glint in her eyes replaced by understanding. "Claire, honey, you're human. You're allowed to struggle with forgiveness."

"But how can I counsel other people about faith and love when I'm holding on to eight years of hurt?" I bit my lip. "How can I take perpetual vows when I'm not sure I can practice what I preach?"

"Remember when I was terrified to come out?" Jasmine asked. "How I thought I had to choose between my identity and my faith?"

I nodded, the memory of those painful years still raw.

"You were the one who told me God made me exactly as I am. That questioning didn't mean I was turning my back on Him. Maybe it's time you gave yourself the same grace you've always given everyone else. Perpetual vows are forever, *ate*. If you're having doubts now, they won't just disappear after you say some words," she said.

Damn it, my vision started to blur. "I love this job, Jaz. The kids are so eager to learn about God and their faith. Their parents can be a handful, but I wouldn't change anything."

"No one's saying you have to give that up," she said. "The Church pushed me away, but I still have my faith. It just looks different now. You can still teach those kids about God without the habit. You can still serve without denying parts of yourself. Maybe that's exactly what you're meant to do—show them that loving God doesn't mean you have to be perfect."

I inhaled deeply. "God, I hate when you're right." A grin curved my lips despite everything. "Seems I have a lot to think about."

"Seems so."

My entire identity and the life I'd built these past years were hanging by a thread. The scariest part wasn't even the possibility of losing it all—it was realizing I might be okay if I did.

"Also . . ." I hesitated, the words catching in my throat. The weight of what I was about to say pressed against my chest like a stone sinking to the bottom of the Pacific Ocean.

"There's more?" Jasmine quipped, eyebrows raised as she tucked a strand of dark hair behind her ear. But I caught the concern beneath her casual tone.

I took a deep breath. "The guy who hit Rico turned himself in a few weeks ago." The memory of Damian's face when he'd told me— raw with grief and something like relief—flashed through my mind.

"Seriously? That's some heavy shit, *ate*," she said.

"I'm going with Damian to meet him."

"Willingly?" Jasmine asked, her eyes searching my face intently. "Why would you do that to yourself?"

I shrugged. "Damian shouldn't have to face this alone. Rico was like a brother to me too, and . . ." I struggled to articulate the tangle of emotions. "I was there that night at the hospital. It feels right to be there for this too."

A knowing smile played at the corners of Jasmine's lips. "Mm-hmm. And this has nothing to do with those lingering feelings you clearly still have for Father Hot Stuff?"

Heat rushed to my cheeks. "It's not like that," I protested, though the words sounded hollow, even to me. "We're just finding closure. Together."

"Sister Claire," Jasmine started. "You might have everyone else fooled with that habit, but I've known you since you stole my Barbies. That look in your eyes when you say his name? That's not 'closure.'"

I rolled my eyes but couldn't stop the small smile tugging at my lips. "Fine, it's complicated. But we both made our choices."

"Did you though?" She raised an eyebrow.

Desperate to shift the focus away from my complicated feelings about Damian, I cleared my throat. "How're things with Rhea?" I asked, noticing how Jasmine's expression changed at the mention of her wife's name—a subtle tightening around her eyes that spoke volumes.

Her smile faltered. "Rough. We've been fighting a lot lately. Small things mostly, but . . ." She ran a hand through her dark hair. "Marriage is a lot harder than I thought it would be. We've been talking about going to counseling."

"We're organizing a marriage retreat in January. You two should come." The words slipped out before I could stop them. "It might help to talk to other couples who've gone through rough patches."

"A Catholic marriage retreat?" Jasmine let out a humorless laugh. "I don't know. The last thing Rhea and I need is more judgment."

"Just think about it?" I urged. "The parish has changed. More progressive. They're more welcoming now. Why don't you come to Sunday Mass as well? Reintroduce yourself to the congregation." I'd for sure need to keep her away from Mrs. Fontana.

Jasmine sighed. "You know what happened last time. The looks I got. I can't sit there and feel like I'm dirty for being who I am."

I bit my lip, the memory of that Sunday morning coming back.

She had been so hopeful, trying to reconnect with the faith we'd grown up with. But the whispered comments and cold stares had crushed her. And seeing it had crushed me too. "Damian wouldn't let that happen," I assured her.

"I know," Jasmine said. "But it's not about one priest. It's the system, the people. It's hard to feel welcome when who you are is the very thing they don't accept."

Watching her pain carve through the facade of faith made my own doubts surface, forcing me to confront the growing chasm between what I preached and what I lived. Could the Church ever truly embrace people like Jasmine, or were we all pretending at acceptance?

"I wish it didn't have to be like this," I said, more to myself than to her. "I wish I could do more."

She was quiet for a moment. "You can't change an entire system, *ate*. But you can change the way you live in it. And in my book, that's more than enough."

She was right. Change didn't come at once. It started with small steps. But where did that leave me? Where did it leave Damian?

Every time I walked into Saint Anthony's, I felt like I was being watched by everyone. Like they could somehow sense the flame burning between me and Damian.

I traced the rim of my coffee mug. "You'll never guess who's still at Saint Anthony's."

Jasmine's eyebrow rose, and she guessed, "Jesus Christ?"

I let out a short laugh. "Jessica Reed."

She huffed. "God, I remember that drama queen. She always did have a thing for Damian."

"I think she still does." I tried to keep the bitterness out of my voice. "She's married now. Has a kid. Attends every church function and helps with PTA meetings too. But the way she looks at him during Mass..."

"Some things never change," Jasmine said with a knowing look. "Listen, I gotta go. I'll talk to Rhea about coming next Sunday and the marriage retreat. Maybe you're right. Maybe it'll be different this time."

I smiled. "I pray it will be."

We said our goodbyes and hung up, but my mind was still racing. My confusion had deepened, but one thing was clear: I couldn't keep living like this. I needed to face reality. The parish was changing, but not fast enough.

And while Damian had brought a more progressive spirit, there were still those who struggled with the tension between appearance and authenticity. I recognized it in Jessica Reed—how she presented a perfect Catholic life to the world while her eyes held a quiet desperation. I'd seen that look during Mass, the way she glanced at Damian, searching for meaning beyond the ritual.

But who was I to judge? We were all pretending in our own ways, weren't we? Me with my habit and prayers that sometimes felt hollow, Jessica with her polished smile and coordinated outfits. All of us hiding behind different veils, afraid of what might happen if we showed the world who we really were.

Chapter Fourteen

CLAIRE

The last rays of sunlight filtered through the windows, transforming my quiet classroom into a canvas of dark angles and fading warmth. I slung my bag over my shoulder and grabbed my skateboard. I'd missed morning Mass, but at least I'd made it to my first class of the day on time. Barely. As I stepped into the hallway, the only sound was the steady tick of the clock that hung at the center of the corridor.

Jessica stood in front of one of the bulletin boards, half hidden in the shadows. Gone was her usual polished smile, the one she flashed to parents and colleagues alike and that said she had everything under control. Her usual perfect posture drooped, and her typically pristine designer blazer was wrinkled at the elbows. A few loose strands of blond hair had slipped free from her careful bun, softening her face.

I stopped, taking a steadying breath. *Mother Mary, help me approach her with an open heart*, I prayed, pushing aside memories of the past that still stung. *Give me grace*. Despite our history, everyone deserved a little kindness.

She hadn't noticed me yet, her gaze fixed on the board of announcements, brows drawn together like she was deep in thought.

I cleared my throat gently, not wanting to startle her. "Jessica?"

Her head snapped up, her blue eyes unguarded, like she'd been caught without her armor. Then, just as quickly, she pulled herself together, smoothing her face into a semblance of composure.

"Sister Claire," she said, managing a tight-lipped smile. "Didn't expect to see you here this late."

She was probably waiting for Sadie to get out of catechism class. "Got a late start today. Had some papers to grade." I offered a gentle smile, noticing the tension in her shoulders. "Is everything okay?"

She hesitated, the polished mask slipping just enough to reveal a glimmer of fragility underneath. Then she shrugged, looking away. "It's just one of those days, I suppose."

I stepped closer, hoping she might fill the stretching silence. Our past interactions hadn't always been easy, and some less-than-kind comments still hung between us. I almost turned around and left, the lingering quiet uneasy. But something in her posture and the slight tremor of her hand made me pause. Mother Superior had always said, *Everyone carries burdens we can't see.*

"Sadie's doing well in class," I said with a genuine smile. "She has a real knack for creative writing. Her story about the mermaid who saved her village was beautiful. You should be proud."

"Really?" Jessica's laugh was hollow, brittle as thin ice. "That's good. At least someone in our family is doing well."

The bitterness in her voice caught my attention. I didn't know what came over me when I asked, "You want to talk about it?"

She faced me, and her eyes widened as though the thought of me being concerned about her was preposterous. "You don't really want to know."

"I do," I said, my voice gentle. "Sometimes it helps to talk to someone."

She continued staring. "Sure you're not talking to me out of obligation?"

It might have started that way, but I genuinely wanted to know what was troubling her. "I'm sure. All ears."

She let out a slow breath, shifting her gaze to the bulletin board again. "Everyone thinks they know me. The pretty cheerleader who married well with this perfect life. They look at me and see exactly what they expect."

"And what do they miss?"

Her blue eyes met mine, and for a moment, something familiar and painfully human broke through her facade. "They miss the part where I cry myself to sleep because my husband hasn't touched me in months. How lonely it is to be someone's trophy instead of their partner. Their equal." She laughed, but it came out more like a sob. "They don't see how much I hate myself for wanting more. Something real."

I dipped my chin, the reality of who she was settling into place. "That sounds incredibly difficult."

"Want to know why I flirt with Father Damian?" she continued. "It's not because I actually expect anything to happen. When he looks at me, I feel seen. Not as Blake's wife or Sadie's mom or the woman who peaked in high school. He sees *me*."

I'd held on to my assumptions about Jessica for so long, but witnessing her vulnerability, a budding shift between us started to form.

"I know what you must think," she said, wiping her eyes with a crumpled tissue from her blazer pocket. "The way I act around him, especially now that he's a priest. The comments, the flirting. God, I must look like such a hussy." She swallowed hard. "And after what happened back then, with you and him—"

I raised a palm to her. "You don't have to bring that up."

"No, I do," she insisted. "I've carried this guilt for years. I knew you two were having problems back then, but I was so desperate to *feel*. Anything." She clasped her hands, letting them hang loosely in front of her, and looked down. "I still am, I guess. Just in different ways now."

My resentment eased—not gone, but its hold slipping one stubborn thread at a time. "I understand more than you might think. We all look for ways to *feel* when we're numb." Letting out a slow breath, I asked, "Have you talked to Blake about any of this?"

"How?" Her voice was small, childlike. "How do I tell him I'm drowning in what he thinks I should be?" She wrapped her arms around herself. "Blake has this image of me. This perfect, put-together wife who hosts dinner parties and chairs PTA meetings, never complaining about anything. If I break that image . . ." She shuddered. "I'd rather be lonely than empty."

Her words resonated more than I wanted to admit. "That's a heavy burden to carry alone," I said, understanding the weight of donning a mask to present to the world.

Jessica's eyes filled with tears again, mascara tracking down her cheeks. "I don't even know who I am anymore. When I'm being real. That person got lost somewhere between homecoming queen and trophy wife."

Without thinking, I took her hand. She stiffened for a moment, then relaxed, her fingers curling around mine.

"These girls," she whispered, gesturing to the closed classroom door across from us. "They haven't learned that they're supposed to be quiet. Expected to be nice when it's the last thing they want to do. That they're meant to somehow accept being less. They take up space so beautifully. I want to tell them to never stop, to never become—" She cut herself off with a deep inhale and smoothed her blazer.

"You're being too hard on yourself," I said. "You're brave enough to stand here and be honest. That counts for more than you know. Maybe it's the first step to finding yourself again."

"I'm sorry," she whispered, squeezing my hand. "For everything. For being the person everyone thinks I am. For not being brave enough to be anyone else. For that night with Damian."

Behind the flawless act, there she was, and despite all the resentment I'd built up, I leaned toward her. "You don't need to carry this anymore."

She was quiet for a long moment, her thumb brushing absently over her wedding ring. "You know, Damian was so drunk that night," she said, her voice barely audible. "He kept talking about you and his brother. How everything was falling apart. I thought I could make him forget. Make myself forget." Her gaze met mine. "But I couldn't. Not like that. Not when he was so broken." She sniffled. "I want you to know when he kissed me, it was empty. Pain looking for somewhere to land. I took him home after. Made sure he got inside. That was it." She gave a watery laugh. "Probably the one decent thing I've done in my life."

Her honesty settled between us. "That was more than decent, Jessica. Thank you," I said, surprised by the genuine gratitude I felt.

She rolled her shoulders back and inhaled. "This stays between us?" she asked, a hint of her old smile returning. "God forbid anyone discover I have actual feelings buried under"—she gestured at herself —"whatever this is."

I let out a soft laugh. "Relax—I'm not in the business of gossiping, let alone outing ice queens."

Her armor fell back into place—the smile, straight back, smoothed hair—but now I could see the gentle heart it protected.

Jessica glanced toward the classroom door, where Sadie gathered her things. "I read about the man who killed Rico Bellucci online this morning." Her voice softened. "Thomas something?"

"Thomas Mercer," I said, my stomach twisting at the mention of his name.

Jessica nodded. "Must be difficult for Father Damian. For all the

Belluccis." She adjusted her purse strap. "I always wondered if they'd ever find who did it. Eight years is a long time to wait for answers."

"It is," I agreed.

She called out to Sadie, asking her to wait in the SUV. Once her daughter was out of earshot, Jessica turned back to me. "You were there that night, weren't you? At the hospital?"

I nodded, the unwelcome memories flooding back in—sterile waiting room, overhead lights crackling with static energy, Damian's hand in mine as we waited for news that would devastate us all.

"Tell him," she started, then hesitated. "Just tell him people are praying for him."

"I will," I promised.

"You know what's really ironic?" she asked. "You're probably the first person in years who's actually listened to me. Maybe God knows what He's doing after all."

After Jessica made her way toward the exit, I stayed in front of the bulletin board, my thoughts spinning between Jessica's unexpected vulnerability and the weight of Thomas Mercer's arrest hanging over the parish. Over Damian.

My heart ached for him in a way that went beyond our complicated history. I'd seen the shadows in his eyes these past few days, the tension in his shoulders whenever someone mentioned Rico's name. He was carrying the burden so privately, so stoically. Classic Damian, shouldering his pain alone rather than letting others help him bear it.

What was I supposed to do when someone I cared about was hurting, but the very thing that might comfort them—my presence, my touch, my unconditional support—was precisely what I wasn't supposed to offer?

My fingers itched to reach for my phone, to text him. But what could I possibly say that wouldn't cross the lines we'd been so carefully maintaining?

The hit-and-run had shaped Damian in ways I was only beginning to understand. It had driven him to a life dedicated to finding meaning in suffering.

I wanted to help him through this. God, I wanted to be there for him in all the ways that mattered. But I didn't know how to separate *Sister Claire* from the *Claire* who still cared too much, whose heart raced when he entered a room, and who still woke from dreams where his hands and lips found all the places they shouldn't.

I touched my thigh absently, a habit from when I used to trace the scars hidden beneath my skirt. We all carried wounds, visible and invisible. Perhaps grace wasn't about being perfect. Maybe it was about seeing each other's humanity, rough edges and all, and offering understanding instead of judgment. But with Damian, every act of grace, every moment of honest connection, felt like walking a tightrope over a chasm neither of us could afford to fall into.

In that moment, my phone vibrated with a text, the cheerful chime cutting through my swirling thoughts like a bell calling me back to the present.

DAMIAN

Planning session Friday in the church hall @3:30. Just us.

I raised an eyebrow, a smile tugging at my lips despite the thoughts swirling around in my head. Of course he'd choose Friday— our lightest workday, when the weekend exodus began and half the admin staff started sneaking out after lunch like kids escaping detention.

Even Mrs. Walker, who usually stayed glued to her desk until precisely 5:00 p.m., had a habit of mysteriously "remembering errands" around 2:30 on Fridays. The teachers weren't much better, racing to their cars the moment the last bell rang, already mentally checked out and planning their weekend adventures.

It was clever timing, if I was being honest. The school would be quieter than Sunday morning Mass, with just the die-hard workaholics and whoever drew the short straw for after-school supervision still hanging around. We'd have the church hall to ourselves without Mrs. Fontana's hawk eyes tracking our every movement or some overeager parent volunteer "accidentally" wandering by to see what the priest and the nun were up to behind closed doors.

Smart man.

My stomach did a little flip at the thought of being alone with him again after what had happened in the rectory. After the blessing and then his lips lingering on my forehead.

But then I thought about Sarah and Tod, looking so lost and broken. They needed this retreat. They needed hope, and guidance, and the reminder that love was worth fighting for.

I thought about all the other couples out there struggling in silence, convinced their marriages were beyond saving because no one had ever told them that faith and love could coexist with doubt and imperfection.

Rise to the challenge. The bishop's words echoed in my mind, and that spark of purpose lit up in my chest—the same one that had guided me into teaching, ministry, and believing I could make a difference in people's lives.

This wasn't about me and Damian and whatever complicated mess we'd stumbled into. This was bigger. It was about showing people that love—messy, complicated, beautiful human love—could be sacred too.

With renewed determination and stubborn optimism that had gotten me through years of religious life, I texted back.

ME

I'll be there.

DAMIAN AND I SAT ALONE IN THE CORNER OF THE PARISH HALL, BURIED UNDER a mountain of Advent preparation materials alongside our retreat-planning documents. With Christmas approaching, parish activities had doubled with decorating committees, youth-pageant rehearsals, and marriage-retreat-planning sessions.

Earlier that week, we had chaperoned my eighth graders' field trip to San Carlos Mission. Walking through the ancient stone courtyard, I'd watched him patiently answer the students' endless questions about the missionaries' lives. He'd rolled up his sleeves in the afternoon heat, revealing strong forearms that reminded me of senior year when he'd drag me to the beach just to watch the sunset.

At one point, he caught a student's journal before it blew away, his reflexes quick as lightning—just like when he used to catch me whenever I'd slip on my skateboard. "Always falling," he used to tease, his hand lingering on my waist a heartbeat too long. That annoying flutter had returned to my stomach, and for a moment, the years between us collapsed into nothing.

Each interaction was an exquisite type of torture, my penance for all the forbidden thoughts I'd been having as of late.

The building settled around us, creaking and sighing, as I tried to focus on the volunteer list in front of me. But all I could think about was how Damian's arms had felt around me. Safe. Warm. The memory of his body pressed against mine haunted me, along with the knowledge that I hadn't pulled away when I should have.

He looked different today in jeans and a worn gray long-sleeve shirt, his dark hair slightly disheveled. Less like the untouchable Father Bellucci and more like the boy I used to know. His emerald eyes drifted toward me more than they should. Intense, thoughtful, lingering too long. Every time I glanced up, I caught him watching, though he'd quickly look away.

I stood, the metal chair scraping against the white floor tiles, desperate to focus on anything else besides the dangerous spark catching fire between us. Grabbing a marker, I walked to the whiteboard and started outlining the retreat schedule. "We should split up the groups," I said, forcing steadiness into my voice. "One session for—"

"Those jeans look good on you," Damian cut in, his voice low and rough.

I froze, marker hovering mid-stroke. When I turned, his eyes locked on to mine, dark with barely contained hunger. My heart stuttered as warmth rushed up my neck. I glanced down at my outfit—old skinny jeans, a band tee, and sneakers. Nothing special by any means.

"*You're* not supposed to be looking, Father," I teased, but my traitorous voice wavered.

His lips curled into a devastating smirk. "You make it very *hard* not to."

My stomach flipped, heat pooling in the pit of my belly. *God, give me restraint.*

Damian stood, slow and deliberate, and rounded the table. Every step he took toward me was measured, his eyes never leaving mine. I stepped back.

"Don't move." His voice was firm, a command I hadn't expected.

My pulse hammered in my ears. "What're you doing?"

"Just stay still," he repeated. "I want to try something."

I nodded.

He closed the space between us with one final step, my skin prickling at his proximity. His hand found my waist, his firm touch sending hot pulsating ripples through me. My breath caught in my throat.

I should've pulled away. Should've told him to stop. But—God forgive me—that was far from what I wanted.

His lips grazed the curve of my neck, the contact featherlight, fleeting, like lightning racing down my spine. He inhaled deeply, as though he were trying to memorize my scent. Or memorize me.

"Claire," he whispered, his voice a soft prayer.

I bit my lip, fighting every instinct that screamed at me to give in, to turn my head and let his lips meet mine. But I stayed still and dropped the marker. My fists clenched at my sides, nails digging into my palms, fighting his insufferable magnetism.

His mouth hovered near my ear. "Can I taste you?"

"Father," I murmured, hoping the title would snap us both out of this forbidden haze, but it didn't. I gave in to his request, tilting my head to give him better access.

He wrapped an arm around my waist, pulling me flush against him, his mouth moving to the base of my neck. His lips and tongue worked in tandem, tasting me like I was the first drop of water after a drought.

A breathy moan escaped me before I could stop it, and he responded with a low, guttural sound, his hand trailing up my side, stopping at my breast. He squeezed, and my body arched into him.

He ground himself against me, the hard length of him pressing into my lower stomach.

I gasped.

"We should stop," he said, but showed no effort.

My hands found his shoulders, and he lifted me, my legs wrapping around his waist as he pushed me against the wall. His lips continued to work their way up my neck, his breath hot against my skin.

This is sinful, my mind screamed, but my body didn't care.

His teeth teased a bite, never quite committing, a calculated torment that danced right at the border of too much, sending sparks of warmth down my spine. A whimper escaped me. The sound, the vulnerability, seemed to snap him out of it.

Damian stopped, panting, his forehead resting against mine.

"Fuck. I'm sorry," he whispered, his voice shaky as he released me, sliding me down his body to the floor.

My sneakers hit the tiles, and I wobbled, dazed, with my hand over my neck. "Did you just bite me?"

He stepped back, his hands still lingering on my waist. His gaze bored into mine, filled with the same turmoil that was raging inside me. "I'm sorry," he repeated.

I stared at him, my heart racing as he backed away, the distance between us growing too quickly. What could I possibly say to make this better?

Another moment passed, and then he turned and ran out of the hall without another word, leaving me standing there, trembling, my body aching from the loss of him.

I hugged myself, trying to calm the wild thrum of my heart, but all I could think about was how much I had wanted him to kiss me—how badly I had wanted to fall apart in his arms.

The whiteboard still had my half-finished schedule outline on it, and I'd dropped the marker somewhere on the floor, evidence of how quickly everything had spiraled from professional to whatever the hell that was.

Dear God, send help!

Chapter Fifteen

DAMIAN

The priest in me screamed for space, air, anything to stop me from fucking her right there in the church hall. I just wanted a taste. One moment to indulge in her scent. The feel of her. But once I did, heaven help me, I couldn't stop. It was like all my control snapped and crumbled the second my tongue tasted her salty-sweet skin.

I was no stranger to situations like this. Plenty of women in the parish had tried—subtle touches, lingering glances—but I'd resisted them all without thinking twice. It wasn't hard. I knew my vows, knew where my boundaries were.

But I couldn't reduce Claire to mere temptation. She was more than that. She was every choice I hadn't made. The path I hadn't taken. The what-if that haunted my prayers.

Cool air hit me as I burst through the heavy wooden doors of the church, the sanctuary empty and silent. My footsteps echoed on the stone floor as an uneasy stillness pressed in on me from all sides. With trembling hands, I headed straight for the confessional, a place I'd offered absolution to so many.

The door creaked as I closed it behind me, the small space enveloping me in darkness save for the faint light streaming through the wooden slats. I sat on the bench, my breathing shallow, trying to calm my raging hard on.

The way those jeans hugged Claire's sexy curves, the teasing lilt in her voice when she said, *You're not supposed to be looking, Father.* But how could I not? How could I stop myself from wanting to?

I tried to center myself, but my thoughts tangled between desire, dancing with guilt, and lust, all battling against my vows.

My breath hitched. I shifted in the suffocating tight space of the confessional. I should've left, gone somewhere else, prayed harder, done anything but sit here and let these thoughts consume me. But I couldn't leave. Not yet. Not until I had some release.

I closed my eyes and exhaled. My hands betrayed me, reaching for the tissues parishioners used when a confession became too emotional.

I'm going to hell for this.

Unbuckling my cheap pleather Target belt, I unbuttoned my jeans and pulled the zipper down, releasing my throbbing cock. Visions of Claire swam through my mind as I gripped it and started stroking, hard. The way she bit her bottom lip when deep in thought. How she flipped her wavy dark hair to one side. Her sultry gray eyes.

I increased my pace, a deep shame settling in my chest as I fucked my fist. My orgasm built with every stroke, my breaths coming in ragged gasps.

"Claire." Her name slipped from my lips, soft and reverent. God, I wanted to touch more of her. Every part of me ached for it—my cock, my mouth, my soul. I wanted to feel the warmth of her skin beneath my fingertips, the curve of her body pressed against mine. I wanted it all. Her laughter, her frustration, every broken piece she tried to hide from me.

I want to taste her more.

Touch her.

Fuck her until she comes, hard.

Pressure built low in my stomach, and my balls began tightening. "Fuck. I'm sorry." I stifled a moan and released spurts of white liquid into the tissues, my heart pounding in my ears. Leaning back against the wooden wall, I stared up at the shadowed ceiling of the confessional. *What the hell have I done?*

I could barely breathe as I whispered, "Forgive me, Father. I have sinned." The words fell from my lips in the same hollow tone I'd heard from so many others, but this time they felt heavier, more real than they ever had before.

The desire didn't disappear. Claire lingered in my mind, no matter how much I tried to push her away.

I needed to regain control. Every time I saw her, every time she smiled at me or teased me with that light in her eyes, I was slipping further away from the person I was supposed to be. The priest. The guide.

But I was just a man wrestling with feelings I'd thought I'd never have to face again.

"None of the trials which have come upon you is more than a human being can stand. You can trust that God will not let you be put to the test beyond your strength, but with any trial will also provide a way out by enabling you to put up with it." —1 Corinthians 10:13 (New Jerusalem Bible)

SUNDAY ROLLED AROUND, AND I STOOD AT THE ENTRANCE OF SAINT Anthony's beside Deacon Mel, greeting parishioners as they arrived for Mass. The morning sun warmed my back as I shook hands and exchanged pleasantries with familiar faces I'd come to care for over my time as parish priest.

"Beautiful morning, Father," Deacon Mel said between greetings, his weathered face crinkling with a smile.

I nodded, about to respond, but movement in the parking lot caught my eye. Claire was walking across the asphalt, her habit stirring slightly in the breeze. But she wasn't alone. My pulse quickened as I recognized her sister, Jasmine, walking beside her with another woman—presumably her wife, Rhea. Their hands were laced together, and even from this distance, I could see the hesitance in Jasmine's posture, the way Rhea's thumb traced reassuring circles on her hand.

Claire had mentioned how Jasmine's last visit to Mass had ended with subtle barbs and not-so-subtle stares from some of the older parishioners. I straightened my shoulders, making a quick decision.

"Good morning, Sister Claire," I called as they approached, making my voice deliberately warm and welcoming. "Hey, Jaz, it's been a while."

"What's up, *Father* Damian," Jasmine replied with a hint of her usual spark, though I caught the wariness in her eyes. She gestured to the woman beside her. "This is my wife, Rhea."

"Welcome, Rhea," I said, extending my hand. "I'm glad you both could join us today."

They exchanged a surprised glance before Rhea took my offered hand, some of the tension visibly leaving her shoulders. "Thank you, Father."

I noticed Mrs. Henderson and Mrs. Fontana watching from nearby, their hymn books clutched tight against their chests, whispers already forming on their lips. Several other parishioners slowed their pace, glancing over with poorly disguised curiosity.

"Please come in," I said, placing myself beside the women as they entered. "We're about to begin, and I'd hate for you to miss the opening hymn."

Claire's grateful smile warmed my chest as she led her sister and Rhea toward a pew. I caught several disapproving glances from the congregation, but I held my ground, my expression making it clear that everyone was welcome in God's house—regardless of who they loved.

Deacon Mel leaned closer as the last stragglers filed in. "Bold move, Father," he murmured, but his tone held no judgment.

I shot him a grin but didn't respond.

As Mass began, I let the tension simmer for a moment, my mind turning over what I'd seen. The stares, the whispers—it was a recurring battle. And it wasn't just about Jasmine and her wife or Claire. It was about all the ways people ostracized one another for reasons that had nothing to do with faith.

I stood at the pulpit, gazing out at the congregation, the green vestments of Ordinary Time draped around my shoulders. The Gospel of Luke had just been proclaimed—Christ's words about loving our enemies, about showing mercy as our Father is merciful. As I looked at the faces before me, I felt the Spirit moving, urging me beyond my carefully prepared notes toward a rawer, more urgent message.

"Brothers and sisters, Christ calls us today to love without conditions, to show mercy without reservation. But what does that look like in practice? How do we love those who have hurt us? How do we show mercy when our hearts cry out for justice?"

I glanced toward their pew, seeing how Jasmine and Rhea sat close, drawing strength from each other's presence. Their quiet dignity, their refusal to be shamed, struck me deeply.

"Christ didn't say love was easy. He said it was necessary. When

He walked among us, He didn't turn away the broken, the lost, or the misunderstood. He broke bread with tax collectors, touched lepers, and spoke to the woman at the well. He embraced those society had cast aside."

My voice grew stronger, steadier. "Love means opening our doors to those we don't understand and welcoming those who feel they've been pushed away. It means choosing compassion over judgment. Mercy over condemnation."

I could see the shift in the congregation, some heads nodding, some still looking skeptical. But I pressed on.

"God's love knows no bounds, and neither should ours. If we are truly to be His hands and feet on this earth, we must make sure no one feels like a stranger in His house. We must love as we have been loved—completely, without reservation, without exception."

The morning light streamed through the stained glass, painting the congregation in jeweled colors. "This is our calling, not just as Catholics, but as human beings. To love. To forgive. To welcome. To serve. Because that's what Christ did, and that's what He asks of us."

When communion began, I took my place at the altar, the chalice cool against my palms as parishioners formed a line down the center aisle. One by one, they came forward, hands outstretched or crossed over their chests for a blessing.

My heart quickened when Jasmine and Rhea rose from their pew and joined the line. I glimpsed Mrs. Fontana's sharp intake of breath and the way her back stiffened as they passed her row. But they held their heads high.

When they reached me, they crossed their arms over their chests, the traditional sign for those who wish to receive a blessing rather than the Eucharist. Jasmine's eyes met mine, uncertain but resolute.

"May the Lord bless you and keep you," I said, making the sign of the cross over them both. "May His face shine upon you and bring you peace."

"Amen," Rhea whispered, her expression one of genuine gratitude.

They returned to their seats, the simple dignity in their steps a silent rebuke to the whispers around them. Claire caught my eye from her pew, her face alight with what looked like appreciation.

The rest of the Mass continued without issue, but the tension hadn't completely dissipated. By the time it ended, Jasmine and Rhea were already making their way out. Claire watched them go, worry still apparent on her angelic features. I offered her a small nod, as if to say, *I've got this.*

As soon as the church began to empty, Mrs. Fontana approached me, her lips pressed into a thin line. "Father," she began, her voice hushed but firm, "I worry about the message we're sending to the children. You understand."

I followed her gaze to the back of the church, where Jasmine helped an elderly Mr. Rodriguez with his coat. "Yes, it's wonderful to see our younger members setting such a good example of kindness, isn't it?"

Her fingers tightened around her purse. "That's not what I meant, Father." She lowered her voice. "Have you considered what this looks like? Saint Anthony's has always been a respectable parish."

"And welcoming all of God's children somehow makes us less respectable?" I kept my voice low, though anger simmered beneath my practiced calm.

She glanced around before stepping closer, lowering her voice. "My family has supported this church for generations."

"And we're extremely grateful. But there's no price on faith."

Her face flushed. "I didn't mean it that way."

"You didn't?" I gentled my tone, though my resolve didn't waver. "You're suggesting we should turn people away to maintain appearances? To keep the money flowing?"

"I'm saying we have standards," she hissed. "Traditions. If word gets out that we're encouraging this kind of lifestyle, other parishes will talk. Families might leave. My own contributions—"

"Then withhold them," I said. "If that's what your conscience dictates. But I won't turn anyone away because their love makes you uncomfortable."

"You're making a mistake," she warned, fingers clutching her rosary.

"The Church teaches love above all else, Mrs. Fontana. When Jesus sat with tax collectors and sinners, the Pharisees questioned Him too. But He said it's not the healthy who need a doctor, but the sick. Though in this case," I added, unable to keep the edge from my voice, "I'd argue the sickness lies more in our judgment."

She drew back as if I'd slapped her clear across the face. "Well. I see you've made your choice."

My tone softened. "I have. And I pray you'll make yours with love rather than fear. You're welcome here too, Mrs. Fontana. But so are they. That's not negotiable."

She opened her mouth, then closed it. Without another word, she turned and walked away, her heels clicking against the stone floor. I watched her leave, my heart heavy but my conscience clear. Some things were worth more than money. Worth more than reputation. Worth the whispers that would surely follow.

As silence settled over the sanctuary, I spotted Claire, her figure backlit by the morning sun streaming through the doors. Her beautiful gray eyes held mine with a mix of gratitude and an emotion that made my skin prickle beneath my robes. My pulse raced against the confines of my white collar. Even across this distance, she pulled at me like the moon pulls the tides. Constant. Inevitable.

God help me, I don't know how much longer I can resist this.

Through the open doors, Jasmine and Rhea waited near their car, their love on display without shame or hesitation. They had chosen authenticity despite what others thought. And seeing Claire's quiet pride in her sister's courage, I felt another shift, a certainty taking root beneath all my carefully constructed walls.

In the end, wasn't that what faith was really about? Not judgment, not exclusion, but love in its purest, most unconditional form. The kind that made people question everything they thought they knew. The kind that Claire stirred in me with one look. She made me wonder if some calls were stronger than others.

Chapter Sixteen

CLAIRE

Damian was standing near the front, his back to me as he spoke with parishioners exiting the church. His posture was relaxed, though I knew the burdens he was carrying. I shifted, my sneakers scuffing against the gray stone floor. *I can't do this. This is physical attraction*, I reminded myself for the millionth time. But then my chest constricted as the memory flooded my mind.

I'd let him put his lips on me, let him touch me. And the most sinful part of it all was I wanted more. If he'd wanted to fuck me in the church hall, I would've let him.

Sister Agnes's words invaded my thoughts. *Child, passion isn't something to be feared or crushed. It's fire from God Himself. The question isn't whether you feel it, but what you do with it.*

I glanced around, taking in the Mass goers who still lingered. Most had been surprisingly welcoming to Jasmine and Rhea. Deacon Mel had even invited them to the next parish potluck. Only Mrs. Fontana and her tight circle had maintained their icy distance. I felt a flicker of pride at how things had changed since Jasmine's last visit, though there was still more work to be done.

My gaze drifted back to Damian. He had a way of making people feel understood. It was one of the reasons I'd fallen for him all those years ago. And it was one of the reasons I couldn't seem to completely let go.

I turned to leave before I could spiral further into my thoughts. But before I reached the double doors, I stole one last glance at him. He was standing there, still staring at me.

"Claire, we're heading to Mom and Dad's. Want a ride?" Jasmine asked as she and Rhea stood a few feet from their car.

"Yeah," I said too quickly.

Jasmine strode over to me, linked her arm through mine, and tugged me toward the forest-green sedan. "Mom's making pancit. And you know how she gets if we're late."

The cool midmorning breeze brushed my cheeks, a startling contrast to the suffocating warmth of the church. But even as I climbed into the car, rolled down my window, and breathed in the fresh salty air, I couldn't shake the feeling that no matter how far I tried to run from this, I'd never truly escape.

The ride to my parents' house was long, winding along the coast for nearly an hour, but the back seat of Jasmine's car offered some sanctuary from . . . everything. The Pacific stretched out beside us, the late-morning sun casting a soft glow on the water.

"You okay?" Rhea asked, glancing at me in the rearview mirror. "You seemed a little off during Mass."

I forced a smile, pushing away the memory of Damian's intense gaze from earlier. "I'm fine. Shouldn't I be the one asking that?"

"You were right, *ate*. It was different this time," Jasmine said, turning to face me from the passenger's seat. "I actually felt welcome. Like we belonged there."

Rhea nodded, her hands relaxing on the steering wheel. "When Damian greeted us at the door, I was bracing myself for that polite but distant priest smile, you know? But he was genuinely happy to see us."

"He remembered me," Jasmine added. "After all these years, he remembered me. And there was no awkwardness when I introduced Rhea as my wife."

"That meant everything," Rhea said softly. "I've been to churches where priests barely acknowledged my existence. But he made sure we felt seen—included."

"And his homily," Jasmine continued. "He was talking directly to us. About love without conditions, about opening doors instead of closing them. I kept waiting for the 'but' or the fine print, and it never came."

"The way he looked right at us when he said no one should feel like a stranger in God's house," Rhea added, her eyes meeting mine in the mirror. "I teared up. When's the last time a priest made me cry happy tears?"

Jasmine reached back and squeezed my hand. "Whatever you've been doing there, whatever influence you've had on him, it's working. The whole atmosphere was different. Lighter. More loving."

"Even Deacon Mel came up afterward and chatted with us," Rhea said with a laugh. "Asked if we were planning to come back, said the parish could use more young couples."

"We want to come back," Jasmine said, her voice firm with decision. "Not just for you, but for us. I've missed this, *ate*. I've missed having a spiritual home where I don't have to hide who I am. Missed feeling God's love reflected in how people treat each other."

Tears pricked at my eyes, and I was overwhelmed by the hope in their voices. "I'm glad your experience back was a positive one," I said, my smile genuine this time.

When we pulled up to my parents' house, the old yellow siding welcomed us. Dad's cooking filled my nose as soon as we opened the front door. The small Santo Niño still watched over the entryway, just as it had throughout our childhood.

"Girls!" Mom called from the kitchen, where she was organizing papers at the counter—probably grading or planning lessons. As a high school English teacher, she never seemed to stop working. "Perfect timing. Lunch is almost ready."

I stepped into the kitchen. Dad stirred a pot of sinigang, the scent making my mouth water. Mom looked up from her stack of papers, her eyes immediately going to my habit with that expression of gentle disappointment.

"There're my overachievers," Dad said, opening his arms for hugs. "How are my brilliant girls doing?"

"We've been good, Pop," Jasmine said, settling into her usual spot at the table. Rhea sat beside her, comfortable in the warmth of our kitchen.

Mom set aside her red pen and really looked at me. "Are you getting enough sleep, *anak*? Eating properly? I know how you get when you're stressed. You forget to take care of yourself."

Classic Mom—caring but delivered with the underlying message that I wasn't managing well enough. The observation hit an old nerve, the one that used to send me spiraling in college when every phone call home felt like a performance review.

"I'm fine, Ma. Just busy with the new school year."

"Hmm." She studied my face critically. "You've lost weight. I can tell. And working at a parish school . . ." She shook her head. "Claire, you have a master's degree in education. You could be teaching at any prestigious private school, maybe even working toward administration. Instead you're—"

"Following her calling," Dad interjected. "Which takes more courage than climbing any corporate ladder, Bea."

Mom sighed, the sound heavy with years of watching what she saw as wasted potential. "I just think Claire is capable of so much more. Remember your test scores? Your GPA? You were valedictorian, for heaven's sake. You could have gone to any graduate program, could be running your own school by now."

There it is. The repeated litany of my achievements, each one a golden weight around my neck. I remembered the way she'd beam when I brought home perfect report cards, the way her eyes would light up when teachers praised my work. But I also recalled the subtle disappointment when I came in second at the science fair, the gentle but persistent questioning when my SAT scores were merely excellent instead of perfect.

"She *is* making a difference," Jasmine muttered. "She's teaching kids about faith and love."

"Of course she is," Mom said, voice softening. "I'm not saying the work isn't meaningful. It's just . . ." She looked at me with eyes that held both love and frustration. "I've watched you excel at whatever you put your mind to since you were little. Science fairs, debate team, honor roll every semester. You were going to change the world, Claire."

The memories crashed over me: staying up until 2 a.m. in high school to perfect projects that were already A-level work, the panic attacks before big tests because anything less than perfect was deemed a failure, the way I'd learned to measure my worth by external validation.

Mom had never meant to create that pressure. She'd believed she was nurturing my potential, celebrating my gifts. But somewhere along the way, her love had become conditional on my performance, and I'd internalized that until even breathing felt like a skill I had to excel at.

"Maybe I still am," I said quietly. "Just not the way you expected."

Dad placed a bowl of rice in front of me. "Your mother's proud of you, *anak*. She just shows it by worrying you're not reaching your full potential."

Full potential. Those words used to follow me into my dorm room at college, where I'd sit on my bathroom floor with a razor blade, trying to find some way to feel in control when the pressure became unbearable. Mom had never known about the cutting. Would be horrified to find out. She'd blame herself, and that wasn't fair. She'd loved me the only way she knew how.

Mom's mouth tightened; she hated being psychoanalyzed, even gently. "I'm not worried. I'm realistic. Claire has gifts that could take her anywhere. Instead, she's . . ." She gestured vaguely at my habit.

"Serving God and teaching children," Dad finished for her. "Sounds pretty successful to me."

"And now you're working with Damian Bellucci," Mom continued, unable to let it go. "I always liked that boy. But a priest? Really? With his potential?"

Pursing my lips, I glanced at my plate. I'd spent years in therapy learning that my worth wasn't tied to achievement, only to end up back in this kitchen where love remained measured by potential reached or wasted.

I released a slow breath, calling on God to give me patience. "He's doing important work too."

"I'm sure he is. But you have to think practically. What happens in ten years? Twenty? You're both brilliant people limiting yourselves to—"

"To a life of purpose?" Dad suggested.

Mom shot him a look. "To a life without advancement and financial security. A life without options."

The weight of her expectations settled onto my shoulders. This was the dance we'd done my whole life: Mom seeing endless potential, me trying to live up to it, never quite meeting the vision she had of who I could become.

The difference now was that I understood her love, even if I couldn't change how it affected me. She wasn't trying to hurt me; she was trying to ensure I never settled for less than she believed I deserved. The problem was that her definition of "deserving" and mine had never quite aligned.

"How was Mass today?" Dad asked, clearly trying to redirect.

"It was beautiful, Dad," Jasmine said. "Father Damian gave a wonderful homily about acceptance and love."

Mom perked up slightly. "Well, that's good. At least he's putting that intellect to use. Though I still think he would have made an excellent lawyer or professor."

Dad's expression grew more serious as he passed the rice. "Speaking of Damian, I read about Thomas Mercer in the newspaper. After all these years, he finally turned himself in."

My spoon froze halfway to my mouth. The mention of *him* always hit like a punch to the gut, but hearing it here, in my parents' kitchen, made it feel even more surreal.

"Terrible thing," Mom said, shaking her head. "That poor family. Eight years of not knowing, and now this. I can't imagine what Damian must be going through."

"The article said the man's wife was dying of cancer," Dad continued. "She made him promise to confess before she passed. What a burden to carry all those years."

Jasmine glanced at me, concern flickering in her eyes. "How is he handling it? Damian, I mean."

I forced myself to take a bite of sinigang, buying time. "It's difficult," I said. "For everyone at the parish."

What I couldn't tell them was that Damian had asked me to go with him to visit Thomas Mercer tomorrow. That we'd be sitting across from Rico's killer, facing the man who'd changed both of our lives.

Mom would have a field day with that information—analyzing every aspect of why I'd agreed to go, what it meant for my vows, whether I was making sound decisions.

"I suppose there will be some kind of service?" Mom asked. "For healing or closure?"

"Yes, this weekend," I said, grateful for the safer topic. "A prayer service for justice and healing."

"Good," Dad said. "The community needs that. Damian too, I imagine."

I caught Dad's eye across the table, and he gave me a small understanding smile. He'd always been the one to celebrate what we were rather than mourning what we weren't. He was the one who'd taught me that love didn't require a list of perfect achievements.

After lunch, we lingered around my parents' table for nearly two hours, the conversation shifting to lighter topics. Dad told stories about his construction job while Mom graded papers with one ear on our discussion, occasionally chiming in with corrections or observations.

Jasmine and Rhea helped clear the dishes, and we all ended up in the living room, where Mom showed off photos from her latest school field trip and Dad shared gossip about the neighbors.

It was almost four o'clock by the time we started gathering our things to leave. Mom packed us leftover sinigang in containers she insisted we take despite our protests that we couldn't finish it all. Dad hugged each of us twice and made Jasmine promise to bring Rhea back soon.

"Drive safely," Mom called from the doorway as we walked to the car. "And, Claire, get some rest. You look exhausted."

Even her parting shot came wrapped in concern.

The ride back to my cottage took about an hour along the winding coastal highway. Jasmine had put on a playlist of soft R & B that filled the comfortable silence as we passed the usual landmarks: the beach where we used to have family picnics, the ice cream stand that only opened in summer, the overlook where teenagers still parked to watch the sunset. The warm golden late-afternoon light painted everything in that dreamy California glow that made even ordinary moments feel cinematic.

When we pulled up to my place, Jasmine turned in her seat, glancing over her shoulder at me. "Mom was especially *Mom* today."

I shrugged, trying to seem unaffected. "She means well. She just wants the best for us."

"The 'best' according to her definition," Rhea said from the driver's seat. "But teaching those kids, helping families like ours feel welcome at church again? That's incredible. That's changing the world in ways Mother doesn't understand, but it matters."

Jasmine nodded. "Seriously, *ate*. You and Damian are making Saint Anthony's a place where people like us can actually belong."

My throat tightened. "Thanks, guys. Sometimes it's hard to remember that when Mom starts listing all the things I could've been."

"Your potential isn't wasted," Jasmine said. "It's being used exactly how it should. Mom measures success by titles and salaries, but you're measuring it by changed hearts and healed souls. There's no comparison."

We sat in comfortable silence for a moment before Jasmine cleared her throat. "So, how are you doing? With everything?" She didn't conceal the careful concern in her voice.

"What do you mean?"

"I just . . ." Jasmine glanced at Rhea, who gave her an encouraging nod. "You seemed a little, I don't know, tense today. During Mass and after."

Shit. "I'm fine. Just adjusting to working at the parish, you know? Lots of memories."

"That makes sense," Rhea said. "It must be strange being back there with Damian—sorry, Father Damian. Given your history."

I felt heat creep up my neck. "We're colleagues now. Nothing more."

Jasmine turned in her seat to look at me more directly. "*Ate*, you know you can talk to us, right? About anything?"

The gentleness in her voice nearly undid me. "I know."

"Look, I want you to know, if you did decide that this wasn't the life for you, I wouldn't fault you for it, and I don't think God would either." Jasmine reached back and touched my leg, squeezing it. "But don't let Mom's disappointment make that decision for you."

"You're not failing at some imaginary standard," Rhea added, meeting my eyes in the rearview mirror. "You're succeeding at being exactly who you're meant to be."

The corners of my mouth rose as warmth spread through my chest. "Thanks. Both of you."

I stepped out of the car and stood next to the driver's side window. "Are you two signing up for the marriage retreat?"

"I think we might," Rhea said. "After today, I'm actually excited about being part of Saint Anthony's again."

"Awesome. I'll message you the link."

We said our goodbyes, and I stepped away from the car. As I watched them drive away, my chest tightened—not just at the thought of spending more time alone with Damian, but at the realization that maybe my struggle wasn't just about him. Maybe it was about finally learning to measure my worth by my own standards instead of everyone else's. One thing was abundantly clear: This wasn't going to get any easier.

Chapter Seventeen

DAMIAN

Monday morning, the early fog clung to the coastal highway as I kept my hands anchored on the wheel, focusing on the weight of it beneath my palms rather than the knot tightening in my chest.

Claire sat beside me in the passenger's seat. She wore her glasses today. When we were younger, she'd switch to frames when her allergies acted up. My lips curved up at the memory.

God, I wanted to reach over and cover her hand with mine like old times. But I pressed my lips together and kept my eyes on the road ahead, pretending the county jail was just another destination instead of the place that might change everything.

I kept stealing glances at her, noting the careful way she held herself, the deliberate space she maintained between us. After what had happened in the church hall, I didn't blame her.

"About what happened Friday," I said, the words thick in my throat. "In the hall, when I—"

"Moment of weakness," Claire said, voice crisp and professional. She didn't look at me, keeping her gaze fixed on the road ahead. "For both of us."

I nodded, my grip tightening on the steering wheel. "It was inappropriate. I crossed a line."

"We both did." She adjusted her glasses, a nervous gesture I remembered from high school. "Let's just call it nostalgia. Old sensibilities getting confused with present circumstances."

Nostalgia. The word stung more than it should have, reducing what I'd felt to safe and dismissible. But maybe that was what we both needed.

"It won't happen again," I said, meaning it.

"Good." She finally glanced at me, her gray eyes steady but holding a flicker of what I thought might be regret. "We're both wearing the uniform now," she said, adjusting her veil with a rueful smile. "Guess that comes with a pretty strict dress code for the heart too."

"I know." The weight of my collar was heavier, a physical reminder of the promises I'd made. "I'm sorry for putting you in that position."

Claire nodded once, a sharp movement that suggested the conversation was over.

The boundaries were drawn, clear and unmistakable. Professional distance. Sacred duty. The past firmly where it belonged.

And yet my body refused to compute the memo. My fingers burned with the memory of her skin, the way she'd felt beneath my hands when I'd lost control and pressed her against that wall. The taste of her neck lingered on my tongue like communion wine, sacred in its sweetness, damning in my hunger for more.

Christ, what is wrong with me? Here I was, driving to confront my brother's killer, and all I could think about was how Claire's pulse had fluttered under my lips like a trapped bird.

I shifted in my seat, trying to focus on anything else. The road, the ocean, the weight of what we were about to do.

Focus. Rico. Thomas Mercer. That's why you're here.

"Thanks again for coming with me today," I said, grateful for the shift to safer ground, even as my voice came out rougher than intended. "This isn't exactly how most people would choose to spend their day off."

"Well, it was this or reorganizing my already-perfectly-organized book collection," she said with a slight grin. "And honestly? Facing down your demons seemed like the more productive use of the Monday holiday." Her teasing tone lightened the heaviness in the truck, though I caught the way her fingers worried the edge of her skirt.

I grinned despite the twisting in my stomach. "Tough choice."

"Seriously though," she said, her voice gentling but maintaining that careful distance. "When you first told me about Thomas, I couldn't let you do this alone. Rico deserves that much."

Rico deserves that much—not *You deserve it* or *I want to be here for you.* The distinction hit me like a small blade between the ribs. I deserved that. I'd earned it the night I walked away from her.

The road stretched out before us, winding along the coastline, glimpses of the ocean appearing between buildings. The salt air should have been calming, but my chest was tight, like I was wearing a collar two sizes too small.

"Nervous?" Claire asked, her voice neutral.

"That's one way to put it." I could feel sweat gathering at my temples despite the cool morning air. "I've been dreaming about confronting this man for eight years. And now that it's happening . . ."

"You're wondering if it'll change anything," Claire finished, her gaze thoughtful as she watched the scenery pass. "If seeing his face will make the pain any different. Less."

I nodded.

Claire reached over, her fingers brushing mine on the steering wheel. It was a brief, careful touch that somehow contained both comfort and clear boundaries. "Whatever happens in there, you're not facing him as Father Bellucci. You're Damian, Rico's brother."

The simple contact grounded me for a moment, even as it reminded me of how different things were between us now. Professional. Distant. Safe.

As she withdrew her hand, I caught her studying my profile with that look she used to get when she was calculating risk—the same expression I'd seen before she'd climbed the old oak behind her house or snuck out for midnight drives.

"This man is a former chemistry teacher," Claire said. "He had a wife. Has kids that are grown. He's not exactly the criminal mastermind I built up in my head."

"Yeah. It would be easier if he were a monster."

Claire nodded, her profile sharp against the window. "Monsters don't turn themselves in. People do. People who make terrible mistakes and have to live with them." She paused. "Like we all have, in different ways."

We lapsed into silence as the county jail, a gray concrete building surrounded by high fencing that looked like it could swallow hope whole, came into view.

I gripped the steering wheel until my knuckles blanched, the walls of the prison rising before us like a fortress of judgment. My heart rate picked up as it grew closer and closer. The visitor's parking lot stretched around us, filled with other cars carrying other people's shame and worry. I pulled into an empty space and cut the engine, the weight of my truck keys heavy in my palm.

Get it together, Bellucci.

The engine ticked as it cooled, but I couldn't make myself move. Each breath felt measured—deliberate—the way I'd trained myself to breathe through difficult moments at the pulpit.

Can I do this? In the confessional, there had been a screen between Thomas and me. Safety in anonymity and ritual. Here, I'd be face-to-face with him. I tugged at my collar again, feeling like it was strangling me.

Claire must have noticed because she turned to me, her gray eyes intense but careful. "Hey," she said. "I'm right here. Okay?"

I could only nod, my voice buried somewhere beneath eight years of grief and self-recrimination. As we walked toward the entrance, our footsteps fell into sync, a rhythm that spoke of the shared history neither of us could completely erase or ignore.

Claire had called ahead, explaining she was providing spiritual support as Rico's former friend. The bureaucracy of grief, she'd called it wryly, but it had gotten us both cleared for the visit.

Security was unpleasant—metal detectors that beeped accusations, pat downs that felt invasive, the echo of gates sliding shut behind us with the finality of a tomb sealing. The institutional scent of disinfectant and despair made my stomach turn.

Claire didn't flinch, even as the guard's hands skimmed over her with professional detachment. Her quiet dignity in this sterile, dehumanizing place was admirable.

The visiting room was nearly empty, white lights humming overhead like angry wasps, making the walls, chairs, and tables appear harsh and bleached. One other family huddled in the corner, speaking in hushed voices to a young man with tattoos crawling up his neck.

"The lights in here could use some warmth," Claire murmured, her eyes scanning the bare walls with that instinctive need to nurture, to improve. "Maybe some plants. Something alive."

I almost smiled at her automatic assessment and the way she couldn't help but see potential for beauty even here. Before I could respond, the door buzzed open. Thomas Mercer appeared, escorted by a guard, and my breath caught.

He was smaller than I'd imagined based off the pictures I'd seen online. Thin, gray at the temples, shoulders curved under the weight of guilt. Just a man. A broken, ordinary man who'd made one terrible choice on one terrible night. His eyes widened when he saw Claire, confusion flickering across his features.

"Mr. Mercer, I'm Father Damian Bellucci. I'm Enrico's brother," I said as he sat across from us. "This is Sister Claire Vergara."

Thomas nodded, and his dark eyes met mine with a clarity that hadn't been there before. He knew I'd been the priest who'd heard his confession and desperate pleas for guidance. "Father. Thank you for seeing me today." He turned to Claire, his gaze questioning. "Are you a cousin?"

"No," she said, her voice gentle but clear. "I was Rico's friend. He made everyone feel like family—especially awkward teenagers who tried too hard and burned dinner more often than not."

Thomas swallowed visibly, his eyes dropping to his cuffed hands. "I see. And you're both . . ." He gestured vaguely at our clerical clothing.

"We serve at Saint Anthony's parish," I said, feeling oddly compelled to explain. "Claire was a huge part of our lives back then. She still is."

Claire's eyes met mine, an unreadable emotion flickering there before she looked away.

Thomas shifted in his seat, the metal chair creaking under his weight. "Saint Anthony's," he said. He paused, seeming to consider his next words. "That's a beautiful church. I used to drive past it sometimes on my way to work." His voice was tentative, as if he was testing whether normal conversation was allowed in this place. "I taught chemistry at the high school for fifteen years before . . . Well, before everything changed."

"Chemistry," Claire said, her pastoral training kicking in as she recognized his attempt at normalcy. "That must have been rewarding. Working with young people."

"It was." A ghost of a smile crossed Thomas's face. "They kept me on my toes. Always asking questions I hadn't thought of." The smile faded. "I miss it. The classroom. The students who actually wanted to learn."

Tension grew within me with each passing statement. Here was this man—Rico's killer—talking about his job, his life, as if he deserved the courtesy of small talk.

"How long have you both been . . . ?" Thomas gestured again at our religious garbs. "I'm sorry. I don't know the proper way to ask about your vocation."

"Eight years," I said, clipped. "I entered religious life eight years ago."

Thomas's face went pale. "Eight years." He repeated the words like a prayer or a curse. "The same time that . . ."

Claire interjected, "I entered religious life four years ago."

Silence settled between us. The artificial normalcy of the conversation crumbled, leaving us staring at the real reason we were here. Thomas cleared his throat, his fingers drumming nervously against the metal table.

"I couldn't let Damian come alone," Claire said, her voice neutral. "We're better together when facing difficult situations."

Better together. The phrase wrapped around my chest like a vise and squeezed until I couldn't breathe. I'd been missing this sense of partnership, of facing life's storms with someone who understood the demons haunting me.

Thomas glanced at me, then met Claire's gaze again. "I need to ask, and I know I don't have the right." His voice was barely above a whisper. "What was *he* like? The person, not just"—he swallowed thickly—"not just the victim in a police report."

I tensed, my jaw clenching involuntarily, but Claire laid a hand on my arm, a grounding pressure that somehow contained both restraint and permission.

"He was brilliant," she said, and for the first time since we'd arrived, a genuine smile touched her lips. "The kind of person who lit up when explaining a topic he loved. Whether it was calculus or theology or why the 49ers were definitely going to win the Super Bowl this time." Her voice grew gentler with remembrance. "He never made you feel small for not understanding. He just got excited about sharing what he knew."

The memory crashed over me like a rogue wave: Rico sprawled on our kitchen floor, surrounded by textbooks, his dark hair falling into his eyes as he leaned over Claire's shoulder. He'd been walking her through the same calculus problem for the third time, his voice growing softer with each explanation, never a trace of frustration.

"You've got this, Claire," he'd said, tapping the pencil against the paper in a rhythm that meant he was thinking. "Just think about it like this: Imagine the curve as a mountain, and we're finding the steepest part of the climb."

When she'd finally gotten it, his face had lit up like Christmas morning, and he'd pulled her into one of his bone-crushing hugs. "See? I told you that brilliant brain of yours would figure it out." He'd never once made her feel stupid, never showed the slightest impatience.

Claire's voice snapped me back to the present. "He had this profound desire to help people." Her voice was thick with grief and love that she was trying to control. "That's why he was going to become a priest. He believed in people's capacity for good, even when they couldn't see it in themselves."

Thomas nodded slowly, taking it in. "And he was studying to become a priest?" He glanced at me. "Like you?"

"Yes," I said, my throat like sandpaper. "Though he was certain of his calling in a way I—"

In a way I never was.

Thomas's gaze moved from Claire to me, understanding dawning in his eyes.

"I should have stopped," he said suddenly, all pretense of small talk abandoned. "I've relived that moment every day for years, imagining a different choice. The what-ifs. But I can't change what I did."

"None of us can," I said, hoarse. "We can only decide what to do now."

He nodded, staring down at his cuffed hands. The stark lighting accentuated the deep lines around his eyes and the way guilt had carved itself into his features.

Claire maintained her careful composure, keeping herself together, even as unshed tears shimmered in her eyes. Something inside me shifted, a realization building like pressure behind a dam.

I need to stop running. From the pain. From the truth. From who I really am.

"I want you to know I'm pleading guilty. No deals, no reduced charges. I won't put your family through a trial," Thomas said.

"Thank you," I said, meaning it.

He looked at Claire. "Thank you for telling me about Rico. For helping me understand who he was, not just what I took from this world."

Claire nodded. "He was a beautiful person."

Thomas swallowed hard, his Adam's apple bobbing. "I know it's unfair of me to ask." He glanced from Claire to me. "Can you ever forgive me?"

The question hung in the air, thick and potent as incense. I thought about Rico and his easy laughter. He'd forgiven me for every stupid thing I'd done as his annoying younger brother. Never held grudges.

"Rico would have forgiven you already," I said, steadier than I'd expected. "That's who he was. As for me . . ." I paused, Claire's presence beside me like an anchor. "I'm working on it."

He focused on Claire. "And you? Can you forgive me?"

She was quiet for a moment, considering. "I'm working on it," she said honestly. "Just like Damian. Just like you're working on forgiving yourself."

Thomas remained quiet as the heavy sound of keys jangling echoed down the sterile hallway. The guard's footsteps were purposeful, each step marking the end of a chapter I wasn't sure I was ready to finish.

"Time's up," the guard announced.

We all rose from the metal table, the chair legs screeching against the concrete in a way that made my teeth ache. The too-bright lights overhead hummed their constant tune, casting us in that sickly institutional glow that made even healthy skin look corpse pale.

As Thomas was being led away, he turned back to us. His watery red-rimmed eyes found mine, then Claire's.

"Thank you both for coming here," he said, his voice barely above a whisper but carrying across the room with startling clarity. "For seeing me as more than just the man who killed Enrico."

Molten heat flooded my veins, starting in my chest and radiating outward until every nerve ending electrified.

More than just the man who killed Enrico.

Those words echoed in my skull like a death knell. As if eight years of shattered dreams and sleepless nights were just inconvenient details. As if Rico's stolen calling, his capacity for goodness I could never match, was negotiable against this man's need for forgiveness. That single act had obliterated my life. Rico's dreams of priesthood, my parents' marriage, my own faith, Claire's trust in me. This man— this *ordinary* stranger—with his guilty conscience and trembling hands, had destroyed everything I'd ever loved with one cowardly decision.

My hands curled into fists at my sides, fingernails digging crescents into my palms as the rage built inside me, wild and consuming. The bleak metallic air of the jail mixed with the bitter fury that had been dormant for years.

The walls of the visiting room closed in, the recycled air suffocating. I didn't wait for Claire. My legs carried me through the maze of hallways on autopilot, past the metal detectors and armed guards, past the heavy doors that clanged shut behind me with the finality of a coffin lid.

"Dames, wait," Claire called across the parking lot, breathless and urgent.

But I couldn't stop. My stride lengthened as I made my way toward the truck, keys already in my hand, though I didn't remember pulling them from my pocket. The late-afternoon sun beat down on the asphalt, shimmering in waves that made the distant mountains look like mirages.

She caught up to me just as I reached the driver's side door, her habit disheveled from running, wisps of wavy dark hair escaping from beneath her veil.

"What happened back there?" she asked, searching my face.

I yanked open the truck door. "Get in."

"Don't do this. Don't shut me out."

"Just get in, Claire."

Her chest rose and fell, breaths heavy, but she made her way to the passenger's side, climbed in, and buckled up.

The drive to her cottage passed in tense silence. My fingers were tight to the point of aching around the steering wheel, jaw clenched. Every few seconds, Claire peeked at me, but I kept my eyes fixed on the road ahead, watching the familiar coastal scenery blur past without really seeing any of it.

I pulled into her driveway. Her hand hovered over the door handle, but then she turned to face me.

"Hey," she said. "You know that thing Rico used to say? About how storms don't last, but sturdy trees do?" Her gray eyes met mine with quiet determination. "You don't have to weather this alone."

"I need to be alone."

She flinched, and my heart wrenched in my chest—guilt mixing with the rage until I couldn't tell where one ended and the other began. But I couldn't deal with her concern, her attempts to calm me down.

She studied my face for another moment, then nodded slowly. "Okay." She climbed out of the truck, and I waited just long enough to make sure she made it safely inside before peeling out of her driveway with more force than necessary.

As the sun made its decent over the horizon, I found myself standing at the edge of Cliff Overlook, the secret place that Rico had first revealed to me and that had later been claimed by Claire and me as our own. This precipice held the echoes of every promise we'd whispered beneath God's stars. It was where I'd first confessed my love to her. Where the future had stretched before us like an answered prayer. Now it was a shrine to all I'd lost: first Rico, then Claire, then myself.

The Pacific stretched endlessly before me, dark water meeting darker sky in a line so perfect it looked drawn by God's hand. The wind whipped across the clifftop, carrying the scent of salt and seaweed, tugging at my collar like demanding fingers.

Below, waves crashed against the jagged rocks with the relentless rhythm of eternity. The cypress trees that clung to the cliff face bent under the coastal breeze, their branches twisted into shapes that spoke of survival against impossible odds.

I closed my eyes and breathed deeply, tasting salt on my lips, the ancient power of this place settling into my soul.

Eight years of suppressed rage and grief and guilt tore from my throat, part roar, part sob.

"Why?" I screamed at the darkening sky. "Why did You take him? Why am I the one You left to clean up the mess?"

The wind swallowed my words, carrying them out over the water, where they dissolved into nothing. But I wasn't finished.

"He was going to be *Your* priest. He was the one with the calling. The one who could *actually* help people." Tears streamed down my face, hot and bitter. "I'm a fraud. A goddamn fraud."

My legs gave out, and I dropped to my knees in the coarse grass, hands flat against the earth as if I could somehow anchor myself. The indignation consumed me from the inside out, leaving nothing but ash and cinders in its wake.

"I want to feel more than this hollow ache," I whispered to the gathering darkness, the words torn from somewhere deep in my chest.

The confession hung in the air between me and whatever remained of my faith. Raw, terrible, and true.

"I want to love without feeling like I'm betraying You."

The sound of a car door slamming echoed across the clifftop, followed by soft footsteps whispering through the grass behind me. I didn't need to turn around to know it was Claire. Her floral scent carried on the wind, her presence a warmth against my back.

She didn't speak, just stood there in the setting sun, her shadow long and dark across the grass. After several minutes, she arranged her black skirt carefully as she settled onto the grass next to me. Even in the simplicity of her habit, she carried herself with a grace that made my chest tighten with longing.

"How did you find me?" I asked, hoarse from screaming.

"I know you," she said. "This is where you always come when the world becomes too big to carry."

We sat in silence for a long moment, the last rays of sunlight casting long shadows across the cliff, its slanted light gentling the harsh edges of the day.

"I can't do this anymore, Sparrow," I said finally, the words barely audible over the waves crashing against the rocks below. "I can't pretend to be at peace when I'm burning inside."

She took my hand, her fingers cool and grounding against my overheated skin. "Then stop carrying it all alone," she said, with the same gentle authority I remembered from watching her with the youth group. "Rico wouldn't want you to destroy yourself trying to honor his memory."

"It's not that simple."

"Why?" She turned to face me.

I looked away, out at the endless Pacific, my throat constricting. "Because everyone's watching. My parents look at me and see the son who lived. The son who has to make up for Rico's lost potential. Because the entire parish thinks I'm some kind of saint when really I'm just a coward hiding behind a collar."

I pulled my hand from hers, running it through my hair with trembling fingers. "Because if I walk away from this, what was it all for? Eight years of trying to honor him, of convincing myself this was my calling. What if I'm wrong? What if this is just another way of running from responsibility?"

My voice wavered. "I made promises to God. Sacred vows. And breaking them doesn't just damn me. It destroys everything people believe about me. My parents have already lost one son to tragedy. How can I make them lose another to scandal?"

Claire's eyes brimmed with tears. Her fingers caressed my cheek. "Dames," she whispered, her voice breaking. "Listen to me. The hardest person to forgive is always yourself."

Her thumb brushed away a tear I hadn't realized had fallen. "You think breaking your vows would be the ultimate unforgivable sin? But what about the sin you're committing against yourself right now? The way you're crucifying your own heart?" She pulled back. "Jesus forgave the thief on the cross. He forgave Peter for denying Him. He forgave everyone who asked. But you . . .” She shook her head. “You won't even give yourself the grace to be human.”

Christ, she was right, and that made it worse. Even through the haze of my anger, her words found their mark, like always—gentle but unflinching, loving but uncompromising.

I stood slowly, then smoothed my black button-down. Each movement was like putting armor back on piece by piece. “I should go. Got some errands to do before evening Mass.”

She nodded. “Yeah, I've got papers to grade.”

I offered her my hand, steady despite the chaos in my chest. But I made the mistake of looking into her eyes—beautiful and gray. They had always stripped away every defense I'd carefully constructed.

“You know what I've always loved about you, Sparrow?” I rasped. “You see light in the darkest places. Even in me.” My fingers found a strand of hair that had escaped her veil, tucking it back from her cheek. “Sometimes I envy how pure your heart is. How you can still believe in goodness after what we've been through.”

She bit her bottom lip, tilting her head slightly. For a moment, neither of us moved, suspended in that dangerous space where truth lived.

I dropped my hand and stepped back, breaking the spell before it could destroy what little resolve I had left. As I headed toward my truck, every instinct screamed at me to turn around, to go back to her. But I kept walking because duty demanded it, even if my heart refused to follow.

Chapter Eighteen

DAMIAN

Two days after my visit to the county jail, I drove to my parents' house after evening Mass. The road was familiar, and the closer I got to my parents' house, the tighter my chest constricted. The faint outline of my childhood home came into view, nestled in the same spot it had always been.

I parked in the gravel driveway, the crunching stone beneath the tires jarring in the stillness. I sat in the truck for a couple minutes, trying to motivate myself to walk through that front door.

Telling them about my visit with Thomas Mercer could go a few different ways. My mother would probably go quiet, her hands folding in her lap as if in prayer—her silence always louder than words. My father, on the other hand . . . He was the wild card.

Rico would've handled this way better than me.

I took a deep breath and released it slowly, closing my eyes for a second before grabbing the small bouquet I'd picked up for my mom.

The hinges groaned as I pushed open the front door, and the scent of garlic and herbs hit me. The TV droned from the living room, Fox News turned up too high, like Dad always had it these days.

He was in his leather recliner, the worn armrests molded to the shape of his hands through the years. His silver hair was longer than usual, unkempt in a way that would've bothered him before. A half-empty mug of coffee sat on the side table, probably cold by now. It was the same 49ers mug Rico had given him for Father's Day years ago.

When I walked in, he muted the TV and turned toward me—a small gesture that caught me off guard. It had been months since he'd given me his full attention. He hadn't bothered, even on the day the detective visited and told him about Thomas Mercer. His dark eyes were tired but more present than I'd seen in years, as if a shift had occurred since Detective Alvarez's visit.

"Hey, Dad," I said. "Where's Mom?"

"Out back," he said.

I nodded, swallowing the lump in my throat. The man sitting in that chair wasn't the same dad I'd grown up with. Rico's death had turned him inward, made him retreat into himself.

I made my way through the house and out to the backyard, the flimsy screen door creaking shut behind me. My mom was sitting on the old wooden bench beneath the weeping willow. Her hands were folded in her lap, her eyes distant, as if she wasn't really there. I approached her, flowers in hand.

"Hey, Mom," I said, crouching down beside her and offering the bouquet of white lilies. "I brought your favorites."

She blinked, her gaze shifting to the flowers. A smile graced her lips, but it didn't reach her eyes. She took them, fingers brushing against mine for a second before she set them down beside her.

"Thank you, *tesoro*," she murmured.

I sat next to her, not really sure what else to say. She was having a bad day, missing Rico most likely.

"How've you been?" I asked, knowing it was a useless question.

She didn't answer right away. "Fine."

I knew she wasn't. Clearing my throat, I forced the words out. "Let's go inside. I want to talk to you and Dad together."

"Okay." Mom picked up the lilies, holding them against her heart.

When we walked back inside, I found Dad standing by the window instead of in his usual chair, as if he'd been waiting for us. He took in Mom's petite frame and the flowers clutched against her chest, and his expression shifted—a crack in the wall he'd built around himself.

"What's going on?" he asked, sitting down in his recliner.

"Dami has something to say," Mom said.

Not knowing how else to start this conversation, I brushed my fingers through my hair. "I visited Thomas Mercer with Claire Vergara."

Dad's eyes widened, then narrowed as he looked at me. "When?"

"Monday," I said, helping Mom settle on the couch. "I should have told you both, but I needed time to process it."

"And Claire went with you?" Dad asked. "That's good. You shouldn't have had to face that alone."

I nodded, grateful for his understanding. "She needed to see him too. For her own closure."

Dad's jaw tightened. "And did she get it? Did you get it?"

"I think she did. For me, it solidified what I told you before. About my calling."

Dad's eyes flickered, empathy crossing his face.

"And Thomas is pleading guilty," I added. "No trial. No dragging it out."

Dad nodded, his fingers tightening around Mom's. "Good. Smart man."

The three of us sat in silence for a moment, each wrestling with our thoughts. It was Dad who broke it. "You know what I've been watching you do all these years? You've been trying to fix everything —our grief, our marriage, our faith. Hell, you even became a priest, thinking you could fix God's plan."

My chest tightened, and I found myself clenching my fists before forcing them to relax. "I—"

"You've been carrying so much, *tesoro*," Mom said, her voice gentle but firm. "But fixing our pain isn't your job. It never was. We have to do our healing on our own." She squeezed my hand. "You can't love someone back to life, and you can't sacrifice your way out of grief."

I wanted to protest, to explain that I had to do it, but the words wouldn't come. The constant tension I carried started to ease.

"Does Claire have anything to do with this epiphany?" Dad asked, his perception sharper than I'd given him credit for.

I nodded, unable to hide the truth any longer. "Yes. But I'd been asking these questions before she came back into my life."

Dad's expression softened. "I get it. You had strong feelings for her once upon a time."

I don't think I ever stopped. "I thought choosing God meant giving up everything else."

"I've been waiting for you to say something, do something, become someone that would make the pain go away," Dad said, his voice cracking. "That isn't fair to you. I realize now what I was putting on your shoulders."

My throat constricted.

"You've been trying to be our savior," Mom said, looking between Dad and me. "We just need you to be our son."

Dad's eyes filled with tears. "We lost Rico, and instead of grieving together, we all went to our separate corners. You went to the Church, your mother went into her shell, and I went into my anger. We just needed each other." He shook his head and inhaled deeply, the same way Rico used to when he was choosing his words carefully. "You know, your mother and I have been so focused on what we lost." He looked directly into my eyes. "You're not Rico, Damian. The priesthood was *his* dream."

I nodded but remained conflicted. This life I'd chosen had given me so much. Working with the kids at Saint Anthony's, watching them open up during counseling sessions and youth group, finding their voices. That mission trip to Honduras this past spring, where we'd built a school with our bare hands, the sweat and satisfaction of creating and knowing it would outlast us. Hell, most of the experiences that had shaped who I'd become had happened because I'd taken those vows.

Dad cleared his throat. "You could've had a different life, son." His voice held regret now, the anger of past years burning away to embers and ashes.

Claire drifted to the forefront of my mind. I swallowed hard, blinking back tears. "I know."

"Rico wouldn't want you sacrificing your happiness on his account. None of us do." Dad's voice was rough. "Some things are broken, son. Some things stay broken. And that's okay. You don't *have* to make everything right."

The permission I'd been waiting for eight years crashed over me like a wave. My shoulders sagged. "I don't know how to stop," I admitted, my voice barely audible.

Mom reached for both of our hands, creating a circle of connection that had been broken for too long. "Rico wouldn't want this," she said. "He wouldn't want us frozen in place, afraid to live because he can't." She squeezed our hands. "He'd want us to love, to be happy, to honor his memory by moving forward. Even if it is without him."

All this time, we'd been ghosts in our own lives, haunting the spaces Rico had left behind.

"Yes," I said, my voice thick. "We're still here."

By the time I stepped out of my parents' house, there was a difference I couldn't quite put into words. We weren't magically healed—eight years of grief didn't disappear in one conversation. But for the first time since Rico's death, we were talking to one another instead of past one another. Different as it was, the fact settled in: We were finding our way back to each other.

Chapter Nineteen

After all the heaviness Damian and I had been swimming through lately, I figured my favorite broody priest could use a healthy dose of fun on his day off. I practically bounced out of bed Friday morning, then threw on my favorite pair of well-worn jeans, a soft cotton band tee that had seen better days, and my trusty black sneakers, which had walked more miles than I cared to count. Grabbing my skateboard, I headed over to the rectory with a grin tugging at my lips.

Damian hadn't touched a skateboard since Rico died, and honestly, that just wouldn't do. My heart gave a little squeeze as I recalled the skateboard gathering dust in the corner of his living room. It had been Rico's, and I'd recognize that ridiculous Marvin the Martian sticker anywhere, not to mention the battle scar where Rico had attempted one of his more ambitious tricks and learned the hard way that concrete doesn't forgive.

Rolling up to the two-story building that sat like a loyal guardian next to the church, I hopped off my board and skipped to the front door. The doorbell echoed inside, and within a minute—okay, maybe it was two, but who was counting?—Damian appeared, jeans hugging him like sin, a T-shirt showing every line of muscle I wasn't supposed to notice. I wondered if God just enjoyed torturing me.

Clearing my throat, I asked, "Miss me?"

His eyebrows shot up, and I caught him doing his own little inventory of my appearance. "I wasn't expecting you today."

I took a deep breath, channeling all my best persuasive energy. "Grab your brother's skateboard, Dames."

Those dark brows of his crashed together like storm clouds. "Absolutely not," he said, but I didn't miss the little flicker of . . . curiosity? Longing? It danced behind that stern priest mask he wore so well.

"Oh, come on." I flashed him my most winning smile, the one that used to get me out of trouble with the nuns back in school. "One ride. That's all I'm asking for."

His gaze drifted to Rico's board in the corner, and his throat worked as he swallowed whatever emotions were trying to bubble up. "Claire, I can't."

Stepping closer, enough to see the war playing out in those gorgeous green eyes of his, I softened my voice. "When was the last time you did something purely for the joy of it? And don't you dare say 'celebrating Mass,' because we both know that's not the same."

He glanced toward the church like it might offer him an escape route, then back at me. I could practically see the gears turning.

"One ride," I repeated, putting just enough challenge into my voice to poke at his competitive side. "I promise God's not going to strike you down for remembering the person you were before all of this." I gestured to everywhere around us.

His expression shifted—maybe trust, maybe just exhaustion from fighting himself all the time. "Fine." He walked over to Rico's board, and I pretended not to notice the way his fingers trembled as he reached for it.

Leading him out to the empty church parking lot, I threw him a look over my shoulder. "Try to keep up, old man."

A corner of his mouth lifted. *Progress!* And I caught a glimpse of that competitive spark that used to make our teenage races so much fun.

The coastal path stretched before us, a ribbon of possibility, quiet and peaceful, in the early morning. Most tourists were probably snug in their beds, which meant we had this slice of paradise all to ourselves. Salt air filled my lungs as we skated side by side, and I made sure to keep what the Church would consider "room for Jesus" between us, even though every cell in my body wanted to drift closer. The ocean sparkled beside us, sunlight dancing on the waves.

About fifteen minutes into our little adventure, we rolled up to one of the two coffee shops in our sleepy town. I hopped off my board with more enthusiasm than the situation called for, and Damian followed suit, albeit with more grace.

The café was one of those perfectly imperfect coastal places, with weathered wood, mismatched chairs, and the kind of charm that couldn't be manufactured. It perched just one street back from the ocean view, close enough that you could taste the salt in the air with your morning brew.

As we stepped inside, I overheard the barista chatting with a customer. "Yeah, Ramirez's brother's helping with pickups while the divorce settles. Poor kid's been through it."

The words "Ramirez's brother" snagged, tugging at some corner of my brain I didn't want to examine too closely. That last name sounded familiar. I shook it off and ordered a drink that could raise the dead.

After getting coffee and croissants that were still warm from the oven, we settled at a little table outside. Together, we watched the sun climb higher in the sky, painting everything in shades of gold and promise. And Damian's face in that morning light? It was like watching a master painter work with actual sunbeams.

Focus, Claire. Coffee. Conversation. Not the way the light hits his cheekbones.

After our caffeine fix, we skated farther down the road to the old pier we used to frequent as teenagers. Hopping off our boards, we strolled onto the weathered boardwalk, which creaked with greetings beneath our feet just as it had all those years ago. I glanced up at the sky and noted clouds gathering like gray cotton balls. Naturally, I'd forgotten to check the weather forecast. *Classic me.*

"Rico taught me how to skate here," Damian said, kicking at a loose plank absentmindedly. "Spent hours watching me eat pavement until I finally managed to land a decent kickflip."

My heart did that melting thing it always did when he talked about his brother. "He was always so patient with you. Saint Rico, we used to call him. Remember? Though never to his face because his ego was already big enough."

"Yeah." Damian's fingers traced the edge of the board, reverent as any prayer he'd ever offered. "I couldn't touch it after . . . well, everything. Didn't feel worthy."

Oh, honey. I stepped in front of him and started walking backward while he walked forward, a move that had gotten me in trouble more times than I could count, but old habits die hard. "Want to know what I think?"

His lips curved up. "Do I have a choice?"

I rolled my eyes. "I think—shit!"

And because God has a twisted sense of timing, my feet tangled together like some kind of coordination-challenged flamingo. But before I could introduce my backside to the wooden deck, Damian's arms swept around my waist, pulling me against his chest.

Sweet mother-of-pearl. The man was solid muscle and warm skin and everything my vows said I shouldn't be noticing right now.

"You okay?" he asked, his voice soft and concerned.

Looking up into those emerald eyes of his, I bit my lower lip and nodded, not trusting my voice when my heart was doing its best impression of a hummingbird on espresso.

Amusement sparkled in his expression as he brushed a strand of hair from my face with fingers that were far too gentle for my sanity. "This is the Claire I remember. Always rushing headfirst into trouble."

"Well, when you put it like that, I sound absolutely charming," I managed, trying to inject some lightness into the moment. "Thanks for the save, by the way."

"I should be the one thanking you, Sparrow," he said.

He released me, thank God.

What did he mean by that? And, more importantly, why did I desperately want to know? This was definitely venturing into dangerous territory, the kind that led to heartbreak and broken vows and a conversation with the bishop that I really didn't want to have.

"Anyway," I said, clearing my throat and trying to remember what we'd been talking about before my coordination decided to abandon ship. He helped me straighten and we continued our walk. Reaching the end of the pier, I stared out at the endless expanse of ocean, gathering my thoughts like scattered seashells. "What I was trying to say before I nearly became one with the deck was you need to forgive yourself, Dames."

He glanced down at the skateboard in his hands, and I could see a weight pressing on his broad shoulders. "Yeah. Trust me, I'm working on it."

"Good," I said, because sometimes the simplest words carried the most sincerity. "Keep working on it." Maybe it was about time I took my own advice. But wasn't the saying "do as I say, not as I do"?

He nodded, staring out at the white-capped water that stretched toward forever. For a moment, we just stood there in comfortable silence. Two people carrying their own complicated histories, trying to figure out how to move forward without forgetting where they'd been.

I studied his profile as he watched the storm clouds gather. Damian had always been a man of few words, which used to drive me crazy when we were dating.

Rain clouds were starting to block the warmth of our perfect midmorning sun, but honestly? I didn't want this magical little bubble we'd created to end.

"You know what Rico would say if he could see you denying yourself this kind of joy?" I asked as we started heading back toward shore, our boards tucked under our arms.

Damian's eyes met mine. "He'd kick my ass from here to Sunday."

"Exactly." I had to physically stop myself from reaching for his hand, reminding my traitorous fingers that we weren't those carefree teens anymore. "I've discovered that the best way to honor his memory is by remembering the joy he brought to life. Rico never half-assed anything, especially happiness."

When we reached the shore, we found a perfect little spot on the beach and settled into the sand, our boards resting at our feet. I couldn't help but notice that the rigid set of Damian's shoulders had finally softened. His chest rose and fell with deep, peaceful breaths, and his dark hair danced gently in the salty breeze. In that moment of perfect stillness, God's presence was as clear as the night Damian held me while we prayed the Our Father together.

"You feel Him here, don't you?" I murmured.

Damian nodded, his gaze fixed on the endless horizon. "I do." He faced me, and the intensity in his expression made my breath catch in my throat. "Thank you. For knowing exactly what I needed before I even knew it myself."

I fought every instinct I had to lean into him, to offer the comfort we both desperately craved but couldn't allow ourselves to have. Instead, I closed my eyes and let myself get lost in the symphony around us: the rhythmic crash of waves, the way our breathing had somehow synchronized, and that quiet voice deep inside me whispering that this moment was sacred.

"Rico would be proud of you," I murmured, glancing at him.

Damian's hand twitched toward mine before he caught himself. "He'd be proud of both of us."

I honestly couldn't remember which one of us suggested heading down to the water, but somehow we ended up strolling along the beach. It was like muscle memory from all those countless afternoons we'd spent here as teenagers, when the world felt infinite and uncomplicated. The sand was still wonderfully cool beneath my bare feet as we kicked off our shoes, abandoning them beside our boards like we were shedding our adult responsibilities.

The hem of my jeans collected sand with every step, but I couldn't bring myself to care even a little bit. The ocean stretched endlessly before us, waves rushing in and retreating like the tide of emotions I was desperately trying to keep contained.

"Remember when we used to come here after school?" Damian asked. "You'd read poetry out loud while I practiced my tricks, convinced I was going to be the next Tony Hawk."

The rain started as just a gentle sprinkle, but within seconds it was coming down like the sky had opened up and decided to dump everything it had been saving. We grabbed our shoes and skateboards, getting absolutely soaked, and took cover at a nearby bus stop that looked like it had seen better decades.

"Want me to call for a ride?" I asked, slipping my completely drenched sneakers back on and trying not to shiver.

Damian was doing the same, wringing water out of his shirt. "The church is only half a mile up the road. Easy run."

"Okay. Have fun with that." I gave him a little wave. "There's no way in heaven I can keep up with you. You run every single day."

His soaked T-shirt clung to every muscle in his shoulders and chest. *Focus on the rain, Claire. The very wet, very cold rain.*

"Come on, Sparrow. After all, this whole adventure was your brilliant idea." He grinned at me, and I sensed the guilt trip he was laying on me.

I huffed. "Fine, but if we're running, I'm heading straight to my cottage."

He shrugged like it was no big deal. "Works for me. I'll follow your lead."

Taking three deep breaths, I mentally prepared myself to jog through this absolute downpour like some kind of crazy person. Before I could lose my nerve, I sprinted out from our little shelter and headed toward my cottage.

The freezing rain was oddly refreshing, and I couldn't help but start laughing at the sheer ridiculousness of it all. Here I was, a twenty-nine-year-old nun, running through a downpour with a skateboard tucked under my arm. And right beside me was my ex-boyfriend, who happened to be a priest. If that wasn't a setup for a cosmic joke, I didn't know what was.

"What's so funny?" Damian shouted through the sound of rain absolutely hammering the pavement.

"How completely absurd this is," I called back.

We reached my neighborhood with the cottage finally coming into view, looking like a beacon of warmth and dryness. Breathing hard—okay, maybe gasping was more accurate—I managed to maintain what I thought was a pretty impressive pace toward my front porch. Once we reached safety, I dropped my skateboard and tried to catch my breath while Damian stood there looking like he'd just taken a leisurely stroll.

Damn him and his stamina.

He shook his hair out like an overgrown puppy, sending water droplets flying everywhere.

I couldn't help but giggle as I unlocked the front door. "You're going to freeze if you stay in those wet clothes. Come in and get warm. The last thing I need is to have to explain to the parishioners why I let their favorite priest catch pneumonia."

Damian followed me inside, closing the door behind him. He stood somewhat awkwardly in my small foyer, dripping all over my hardwood floors.

"Let me toss your clothes in the dryer." I placed my skateboard in the coat closet, already mentally rummaging through my limited wardrobe for clothes that might fit him.

"I don't think that's such a good idea." He crossed his arms over his chest, which emphasized exactly how broad his shoulders were.

I wanted to have a serious conversation with God about why He had to make Damian so magnificent to look at. "Don't worry, I've got something you can wear while they dry. Be right back."

Practically fleeing to my bedroom, I changed into dry fitted shorts and a long comfortable tee and then grabbed my oversized pink hibiscus robe from behind the door. It was huge on me, so it should fit Damian just fine.

I brought it out to him with what I hoped was an innocent smile, pointing toward the bathroom.

"You seriously expect me to wear this?" He held it up against himself, looking somewhere between amused and horrified.

"It's not like you're planning to parade around town in it." I rested one hand on my hip, channeling my best no-nonsense voice.

Teeth chattering, he thought it over for what felt like an eternity before finally releasing a long-suffering breath and then heading toward the bathroom.

"Underwear too," I called after him just as he closed the door.

Minutes later, he emerged with his wet clothes in hand, and I had to cover my mouth with both hands to keep from absolutely losing it with laughter.

"Not. One. Word," he warned, handing me his soggy clothes with as much dignity as a man wearing a pink hibiscus robe could muster.

I pressed my lips together, trying my best to look serious. "I didn't say anything."

His eyes narrowed. "I know what you're thinking."

"Oh, so you're a mind reader now?"

"No. I'm a Claire reader." His gaze darkened as his eyes perused down the length of my body, making me very aware of every inch of skin my shorts weren't covering.

I swallowed hard, my mouth going completely dry. "I should get these in the dryer. You want a drink?" I gestured toward the sofa. "Water? Coffee?" *Something stronger?*

He settled onto the cushions, the pink robe somehow making him look even more masculine by contrast. "Water please. Thanks."

As I stood there for just a moment longer than necessary, I noticed his gaze had found my legs. More specifically, my thighs. *Shit.* I'd completely forgotten that these shorts showed my scars. I spun away, hoping he hadn't seen, and all but ran to the laundry room.

How could I be so careless? I tossed the wet clothes into the dryer with more force than necessary, slammed the door, and turned the machine on. Tugging at my shorts to try to cover more of the faded lines, I grabbed a mason jar from the kitchen and filled it with cold water, taking a few deep breaths to collect myself.

When I returned to the living room, I handed him the water and settled beside him on the couch, making sure my oversized tee covered as much of my thighs as possible. But I had a sinking feeling he'd already seen what I'd tried to hide.

He took a long drink, then set the glass carefully on the coffee table. "Claire." His voice was gentle, careful. "Your thighs."

My entire body went rigid.

He turned to look directly into my eyes. "When?"

I focused on the raindrops streaking down the big bay window, creating little rivers of distortion. "College. It felt like the only way I could breathe when everything else was suffocating me."

"I'm so sorry," he whispered, and the pain in his voice nearly undid me.

"Maybe 'broken' is just another word for 'human,' " I said, finally meeting his gaze and letting him see past the careful mask I usually wore. "Sometimes it still hurts to breathe."

He reached for my hand, his thumb brushing softly over my knuckles. "If you ever need me to, I could breathe for you."

Did he really just say that? A tear slipped down my cheek before I could stop it. I moved to wipe it away, but he caught my hand, stilling the movement.

"You're not allowed to say things like that to me," I whispered.

The faintest smile curved his lips. "You want to know something else?"

Despite everything, my lips quirked upward. "What?"

"You're the bravest person I've ever known." He held my gaze for another long moment before pulling away and adjusting the pink robe to maintain some semblance of modesty.

Nope, get your mind out of the gutter, Sister Claire. But I couldn't help wondering what I'd missed out on all these years. My mind drifted treacherously back to the way his lips had moved against my neck in the church hall.

"How did you end up at the convent?" Damian's question cut through my completely inappropriate thoughts. "What led you there?"

My eyes widened at the directness of his question. I looked down at my clasped hands and took a shaky breath. "After college, after the cutting got worse, I ended up in the hospital."

He leaned closer, giving me his complete attention.

"Jasmine found me. I'd gone too deep one night. Didn't mean to, but . . ." I shrugged like I was discussing a missed coffee date.

"Hospital policy says after a suicide attempt, you stay for observation. I met a nun there. Sister Agnes. She was the hospital chaplain." A genuine smile touched my lips at the memory. "She didn't preach at me or tell me I needed to pray harder. She just sat with me. Even when I refused to talk for days."

He nodded, and I could see him processing every word.

"I'd been searching for a solid path to walk after graduating. Tried teaching for a while, but it wasn't enough to fill the emptiness." I shifted on the couch, pulling my legs closer to my chest. "I'd been drowning for so long, and the Sisters of Divine Light were the first people who didn't try to *fix* me. They gave me space to heal at my own pace."

"When did you join them?"

"I stayed in therapy for almost a year after the hospitalization. Dr. Cohen suggested I needed structure and purpose." I laughed softly. "It's pretty ironic when you think about it. I'd spent years running from the Church's rules, and here I was, actively seeking out its most structured lifestyle. The Sisters aren't like other orders though. They believe in serving communities by living among the people they help. It felt real—not like I was hiding from life, but finding a completely different way to live it meaningfully."

"When are you supposed to take your perpetual vows?"

My gaze drifted back to the rain-streaked window. "I'm in my third year of temporary vows. This year, I'm supposed to decide if I'm ready for the permanent commitment."

"Are you? Ready, I mean?"

I turned back to him, searching his eyes. "I thought I was."

The dryer's buzzer chose that exact moment to go off, making us both jump like we'd been caught doing something we shouldn't. I bounced up off the couch and hurried through the kitchen to the laundry room. Opening the dryer door, I pulled out his warm, dry clothes and spun around, only to collide directly with Damian's very solid chest.

He caught me by the arms, steadying me. "We really need to stop doing this." The intensity blazing in those green eyes completely caught me off guard.

"Doing what?" My voice came out breathier than I intended.

He leaned in, and I should have stepped back. Should have put my hands up between us. Should have remembered every single reason why this was dangerous territory that could destroy us both. But instead, I tilted my face up to his, dropping his clothes.

When his lips met mine, it was like coming home after years of wandering. The kiss started gentle, tentative, as if he was giving me one last chance to come to my senses and push him away. But then I made the mistake of sighing into his mouth, and that small sound seemed to snap whatever restraint he'd been clinging to.

His hands found my waist with a reverence that made my knees weak, fingers pressing into my skin through the thin fabric of my shirt. He lifted me onto the washer, leaving me weightless, suspended between earth and heaven in the most literal sense. The metal was cool against my bottom, a sharp contrast to the heat radiating from everywhere his body touched mine.

His mouth moved against mine with a hunger that matched the ache I'd been carrying since the day he'd chosen his guilt over our future. I could taste the rain on his lips, smell that uniquely Damian scent of soap and the indefinable warmth that had always made me feel safe.

Damian released a low rumble of pure pleasure that vibrated against my mouth, sending liquid fire racing through my veins and pooling low in my belly. My hands fisted in the pink hibiscus fabric of my robe he was wearing, pulling him closer until there wasn't a breath of space between us.

The kiss turned demanding, and my toes curled. His lips were achingly familiar, like muscle memory. My body remembered exactly how we fit together. One of his hands slid to the base of my throat, and his fingers wrapped around my neck. His other hand found its way to the small of my back, fingers splayed wide and warm through my shirt, anchoring me to him like I might float away if he let go.

God forgive me for missing this.

His lips traced the line of my jaw, and I couldn't stop the small gasp that escaped me when he found that spot just below my ear that had always been my undoing. His hard length pressed into my hip through the robe, and I wrapped my legs around him. God, I wanted his dick inside me, thrusting in, pulling out, over and over.

Reaching beneath my shirt, he cupped my bare breast and rolled my pebbled nipple between his fingers, eliciting a moan from me. He trailed his mouth down my collarbone and started sucking and using his tongue. I gasped. *That* was a sensitive area I hadn't known about.

Damian isn't just any man. He's a priest. What am I doing? The thought hit me like cold water. *What am I doing?* I pushed him away, my hands flat against his chest. "What're we doing, Dames?"

"Shit. I don't know." He brushed his fingers through his still-damp hair before setting me back on my feet.

I bent to pick up his clothes, which had scattered across the floor during our little make-out session. "Maybe we should try not to be alone anymore," I said, handing him his clothes and trying to ignore the way my lips continued tingling.

He took them from me, our fingers brushing briefly. "You're probably right. Public places from now on."

"That would be wise."

Damian nodded and headed toward the bathroom to change. By the time he emerged, the rain had finally let up enough for him to make the walk back to the rectory.

As for me? My carefully constructed self-control was slipping away like sand through my fingers. I was starting to forget I was supposed to be holding a grudge against him. Forgetting exactly why I'd joined the convent in the first place.

But then I remembered Jasmine's words: *You can still serve without denying parts of yourself. Maybe that's exactly what you're meant to do—show them that loving God doesn't mean you have to be perfect.*

Maybe she was right. There had to be a way to honor both my faith and my heart without destroying either one.

Chapter Twenty

CLAIRE

Seven Years Ago

The blade's cool edge glinted in the bathroom light as I turned it over in my fingers. My hands shook. They had been for weeks now. *I need this.* The voices in my head keep screaming at me. *I'm not enough. I'll never be enough.*

Salt air drifted through my dorm window, carrying the distant sound of chapel bells from the campus ministry building. A reminder of home, of the ocean I'd left behind. Of Sunday mornings at Saint Anthony's, when life made sense, when Damian's hand in mine felt like the only prayer I'd ever need.

Before Rico died. Before everything fell apart.

I glanced at my phone. Three missed calls from my academic advisor. Two unread emails about my falling GPA. And on my desk was a growing pile of assignments I couldn't bring myself to look at, the words blurring together.

The scholarship review board meeting was tomorrow. Twenty-four hours to somehow prove I deserved to keep my full-ride scholarship. Without it, I'd have to leave school, go home, and face the questions I couldn't answer. *What happened to you,* anak? *You used to be so strong.*

I could already hear my mother's voice, the way it would get when she was trying not to cry. *We sacrificed so much for you to have this opportunity, Claire. Your father works double shifts, I'm a teacher in addition to cleaning houses for families who look through me like I'm invisible, all so you can have a secure future, a profession that won't leave you struggling like we have.*

The disappointment in her eyes last Christmas when I'd changed my major from accounting to religious studies flashed in my mind, along with her words. *Why are you throwing away your future? What will people think?*

Perfect grades weren't enough—I also needed to work. Working wasn't enough—I also needed to volunteer. Being strong wasn't enough when Damian needed me to be stronger. Being faithful wasn't enough when God felt absent. Being myself wasn't enough when everyone needed me to be someone else.

I used to be a lot of things.

Just one more, I told myself, fingers trembling against the metal. *One more to make the noise stop. To numb it.*

I'd managed to stop for a month. Sort of. I'd started again when I'd been cleaning up broken glass in my dorm room. It was a picture frame I'd thrown during another breakdown. One of Damian and me at junior prom. A sharp edge had caught my thigh as I'd knelt to pick up the pieces, and the pain had been sudden. Bright. Clarifying.

For that moment, everything else had faded away.

The pressure of maintaining my scholarship, the weight of my mom's expectations, the constant ache of missing Damian, the guilt over not being able to help him through his grief. All of it had disappeared in that flash of physical pain.

The memory of that relief had haunted me for days. Until I'd found myself in the bathroom with a razor blade, telling myself I just needed to feel more than this empty void.

That was three months ago. Before I'd stopped going to classes regularly. Before I'd started avoiding phone calls from home. Before I'd tried sleeping with random guys from parties, thinking maybe sex would fill the emptiness inside me. It had only made me feel more vacant and disconnected from myself.

You're supposed to be strong. I pressed the blade against my inner thigh, where no one would see. Where I could hide the evidence of my weakness. The cuts from last week were still healing, pink lines that marked my shame like a roadmap of failure.

Just yesterday, I'd sat in the campus ministry office, supposedly there for guidance about my major. "I don't know what God wants from me anymore," I'd told Father Mark. "I feel so lost."

"God's love isn't conditional on your achievements, Claire," he'd said, his kind eyes crinkling with concern. "Your worth isn't measured by your GPA or your career path. It's in being His child."

The words were warm in the moment. But now, sitting on the cold tile of my bathroom floor, they felt hollow. Like the prayers I recited mechanically each night, searching for a connection to God that slipped further away with each new scar I carved into my skin.

Some Catholic girl I turned out to be.

"Our Father, who art in heaven." The prayer slipped out as I made the first cut, shallow but stinging. "Hallowed be Thy name."

Blood welled up, bright and viscous against my brown skin. That strange relief I'd grown addicted to, like releasing pressure from a valve that had been building for months, washed over me. My breathing steadied, the voice in my head quieting just a little.

Another cut. Deeper this time.

"Thy kingdom come, Thy will be done." My lips moved around the familiar prayers, but my chest tightened as each word scraped against my throat.

My phone buzzed against the tile. Probably another email from the financial aid office. Or maybe a text from my mother, wondering why I'd been so quiet lately. She'd called yesterday, her voice tight with worry and something else—frustration, maybe.

Claire, you sound different. Are you eating enough? Are you praying? Your cousin Chantel just got into nursing school, and she's working two jobs to pay for it. She doesn't even have a scholarship like you do.

The unspoken comparison hung between us, like it always did. Chantel, who never complained. Chantel, who appreciated her opportunities. Chantel, who hadn't disappointed her family by abandoning a practical degree for religious studies.

I couldn't bring myself to look at the phone. Couldn't face another reminder of how I was failing everyone who believed in me—everyone who saw potential in me that I couldn't even see in myself anymore.

Even Damian. There were so many nights I'd lain awake wondering if that was one of the reasons he'd broken up with me.

Maybe if I'd been better, stronger, more faithful—maybe he wouldn't have left.

The thought sent a fresh wave of self-loathing through me, and I pressed the blade down, harder this time. The prayer continued to fall from my lips, automatic and desperate.

"On earth as it is in heaven. Give us this day our daily bread."

Tears burned my eyes, but I blinked them back. I didn't deserve to cry—not when I was doing this to myself and failing at everything else. The girl who used to lead youth group, who'd been so sure of her faith, her future, her place in the world. She was a stranger now.

"And forgive us our trespasses." The words caught in my throat.

What would Father Mark think if he could see me now?

What would my parents think?

What would Damian think?

The door to the dorm room burst open, keys jangling. My heart hammered against my ribs as I froze, the blade still pressed against my skin.

"Claire?" Michelle's voice carried through the thin bathroom door. "You in there? I grabbed coffee. The good stuff from off-campus."

"Yeah," I called back, surprised by how sure my voice sounded despite the tremor in my hands. "Just . . . give me a minute."

"No rush. I'm heading to the library after this anyway. You still coming to study group tonight?"

Study group. Right. I'd promised to attend, hoping it could help me salvage what was left of my semester. But I would probably skip it, because the thought of pretending to be okay for three hours felt impossible.

"We'll see," I said, which was code for no, and we both knew it.

I waited until her footsteps faded before letting out a shaky breath. Blood trickled down my thigh, and I grabbed toilet paper to clean it up, movements practiced. Too practiced.

The mirror above the sink caught my eye, and I stared at my reflection. I looked . . . normal. Tired, maybe, but normal. No one would guess that the girl who'd been valedictorian of her Catholic high school, who'd had her whole life mapped out in neat, perfect steps, was falling apart one cut at a time.

I pulled on my jeans, wincing as the fabric rubbed against the fresh cuts. The physical pain would fade, but that cursed emptiness? That would linger. It always did.

Standing at the sink, I washed my hands, watching the water run pink, then clear. My reflection stared back at me, and for a moment, I searched for the girl I used to be. That girl who believed in love and faith and happy endings. That girl who thought she could save everyone, including herself.

Just get through today. Make it through one more day. It was the same lie I'd been telling myself for months now. But tomorrow my demons would return, and so would the blade.

Maybe Father Mark was right. Maybe God's love wasn't conditional. But standing here, surrounded by the evidence of my shame, I couldn't feel that love anymore.

"I'm sorry," I whispered to the mirror, though I wasn't sure who I was apologizing to.

God? My parents? Damian? The person I used to be?

My reflection offered no comfort, only the certainty that I'd disappoint my mother. Again.

"I don't understand, *anak*," she'd said during our last real conversation, her voice cracking. "You had everything. Good grades, a good boy who loved you, a future that was guaranteed. How did you let it all slip away?"

Her idea of "perfect" was unattainable. When tragedy struck, I crumbled. So I apologized, promised to do better, and somehow, that had to be enough.

Chapter Twenty-One

CLAIRE

Present Day

The weekend dragged by like penance—rain on Saturday, more rain on Sunday, as if the heavens were crying right along with my confused heart. But Monday morning brought sunshine, and I pulled into Saint Anthony's parking lot with what I desperately hoped was renewed energy.

Please, God, let today be different. Help me be stronger.

I gathered my things from the trunk, mentally cataloging the week ahead: lesson plans to finish, marriage retreat details to coordinate, and a stack of permission slips for the next youth event.

My hands fumbled with my teaching bag. I'd barely slept, my mind a battlefield between duty and desire—between the vows I'd made and the memory of Damian's lips on mine. Just thinking about it sent heat flooding through me, pooling low in my belly in a way that made me want to press my fingernails into my palms until the sharp sting reminded me who I was supposed to be.

I was furious with him for kissing me. Absolutely livid that he'd shattered the careful distance I'd built between us with one reckless moment. But God help me, I was even more furious with myself for not stopping him. For melting into him like I was a teenager again, all breathless want and desperate hands. For the way my body had betrayed every sacred promise I'd made when his mouth claimed mine.

I slammed the trunk harder than necessary, the sound echoing across the parking lot.

Taking a shaky breath, I forced myself to stand still, letting the morning sun warm my face. *It's all going to be okay*, I repeated like a mantra. We'd agreed to meet only in public spaces from now on. That moment of beautiful, terrible madness would be the last time.

It had to be.

The alternative would destroy everything. Would mean confessing that eight years of prayers and penance had all been one grand performance to convince myself I was over Damian Bellucci. It would destroy the careful sanctuary I'd constructed from the rubble of our shattered dreams. And despite every reckless cell in my body screaming otherwise, I wasn't ready to crumble again.

"Claire Vergara."

I froze at the sound of the familiar voice. A voice I hadn't heard in years. My stomach dropped as I turned around slowly, praying I was mistaken.

Spoiler alert: I wasn't.

Preston Kane leaned against a sleek black car, sunglasses pushed up on his head, grinning like he'd just won the lottery. He looked exactly as I remembered him—tall, confident, with that same smirk that had once made my heart race for all the wrong reasons.

"Preston," I managed. "What're you doing here?"

He pushed off his car and sauntered toward me, eyes traveling down my habit in clear disbelief. "My niece has been talking nonstop about her new teacher. Had to see it for myself."

My mind raced through all the classes I taught, from elementary to high schoolers, but it was impossible to keep track of them all. "And your niece is?"

His grin widened at my obvious discomfort. "Emma Ramirez. Blond pigtails, unicorn backpack."

Emma—sweet, quiet, always sat in the front row and asked thoughtful questions about Bible stories. The thought of Preston being connected to her made my stomach turn. "I—yes. She's lovely. Very smart."

"Takes after her mother, my sister," he said with a low chuckle. "I'm helping out with pickups while she's dealing with her divorce."

I adjusted the strap of my bag. "Kinda early for pickup. You're a dedicated uncle."

"I wanted to catch you before school started. Perfect timing, wouldn't you say?" He winked at me.

I glanced around, acutely aware of how exposed we were in the parish parking lot. Anyone could see us, could hear us. Other parents would be arriving soon for drop-off. "I should go. It was good seeing you."

Before I could walk away, he said, "You've been teaching my niece about saints and salvation while hiding your own colorful past? That's rich, even for you."

Leaning back against the trunk of my car, I asked, "Why're you here, Preston?"

"Come on, Claire." He stepped closer, invading my space in that entitled way I'd once found arousing. Now? Not so much. "I just want a moment of your *sacred* time. For old times' sake."

My blood ran cold—like our history was a shield he could hide behind. "That was a different life," I replied, clutching my bag tighter.

His laugh was sharp. "Baby, you can change your clothes, but we both know what's underneath. You're as filthy as they come." His gaze lingered on me. "Remember that weekend in Santa Barbara? The hotel room? The hot tub?"

My cheeks burned. "Stop."

No shame. Just the constant irritation that my first time hadn't been with the only man who ever really mattered.

"What's fascinating," Preston continued, clearly enjoying my discomfort, "is you playing the *good Catholic teacher* with my niece every day. What would everyone think if they knew about the things we've done?"

"Sister Claire," Damian called out, crossing the lot from the rectory—his face calm, his eyes anything but. He wore his clerical clothes, the white collar stark against his black shirt, but there was nothing *holy* about the look he gave Preston.

"Father," I acknowledged, my heart hammering in my chest. I shot him a look that said, *Please don't do anything stupid.*

"Everything all right here?" Damian asked, his voice carrying that quiet authority he used during difficult parental confrontations.

Preston sized Damian up, his smirk widening. He extended his hand. "Preston Kane. I'm Emma Ramirez's uncle—she's in one of Sister Claire's classes."

"Father Bellucci," Damian replied, shaking Preston's hand with what looked like unnecessary force.

"You've got a nice little gig here, Father," Preston said, glancing between us with knowing eyes. "Claire always did have a thing for authority figures. Hope that's not affecting her teaching methods."

I stepped between them before Damian could respond. "Mr. Kane was just leaving," I said firmly, trying to regain some professional composure.

Preston leaned against my car. "Actually, I was hoping to discuss Emma's progress. Maybe take Sister Claire out for a coffee? To talk about my niece's spiritual development, of course."

"Sister Claire has office hours posted for parents," Damian said, his voice like ice. "I'm sure she'd be happy to schedule an appointment during appropriate hours."

A flare of irritation spiked through me despite my gratitude. I didn't need Damian fighting my battles.

"Excuse me, *Father Damian*," I snapped.

His mouth shut, and a muscle in his jaw worked as he crossed his arms over his chest.

I turned to Preston, forcing my voice into a professional tone. "If you have concerns about Emma's education, we can schedule a proper conference with her mother present. What happened in college has no bearing on my qualifications as an educator."

Preston's expression hardened. "Right. Saint Claire now, huh?"

"I was lost," I replied, refusing to be intimidated. "I'm not anymore."

He stared at me for a long moment before shrugging. "The Claire I knew was a lot more . . . flexible." He slid his sunglasses back over his eyes. "I'll be sure to mention to my sister how devoted you are. Are you sure I can't convince you to go for coffee with me?"

"I'm afraid Sister Claire's day is full," Damian cut in, stepping forward.

Preston laughed, backing toward his car. "Easy, Father. Just a concerned uncle here. My sister appreciates me staying involved." He opened his car door. "See you around, *Sister* Claire. Emma's really looking forward to your lesson on Mary Magdalene. I might even sit in to see you in action."

"Goodbye, Preston," I said with the kindest smile I could muster.

He started his car and drove away. My hands trembled with anger and humiliation. The implication was clear, and there would be little I could do to stop him. When his car faded from view, I rounded on Damian.

"What the hell was that?" I demanded.

Damian flexed his neck. "He was threatening you."

"And I was handling it," I gritted out. "I have to work with these families. I can't have you inserting yourself into every difficult situation."

"Difficult situation? He was blackmailing you into going to coffee with him."

I rolled my eyes. "So? What if I go?"

A smug grin curved Damian's lips. "You don't mean that."

"You're impossible."

The drop-off line of cars began to form in front of the school. I needed to end this conversation.

"What did he mean by 'flexible'?" he asked, voice low.

Was he really asking me this in the church parking lot? I let out a long breath. "Are you asking as my priest or my ex?"

His gaze darkened. "Which do you think?"

I laughed. "You really want to play this game? Fine." I leaned closer. "Preston used to fuck me."

Damian didn't flinch, didn't look away—stoic to the bone. But I caught his pulse hammering in his throat and the way his breath snagged for half a second.

"Is that supposed to shock me?" His voice was low and even, betraying nothing but restraint stretched too thin. "All it does is make me wonder how much you wanted it. And how much of you is still burning for someone who isn't me."

I tilted my head. "Jealous, Father?" My voice dropped to a whisper meant for him alone. "Because you look like you want to pin me against the nearest wall and erase every trace of him."

His hands flexed at his sides as if he was praying for strength. He stayed silent, holding himself perfectly still, but the storm in his eyes told me everything: I'd lit the fuse.

And then—because the drop-off line was crawling forward and neither of us could afford to let anyone see what was burning between us—I tore my gaze away first.

"This is ridiculous," I murmured, turning on my heel and starting toward the brick building.

He grabbed my forearm, stopping me. "Wait."

"Don't do that." I yanked my arm away, looking toward the school to make sure no one was watching us.

His voice was quieter now, uncertain. "Can we talk about what happened?"

Every muscle in my body stiffened. The memory hit me: his hands on me, his dick grinding against me, the desperate way we'd kissed.

That was the last thing I wanted to talk about. "No."

"I know we agreed to public spaces, but—"

"What, Damian?" I asked, cutting him off. I tried to steel my heart as it fractured. "You'd do well to keep your distance from me from now on. For both our sakes."

I rushed toward the school building, refusing to look back even though I could feel his eyes on me. But I couldn't ignore the look of hurt that had flashed across his face, raw and wounded.

Preston's visit had ripped open a door I'd thought firmly closed, forcing me to confront not just the woman I'd been before the veil, but how that woman could still damage the life I'd built.

But it was more than that. I felt stupid for inviting Damian to spend last Friday with me. For thinking we could recapture the innocence of our past. For convincing myself that one day of normalcy—skating, laughing, pretending we were just old friends— wouldn't lead exactly where it had: to me sitting on my washer, his mouth on mine, eight years of separation dissolving in seconds.

I couldn't bring myself to regret it though. That was the worst part. Like I was still *his* Claire, not *Sister* Claire. Like the vows we'd both taken were just words and the love between us was the only truth that mattered.

God is love, I reminded myself as I stepped into my classroom. So why did love, past and present, have to hurt so damn much?

Chapter Twenty-Two

CLAIRE

A full week had passed since Preston's unexpected visit, and honestly? I was grateful for the distraction. Better to wrestle with the sour taste he'd left in my mouth than to sit too long with the silence that followed me home at night. At least Preston gave me something solid to direct my anger at. Enmity was easier to carry than the ache I couldn't name. It was simple. Grief, guilt, longing—those were the emotions that clawed at me when the house got too quiet.

Damian had texted earlier in the week that he'd caught a cold—probably from our Friday outing in the rain—so I'd taken over tasks for the marriage retreat. My plate was fuller than at a potluck dinner, but thankfully, Jessica had swooped in like some kind of catering fairy godmother and helped me find an affordable company. Crisis averted, at least on paper.

But order on the outside didn't erase the mess underneath.

I'd never claimed to be perfect. The people here didn't know *that* Claire—the one before the veil and vows. They didn't need to know about how I had enjoyed pleasure, the electric thrill of desire, or the simple joy of skin against skin, so the last thing I needed was Preston outing me as some modern-day Mary Magdalene with a heart full of passion and zero interest in playing it safe.

Desire, whether everyone wanted to believe it or not, was part of the beautiful, messy tapestry of being human. God created every thread of who we were as people, including the parts that made us blush.

They say time heals all wounds, but they also say absence makes the heart grow fonder. What was "time" if not absence in this case? I believed time, or *absence*, made the heart more stubborn. And Damian fucking Bellucci had awakened what I thought I'd successfully tucked away, like Christmas decorations in the attic.

I used to believe there was no contradiction between faith and wanting and that the two could dance together in perfect harmony. Was fighting my desire really honoring God's will, or was I just following rules written by people who were probably as confused as I was?

And what *had* Damian wanted to talk about in that parking lot? The mystery was driving me absolutely—

"Good morning, Sister Claire!" The chorus of preteen voices bounced off my classroom walls like Ping-Pong balls, snapping me back to reality.

I stood at the front of the room, fingers tracing the well-worn edges of my Bible, a book that had seen more late-night wrestling matches with faith than a WWE championship.

"All right, my little stars," I called out, raising my voice just enough to surf above their chatter. "Today we're diving into love— but not the kind that makes you write terrible poetry in your diary. We're talking about God's love. The kind that shows up when you least expect it, like finding twenty bucks in your winter coat pocket."

I flipped to 1 John 4:7-8, a passage I'd probably read more times than I'd watched my favorite rom-com, which was saying a lot. " 'Beloved, let us love one another, for love is from God, and whoever loves has been born of God and knows God. Anyone who does not love does not know God, because God is love.' "

If only faith came with an instruction manual as clear as IKEA furniture. Well, maybe *clearer* than IKEA furniture. At least then we'd only be missing a few screws instead of questioning our entire foundation.

"So," I began, pacing slowly between the desks, "what do you think this tells us about love? About how God sees it?"

Michaela's hand shot up like a rocket—that girl always had thoughts percolating. "It means if we love other people, we're basically getting a masterclass in knowing God? Like, love is the ultimate study guide?"

My lips curved up as I snapped my fingers. "Exactly! Love isn't just a warm fuzzy feeling you get when someone brings you coffee. It's how we experience God's presence in our lives."

Even when it upends every certainty you've been clinging to.

Luke raised his hand, which was rarer than a unicorn sighting. "Does that mean God loves everyone the same? Even people who love differently than some people think they should?"

Bingo. Right to the heart of it. I thought of Jasmine, of my winding journey, and of all the beautiful, complicated ways love shows up in the world.

"God's love isn't a checklist," I said. "He calls us to love in all its raw forms—flawed, unpolished, but true."

The discussion flowed like a river finding its way to the sea, but my mind kept drifting to Damian. To the way he'd made me question everything I'd thought I understood about faith, love, and the space where they intersected. These kids were asking the same questions I grappled with every night, and their honesty was as refreshing as an iced taro milk tea with boba.

When the bell rang, they filed out, still chattering about love and God and whether it was possible to love pizza as much as you loved your family—Dylan's contribution to our theological discussion. They were wrestling with these big ideas so openly, without the weight of "shoulds" and "should nots" crushing their curiosity. That was what faith was supposed to look like—not certainty, but the courage to ask questions, to seek, and to love without fear.

I was scribbling notes in my lesson plan when the door to my classroom creaked open. Laura stepped in carrying two steaming cups of coffee. She'd been doing this lately—little gestures that created pockets of warmth in my otherwise chaotic days.

"Thought you might need some fuel," she said, setting one cup on my desk. The rich aroma filled the air, better than any scented candle ever made. "That was quite the theological discussion today. Those kids are lucky to have you."

I tucked a rebellious strand of hair back under my veil and wrapped my fingers around the warm mug. Laura had somehow figured out my coffee preferences with detective-level precision: splash of cream, no sugar, perfect temperature.

"Well, if God is love, it stands to reason He'd want to bless people who experience it, right?" I said before taking a cautious sip.

She settled against one of the student desks, cradling her own cup like it held the secrets of the universe. "I refuse to believe God wants His people to choose between devotion and love. It's like asking someone to choose between breathing and having a heartbeat."

The gentle understanding in her voice reminded me of my *lola*—if she had been the type to have deep theological discussions instead of worrying about whether I was eating enough vegetables.

"I used to think that too. But maybe sacrifice gives weight to devotion? Though lately, I'm questioning what I thought I knew. It's like someone rearranged my entire spiritual GPS, and now I'm stuck asking for directions at every intersection."

She let out a soft laugh. "How can the Church ask someone to deny a part of themselves that feels as natural as breathing? Why wouldn't God want everyone to experience what He literally *is*?" She paused, studying me with perceptive brown eyes. Laura had a superpower for reading between the lines—for seeing the stories people tried to keep hidden.

"What am I supposed to do when every instinct in me is telling me to reach for connection? For love?" I asked, staring at the trees swaying in the breeze through the window.

She set her coffee down and moved closer, bringing a warm, calm presence that she'd earned through years as an educator and made everything feel a little less overwhelming. "When love and faith are at odds, maybe it's not the love that needs examining. Maybe it's the fence we've built around faith." Principal Omura spoke without judgment, just compassion so pure it made me want to spill every secret I'd ever kept.

I rested my forearms on my desk. "Trust me, I know. The Church's stance on celibacy has been debated since, well, probably since the first priest fell in love. There're centuries of tradition behind it, and unfortunately, I don't see it changing anytime this millennium."

Laura's eyes softened as she reached out and squeezed my hand. Tears pricked at the corners of my eyes—happy tears, grateful tears, tears that said, *Finally, someone understands.* "You talk about love like it's a gift instead of a burden. Like it's worth celebrating, not fearing. And you're absolutely right."

Her words wrapped around my heart. She had no idea how close to the truth she was. Or maybe she did.

"Love, in all its forms, is a gift," I said, the words feeling truer each time I spoke them.

She studied me for a few seconds, then pulled me into a gentle hug. "Change isn't as impossible as you think, Claire. But maybe it's not the kind of change you're expecting."

I melted into her embrace, accepting her comfort. When she

pulled away, her dark eyes held so much warmth I thought I might spontaneously combust from pure human kindness.

She gathered her coffee cup and headed for the exit, pausing in the doorway. "You know where to find me if you need to talk. About anything."

As the door closed behind her, I sat at my desk, watching my coffee steam curl toward the ceiling like tiny prayers. Laura had become more than just a principal—she'd become a friend who seemed to understand the language of my struggles without a translator.

I was supposed to be focused on my faith, vows, and calling. But truthfully, the tension between love and duty had always felt like a daily wrestling match with my soul. And honestly? Some days I wasn't sure which side I wanted to win.

Chapter Twenty-Three

CLAIRE

I didn't know what had gotten into me. Maybe my conversation with Laura had loosened some screws in my brain, because after my last class, I rushed home and was now elbow-deep in my cottage's tiny kitchen making arroz caldo for Damian. I'd spent the better part of three hours channeling my inner *lola*, stirring rice porridge while the comforting symphony of ginger, garlic, and green onions filled every corner of my space.

I chopped vegetables with the precision my *lola* had drilled into me since I was tall enough to reach the counter. *Every Filipina should know how to make arroz caldo*, she'd said, though I was pretty sure she had visions of me feeding my future husband, not a Catholic priest.

Once it was done, I headed for the rectory. I stood outside Damian's front door, clutching a container of homemade soup with a little ramekin of green onions stacked on top, while the November wind rattled the windows. I'd convinced myself this was just normal human decency—what any concerned friend would do. *Nothing scandalous about bringing warm and yummy food to a sick person, right?*

I knocked, half hoping he wouldn't answer so I could leave the container on his doorstep. But of course, the door creaked open, and there he stood. He was wearing gray sweatpants and a faded Metallica T-shirt that clung to his broad shoulders. His dark hair was perfectly disheveled. Even sick, his handsomeness was devastating, making my brain short-circuit even more.

"Claire, what're you doing here?" he rasped.

I held up the container. "I thought you might need something warm to chase away the plague."

He stepped back to let me in. "What is it?"

I scanned the living room. A blanket lay crumpled on the couch, and an empty mug sat abandoned on the coffee table.

"Arroz caldo," I announced, making my way into his kitchen with the confidence of someone who definitely belonged there. "My grandma's secret weapon against all earthly ailments. It's Filipino chicken soup with magical healing properties." I tried to ignore the weird domesticity. "Please tell me you've had more than coffee and misplaced hope today."

He leaned against the counter, tracking me with those green eyes as I rummaged through his cabinets. "This morning? Maybe? Time is a social construct when you're dying."

"Damian." I shot him a look that would've made my mother proud—pure Filipino guilt mixed with genuine concern. He managed a weak smile, and my heart decided that was the perfect time to do the fluttery thing I absolutely did not have time for.

"I've been sleeping mostly."

I found a bowl in the cabinet above the sink and popped the container into his microwave, because even sick priests deserved properly heated food. The kitchen filled with those soul-warming scents that transported me straight back to childhood —Grandma humming while she chopped green onions, the sound of rain on our old roof, the way food was love made tangible in our house.

"It smells like heaven decided to open a restaurant," he

murmured, stepping closer. *Too close.* Close enough that I could feel the heat radiating from his body.

The microwave beeped its cheerful completion, and I carefully extracted the bowl, stirring the porridge with the same reverence my *lola* had taught me. "The ginger and garlic works miracles," I explained. "*Lola* used to say this could cure everything from heartbreak to the common cold. Though she might've been slightly biased."

"Your grandma taught you this recipe?"

"Mm-hmm. She conscripted me as her sous-chef from the time I could hold a knife without immediate bloodshed." I sprinkled chopped green onions from the smaller container on top with the kind of precision that would've made Gordon Ramsay weep. "Said every Filipina should know how to make arroz caldo, though I think she had visions of me nurturing a husband and babies." I gestured vaguely between us. "Not whatever this is. Here, eat this before it gets cold."

Our fingers brushed as he took the bowl, and that same electric shock that had plagued me since high school shot through me. He settled onto the couch and took his first spoonful, color immediately returning to his face.

"Your *lola* taught you well," he said, looking like he'd just discovered the meaning of life in a bowl of rice porridge. "This is incredible."

I tried not to think about all the times I'd watched *lola* make this exact dish for my grandpa, *lolo*, when he was under the weather. How she'd hover nearby like a concerned guardian angel until he'd finished every last bite, love expressed through wonderfully seasoned comfort food. And here I was, apparently following in her footsteps with a man who'd taken vows of celibacy. *Oh, the irony.*

"The secret is toasting the garlic until it's golden perfection," I said, perching on the arm of the couch. "And the ginger has to be fresh

—none of that powdered nonsense they try to pass off at the grocery store. *Lola* would rise from the grave to lecture anyone who used dried ginger."

He slurped another spoonful with zero shame, and I was mesmerized by the ridiculous simplicity of watching him swallow. *Stop it.*

"I don't think I've ever had this before," he admitted.

"Seriously?" I smiled, my mind automatically filling with memories of Sunday gatherings at my parents' house—tables groaning under the weight of pancit, lumpia, and adobo, the beautiful chaos of family meals where food and faith intertwined. "Maybe when you're feeling less like death warmed over, I could introduce you to chicken adobo or—" I caught myself mid-sentence, a reality check slapping me upside the head. "Sorry. I shouldn't be making dinner plans with you. That's probably several kinds of inappropriate."

"Claire." His voice went soft, thick with something that definitely wasn't just congestion. He set the empty bowl down with the kind of care usually reserved for precious artifacts. "Come here."

Every rational cell in my body screamed that I should politely decline, gather my empty container and my questionable life choices, and make a dignified exit. Instead, I slid onto the couch beside him like my common sense had taken a permanent vacation. He was fever-warm, heat pouring off of him like a human furnace, and when he leaned against me, my resolve crumbled.

"Thank you," he murmured, his head finding my shoulder. "Not just for the food. For caring enough to show up."

"Of course I care." *More than I should.* But thankfully, those words stayed locked in my chest.

He shifted until he was lying down, his head resting in my lap, and I started running my fingers through his hair. Outside, the wind howled as if it were having its own existential crisis, and rain spattered against the windows. But inside this little bubble we'd created, all was warm and safe.

"It was driving me insane," he said drowsily, already half asleep.

"What was?"

His eyes had drifted closed, but they fluttered open to meet mine. "Seeing you with Preston."

My eyebrows shot up somewhere near my hairline. I knew I shouldn't ask, that it would open a whole can of worms, but my mouth had other plans. "Why?"

His gaze held mine with startling intensity for someone who was supposedly dying of the common cold. "You know why."

I tilted my head, channeling my inner innocent angel even though we both knew better. "Do I?"

He huffed out a breath that was part frustration, part amusement. "I was jealous as hell. I had no right to be, but I was. You're supposed to be mine."

And there it was: Pandora's box cracked wide open, spilling all kinds of complicated feelings into the space between us.

"Maybe we should save the life-altering confessions for when you're not sick and potentially hallucinating."

"Is it terrible that I want you to be my safe harbor again?"

I held my breath to keep from gasping. He remembered our promise, the one we'd made under starlight when we thought we had forever figured out. *By the light that guides us, I promise to always find my way back to you, no matter how lost I get.*

But that was then, and this was now, and now came with vows and complexities and enough emotional baggage to sink a freaking cruise ship.

I continued combing my fingers through his hair, hoping the gentle motion would soothe both of us. "Shh. Rest now, you dramatic, feverish man."

He caught my wrist gently, his thumb tracing small circles on my palm. "I need to tell you something," he murmured. "It's been weighing on me since you came back into my life."

"What is it?"

"That night at the party. Jessica told me you were there." His glassy eyes found mine. "I know what you saw, and I know what you must have thought all these years. The story you've been carrying around in your head."

My heart stuttered in my chest like a broken CD player. We'd never spoken about it—this betrayal I'd carried around like a stone in my shoe for the past eight years.

"Dames," I started, not entirely sure I wanted to excavate old graves.

"No, please. Let me say this." He struggled to sit up a little, his shoulder pressing against mine with warm insistence. "I was so drunk that night. After Rico, I just wanted to stop hurting for five minutes. Wanted to crawl out of my own skin."

I nodded, remembering the hollow-eyed boy he'd become in those awful weeks after the funeral, like grief had carved out everything bright inside him.

"Jessica was there, and yes, we made out. Not my proudest moment." His voice dropped lower, more serious than I'd heard it in years. "But that's all it was. She took me home after, made sure I didn't choke on my own misery. Nothing else happened. Nothing."

"I talked to her," I admitted quietly, the words slipping out before I could stop them.

Surprise flickered across his face. "When?"

"Earlier in the school year. She told me all of it." I paused, gathering the scattered pieces of that conversation. "Said you kept talking about me, Rico. That you were both just drowning in different kinds of pain."

He exhaled slowly, as if he'd been holding his breath. "All these years, I thought you hated me for that night."

"I did hate you for a while," I confessed, the honesty tasting bitter and sweet at the same time. "Being angry at you was easier than admitting how much it broke me."

His fingers found mine—tentative, warm. "I'm sorry for adding that to everything else you were carrying. You deserved so much better than a broken boy who didn't know how to grieve without destroying all the good around him."

For years, I'd held on to that moment as proof that I'd never really mattered to him. That his grief had made him careless with my heart. But sitting here now, the last of that old anger dissolved like cotton candy in rain and was replaced by understanding. Two souls just breaking into adulthood, crushed beneath a sorrow too vast to contain.

"We were so young," I whispered. "Neither of us had the first clue how to handle losing Rico."

He nodded, his thumb still tracing gentle patterns on my palm. "Still doesn't excuse the hurt I caused. I should have tried to explain instead of pushing you away."

"Would I have listened?" I asked, and we both knew the answer.

A melancholic smile curved his lips. "Probably not. You were always stubborn as a mule when you were hurt."

I squeezed his hand. "Well, I'm listening now. Better late than never, right?"

His eyes held mine for a long moment. "Better late than never." He lay on my lap once more and drifted back to sleep.

The heaviness hadn't gone away but had changed shape. Where there'd been a wall, I could almost see a bridge, and this time, we found our way over. Except that was dangerous, wasn't it?

I ran my fingers through his hair, watching his chest rise and fall with each peaceful breath. The rain continued its gentle percussion against the windows, but in here, the air had finally cleared. Like the storm had passed, leaving everything washed clean and new.

THE LEATHER SOFA CREAKED SOFTLY AS I STIRRED AWAKE, AND MY FIRST thought was that this was either the best or worst way to wake up. Damian lay sprawled between me and the back of the couch, his head pillowed on my abdomen, one arm anchoring me close.

Somehow during the night, we'd become an impossibly tangled knot of limbs, his body curved around mine like he was trying to protect me from the world or maybe from my common sense.

In the quiet sanctuary of early morning, I allowed myself the dangerous luxury of staring at Damian. His dark hair was mussed from sleep, falling across his forehead in a way that made him look like the teenager I'd once known, before grief carved lines around his eyes and he learned to carry the weight of other people's faith on those broad shoulders. His lips were slightly parted, warm breath ghosting through my cotton tee in a rhythm that should not have been as hypnotic as it was. Even the weight of him felt achingly right —solid and grounding.

That was when Damian shifted. I thought he was going to wake up and break this spell we'd woven in sleep. Instead, his mouth pressed against my stomach through my shirt, and I froze.

Oh God—is he awake?

His warm lips wandered lower with sleepy exploration, each touch igniting fireworks beneath my skin. I was supposed to be stronger than this. But apparently, my willpower had clocked out, because when his eyes remained closed and he nuzzled closer, lifting the hem of my shirt, I didn't exactly stage a tactical retreat.

"He'll never touch you again." His tongue traced lazy, devastating circles across my belly, the wet heat making my muscles quiver. Every rational thought I'd ever had abandoned ship as his chin glided against my sensitive skin, the contrast of soft lips and rough stubble drawing a whimper from my throat.

"Who?" I asked.

"Preston."

I tried to move, but his arm locked around my waist with surprising strength for a man who was supposed to be *asleep*. He pressed me deeper into the couch cushions.

This was wrong on so many different levels. He caressed that sensitive spot near my navel and then lower, his teeth grazing the delicate flesh with reverent hunger. My hips lifted without permission, seeking more of whatever this madness was.

"Your body doesn't beg for him the way it begs for me." His hand slid up my side, calloused palm mapping every curve like he was memorizing me, fingertips pressing into my ribs with just enough pressure to make me forget my own name. Each exhale ghosted across my skin, raising goose bumps that had nothing to do with the morning chill.

Damian's mouth pressed at the edge of my waistband, and I couldn't stop the sharp little sound, between a sigh and a whimper, that rose from me and seemed to fill the entire room with my desperation.

His fingers splayed across my ribs, thumb brushing the underside of my breast through my bra, and I was pretty sure I saw stars. Or Jesus. Possibly both.

A sharp knock at the front door shattered the moment, the sound echoing through the rectory, where dawn's first light was creeping through the curtains.

Reality check, courtesy of God's impeccable timing.

"Damian," I whispered urgently, shaking his shoulder while trying to ignore the way my body was still humming from his touch. My heart leaped into my throat as another knock echoed through the space. "Someone's here, and unless you want to explain why there's a nun in your living room at dawn, we need to move. Now."

He stirred against me, those emerald eyes blinking open. "Shit."

"The door. Answer it before they break it down," I hissed, scrambling up and looking for the nearest hiding spot like I was playing the world's most inappropriate game of hide-and-seek.

My pulse racing, I ducked into the coat closet just as Damian stumbled toward the door. The small space was filled with mothballs and starched clerical garments. I pressed myself against his heavy winter coat, trying to quiet my breathing and pretend I wasn't having a complete moral crisis.

Through the slats, I watched Mrs. Fontana bustle in, her arms laden with what smelled like chicken noodle soup. Of course it was *her*.

"Father Bellucci, I know it's early, but I wanted to check on you," she chirped, settling her offerings on the coffee table with the efficiency of someone who'd clearly done this before. "Make sure you have everything you need to recover properly."

"That's very kind of you, Mrs. Fontana," Damian managed, his voice still rough with sleep and probably lingering traces of whatever fever dream we'd just been living.

She fussed with the arrangement of items on the coffee table as if she were staging a magazine photo. But I caught the way her eyes lingered on my empty arroz caldo bowl with the intensity of a detective examining evidence.

"I see someone's already brought you food," she observed, and I could practically hear the gears turning in her head.

"Oh, yeah. Sister Claire dropped off some Filipino soup last night," Damian said.

"Ah." Her lips thinned into a line as she straightened, smoothing her beige cardigan with deliberate precision. "I've noticed you two spending quite a bit of time together lately."

From my hiding spot, I rolled my eyes so hard I was surprised they didn't fall out of my head.

Damian crossed his arms, and even from the closet, I could see his biceps bulge with the movement. "She's helping me plan the marriage retreat. It's church business."

"Of course, of course." Mrs. Fontana rested on the edge of the armchair, folding her hands in her lap with practiced patience. "It's just that some of us in the congregation have been here a long time, Father. We have long memories. And we remember how close you two were before the vows."

He stiffened. "Mrs. Fontana—"

"I just worry, dear." The endearment dripped from her lips. "A young, handsome priest like yourself, and she's quite beautiful, isn't she? Even hidden away in that plain habit."

Oh, you've got to be kidding me.

"Sister Claire is one of the most dedicated people I know," Damian said, his voice carrying an edge that could've sharpened knives. "She deserves more respect than whatever you're implying."

Mrs. Fontana's gaze drifted back to my empty bowl. "I'm sure she means well, Father. But kindness can be dangerous, especially from someone with her particular charms."

I pressed my hand harder against my mouth to keep from either laughing or screaming. She was talking about me like I was some kind of temptress sent from hell to corrupt their precious priest, not the same person who'd helped her hang Christmas garland every year until I left for college or the same person who'd held her hand during her husband's funeral Mass and brought her casseroles when she was too grief-stricken to cook.

The worst part? She wasn't entirely wrong. I had crossed lines with Damian that proved every single one of her suspicions. That shame burned hotter than my indignation.

"Mrs. Fontana"—Damian's tone went full priest mode,

authoritative despite his illness—"I appreciate your concern, but Sister Claire is above reproach. If you have issues with the way we're conducting church business, you're welcome to speak with Bishop Valenti."

She sighed as if the weight of the world rested on her cardigan-covered shoulders, patting his arm with maternal condescension. "Just be careful, Father. That's all this old woman is saying." She headed for the door, pausing for one final dramatic flourish. "Remember, the devil's greatest trick isn't tempting us with obvious evil. It's making sin look beautiful and good."

With that cheerful thought, she swept out, leaving behind the scent of disapproval and Bengay.

The door clicked shut, and I emerged from the closet like some kind of disheveled jack-in-the-box, trying to shake off Mrs. Fontana's words.

"Well, that was absolutely delightful," I said, attempting to inject some lightness into the stuffy atmosphere. "Nothing like a good old-fashioned guilt trip to start the morning."

"That was too close for comfort," Damian said, running a hand through his hair.

"I should go." I straightened my rumpled T-shirt, avoiding his gaze. "I'll take the back exit, do the whole walk-of-shame thing without the actual shame. Well, less shame. Some shame is unavoidable."

"Wait." He stepped closer, warmth still radiating from his skin. "What she said about you—"

"Don't. Please." I held up a hand like I could physically stop his words. "Just don't."

His jaw tightened. "She's wrong about you, Claire."

"Is she though?" The question slipped out before I could stop it, carrying all the uncertainty I'd been trying to ignore. "Maybe she sees something we've been working really hard not to acknowledge.

Maybe this"—I gestured between us—"has to stop before we do something we can't take back. For real this time. And I really need to start taking my own advice," I said, remembering that it was me who'd told him to keep his distance.

I turned to leave, but he caught my hand with gentle insistence. The touch sent electricity racing up my arm, settling somewhere low in my stomach. His thumb traced over my pulse point tenderly before he pressed his lips there, soft and reverent and absolutely ruinous.

"We passed the point of stopping the moment you walked back into my life," he murmured against my skin, his words vibrating through me.

My eyes widened, and I pulled away before I did something stupid —like kiss him senseless at seven in the morning. "Get some rest, you impossible man."

Sneaking out the back exit was the most ridiculous thing I'd ever done, but there I was, creeping around like a teenager avoiding curfew. Mrs. Fontana's parting words echoed in my head as I walked home in the crisp morning air. *Making sin look beautiful and good.*

But wasn't that exactly what faith was supposed to teach us? Finding the sacred in unexpected places, recognizing God's love in human form? The line between holy and profane had never felt so impossibly blurred.

The salty ocean breeze filled my lungs as I walked the mundane path home, my fingers unconsciously circling my wrist where the warmth of his kiss refused to fade. Despite everything, I couldn't deny the truth that was blooming in my chest like spring after a long winter.

I was falling for him all over again, tumbling headfirst into the same beautiful disaster that had wrecked me once before.

God help me. But even that felt like a lie. Because deep down, in the honest corners of my heart, I wasn't sure I wanted His help. Not when falling felt less like sin and more like coming home.

Chapter Twenty-Four

Christ, I'm falling apart.

She held me on the edge, and I kept walking toward whatever came next. The sliver of control I'd fought so hard to maintain was crumbling faster than I could rebuild it. In private, I was already lost. But now? I couldn't even keep it together during Mass, of all places.

My eyes would find her without permission, drawn to the way morning light caught the curve of her cheek, the gentle bow of her lips as she sang the hymns. I'd catch myself staring and tear my gaze away, my heart hammering against my ribs like a caged animal.

Did anyone notice?

There was only one place I could think of to clear my head—though God knew if it would work anymore.

Earlier that day, Detective Alvarez had called with an update on Thomas Mercer. "The case is officially closed," he'd said. His words echoed in my mind as I continued down the sidewalk to the cemetery. It was over. The breath I drew felt deeper than any I'd taken since that night at the hospital.

The worn path to Rico's grave seemed longer today, each step heavier than the last. His tombstone looked the same as always. Simple. Clean. *Enrico James Bellucci. Beloved Son and Brother. Gone too soon.* The words were etched deep in the granite, but they didn't say enough. Didn't tell how his laugh could fill a room, or how he'd stay up all night helping me study for exams. They didn't mention that he dreamed of becoming a priest and helping people. They didn't say how much we all lost when he died.

I sank to my knees in front of the stone, not caring about the dampness seeping through my slacks. "It's been a while." I traced the grooves of his name with my finger. "I don't know what I'm doing anymore."

A crow cawed somewhere in the distance, the sound sharp against the quiet.

"I met him, Rico. The man who—" My voice caught. "The man who hit you. Thomas Mercer. Just a regular guy. A chemistry teacher of all things." I let out a bitter laugh. "The fucked-up part is he confessed to me before he turned himself in. And I had to give him absolution."

I stared at my brother's name, my vision blurring. "That was the hardest fucking thing I've ever had to do in my life." I swallowed hard. "Everything I thought I knew, everything I built after you died, is crumbling. I'm crumbling."

Inhaling deeply, I said, "Claire became a nun. Can you believe that?"

A chilly breeze stirred the white lilies Mom had left. The sweetness of the flowers mixed with the sharp air reminded me of altar boy training, Rico teaching me how to light the incense without burning myself. *Steady hands, little brother.* He'd guided my movements until the smoke curled just right.

"Remember how you used to tease me about her?" I choked out a laugh. "You knew before I did. You always knew."

He'd caught me staring at Claire in the cafeteria one afternoon, a knowing gleam in his eyes as he nudged my shoulder. *That girl's got you wrapped around her finger, and she doesn't even know it.*

I leaned back against a tree a few feet from his marker, its rough bark digging into my skin through my black shirt, anchoring me to the present. My fingers dug into the earth beside me, desperate for something solid to hold on to.

"You were so sure we'd end up together. Called us soulmates. Said it was written in the stars or some romantic bullshit like that. But then you left us. Left me. And I broke. Every aspect of my life fell apart."

I thought if I gave enough of myself away, if I denied every selfish want and human need, somehow it would equal the life that had been taken from us. Like I could bargain with God. My life of service in exchange for some peace for Mom, some forgiveness from Dad. Some sign that Rico's death meant more than some senseless tragedy. I ripped at the grass beneath my hands, watching the green blades scatter in the wind.

"When I sat across from Thomas, I realized I've been punishing myself for surviving. Building walls around my heart like somehow that would balance the scales. But you wouldn't have wanted that, would you?

"I wish you were here to tell me what to do." Tears burned my eyes. "I don't know how to be the man you always believed I could be. How do I love her the way she deserves when I'm still so broken? I pushed her away, pushed everyone away. I was a fucking coward. Scared of loving someone again and losing them too."

The cemetery brightened around me, shadows retreating like sinners from confession, leaving nowhere to hide from the truth I'd been avoiding. I pulled out my collar, turning it over in my hands. The white plastic was cold and artificial. "Somehow, I feel alive again." My chest tightened. "And I'm terrified, Rico. Because what if I'm wrong? What if this isn't what God wants for me?"

I could almost hear his response, could picture the way he'd roll his eyes and call me an idiot. He'd always been the brave one who went after what he wanted without hesitation.

A car passed on the nearby road, the faraway sound muffled. A sparrow hopped onto Rico's headstone across from me, tilting its head as if it were listening. *My Sparrow.* The nickname for Claire had come easy—she'd been so light on her feet, always darting from one thing to the next, quick to startle but never gone for long. Fragile and fierce all at once. The sight pulled a smile from me, though it hurt to hold it.

"You would've known what to do. You always did. Would've told me to stop overthinking and follow my heart." I laughed, but it came out more like a sob. "God, I miss you. Every single fucking day."

I stood slowly, my knees protesting. Dew had soaked through my pants. "Maybe it's time I stopped trying to fill the space you left behind." I pressed my palm to the top of his headstone, the warmth where the sun had touched it seeping into my skin.

Looking down at my brother's grave, I saw him as he had been clearly in my mind: Twenty-two and full of life, that crooked grin on his face, the one that always meant trouble. The way he used to ruffle my hair. How he'd drop everything to help me, no matter what.

"I'll always carry you with me, Rico. But I can't keep using your death as a reason to hide from life. From love." I stepped back, straightening my shoulders. "Claire brings a fullness to my world. When I'm with her, I can imagine a future that doesn't revolve around atonement."

I turned to leave, then paused, glancing back one last time. The gravestone stood silent in the afternoon light. The breeze picked up again, rustling through the trees, and for a moment, it felt like an answer. A blessing. Like Rico was there, telling me it was okay to let go.

"I love you," I whispered.

As I walked away, each step was lighter. Meeting Thomas Mercer had done what eight years of prayer couldn't. It had forced me to see the prison I'd built for myself. I was ready to stop living in the shadow of what I'd lost and start reaching for what I could have. All that was left was deciding what that looked like.

Chapter Twenty-Five

CLAIRE

The late-afternoon air had a crispness to it, a slight chill that lingered as the sun broke through the clouds, casting a golden hue over Saint Anthony's courtyard. The bake sale was massive—at least ten tables overflowing with cookies, cakes, and pastries, all arranged in a circle in the middle of the courtyard.

Parishioners and nonparishioners alike crowded around, eagerly buying up the baked goods. Their chatter blended with the clinking of coin boxes. The sweet scent of sugar and cinnamon filled the air, mixing with the salty breeze from the ocean.

A few of the kids from the parish school ran around, their laughter ringing through the air. My lips curved up, even though anxiety knotted my chest.

As I arranged another tray of cookies, my mind drifted to Sundays at home, helping Mom prep pan de sal while she gossiped about the latest church drama. The memory of her hands working the dough and the way she'd slip me an extra roll still warm from the oven made my chest ache. I'd learned at an early age that food was its own kind of prayer, a way of showing love without words.

Parish women bustled around me, reminding me of my *titas* at family gatherings, their conversations oddly comforting even as their scrutiny made me squirm. That was the thing about small Catholic communities. They saw everything. Judged everything.

Damian was finishing up evening Mass. He'd been stopping by to check on everyone whenever he had free time. We had fallen right back into that delicate dance of pretending we were fine, as though nothing had ever happened between us.

No matter what Damian had said, some chapters were better left unfinished. Those moments had to stop. We were matches and gasoline, destined to burn everything around us if we got too close again. Better to stay what we were: a cautionary tale about timing and choices.

"Sister Claire, these cookies are adorable," Mrs. Walker exclaimed, pointing to a tray of sugar cookies shaped like little confectionary crosses.

I laughed, adjusting a plate of brownies next to them. "Mrs. Lim made those. She's been baking since Friday."

Mrs. Walker chuckled. "She never does anything halfway, does she?"

Before I could respond, the familiar tenor of Damian's voice caught my attention, and my body tensed. I didn't even have to look to know he was here—not when the energy shifted when he walked into a room.

I turned, and there he was, striding toward me. His black slacks brushed softly with each step. He was carrying a couple large boxes, his face flushed from the brisk walk across the parking lot.

"You're late," I teased, trying to keep my tone light as he approached the table.

He set the boxes down before running a hand through his dark hair. "Mrs. Fontana cornered me after Mass with twenty questions."

I rolled my eyes. "Of course she did. I swear, she could run this parish if she wanted to."

Damian chuckled, and for a moment, the tension between us eased.

He started unpacking one of the boxes, pulling out more donated cupcakes. I watched him for a second, trying to ignore the way my heart skipped a beat when his lips tilted into that boyish smile.

God, give me grace to deal with him.

"So," Damian said as he stood next to me behind the table, "would it be a sin if I stole one of your cookies?"

My eyes narrowed as I pointed my index finger at him. "Don't you dare."

A corner of his mouth quirked up. "Oh, come on, Sister Claire. Just one little *taste*."

My breath hitched, lips parting ever so slightly. "I think you've had more than your fill," I whispered.

He cocked an eyebrow. "That's not what I meant, but if you're offering . . ."

I groaned and busied myself arranging a new batch of cookies at another table. The kids ran past us again, giggling as they played a game of tag. One of the younger girls, Sophie, skidded to a stop near me, her cheeks reddened from running.

"Sister Claire! Can I have one of those cupcakes?" she asked, pointing to the tray.

I crouched down to her level, smiling. "You have to ask your mom first, okay? If she says yes, I'll give you the best one."

Sophie grinned wide and ran off toward her mom. I stood, only to catch Damian watching me, a soft smile on his face. I cleared my throat, feeling self-conscious under his scrutiny.

"What?" I asked, raising an eyebrow.

He shook his head, his smile fading into thoughtfulness. "Nothing. You're good with them."

I blinked, not expecting the sudden shift in tone. "With the kids?"

"Yeah," he said. "You would've been an awesome mom."

My cheeks heated. His eyes locked on me, and my pulse stumbled. It was the look I remembered from before—when loving him hadn't felt like stepping into brimstone and fire.

I swallowed, forcing a smile to curve my lips, and brushed off the moment. "It's easy when sugar's involved."

Damian's grin widened. We went back to speaking with the people and organizing tables, but his presence loomed over me. The way he moved closer than he needed to, the way our hands brushed against each other when we reached for the same plate.

After another rush of customers, I glanced in Damian's direction, who gazed off into the distance.

He seems . . . lost? Conflicted?

"What's going on in that mind of yours, Father Bellucci?" I stepped closer, tucking a strand of hair back into my veil. *It's always this same damn strand.*

Damian shrugged, his brow furrowed as he straightened a stack of disposable plates. "Just thinking."

"About?" I pressed, trying to remain casual.

He hesitated for a second, his eyes flicking up to meet mine. "That morning in the rectory."

I hadn't expected him to talk about *that* out in the open. I forced my lips to curve up and said, "Can we just pretend it never happened?"

We just stood there, the space suddenly too small. The heat from his body seemed to seep into the air between us, a quiet hum of energy that made my skin tingle.

"Is that what you really want?" he asked.

Did he seriously want to continue this? I crossed my arms and gritted out, "We shouldn't be talking so openly about this."

Damian's green gaze lingered on me for a beat too long before he nodded. "You're right. Later, then."

A young woman with long blond hair traipsed toward Damian with a wide smile. Her dark eyes flicked over him with a boldness that twisted my gut.

I tried to focus on throwing away empty pastry boxes, but it was impossible not to overhear their conversation. Her voice was light, casual, but there was a sultriness underneath it—a subtle flirtation that made my skin crawl.

"Father Damian," she said, her tone soft and sweet. "Do you think you could make some time for a confession after the bake sale?"

I didn't have to look to know Damian was smiling. He always smiled when someone asked for help. It wasn't just a priestly duty to him; he genuinely cared. He'd always been warm and approachable, and that was what made him so *him*. But right now, it was too much.

"Of course, Lilia. Meet me in the church confessional afterward." He glanced at his wrist watch. "In thirty minutes?"

"Sounds good. Thank you, Father. I'm looking forward to it."

I bit my lip, copper trickling onto my tongue. He was doing his job. Being kind. But my skin pickled with irritation at the way her hand brushed his arm as she walked away. I wasn't supposed to care who flirted with him. Wasn't supposed to care how many young women asked for his time. But here I was, annoyed at the way she'd lingered a second too long and how his lips had curved up at her.

To try to keep myself distracted, I straightened the already-neat row of pastries.

"Sister Claire, dear?" Mrs. Walker's voice jolted me back to the present. She stood next to me, her brow furrowed in concern. "We're out of registration forms in the church lobby. There are still a few couples asking about the retreat."

I pursed my lips. "They can register online, Mrs. Walker."

She shook her head. "Some of our older generation don't do well with computers, you know. We really need more *physical* forms out there."

I started to argue—to explain that we had enough online options to make the process seamless—but I could tell by the set of her jaw that Mrs. Adeline Walker wasn't going to budge. She was old-school, and that meant paper forms, no matter how much easier the digital ones were.

This is penance. I exhaled, wiping my hands on a towel and nodding. "All right, I'll go make more copies."

Mrs. Walker smiled. "Thank you, dear. I'll handle cleaning up here."

I gave her a grateful grin and glanced in Damian's direction one last time. He was still standing where I'd left him, talking to another parishioner. Lilia had immersed herself in conversation with Mrs. Fontana a few tables away.

Turning on my heel, I headed for the church office. As I walked across the courtyard, I couldn't help but think about how ridiculous it was to feel like I had any claim on Damian. *Then again, he admitted to being jealous of Preston.*

I could recite a thousand Hail Marys, but they wouldn't drown out the way my heart raced when he was near. Even wrapped in this habit, bound by sacred promises, a piece of my soul whispered his name.

That was why I needed space—distance. Because the second I let my guard slip, even a fraction, it all came back. The jealousy, the desire, the jumbled mess of emotions.

I made my way through the church hallway, incense invading my nose. Pushing open the office door, a cool draft brushed past me as I stepped inside and headed straight for the bulky donated copy machine.

It whirred to life, the quiet hum of papers feeding through filling the small room. I leaned against the counter, fingers tapping against the cool surface.

Once the copier stopped, I gathered the stack of warm pages in my hands and decided to drop a few off in the sacristy. *Stay moving. Keep busy. Don't stop to think.* That was my new mantra. Because the moment I slowed, all those unholy desires would catch up and pull me into their undertow.

Chapter Twenty-Six

DAMIAN

The bake sale had wrapped up, the lingering scent of sugar and cinnamon still hanging in the early-evening air. We'd raised more than enough money for the marriage retreat, and I was grateful to everyone who'd helped. The last of the volunteers stacked chairs and put away the tables.

Fuck, I still need to hear Lilia's confession.

I exhaled and headed toward the church to meet her. As much as I wanted to keep my head clear, my thoughts kept drifting back to Claire. The softness of her skin beneath my fingertips haunted me. The way she'd melted against me that night in the rectory burned in my memory. I'd fallen asleep with my head on her stomach, one arm wrapped around her waist. And I'd had the best sleep in years with her fingers brushing through my hair.

The warmth she carried went beyond physical attraction; it radiated from within, visible in the gentle way she smiled at the kids and how her eyes lit up as she taught. I couldn't stop remembering how her body melded to mine and how *right* it had felt to hold her.

The stained glass cast fractured colored light across the pews of the dim sanctuary. A soft shuffle of movement from the sacristy caught my attention midway to the confessional.

My heart picked up, instinct kicking in as I veered off course toward the noise. I pushed open the door, half expecting to find someone who'd stayed behind after the bake sale.

And *someone* collided into my chest and squealed. I peered down, my gaze landing on Claire. On instinct, I wrapped an arm around her waist, steadying her. I braced my other hand against the door.

Her wide gray eyes met mine just as the stack of forms she was carrying tumbled from her arms, scattering across the floor.

"Fuck, Claire," I breathed, more out of shock than anything. "What are you doing back here?"

"I was—" She pushed out of my grasp and gestured to the papers on the floor, flustered. "I was putting a few spares in the sacristy."

We both crouched at the same time, fingers scrambling for the pages. It was just me and her caught in this strange, chaotic moment. My hand brushed hers, a tingling shock arcing up my arm.

Then it happened—our crosses, swinging on their chains, collided and tangled together. I froze, heart hammering in my chest. Claire stilled too. Neither of us moved, the space between us shrinking by the second.

Her breaths quickened, and I couldn't stop my eyes from flicking to her lips, just inches away. The weight of the air shifted, a silent awareness that both of us were teetering on the edge. Again.

Before I could say anything, the sharp slam of the lobby door echoed through the church. My muscles tensed, every instinct firing at once, and my chest tightened.

Someone was coming. *Probably Lilia.*

With my heart hammering in my ears, I grabbed Claire by the arm and pulled her toward the nearby built-in confessional booth. Our crosses still tangled, we slipped inside.

Seconds passed, the footsteps drawing closer.

The space was small—too small for two people. Claire ended up straddling my lap, her knees on either side of my hips as we squeezed onto the narrow bench. Her body pressed against mine, breath hot on my neck.

My hands landed on her waist—whether to keep her still or guide her down onto my throbbing dick, I wasn't sure.

An aching need sparked low in my stomach and spread outward, leaving my body taut with desire. Between shallow breaths, I closed my eyes in an attempt to will away the urge to unbuckle my belt, free my cock, and thrust into her.

Claire started untangling our crosses, and the door on the other side of the confessional clicked open. I knew it was Lilia, always prompt, ready for her confession. I thanked God the screen between us was thick enough to obscure my and Claire's situation.

"Father?" came her soft voice from the other side. "I'm ready."

I swallowed hard, my throat dry. "Go ahead."

Claire shifted on my lap, and I bit back a groan. Who would've thought this confessional would become my own undoing?

With Claire pressed against me, her jasmine scent filling my lungs, I wanted to run my fingers up her curves and taste her delicious lips again.

"Bless me, Father, for I have sinned," Lilia began, but the words felt like a mockery.

I'm the one sinning.

Lilia confessed mundane sins—harsh words to her kids, missed prayers, small deceits. Meanwhile, I was committing far greater sins in my heart, in my thoughts, in the way my body responded to Claire. But I couldn't find the strength to push her away anymore.

Claire moved again, adjusting on my lap as if searching for the most comfortable position. The warmth between her legs grazed me, and my breath caught in my throat. I was supposed to be listening attentively, guiding Lilia in her confession. But with Claire's pussy resting against my twitching cock, all rational thoughts fled my mind.

Somehow, I made it through the next ten minutes. Lilia finished her confession, and I managed to give her a penance, though I couldn't remember half of what I said.

"Thank you, Father," she said, her voice dropping to almost coy. "Would you be available for coffee tomorrow?"

Claire stiffened.

I cleared my throat. "I'm busy with the upcoming marriage retreat. I'm sorry."

There was a small, disappointed pout in Lilia's voice. "Oh. Well, maybe another time, then. Have a good night, Father."

"Good night, Lilia."

The soft click of the confessional door closing behind her signaled her exit, and just like that, Claire and I were alone again.

But neither of us moved.

Her chest rose and fell with each breath. She'd managed to untangle our crosses. But all I could do was stare at her, the dim light casting shadows across her beautiful face.

When I gripped her waist and thrust against her, it wasn't lust consuming me—it was revelation. *This is your weakness*, my guilt said. But after that graveside visit, my soul knew better: *This is your veracity.*

She let out a quiet gasp. "What're you doing?"

I leaned closer, my lips inches from hers. "Please."

"We can't." But she didn't stop me.

"I need you," I breathed, my words a whisper over her mouth. "Help me. Help me find release."

"This is a sin."

"Then I absolve you." I guided her movements, matching her rhythm with my own thrusts.

"We can't," she repeated.

I cupped her nape and crushed my mouth to hers. She opened for me, soft and yielding, and I let myself drown. Her warmth, her breath hitching against me—all that I'd sworn off—seared through every vow I'd made.

My fingers hooked into the edge of her veil, sliding it away in one deliberate pull. Claire unveiled before me—it felt older than vows, older than sin. Like the stars themselves had decreed it. Black hair tumbled down her shoulders, and I buried my fist in it, jerking her head back and baring the line of her throat. I pressed my mouth there, rough kisses marking a trail down her velvety skin. Her pulse thrashed against my lips, frantic and alive, answering to the demand in me I could no longer cage.

Our bodies fused together, fitting like two pieces of a puzzle.

Her hands clamped onto my shoulders, the grinding of her hips urgent and desperate. "Fuck, I'm close."

"Me too." My fingers traced the curve of her waist, memorizing every dip and rise as if it were a map to forbidden treasure.

Reality melted away, leaving only us in this hallowed space where saints once sought solace. But there was no penance here, only desire burning bright and hot between us.

"You're so fucking perfect, Claire." I pulled her in for another kiss. Her body shook against me, and the thought of her coming on my cock sent a wave of heat through me. Her breaths came in short, sharp gasps as she trembled, her orgasm sweeping through her.

With a suppressed grunt, my body tensed, and my hips bucked, grinding against her with a final thrust. My mind blanked, the rush of ecstasy leaving me breathless and shaking.

Oh my God. I leaned back against the confessional wall and stared at her. Her hooded eyes, that sated flush. It turned to guilt in a blink.

"I'm sorry," I whispered on a breath, the word escaping me. But the fucked-up thing was I didn't mean it. I wasn't sorry about what had just occurred between us. Not even a little.

"I should go," she said, her warm breath ghosting across my cheek.

Claire hesitated for a second, eyes searching mine before she slid off my lap. She didn't look at me as she gathered her veil off the floor and hurried out of the confessional, the door clicking shut behind her.

I sat there, frozen, my heart pounding in my chest while the warmth of her lingered. Every nerve ending was alive, hypersensitive to her absence. I pressed my fingers to my hot swollen lips.

Shame and desire tangled in my gut like thorny vines. Not shame for wanting her—that felt too pure, too real to regret—but shame for corrupting this sacred space, for turning a place of confession into a den of primal desire.

And yet I wanted more. How long had it been since every cell in my body sang with the simple joy of touch, of connection?

I should have been on my knees praying for forgiveness. Should have been begging God to take away my unholy thoughts and my carnal desires. But all I could think about was her body writhing against mine.

I ran a shaky hand through my hair, the weight of my collar heavier than ever. These wood panels that had witnessed countless confessions now held one more secret.

I waited until midnight, long after the last parishioner had left and the church had settled into darkness. The only light came from the small battery-powered lamp I'd brought. I made my way toward the confessional, cleaning supplies clutched in my hand.

The wooden door creaked as I pulled it open, the sound echoing through the silent sanctuary. I stood frozen for a moment, staring at the narrow bench where just hours before, Claire had straddled me and I'd tasted the salt of her skin and relished the feel of her body pressed against mine. Where I'd made her come.

A hollow thud resounded as I set the bucket down and dropped to my knees. I poured bleach into the warm water. The harsh chemical scent burned my nostrils. *A fitting punishment.* I plunged the cloth into the solution, wringing it until my knuckles turned white, and began to scrub.

"Forgive me," I whispered, the words catching in my throat. I dragged the cloth across the wooden surface, each stroke penance. The burn of my muscles atonement. This was sacred space, meant for absolution, for mercy—not for my unholy desires.

The bleach seeped into a small cut on my thumb, the burning sting making me wince. *Good.* The pain was deserved. Necessary. I scrubbed harder, moving methodically through the small booth, cleansing away evidence that didn't exist except in my mind.

As I continued scrubbing, my movements grew more deliberate and less frantic. The desperate energy that had driven me here was changing, sharper now. More resolute. I wasn't here to clean the confessional—I was here to prepare myself.

I sat back on my heels, the damp cloth falling from my raw hands. The wood of the bench, polished by time and use, acted as a quiet reminder of how many men had sat here before me.

How many penitents had left this booth unchanged, carrying the same burdens week after week? How many had confessed the same sins, made the same promises, only to return with the same failures?

That's not going to be me.

I could scrub until my hands bled, could pray until my voice went hoarse, could beg God's forgiveness until dawn broke through the stained glass. But it wouldn't change what I was about to do. It wouldn't change what I *wanted* to do.

I touched the bench, my fingers tracing the wood grain. What happened here hadn't been a mistake. I'd felt truly alive—had since *she* found her way back into my life after eight years. She'd upended the hollow, dutiful existence I'd been living and lit a fire that made my soul sing.

My knees protested the slow rise from the hard floor. The bucket and cloth sat forgotten as I faced the crucifix mounted on the wall, my hands folded in front of me. All my choices had led to this moment, my visit to Rico's grave the precursor.

"Forgive me, Father," I whispered, and this time the words carried a different weight—not the desperate plea of a man seeking absolution, but the calm confession of someone who had already made his choice. "Forgive me for what I'm about to do."

I closed my eyes, expecting the crush of guilt or the weight of impending sin. Instead, I felt lighter than I had in years.

"You made me to love her," I continued, steadier now. "You brought her back to me for a reason. I know what I'm about to do goes against all that I promised You. But I can't pretend anymore."

The silence stretched between us, God and His wayward priest. I opened my eyes, looking directly at the cross.

"I'm going to make her mine," I said, the words tasting like both damnation and salvation. "And if that condemns me, then so be it. I'd gladly burn for her."

I gathered the cloth and bucket of diluted cleaning solution. The bleach on my hands would fade, but the decision I'd made tonight would mark me forever.

Chapter Twenty-Seven

DAMIAN

The late-morning sun stretched long shadows over the narrow streets. I climbed the worn stone steps to Max's church, each step echoing. Leaving the usual noise of Saint Anthony's far behind, a sense of relief settled over me.

Father Max's church was smaller than mine, with ivy creeping up the side of the old building. It was tucked in the heart of the town, a place I'd visited countless times during seminary, when Max and I would sit for hours, talking about everything from theology to football.

I pushed open the creaky door, incense and polished wood filling my nose. The sanctuary was empty, the quiet broken by faint music echoing through the space, probably Max finishing his post-Mass duties. I stood in the aisle for a few seconds, running a hand through my hair, nerves settling in. What the hell was I going to say?

As expected, I found him in the sacristy, tidying up after the morning service. He was blasting classic rock on the small speaker that sat behind him while he worked. His blond hair caught the light, his movements methodical, calm. He didn't notice me at first, too focused on folding linens with the same precision he applied to his daily life.

"Max," I called.

He turned, a faint smile playing on his lips as he lowered the music. "I was wondering when you'd show up at my doorstep."

"Back at your altar of chores, huh?"

"You know how it is. The work never ends." Max's grin faded, replaced by a look of concern. He set the linens aside and gestured for me to sit in one of the old wooden chairs by the wall. "What's wrong?"

I sat, not knowing where to start. How could I explain everything that had happened? "I crossed the line with Claire. Not fully, but enough."

Max was quiet for a long moment, a silence that felt like grace rather than judgment. He took the seat next to me. "And . . . are you here for absolution or understanding?"

"I don't know." The words spilled out faster than I'd planned. "I should feel guilty. Should be on my knees begging for forgiveness. But when I'm with her, it feels *right*. I don't know how else to explain it."

"And your vows?"

I huffed. "I love my job. I love counseling those kids and being part of a bigger picture."

Max studied me, his sharp gaze never missing a thing. "But?" he prompted.

"But nothing I've given to God feels as true as what I feel for her. And I don't know what the hell to do with that."

Max pursed his lips, remaining quiet. He had been that way ever since I could remember—letting the silence do the talking until I was ready to say more.

"I keep waiting for someone to tell me what the right choice is. The bishop says to rise to the challenge. You'll probably tell me to honor my commitments. But what if . . ."

He leaned back in his chair. "Go on."

"What if I'm meant to be with her?"

He shook his head, the motion unhurried. "You know what your problem is, Damian?"

I expected judgment. Condemnation.

"You're sitting here asking me for permission to follow your heart. You're a twenty-eight-year-old man. You have the same free will God gave every person on this planet."

My brow furrowed.

He crossed his arms. "You already know your truth. You've known since the moment she walked back into your life."

"But my vows—"

"Are promises you made when you were a different person who was dealing with grief and guilt that had nothing to do with His calling." What he said lodged in me the way incense clung to fabric—permeating, inescapable. "You think God wants you to be miserable? You think He wants you to spend your life denying the deepest part of yourself?"

I opened my mouth to protest, but he held up a hand. "The Church tells you celibacy is required, that you can't serve God and love a woman. But that's the Church talking, not God. And deep down, you know the difference."

"So, you're saying . . . ?"

Max stood, placing a hand on my shoulder. "I'm saying you don't need my permission, or the bishop's, or anyone else's to choose your path. If you want to leave the priesthood, then leave. If you want to stay and honor your vows, then stay. But stop asking other people to make the choice for you."

"And if I choose wrong?"

"There is no wrong choice," he said. "There's only the choice that's true to who you are."

All he'd done was strip away the pretense. I was already set on Claire.

"I think you're one of the most compassionate, caring men I know. You'll serve God whether you're wearing a collar or not. And I think Claire makes you a better version of yourself."

I stood, my mind clearer than it had been in months. "I want her."

"Then you know what you need to do first." His voice was gentle but firm. "Honor your commitments properly. If you're going to choose love, do it the right way."

"Thank you."

"Don't thank me. Thank yourself for finally being honest," Max said.

"I should get back." We said our goodbyes, and I made my way out of the sacristy.

I strolled down the path, passing through the canopy of trees, their branches breaking the sunlight into dappled patterns along the stone. The courtyard stretched silent around me—trimmed hedges, roses blooming red and pink against the gray Gothic walls, ivy climbing higher than I could reach. I lowered myself onto a weathered bench, the scent of earth and flowers heavy in the air. The sun warmed my face as Max's words replayed in my mind.

I'm saying you don't need my permission, or the bishop's, or anyone else's to choose your path.

He was right: I had been waiting for someone to tell me it was okay to want Claire—to love her. I'd been looking for absolution for feelings that didn't need absolving. What I'd been calling sin, Max called love. What I'd been calling weakness, he called revelation.

I stood, the collar pressing taut against my throat, no longer a burden laid upon me but a vow I meant to wrestle into a life I could live with. A life that was mine.

Chapter Twenty-Eight

CLAIRE

Six Years Ago

The afternoon light slanted through Dr. Cohen's office window. I tugged repeatedly at the hem of my long skirt, ensuring it covered the bandages on my thigh. A week had passed since Jasmine had found me—since the emergency room and the rushed prayers and the mandatory psychiatric hold. Now I was in this quiet office full of musty old books and the stench of burnt cheap coffee.

"I'm not crazy," I said, hating how small my voice sounded.

Dr. Cohen's dark brown, almost black, eyes held a calm, kind presence that made me want to spill every word and feeling I'd suppressed. But I'd spent years perfecting the art of keeping it all bottled up, burying the darkness so deep that sometimes I forgot it was there. Until last week, when the pain found its way out through my skin.

She settled into her leather chair, her tablet balanced on her knee. "No one thinks you're crazy, Claire. But we need to understand what brought you to this point."

I stared at my hands folded tight in my lap, while the cross weighed heavy around my neck.

"Can you tell me a little about what happened that night?" Dr. Cohen asked after a long moment of silence.

I pressed my palm against my thigh, over the thick edges of the bandage beneath the fabric. That night flashed through my mind: The sharp blade cutting into my skin. Deep. Not like the other times when I'd been careful, controlled. "I just . . . couldn't take it anymore."

"Take what?"

Such a simple question. The answer was anything but. How could I make anyone understand the relentless ache of never feeling enough, no matter what I did?

"Everything," I whispered. "School, family, Church. Everyone wants something from me. Everyone needs me to be a version of myself I don't know how to be."

Dr. Cohen made a note on her tablet, her stylus tapping lightly against the screen. "That sounds like a lot of pressure."

"The cutting helps. Usually." The words scratched my throat like broken glass. "Helps it all go quiet. All the voices—they stop."

She nodded, giving me space to continue or stop. My choice. When was the last time I'd felt like I had a choice?

"But this time was different," she prompted when I didn't continue.

"I keep trying to pray. But lately, God feels so far away. Like maybe He's disappointed too." The admission burned in my chest. "At least when I cut, I feel *something*."

Dr. Cohen set her tablet aside, leaning forward. "When you say God feels far away, what does that feel like?"

My brows rose. I expected judgment. But she seemed genuine in her curiosity about my relationship with faith.

"It's like . . ." I struggled to find the words. "Standing in an empty church. You know it's supposed to be filled with holiness, but all you hear is silence." Tears pricked my eyes. "I used to find peace there. Now I just feel empty."

A gentle breeze stirred the curtains, carrying with it the distant sound of traffic. Dr. Cohen waited, allowing me to sort my way through my jumbled thoughts.

"That night, I just wanted it all to stop," I whispered, tears finally spilling over.

"What made that night different from the others?" she asked gently.

I closed my eyes, reliving the crushing weight of failure, the scholarship review letter, the disappointed text from my mom. Rico's death. The breakup with Damian. "My life fell apart all at once. And for a moment, I thought maybe it would be easier if I just . . . stopped trying to hold it all together."

"Your file says your sister, Jasmine, found you."

I nodded. "I passed out. She said I was so pale. That there was so much blood." I touched my thigh again and the bandage hidden under my skirt. "The paramedics said if she'd found me twenty minutes later, it would have ended differently."

Dr. Cohen's gaze met mine. "Tell me, Claire. What does peace look like to you? If you could have it without hurting yourself?"

I'd sought peace in churches and whispered prayers my entire life. "I don't know," I admitted. "Maybe . . . being able to breathe without feeling like I'm failing everyone. Being able to make mistakes without hating myself. Existing without having to be perfect."

Dr. Cohen nodded. "That sounds worth working toward."

"I don't even know where to start."

"One step at a time," she said, picking up her tablet again. "One day at a time. Regular therapy sessions. Medication to help stabilize your mood. Most importantly, learning to be gentle with yourself."

I twisted the cross around my neck, the edges pressing into my fingertips. Maybe God hadn't abandoned me after all. Maybe He was just waiting for me to ask for help in a different way.

"I want to try," I whispered.

She smiled. "That's the first step. And, Claire?" She waited until I looked at her again. "You don't have to carry everything alone anymore."

For the first time since that night, a small sliver of hope crept in.

Dr. Cohen reached for a business card from her desk drawer. "There's a retreat center about an hour north of here. The Sisters of Divine Light run programs for people in recovery. Not just from addiction, but from trauma and feeling lost." She held the card out to me. "It's not therapy. More like finding your way back to yourself."

I took the card, running my thumb over the raised lettering. "You think I should go?"

"I think you should consider all your options," she answered. "Traditional therapy, medication, spiritual guidance—whatever combination feels right for you. The question is, What do you want your life to look like six months from now?"

I closed my eyes and pictured mornings where I didn't wake gasping and I could help without pretending. Where the voices stopped telling me I wasn't enough.

"I want to matter," I said finally. "I want to help people. To serve a purpose greater than myself." I opened my eyes, meeting her gaze. "But I want to do it as someone who's whole."

"Then you have some choices to make."

I tucked the business card into my purse as if it were a secret magic ticket to a possibility I'd never considered before.

After we said our goodbyes, I drove back to campus. I rolled down the windows, the crisp coastal breeze filling the car. The same highway stretched before me. The same salt air carried memories of home. But my grip on the steering wheel had eased, as if it was no longer the only thing keeping me tethered to the world like it had been on the drive over.

For the first time in months, I turned on the radio. Fleetwood Mac's "Landslide" filled the tired quietness, and instead of the music drowning me until I wanted to disappear, I wanted to sing along.

The girl who'd sliced that blade too deep was still part of me, but she was no longer the only part anymore.

Chapter Twenty-Nine

CLAIRE

Present Day

The school day had wrung me dry. A wine bottle rested in my firm grip, cool glass pressing against my fingers as I tilted it back for another sip, nursing the growing buzz.

My phone screen flashed, showing it was a little after eight p.m. The streetlight outside cast a soft glow through the big bay window, the curtains drawn back just enough to let in the night.

I shifted on the couch, pulling my knees up and setting the bottle on the end table beside me. The Cabernet Sauvignon warmed my chest, numbing the edges of my anxiety. But not enough to silence the thoughts running laps in my head. I stared at Jasmine's contact icon, hesitating for a second. Taking a breath, I hit the FaceTime button. The screen rang twice, and then her face appeared, framed by her messy bedroom and a pile of laundry in the background.

"What's up, *ate*?" she asked, squinting into the camera. She could probably tell I'd been drinking just by the way I was holding the phone too low and crooked.

"Hey," I mumbled, taking another drink. "You busy?"

"Nah, just folding socks and trying to pretend it's not the most boring thing on earth." Jasmine set the laundry aside and leaned closer to the screen, her brows knitting together. "What's going on? You look like you've got a good buzz."

"Working on it." I took another quick swig. "Something happened between me and Damian."

She didn't respond. Just nodded, waiting. Jasmine knew when to let me get there on my own. Especially when I'd been drinking.

I took a breath. "It's all Mrs. Walker's fault. If she hadn't sent me to make copies, Damian and I wouldn't have—" His name was like lead on my tongue. "God, I don't know how to tell you."

"Just spit it out."

"Okay," I said, squeezing my eyes shut for a second before looking back at the screen. "It happened in the church. I ran into him, and our crosses got tangled. It was *so* stupid. But we were close. Like, really close." *And I'm rambling. Maybe I'm drunker than I think.*

Her eyes widened, but she didn't interrupt.

"And then we sort of maybe ended up in the confessional because someone walked in, and it was such a tight space that I ended up straddling his fucking lap." The more I said out loud, the more ridiculous it sounded, but the way my heart raced just thinking about it was far from hilarious. "We didn't have sex. But we both, you know, *got there*, if you know what I mean."

Jasmine blinked, the corners of her mouth curving up. "Damn, *ate*."

"I know." I heaved a sigh. "But it felt like every inch of me was on fire, and I couldn't think straight. All I wanted was more."

"More?" she asked carefully, testing the waters.

"Yeah," I admitted, a lump forming in my throat. "I've missed it, Jaz. The physical touch. The release. I thought I'd let go of that need, but I guess I haven't. And now I'm falling apart."

"Listen," she started. "You're not a robot. You're human. And that doesn't make you a bad person."

"But it makes me a bad nun."

"Or maybe it just makes you a woman who's learning she doesn't have to be a saint on a pedestal?"

I huffed. "Even the saints did horrible things."

"Well, then, there you go." She bit her bottom lip. "It's okay to question whether or not this is still the right path for you."

"I just . . . I don't know if I can say my perpetual vows when there's a part of me that feels incomplete," I said.

Jasmine's expression softened. "Whatever you decide, it's your choice. Not God's. Not the Church's. Yours."

Tears trickled down my cheeks. "What about my students? What will the parish think?"

"There are other ways you can leave your mark on the world, *ate*. And who the fuck cares what anyone else thinks? This is your life."

All I could do was nod.

We spoke for a few more minutes, the conversation shifting to lighter topics until the buzz of wine and exhaustion began making my eyelids heavy. After we said our goodbyes, I set my phone on the coffee table and sank into the couch.

Jasmine's words lingered. *My choice. Not God's. Not the Church's. Mine.*

The longer I sat there, the more it tugged at the corners of my beliefs, unraveling threads I had always considered unbreakable. I grabbed the bottle of wine off the end table and took another sip, swishing the sweet bitterness over my tongue.

Hey, God, if You're up there laughing at my mess of a life right now, the least You could do is give me a sign. Or maybe another bottle of wine.

A sound a lot like a knock came from the door. I ignored it. *Just my imagination.* Or it was the lingering effects of the wine playing tricks on me.

The knock came again, more insistent this time.

I groaned and pushed off the couch, swaying as I walked toward the door. The buzz of the wine was wearing off, but the exposed fragility persisted. The last thing I needed was someone showing up unannounced.

Peering through the peephole, there he was—Damian. Tall, broad shouldered, and lean, he took up the entire doorway. He didn't look like he belonged here in the real world. It was apparently too much to ask that he stay confined to the walls of the church—too much to ask that he stay a part of the stained glass and the hallowed halls that held all my doubt and guilt.

Is this my sign?

I opened the door. "Father Bellucci." The words came out more sarcastic than intended.

His eyes flicked to the half-empty bottle in my hand, and his lips quirked up. "That kind of night, huh?"

I rolled my eyes, not entirely in the mood for his Damianness. "What do you want?"

He shifted his weight to one leg, glancing past me into the living room before meeting my gaze again. There was a vulnerableness to his expression. "I needed to see you," he said, voice low.

I stepped aside, letting him in, and then closed the door behind me.

I made my way back to the couch and dropped onto the cushion, the fine grooves of the twill pressing into my legs.

Damian sat next to me, the space between us too small and too large all at once.

I took another sip from the bottle and held it out to him. "Want some?"

He stared as if he was weighing some silent internal debate. He reached over and took it after a moment, studied the label, and then brought it to his lips and took a short swig. His face crinkled as he lowered the bottle.

"It's not the communion wine," I said with a half-hearted laugh, trying to break the tension.

"No," he replied, handing the bottle back to me. "Definitely not."

A thick silence settled between us, filling every inch of the room. Clearing my throat, I asked, "So, what's up? Everything okay?"

"Claire." He inhaled deeply. "I don't think I can be strong anymore. I don't *want* to."

My brow furrowed. "You're not making any sense, Dames."

"I want you," he said.

I shook my head. "And how do you think that's going to work?"

Damian's expression softened, but I didn't miss the conflict in his green eyes. "I'm not sure yet."

Letting out a slow breath, I said, "There's just so much that could go wrong, and I won't be responsible for a scandal."

"You won't be. I promise." He wasn't a priest in this moment, but the boy I used to know, who made mistakes and carried regrets. Who used to kiss me like I was the center of his universe.

"Don't make promises you can't keep."

He scooted closer, eyes searching mine. "By the light that guides us, I promise to always find my way back to you, no matter how lost I get."

My breath caught in my throat, and I swore my heart stopped. Damian's handsome face, illuminated by the moonlight and streetlight streaming through the large bay window, held a tentative hopefulness. That familiar spark in my lower belly returned.

I responded, "By the light that guides us, I'll be your safe harbor."

He brought his lips inches from mine and recited a verse from the Bible. From the book of Psalms. " 'Take delight in the Lord, and He will give you the desires of your heart.' "

Before I could speak, he closed the small distance between us, silencing me with his mouth. A surprised squeak escaped me, and his lips tilted up in a smile against mine. He pulled me beneath him and settled his hips between my bare legs. The only layers between us were his black slacks and my oversized tee and underwear.

The thought of fucking Damian in his clerical uniform turned me on more than it should have. *I'm going to hell.*

His lips traced my jawline to the curve of my neck, his tongue working in tandem with his mouth. I couldn't stifle the whimper that slipped free.

"I don't know if I can do this," I said as I ground my pussy against his rock-hard cock.

He drew back, hovering just above me. "Do you want to stop?"

I bit my bottom lip, staring into his green eyes. *Do I?* Some saintly part of me hissed to stop. The other part—the rest of me—arched closer, traitor that it was.

"I should say yes," I whispered, my fingers tracing the line of his jaw. "But I've never been good at doing what I should."

"Say it, Claire." He rested his forehead against mine. "Tell me I can fuck you."

A corner of my mouth rose. *God, I love his dirty talk.* "On one condition."

His lips grazed mine, featherlight, the touch sending shivers down my spine. "Anything."

"You finish inside me."

Worry furrowed his brow.

"I still have my IUD. And I want to feel you completely."

He nodded, trailing kisses down the curve of my neck down to my collarbone, electrifying every nerve. It had been so long that I'd almost forgotten the pleasure behind desire.

My hand drifted to his belt buckle, metal clinking as I undid it. I popped the button of his pants and unzipped them. Using the tips of my fingers, I stroked his length, and a guttural groan escaped his chest. *Was he always this big?*

"Don't," he said in a tone that surprised me. "I need to be inside you. Please."

My lips curled up. "I like you begging."

He grinned, his fingers tracing the hem of my underwear along my inner thigh. "Let's see how ready you are." Sliding the material aside, he plunged one finger into me, and I shuddered, a breathy moan breaking free. "Fuck. You're soaked."

I lifted my hips, and he slid my underwear off. Holding himself above me, he lined up his cock with my entrance. "Spread your legs wider for me, Sparrow," he murmured, staring straight into my eyes.

I obeyed, drawing in a deep breath, letting it out in broken gasps as he parted me. My back arched off the cushions, and the intoxicating, burning stretch made me whimper.

"Shit," I rasped, caught between pain and need. My legs shook, and part of me wanted to tell him to slow down, but I didn't pull away. "Wait," I panted, pressing my palm to his chest, stopping him. "It's too much."

Damian's lips ghosted the shell of my ear. "You can take it. Just breathe, love."

His hands gripped my hips, reverent and claiming. Achingly slow, he slid in farther and farther, holding himself back from thrusting himself into me. "That's it," Damian purred. "You're going to take every inch of my cock."

Bottoming out, he left me so full I could hardly breathe. Every muscle in his body trembled, coiled tight, giving me time to adjust to him. Sweat dotted his forehead. My walls pulsed, clenching, and he swore under his breath.

Once the lingering tinges of pain faded into bliss, I reached up and brought his gaze to mine. "It's okay. Let go."

"Are you sure?"

I nodded. "Yes."

He placed his forehead against mine as he pulled out, languid and unhurried, and pushed back into me. He released a guttural groan, and the slow movement beckoned another moan from me. I didn't care how desperate I sounded.

But Damian was still holding back; it was clear in his tense arms, clenching and unclenching jaw, and shuddering thighs. Each thrust grew rougher—harder—as his restraint seemed to evaporate with every stroke.

He seized my wrists and pinned them above my head. I gasped, and his lips captured mine, hungry and open, tongue searching, teeth biting. Time ceased to exist as I lost myself in him and the sharp, sweet ache where our bodies joined.

We panted half-formed words and expletives between kisses and the sound of flesh meeting, the two of us drawn together by a gravity that allowed nothing extraneous. He gripped my hip with his free hand, the cold metal of his ring biting into my skin. I pretended he'd made that commitment to me while he fucked me faster. Pretended he was mine as he chased pleasure with a focus that bordered on violence. That thought alone pushed me over the edge, and my walls pulsed around his length. The first penetrating orgasm I'd had since . . . God, I didn't even know.

Damian continued to piston his hips into mine, even as my body tremored with waves of pleasure and I spasmed around him. The overstimulation blurred my vision, my mind blanking with ecstasy. For a second, I thought I might faint. But I grabbed his ass and dug my nails in, riding out every aftershock, greedy for more.

"Damian," I gasped. "Oh God." I came again, my body racked with smaller, sharper spasms. I'd never come twice, not with anyone else, and certainly not like this.

"Please," I begged. "Harder."

He buried his face in my neck, breathing me in. "You're killing me, Sparrow." He hooked one of my legs over his shoulder, angling his thrusts, and fucked me deep, again and again, hitting that spot inside me that made me see stars.

Damian continued, unrelenting, until I wasn't sure how many times I came. More than twice. Possibly four. I'd lost the ability to count. He pressed his lips to mine, messy and desperate, swallowing the sounds I made.

With one last brutal thrust, he pulsed inside me, releasing the hot rush of his come. He collapsed onto me, both of us breathless.

I brushed my fingers through his hair, wanting this moment to last forever. But that was wishful thinking.

He pushed up, resting on his forearms. "You okay?"

I nodded. "Yeah."

He straightened and went into the bathroom, and I started to clean up. A few minutes later, he came out with a washcloth and took care of me.

"What're you thinking?" Damian asked, grabbing my underwear off the floor. He slid them back onto me.

We stood there in awkward silence while I considered my words. "I'm thinking you should probably get back to the rectory before anyone notices you're gone."

"Yeah. You're probably right." He stuffed his hands into the pockets of his slacks and started toward the door.

I followed.

He turned to face me. "We'll talk later?"

God knew I couldn't talk about this right now. I needed time to process the impossible turn of events of the night. Nodding, I forced my lips to curve up. "Of course, Dames."

Before he walked out, he placed a chaste kiss on my lips.

I closed the door behind him and leaned against it, my heart racing. The lingering warmth of his touch was like both a blessing and a curse. I traced my lips with my fingertips, swollen and tender from his kisses, and wondered if this was what redemption looked like—messy and complicated and nothing like the clean salvation I'd always imagined. I whispered a prayer, not for forgiveness, but for courage.

Chapter Thirty

CLAIRE

The cold December morning sun cast towering shadows across the highway as Damian drove us to the chancery. We hadn't had time to talk after that night, our duties keeping us busy. When Bishop Valenti had asked to meet with us, it was the perfect opportunity to address the elephant in the room. I just didn't know how.

The blur of pine trees outside the window couldn't hold my attention. My mind kept circling back to the night with Damian that I swore I wouldn't think about.

He'd been rough in all the right ways, yet his touch had carried a reverence that had left me undone as he'd worshipped my body, each thrust a claim on my soul. It had been our first time, and it'd been perfect. I ached for more, craving the heat of him, but the want twisted sharp inside me. I wasn't supposed to feel this way.

Damian sat beside me in the driver's seat, one hand on the wheel, the other resting on his thigh. "You're quiet," he said, breaking the silence that had settled between us since leaving Saint Anthony's.

"Just thinking." I shifted in my seat, hyperaware of the small space between us in his truck. The scent of his cologne mixed with the leather seats made it hard to focus.

"About?"

"Everything." I wrapped my arms around myself, staring out at the passing trees. "Can we talk about what happened?"

He was quiet for a moment. "Of course," he said, tone rough in a way that made my stomach flutter.

Not knowing where to start, I said, "I love teaching."

"And I love my job too. Maybe we don't have to give this up to be together."

I studied his profile. "You really think that's going to work?"

He glanced at me, the sun highlighting his green eyes. "We won't know if we don't try."

"Dames, I don't know. I need time to think about this. *We* need to think about this." I looked out the window again, the chancery building coming into view.

"Think all you want, Sparrow. But my mind's already made up."

Part of me wanted to tell him he didn't get to decide for both of us. The other part—the reckless, traitorous part—wanted to let him.

Damian pulled into the parking lot, but neither of us moved to get out. The building loomed before us. Its beige walls had simple Advent decor that somehow appeared both welcoming and intimidating.

"Everything's going to be okay, Claire," Damian murmured. "Ready?"

I nodded, my throat tight. He didn't seem bothered at all. And here I was inwardly freaking out.

We walked toward the entrance, our footsteps falling in sync. My black sneakers echoed through the corridor, my heart pounding against my rib cage. The strong scent of incense wafted through the air. I took a deep breath, trying to compose myself. This was just a check-in meeting. But that didn't stop the tightness from twisting in my gut.

Damian was right on my heels, his footsteps heavier. We made our way to the receptionist's desk, and she immediately escorted us to the bishop's office.

"Father Bellucci, Sister Claire. Glad you two could make it." Bishop Valenti greeted us warmly, his voice deep and authoritative but with a kindness to it. He gestured to the chairs in front of his desk.

We returned his polite greeting, and my gaze drifted to Damian as I sat. He was quiet, jaw set, with his eyes fixed ahead like he was bracing himself for whatever was about to happen.

I smoothed my skirt over my knees while Damian took the seat beside me, the chair creaking under his weight. Our gazes met, and my pulse spiked. I shifted my attention to the bishop and his expectant gaze.

A small Advent wreath lay on the oak filing cabinet in the corner of the office. The light filtering through the stained glass window cast a soft multicolored glow across the room, adding a kind of quiet sanctity looming over this visit.

"I have to say," Bishop Valenti began, glancing over the notes in front of him, "I'm impressed with how well you two have worked together. The feedback regarding the upcoming marriage retreat has been very positive."

My stomach clenched at the praise. *Positive.* If only he knew how difficult it had been.

"Thank you," Damian said, voice resolute but carrying an edge I knew well. He was struggling despite saying he'd made up his mind.

Bishop Valenti smiled, leaning back in his chair. "You know, organizing a retreat like this is no small task. It requires patience, communication, and trust. You've shown you can work as a team, and that's essential—not just for this retreat, but for the work you do in the parish as well."

A sharp ache bloomed in my chest like a needle pressing into tender skin. *Patience. Communication. Trust.* He needed to stop with all the praise. I was a nun who had broken my vow of celibacy for my high school sweetheart.

I stole a glance at Damian, who appeared calm and unbothered.

"Love and teamwork go hand in hand," Bishop Valenti continued. "Whether it's a marriage or a working relationship, both require understanding and a willingness to see past differences. You both come from different paths and experiences, but you've managed to find common ground. You two should be proud."

I swallowed, the air around me thickening with Damian's presence. The bishop had no idea just how much *common ground* we shared.

Bishop Valenti smiled again, his eyes warm. "I know the couples attending this retreat will benefit greatly from the guidance you'll be providing. You've both demonstrated a deep commitment to your work and to the community. Keep that in mind as you move forward."

Damian nodded.

"Thank you, Your Excellency," I managed to say.

How are we supposed to keep up this charade?

The bishop rose from his chair, signaling the end of the meeting. "Keep up the good work, both of you. God bless."

We stood, offering quiet thanks before making our way to the door. As we stepped into the empty hallway, the silence only amplified the charged air between us. Our gazes met, and my breath caught in my throat. For a moment, neither of us said anything.

Damian's green eyes had turned a shade darker, like the ocean before a storm, his expression caught between frustration and—

"I want you, Claire. I don't care if it's wrong," he rasped.

Before I could respond, he grabbed my wrist and pulled me into an empty conference room. The door clicked shut behind us, and suddenly, he was everywhere—his scent, his warmth, the solid wall of his chest as he backed me against the wall.

"Dames, we can't," I whispered.

His hands found my waist, pulling me flush against him. "Tell me to stop," he breathed, his lips hovering just above mine. "Tell me you don't want this too."

I couldn't. Instead of answering, I wrapped my arms around his neck and pulled him down to me. His mouth crashed into mine. I melted into him, all thoughts of propriety dissolving under the heat of his lips.

Every nerve lit up as his hands traveled up my sides, leaving a trail of heat, until my back arched of its own accord. The rough scrape of stubble against my skin, the press of his chest crushing my back against the door, the way his kiss stole not only my breath but the lies I told myself—it all unraveled me.

"We have to stop," I breathed, even as my body betrayed me, pressing closer.

He pulled back just enough to meet my gaze, his lips swollen and his eyes dark with desire. "Do you really want to?"

I closed my eyes, heart pounding. "No, I don't."

"So, we're doing this?"

I nodded. "Yes, Dames. We're doing this."

My body ached for him, chest tight with the truth I'd buried for years: I still wanted him. More than vows. More than rules. More than the safety of pretending I didn't. This longing was terrifying, but in his arms, it felt inevitable. Like I was made to surrender to him.

Chapter Thirty-One

DAMIAN

The next few days blurred together in a haze of stolen moments and midnight escapes. I spent every free moment I had at Claire's cottage. We'd talk for hours, share takeout on her couch, and make love until we both forgot who we were supposed to be. But around midnight, reality would creep back in, and I'd force myself to leave—though every step away from her felt blasphemous.

I went through the motions of priesthood: confession hours, youth group meetings, even volunteering to help Father Max with his parish's administrative work. But my mind was always with Claire. The way she writhed beneath me, her soft moans echoing in my ears, and the curve of her body molding to mine.

During Mass, my hands shook as I raised the chalice, remembering how they'd traced her skin just hours before. Even in prayer, when I should have been focused on God, all I could think about was her tight cunt clenching around my cock as she came.

She was everywhere. The scent of her perfume on my clothes. The phantom touch of her fingers on my skin. Little pieces of her scattered throughout my day, like breadcrumbs leading me back to her bed every night.

Friday evening, I sat in the confessional, the wooden walls narrowing around me. It was the same confessional where we'd—

No. Don't think about that.

But the memory came anyway—her weight on me, her breath hot against my neck.

"Bless me, Father, for I have sinned," a parishioner began, their voice muffled through the screen.

I started the prayer automatically, but my mind wandered to Claire's cottage, where I knew I'd end up in just a few hours. What kind of priest was I? The kind who spent his nights wrapped around a nun? The kind who couldn't stop even if he tried?

"Father?" The voice pulled me back. "Are you still there?"

"Yes, sorry, Simon. Go ahead," I managed to get out. How could I offer absolution when my own heart was so tangled in sin?

Later that night, I grabbed the spare key that was hiding under the ceramic frog in the garden and entered Claire's cottage through the back door. The house was shrouded in a quiet darkness; the only sound was the soft hum of the refrigerator from the kitchen.

I made my way down the hallway and gently pushed open the bedroom door. Claire was propped up against a mountain of pillows, her face illuminated by the soft glow of her tablet. The screen cast shadows that danced across the walls, and her eyes were focused, moving steadily across the words. With her glasses resting on the bridge of her nose and her dark hair framing her face, she was enchanting, and I was utterly hopeless.

She peered up at me and smiled. "You're not tired of me yet?"

"Fuck no." I shrugged off my shirt and threw it aside without a second thought, the cool air against my skin. I climbed onto the bed, crawled toward her, and pressed my lips against hers. "It feels like forever since I've seen you," I said between peppering her with kisses and pulling her beneath me. Our bodies sank into the plush mattress.

My hand slipped under her tank top, fingertips tracing the silky warmth of her skin.

She giggled. "It's only been a few hours."

God, she's beautiful like this. I wasted no time pulling her underwear off. "Too long."

"What're you doing?"

"Making up for lost time." I kissed my way down her stomach, spreading her thighs. Running my fingers up and down her slit, I teased her before thrusting into her tight wet heat. "This is mine." I glanced at her face, and those beautiful hooded gray eyes filled with desire.

"Yes," she hissed.

"You're going to come like this, Sparrow. Then I'll make you come on my cock."

Positioning myself between her thighs, I pressed my lips to her entrance. Her breath hitched, and a soft gasp escaped her. I parted her folds with my tongue, tracing delicate patterns on her clit.

"Fuck, I love the way you taste."

Her body tensed beneath me. She gripped my shoulders, nails digging in. The scent of her arousal, sweet and intoxicating, fueled my desire even more. She tasted like a mix of salt and honey, an addictive combination. I unraveled her like a tapestry, revealing the raw beauty beneath.

"Oh my . . . I'm close."

"Sweet girl," I murmured. "I'll never get enough of you." Her scent wrapped around me, her thighs quivering as I held her open and licked, every flick of my tongue sending her closer to orgasm.

As I curled a finger in her slick cunt, she tightened around me. Fuck, she gripped me like she was made for this. For me. I moved in and out of her, savoring her whimpers and her hips grinding against my hand. No one would ever get to touch her like this. No one would get to hear her fall apart. *She's mine, and I'll make sure she never forgets it.*

Her moans grew louder, chest rising and falling in shallow gasps.

She was on the edge. I brought my tongue back to her clit, and she sucked in a sharp breath. Her body convulsed as she came, her orgasm coating my tongue.

I studied her flushed face, her gray eyes gleaming with satisfaction. But this was far from over. Grabbing her hips, my fingers squeezed her soft flesh as I flipped her over. She squealed but didn't resist. I yanked her to her knees, positioning her ass in the air. Leaning over the curve of her spine, I brushed my lips against her ear. "I'm not done with you."

She arched into me. I tangled my hand in her hair at the base of her scalp, tugging gently to tilt her head back and catching her moan with my mouth. Her eyes fluttered closed.

I positioned myself at her warm entrance and parted her slowly.

Her hands fisted in the sheets. "Shit."

I pushed into her, a low groan escaping me as her tight cunt gripped my cock. "Fuck, the way you take me . . . I could spend eternity inside you, and it wouldn't be enough."

Her body rocked against mine, meeting each deep plunge of my length with her own desperate need. I kissed her back, her shoulder, tasting the salt on her skin.

Straightening, I gripped her hips tighter, pounding into her more insistently.

Claire looked back at me, her gray eyes wild. "Don't stop," she gasped, wanton. I had no intention of stopping, too lost in her—the feel of her, the sounds she made.

Her walls clamped down on me as she came again, screaming my name. I slowed my thrusts, her orgasm milking me. I wasn't going to last much longer.

"Get on your back," I ordered.

She obeyed in spite of her body shuddering. Her eyes, glazed and spent with passion, met mine. Those luscious lips curved into a satisfied smile.

I settled between her legs and slid into her once more, her wet cunt stretching to accommodate me. Her arms wrapped around my neck, pulling me down to her. Our bodies moved in sync, her hips rising to meet each vigorous thrust.

"Fuck, Claire, I'm going to—"

Pressure built at the base of my spine. I fucked her faster, harder. Kissed her, exploring every inch of her mouth with my tongue. Drawing back, I stared down at her. She was beautiful with her flushed cheeks and hair splayed out beneath her. My body tensed, and I sank into her wet heat one last time, my cock pulsing as I filled her with each wave of my release. I groaned, burying my face in the side of her neck, unable to resist pressing my lips to her skin.

Once my climax passed, I rolled off her and onto my back. Our breaths fell into the same rhythm, our hearts pounding in tandem. Her skin gleamed with a faint sheen of sweat, and her body continued trembling.

"That was . . ."

"Yeah," I agreed. She didn't need to speak. In the sensual moments when we moved as one, something deeper than language passed between us, binding us closer with each breath.

A moment of silence passed as I caught my breath. "Claire. I've been meaning to tell you—" I turned onto my side and found her asleep, her face peaceful in the dim light.

My lips curved up. This wasn't physical desire alone—though God knew that was there, burning through my veins like holy fire. It was everything about her. Her strength. Her brokenness. The way she questioned facts I'd always taken for granted.

I leaned my forehead against her shoulder, breathing in her sweet scent. In a few hours, I'd have to slip away again, back to the silence of my rectory—a place that felt emptier each time I left her. My nights spent with Claire carved deeper certainty into me, undeniable no matter how hard I tried. I would never get enough of her. Not in this lifetime or the next.

"I love you, Claire," I whispered against her skin.

Chapter Thirty-Two

DAMIAN

The weekend of the retreat came faster than I'd expected. Before I knew it, I was standing in the main conference room, looking over a room full of couples. Some held hands. Others sat apart, tension written across their faces. Smaller conference rooms were off to the side for confessions and private counseling sessions. The entire venue was utilized efficiently to give these couples a chance to reconnect and find their way back to forgiveness.

As I greeted the attendees, Jasmine and Rhea walked in, tentative but hopeful, asking if there was room for one more. Without hesitation, I welcomed them, directing them to sign up at the table. A few couples shot disapproving glances their way, and not long after, those couples quietly left. I didn't think much of it. This retreat wasn't about judgment. It was about love, in all its forms. And maybe, if I was honest, it was about learning to forgive for loving against expectation.

I glanced at Claire across the room, radiant even in her plain habit. My lips curved as she made announcements informing everyone we'd be starting soon. The couples took their seats, and after a few icebreaker activities, I broke away with the first pair on the list for a counseling session.

The soft hum of the hotel's air conditioning filled the room, muffling the conversations from the retreaters to a gentle murmur. I sat across from Kyle and Lisa Smith in the small, dimly lit conference room. The space between them seemed miles wide, echoing the hurt that came from years of small wounds that had never quite healed.

Kyle's fingers drummed against his knee, his eyes trained on the floor as if answers might be written in the patterned carpet. Lisa sat with her arms crossed, exhaustion and quiet sorrow mixed on her face. They'd been married for over a decade, but the erosion of time had left them looking more like strangers than partners, two people who'd forgotten how to forgive the small daily betrayals that chipped away at love.

"So, who'd like to start?" I prodded gently. This was supposed to be a safe space for them, a place to unpack years of old wounds and find their way back to grace.

Lisa glanced at Kyle, but he stayed silent, his jaw rigid. Sighing, she spoke first, her voice laced with exhaustion. "We don't talk anymore. We just discuss logistics. Who's picking up kids and who's paying what bill. That's it."

Kyle's head snapped up. "What do you want me to say? Every time I try to bring something up, you shut down or it turns into a fight."

Lisa let out a bitter laugh. "Are you kidding me right now? You don't try to bring things up, Kyle. You wait until you're pissed off and then explode about whatever's been bothering you for weeks."

"Hold on," I said, raising my hand. The leather chair creaked as I leaned forward. "Kyle, can you give me a specific example? Preferably recent."

He wiped both hands down his face. "Last week, she bought another throw pillow. We already have, like, fifteen throw pillows on that damn couch, and I can't sit down without moving half of them. So, I said something."

"You didn't 'say something,' " Lisa snapped. "You walked in from work, and the first words out of your mouth were, 'Seriously, Lisa? Another pillow?' Like I'm some kind of idiot who doesn't know how to manage money."

Kyle's shoulders sagged. "It's not about the money."

"Then what is it about?"

Kyle stared at his hands for a long moment, the AC humming its chorus. "I just . . . I feel like I don't belong in my own house anymore. It's all perfect and pretty, and I'm afraid to touch anything. I come home tired, and there's nowhere I can just exist without causing a mess."

Lisa's expression softened, but her voice remained guarded. "So, instead of telling me that, you attack the pillow?"

"I wasn't attacking the pillow," he said without conviction.

I cleared my throat. "Kyle, what did you want Lisa to hear when you said that about the pillow?"

He paused again, thinking. Longer this time.

"That I miss being comfortable in *our* home. That I miss feeling like she actually wants me there and isn't just tolerating me."

Lisa's breath caught. "You miss . . ." She shook her head. "What? Of course I want you there. I love you."

"I know you love me. But do you *like* me? Do you really enjoy having me around, or am I just an obligation you married ten years ago?"

Lisa's eyes filled with tears, and silence stretched between them. "I . . ." she started, then stopped. "I guess I've been so focused on making the perfect house that I forgot to make it a home for you— for us."

"I miss feeling like we're a team," Kyle said, voice cracking. "I miss laughing with you. I miss feeling like you want to hear about my day."

"I do want to hear about your day," Lisa whispered. "But you come home and you look so tired, and I think, if I can just make everything perfect, then maybe you won't be stressed anymore. But that's stupid, isn't it?"

"No, it's not stupid," I said. "You're both trying to love each other. You're just out of sync."

Kyle finally looked directly at Lisa. "I don't need perfect, Lis. I just need you. I need to feel like I'm your person, not your roommate."

"You are my person." Lisa placed her hand on his arm, tentative. "You're my favorite person. I'm sorry I forgot to show you that."

Kyle and Lisa were both watching me now, their eyes filled with hope.

"Forgiveness isn't a onetime decision," I said, thinking of my own failures and need for grace. "It's a daily choice—especially in the small moments when pride wants to win, and our instinct for self-protection makes us cling to being right rather than being loving."

As the words left my mouth, I realized I wasn't talking just to them; I was preaching to myself—the man who'd been carrying guilt for eight years and had pushed away the one person who might have helped him heal.

When their fingers finally touched, the relief was visible on both their faces. Their marriage wasn't magically fixed, but I could see the start of their healing journey in the careful way they held hands, fragile, like they were afraid to break again.

"We have a lot to work on," Kyle said.

"Yeah," Lisa agreed. "But I want to work on it. With you."

"The thing about forgiveness is that it's not a feeling. It's a decision. And sometimes you have to choose it until the feeling catches up."

Kyle nodded slowly. "Father, how do we make sure this sticks? That we don't just fall back into the same patterns?"

"Practice," I said simply. "Patience. Talk before you're angry. Ask for what you need instead of hoping the other person will guess. And when you mess up, because you will, forgive each other faster than you think you deserve."

An hour passed as we worked through their specific grievances, but underneath it all was a thread of grace—the radical decision to release each other from the debt of past hurts. When they left the room, their hands were intertwined, tentative but real. It was small, almost imperceptible, but it was love.

Left alone in the quiet space, my own words echoed in my mind. I'd always thought forgiveness had to be earned. That love had to be perfect to be worthy. Leaning back in the chair, I scrubbed a hand over my face. Claire flashed through my mind—her laughter from earlier that morning and the way she'd looked at me like I was still worth saving.

I shook my head, trying to clear the thoughts, but they clung to the forefront of my mind.

The door creaked open, and Claire peeked in, backlit by the hallway lights. She stepped inside, and I caught that new scent of vanilla lotion she'd started using, mixed with jasmine.

"Everything okay?" she asked.

Despite the weight on my chest, I almost smiled. "Just thinking."

"Oh no," she said, and there was that way she'd always been able to find light even in dark moments through gentle teasing. But then her expression grew serious. "We're ready for the next activity, but . . ." She hesitated, closing the door behind her with a soft click.

The change in her demeanor made my pulse quicken. "But what?"

She stayed near the doorway, her gray eyes searching my face in the dim hotel lighting. She fidgeted with the edge of her sleeve—a nervous behavior I remembered from when we were young.

"Claire?" I prompted, tone rougher than I'd intended.

"Damian." My name came out soft, almost demure. "I've been meaning to tell you something."

I twisted the ring on my finger.

She took a shaky breath. "I was angry at you for eight years."

The words hit me in the chest, even though I'd known it. "Claire—"

She held up a hand. "Let me finish. I was angry because you left. Because you shut me out. You decided for both of us that what we had didn't matter anymore."

I swallowed hard and straightened. "You have every right to be angry."

"I know." She stepped closer. "But I'm ready to let go *completely* now."

"Claire . . ." I couldn't find words. My chest split in two.

"I'm not saying it doesn't hurt anymore," she continued. "I choose to stop letting that hurt define everything else."

I closed the distance between us then, my hands shaking as I cupped her face. Her skin was warm beneath my palms, and I could feel her pulse racing. "Thank you," I whispered. "You have no idea how much this means to me."

Her eyes fluttered closed for just a moment. When she opened them again, they were bright with unshed tears, but there was something else there too—peace, maybe. Relief.

I leaned down, and she rose up to meet my lips, and it was like coming home. She tasted of mint tea and an indefinable quality that was purely Claire. Her hands fisted in the fabric of my shirt, anchoring us both to this precious moment.

The kiss was soft. Reverent. Not the desperate passion of our youth. A communion of souls that had found their way back to each other across years of hurt and time.

After we broke apart, I rested my forehead against hers, our ragged breaths mingling.

"We need to be careful," she whispered, but there was wonder in her voice instead of worry, like she was marveling at a beautiful landscape rather than a dangerous cliff.

I pressed one last chaste kiss to her lips. "You just gave me the greatest gift I've ever received."

She smiled, remaining silent.

I wanted to hold on to her forever, chain her to me and never let the world, God, or time pry her away again. But I knew how easily she could be taken from me. Her mercy wasn't just a gift; it was the blood in my veins and the breath in my lungs. The thought of losing it—losing her—terrified me more than damnation ever could.

Chapter Thirty-Three

DAMIAN

After lunch, the retreat resumed with a group activity. I glanced at Jasmine and Rhea, their fingers intertwined in quiet defiance in a world that still questioned their love. Next to them, the Andersons sat apart, Mrs. Anderson's perfectly manicured nails tapping against her knee in an anxious rhythm.

Claire stood at the front of the circle, her posture confident despite the questions we were about to ask. She held up a small stack of index cards. "For this next exercise, we're going to focus on authenticity. Each of you will receive a card with a question designed to help you explore the masks we wear, sometimes even with the people closest to us."

She moved around the circle of tables, placing a card face down in front of each couple. Her fingers brushed mine as she set our card down, sending a jolt of electricity through me.

"The goal isn't to solve every problem or find perfect answers," Claire continued, returning to her position. "It's to practice being honest with your partner and with yourselves. Sometimes the bravest thing we can do is admit when we're struggling."

She glanced at me, and I saw a shared understanding of just how difficult this kind of honesty could be flicker in her eyes.

"Take turns reading the questions aloud and answering them. Remember, this is a safe space. What's shared here stays here." Claire settled into her chair beside me. "Father Bellucci and I will be here if you need guidance, but try to listen without judgment and speak without fear."

Kyle picked up his card, turning it over. He cleared his throat and read, "When do you feel the most like you're wearing a mask in your relationship?"

The silence that followed grew heavy with anticipation. Lisa's sharp intake of breath drew my attention as Kyle set the card down and looked at her.

"I look at myself in the mirror each morning and wonder who I'm trying to be: the successful businessman or the perfect husband. It feels like wearing a mask that gets heavier every day." The raw honesty in Kyle's words cracked through the awkwardness and opened the room. The other couples shifted in their seats, recognition flickering across their faces.

"And the worst part," he added, "is that I'm terrified of taking it off. Because what if what's underneath isn't enough?"

My chest tightened. How many mornings had I stood in front of the mirror and adjusted my collar to play the role of *perfect priest*?

"I understand the feeling," Rachel said, her young face earnest. "Malcolm and I are newlyweds, but some days I feel like we're already losing each other. Like we're so busy trying to be what others expect that we forget who we truly are."

Malcolm reached for her hand, and the simple gesture brought tears to Rachel's eyes.

Jasmine leaned forward. "For years, Rhea and I lived behind walls of our own making. The Church told us our love was wrong, so we tried to hide it, to pretend it was less than what it was." She glanced at her wife with affection. "But love doesn't work that way. The more you try to contain it, the more it demands to be seen."

Claire shifted in her chair, and I didn't need to look at her to know those words had hit home.

Love demands to be seen. Refuses to be contained.

"What about you, Father?" Mrs. Anderson's voice cut through my thoughts. "Surely as a priest, you must have insight into how to overcome these barriers."

Clearing my throat, I said, "The hardest walls to break are often the ones we build ourselves. The ones we construct out of duty, or fear, or the belief that denying our hearts somehow makes us holier."

"But how do you know? How do you know when it's time to tear those walls down?" Rhea asked.

"Sometimes the walls become so high that you can't see the sky anymore," Claire reasoned. "And that's when you have to ask yourself: Is it protection or a prison?"

The room fell silent, her words resonating like the last note of a hymn—beautiful and haunting.

Mrs. Anderson dabbed at her eyes with a tissue. "What about commitment? About the promises we make?"

"Perhaps the greatest commitment we can make is to honesty. To authenticity. To love, even when it costs us everything we thought we knew about ourselves," I said.

The buried words dug their way out from that place where doubt and desire had been waging war since Claire had walked back into my life. Every couple in this room was struggling with their own walls, their own masks, but none of them had to stand here and counsel others while their own heart was being torn in two.

Mrs. Anderson's lips pressed into a thin line. "But, Father, surely you're not suggesting that our commitments—our sacred vows—are less important than our feelings?"

Claire tensed next to me, though she kept her expression neutral.

How many nights had I lain awake next to her, questioning what I knew about commitment? About calling? About love?

"Our vows matter," I said, aware of every eye in the room. "But they should bring us closer to who we truly are, not force us to become someone we're not." My gaze drifted to Jasmine and Rhea. "Sometimes the most sacred thing we can do is admit when we're living a lie."

The confession in those words burned my throat.

"But how do you know?" Rachel asked, troubled. "How do you know if you're living a lie or just going through a rough patch?"

I swallowed hard, forcing myself to meet her eyes even as Claire's presence filled every corner of my awareness. "I think, deep down, we always know. The question is whether we're brave enough to admit it."

Kyle nodded. "Like when you wake up every morning feeling like you're putting on armor instead of clothes. Like every word and gesture has to be carefully calculated."

"Yes," I said. "And eventually, that armor becomes so heavy that you struggle to move. Struggle to breathe."

Lisa wiped her eyes. "But taking it off . . . God, it's terrifying. What if people don't like what they see underneath?"

"What if God doesn't?" Mrs. Anderson added.

I closed my eyes as memories of Claire's body pressed against mine washed over me—the taste of her lips, the way she looked at me like I was more than my collar and my vows.

"I believe," Claire started, cutting through and bringing me back to reality, "that God loves us most when we stop pretending to be what others want and start being who He created us to be."

My gaze met hers, and everything else fell away. The masks we'd been wearing, the careful distance we'd tried to maintain.

I glanced down at my hands folded in my lap. "Whether it's love for God, love for another person, or love for ourselves, real love sets us free."

Barriers crumbled. Hands reached across divides. Tears washed away pretense. Love broke through blockades. And in the sacred silence, a fundamental shift happened inside me, settling into place like a cornerstone finally finding its foundation.

I couldn't keep living this lie—pretending that kisses snuck in shadows and late-night trysts would be enough. That we'd be able to keep this hidden forever. Not when every fiber of my being knew the truth. Not when she was right there, her eyes full of the same longing that kept me awake at night.

As the session wrapped up, couples filed out slowly, many of them looking shaken but unmistakably lighter. But I remained rooted to my seat, Claire's words about honesty echoing in my head.

For the first time since she'd walked back into my life, I knew with absolute clarity what I had to do. The cost would be enormous—my position, my identity, everything I'd built my life around. But the cost of hiding, of continuing this charade?

It'll destroy us both.

The moment of reckoning had arrived. I could feel it in my bones.

Chapter Thirty-Four

CLAIRE

The second day of the retreat went smoother than I could've hoped. It was the kind of day where everything just fell into place. Some of the couples who were truly struggling finally opened up and began to work through the issues. Even Jasmine and Rhea, who had been hesitant at first, filled me with a sense of fulfillment I hadn't experienced in a long time.

I wanted that kind of partnership, the willingness to face the mess and stay regardless. But the thought of Damian giving up his calling because of me—for me—made my stomach twist. I couldn't be the reason he walked away from the life he'd built.

The knock on my hotel door was soft, almost hesitant. I squeezed my eyes shut, half convinced it was just the hum of the air-conditioning mingling with the fading edges of slumber. But then it came again, this time louder and more insistent, pulling me from the comfort of my fluffy pillow.

I groaned, dragging myself out of bed, my body heavy. My oversized T-shirt hung loose around me. Silver moonlight spilled in through the open window as I shuffled toward the door, rubbing the last remnants of sleep from my eyes. I opened it without looking through the peephole.

Damian.

His emerald eyes were dark, searching, and for a split second, I thought maybe I was still dreaming. The hallway light cast a soft glow over his face, catching the sharp lines of his jaw, the tension in his posture. He was just standing there, staring at me.

"What are you doing here? Someone could see you," I hissed, then pulled him inside and quickly closed the door. I crossed my arms over my chest instinctively, suddenly aware of how thin my T-shirt was. His eyes roamed my body, and he swallowed hard, Adam's apple bobbing.

"Sorry. I had to see you," he said, voice cracking. He sauntered over to the open window and leaned against the frame.

My eyes drifted over the loose pajama pants slung low on his hips and the cutoff shirt hugging his torso. I couldn't help but notice the way his biceps bulged, the moonlight catching every line and curve. My gaze had a mind of its own, tracing the contours of muscle beneath his shirt before I could remind myself to look away.

"The retreat is a real hit so far," I said.

He shifted. "It is."

I kind of hated how relaxed he seemed about us sneaking around like this. Was he seriously not concerned about the consequences of getting caught? Inhaling deeply, I said, "We can't live like this for the rest of our lives."

He nodded, but the tension didn't leave his shoulders. "I know."

I studied him. His fists clenched and unclenched at his sides, and he stood there as if he were balancing on the edge of a cliff. "You know, and yet you came to me? Here, where you're more likely to be seen?" I asked, my voice softer now, trying to understand what was going on behind those conflicted eyes.

He hesitated. "Well, you haven't exactly sent me away."

Touché. I sighed, leaning against the wall across from him, my exhaustion mixing with confusion. "We should put a stop to this. Figure out how to quit each other."

His eyes locked on mine, something dark and starved flashing behind them. "Is that really what you want?"

Before I could answer, he pushed away from the window and stalked toward me, closing the distance between us in a handful of long strides. His hands gripped my arms as he pinned against the wall. My breath hitched, heart leaping into my throat, but I didn't shove him away.

His mouth crashed onto mine, lips rough and urgent against mine. My body responded before my brain could catch up, hands instinctively wrapping around his neck and pulling him closer as he pressed me harder against the wall.

His hands slid down my waist, and his fingers brushed the thin fabric of my T-shirt, tugging it up. Those fingers glided across my stomach, leaving behind a warm trail of tingles through my nerves. Each touch was more overwhelming than the last. He kissed along my neck, and I arched into him, a soft whimper escaping my lips.

He groaned, his hips pressing into mine with a force that sent my pulse racing. Electric heat shot through me, pooling low in my belly, making my breath shallow and ragged. His hard cock rubbed the cotton of my underwear against my center, and it only fueled the fire raging inside me.

Panting and desperate, he moved his hands to my hips, fingers digging in as he ground himself against me. "I'm sorry. I can't quit you. My heart won't let me," he murmured against my lips.

I whimpered, my head tipping back, mind spinning from the intensity. "We're risking so much."

I instinctively ground my hips against him, and the thin fabric of my underwear did nothing to hide the warm wetness of my pussy.

"I don't want to think about that right now." He trailed kisses down the curve of my neck. "Please. Just let me have you."

This was absolutely ridiculous. Of course, I couldn't resist him either—my body buzzed for him every time he walked into a room. But vocalizing that? Well, it wouldn't solve our problems. It would probably create a whole new beautiful disaster—one that I couldn't let myself be the catalyst of.

His hands slid up to my waist once again, holding me steady as he leaned into my ear. "I want to feel you beneath me, your body arching into me as I thrust into you. I want to hear you beg for more," he growled, low and deep.

Without another word, he crossed the room over to the bed, tossing me down onto the sheets. His green eyes locked on to mine as he crawled over me.

His lips met mine in a devouring kiss, tongue sliding into my mouth with an almost animalistic hunger. He was claiming me— marking me as his—and I couldn't help but surrender to him.

Even as my body responded to his touch, my heart ached with the knowledge that this was temporary. That it had to be. Just another stolen moment that could never be more than that. I wanted to give him everything, but how could I when we both knew this needed to end?

He pulled off my T-shirt, and his fingers traced down my sides, sending a surge of electricity through my veins. The cool air on my skin made me shiver, but it was nothing compared to the heat building in my core.

Part of me wanted to memorize the way his hands felt, the intensity in his eyes, the perfect fit of our bodies together. Because tomorrow, this would all be just another beautiful memory of a relationship I couldn't keep.

He slipped my underwear off, his eyes dipped down to the object of his desire: my bare pussy. He lowered himself down my body, and his licks started slow but escalated, becoming more urgent and demanding with each swipe of his hot tongue across my sensitive flesh. I writhed beneath him, my moans growing louder, and he seemed to feed off my cries for more.

He slipped in one finger, then two, working them in and out of my slit, rubbing and teasing me. My hips bucked to meet his caresses, my body screaming for release. He lapped at the bundle of nerves as his fingers curled, massaging me from inside, bringing me closer and closer to nirvana.

A rushing wave of pleasure crashed over me—through my veins —like a tidal wave, and every inch of my body shook uncontrollably. I cried out, coming hard and pulsing around his fingers.

Damian's eyes were wide with a mix of reverence and pleasure, and I knew I was giving him a sight he would never forget. As my orgasm subsided, he drew his fingers out of me, trailing them along my inner thigh before he stood up and removed his clothes.

Hours spent under the sun or in the gym had left him toned and tanned. He was the perfect specimen of a man, and I marveled at his beauty. As he stood before me on full display, I couldn't help but reach out and trace my fingers along the dips and swells of his muscles. The way they rippled under my touch sent shivers through me.

He was a god among men, and I was about to become his willing sacrifice. His erection stood proudly, and I caressed the silky hardness, fingers trailing along the veins and ridges, each making my heart pound with anticipation. I wrapped my fingers around his girth, its thickness pulsing in my grip. He loosed a hoarse whimper at my touch, and the power of my actions coursed through both of us.

I brought his cock to my lips. My tongue darted out, tracing the lines of his shaft before daring to taste him just below the head. His flavor exploded on my tongue, a mix of salty and sweet that only added to the intoxicating mixture of scents and flavors already filling my senses.

His hands cradled the back of my head, guiding me closer to him as I took him into my mouth. He was big, but I tried to take every inch of him.

His gaze tilted toward the ceiling. "Fuck, that feels amazing."

I pumped him in and out, using my hand to cover what my mouth couldn't reach.

He pulled out of my mouth, his chest heaving with labored breaths. "Wait." Lying on his back on the bed, he said, "Let me fill that cunt as you ride me."

I straddled his lap and positioned myself over him. The heat of his body was like a furnace against me.

"Are you sure?" I gave him one last chance to change his mind. "Once I start, I'm not going to stop."

He gripped my waist, pulling me down. The head of his cock nudged my entrance, parting my folds with ease and plunging into me in one smooth thrust. A sharp broken sound ripped from my throat as pleasure washed over me. I was filled, taken completely by this man, who now owned every fiber of my being.

He held me as he moved, each hard thrust up sending pleasure cascading through my entire body. The bed creaked under the force of our passion, but neither of us seemed to care. All that mattered was our connection and the way our bodies moved together. Two halves of a perfect whole.

Damian's grip on me tightened, guiding me deeper onto his cock with each slam of his hips into mine. "This is yours, Claire. Only yours." His eyes watched me, his expression one of pure bliss and intensity.

I cupped his face in my hands, bringing our lips together in a passionate kiss. Our tongues danced, mirroring the rhythm of our movements as he continued to pound into me. My body was on fire, every nerve ending screaming in ecstasy as I met each of Damian's thrusts.

"I'm close." I rocked my hips against him, chasing oblivion. "Fuck, I'm close."

With a cry of pure bliss, I climaxed around him, my body trembling. My walls clenched tightly around his cock, milking him as he thrust into me again and again with renewed vigor.

In that moment of perfect connection, the truth hit me harder than ever: I loved this man. Completely. Desperately. But I could never have him the way I dreamed. No quiet Sunday mornings making pancakes. No wedding vows exchanged before our family and friends. No children with his green eyes and my smile. We were trapped in this endless cycle of wanting what we couldn't fully have.

Damian groaned, nearing his breaking point, and his movements became more frenzied, every surge of his hips driving him deeper and harder than the last. His breaths came in ragged gasps, each one carrying the raw power of his passion.

I clasped onto him, unable to do anything but ride the wave of pleasure that was now coursing through my entire being.

With a final thrust, Damian's body tensed beneath me. He let out a guttural sound as he came inside me, his hips bucking wildly and then slowing until finally stilling.

For a long moment, we just lay there, pressed together, panting, our bodies trembling with the aftermath of what we'd just done. His heartbeat echoed mine, a steady, relentless rhythm beneath my fingertips. Sweat clung to our skin, mingling in a way that blurred the line between where I ended and he began.

The warmth of his body enveloped me, and his hands left behind an intoxicating tenderness. I stared at him, searching for words, for a way to make sense of this, but nothing came. His lips were swollen, hair disheveled, and my stupid heart twisted inside me at the sight of him like this.

I forced myself to stand, slow and careful, as if breaking the stillness would shatter whatever fragile moment we were clinging to.

I grabbed my tee from the floor and pulled it over my head, avoiding his gaze.

"You should probably go back to your room," I said, trying to keep my voice even. Some of the retreat couples were staying on this very floor, and the last thing we needed was to be caught.

Damian sat up, running a hand through his dark hair, his expression distant, like he was somewhere else entirely. He dressed without a word, slipping on his sweatpants and shirt, but when he reached the door, he stopped. His hand hovered on the knob, and he turned back to me.

His expression shifted to that vulnerable look I knew too well—the one that made my chest tighten every single time. His emerald eyes found mine, and I could see him wrestling with words he wanted to say.

"Claire, I need you to know," he said, voice rough, barely above a whisper, "what's happening between us, it's not just physical. I'm falling—"

"Don't." The word came out sharper than I'd intended, cutting through whatever confession was about to spill from his lips. I stepped back instinctively, wrapping my arms around myself like armor. "Please don't say it."

His brow furrowed, confusion flickering across his features. "Why not? It's the truth."

God, if only that made any of it easier instead of more complicated. I looked away, focusing on the pattern of moonlight spilling across the hotel carpet, anywhere but those beautiful green eyes.

"I can't be the reason you walk away from everything." My voice came out raspy. "I won't carry that responsibility."

"That's not—"

"It is." I met his gaze again, and the pain there nearly undid me.

"You think I don't know what you're wrestling with? You think I can't see it every time you look at me?"

He took a step toward me, and I held up my hand to stop him. If he touched me right now, I'd crumble.

"You have a calling, Dames. You've dedicated your life to serving God, to this parish, and to the people who depend on you. I won't be the person who destroys that."

"You aren't. I was wrestling with this since before you arrived at Saint Anthony's."

My heart hammered against my ribs, every beat screaming at me to run to him, to say yes, to choose love over everything else. But I didn't believe him. I couldn't.

Every option I wanted was destructive—wanting him, keeping him. Unfortunately, love wasn't always about choosing what felt good. Sometimes love meant making a hard choice. Yet the only choice I had left—handing him back to God—tore open my chest and ripped my heart out. But how could I live with myself if I became the reason he walked away?

"Please," I whispered. "You should go back to your room, Dames."

Hurt fractured his expression, spreading across his features like splintered glass. He nodded slowly, understanding passing between us without another word. His hand turned the doorknob, but he paused one more time.

"This isn't over, Claire," he said, and then he left.

As the door closed behind him with a soft click, I knew it had to be. Not because I didn't love him—I loved him more than I'd ever loved anyone—but because wanting him meant destroying him. And if one of us had to bleed, it would be me.

Chapter Thirty-Five

DAMIAN

The stillness of early Sunday morning greeted me as I walked into Saint Anthony's, the weight of the quiet suffocating me. The air was cool, the light filtering through the stained glass windows casting muted hues of red and blue across the wooden pews. Everything about the scene should have brought me peace—this was the sanctuary I had devoted my life to, the place where I was meant to feel closest to God. But today, the calm of the church stood in contrast to the hurricane of emotions inside me.

The events of last night lingered at the edges of my mind. *Claire.* Her name was a prayer and a sin all at once. I had fucked her raw again, and with no remorse. Tasted the bittersweetness of her cunt. Kissed those full lips. My hands clutched the edge of the marble altar as I prepared for Mass, trying to focus, but my mind wouldn't let go of the image of her breathless and writhing on top of me.

There's gotta be a special place in hell for a man like me.

I stepped up to the altar and began, my voice calm despite the longing and the pain swirling in my chest. I moved through the motions, but as I glanced out at the congregation, I couldn't help but notice the couples scattered throughout the pews. An older man gently squeezed his wife's hand, their fingers entwined as if the years had only strengthened their bond. A younger couple sat closer together, sharing soft glances and subtle smiles, the warmth between them palpable.

It was love. And I saw it everywhere this morning. The kind of love I'd spent years convincing myself wasn't for me. The kind I'd told myself was reserved for others, while I devoted myself to a higher purpose. *For God. For Enrico.* But watching them now, the beauty of their connection sacred in a way I couldn't deny, my chest tightened. Love—romantic, messy, human love—was the greatest expression of faith that I'd been denying myself for too long. The contrast between what I was preaching and what was in my heart had never been so stark.

The Mass continued, but I was drifting. My hands moved through the acquainted motions, lifting the chalice, reciting the words I had memorized. My mind was somewhere else—lost in the growing sense of disillusionment that had been creeping up on me for months.

I looked out at the congregation—at the couples who seemed so connected, so in tune with one another. Was that not a form of service too? To love another person fully, to share your life with them, to build something together? The Church said love was sacred, but only when it existed in certain forms—between a man and a woman, between married couples. And priests, well, we were supposed to deny that part of ourselves, as if love and connection were somehow distractions from faith.

But I wasn't sure I believed that anymore. My faith was still strong—I could feel it, pulsing beneath the surface, as constant and alive as ever. But this life of denial, of closing myself off from love . . . It was wrong. Or at least incomplete. Was I truly serving God by barring myself from the human experience, from the very thing that made life beautiful and sacred?

After Mass ended, I stayed in the sacristy longer than necessary.

The church was quiet now, the congregation gone. The silence wasn't comforting today. Simply hollow.

I made my way back to the rectory, my steps heavy. Once inside, I sank into the worn armchair in the corner of the living room, my head falling into my hands. My mind was a tangled mess, consumed with thoughts of Claire, of the Church, of what my life had become.

What if love was another way to serve? What if by denying it I was cutting myself off from what God wanted for me? From what I needed?

I leaned back in the chair, staring at the ceiling. My priestly vows hung heavy around my neck. There had to be a way to live a life of faith, of service, without denying love. Without denying what it meant to be human.

My decision had been made, but Claire's refusal to hear how I felt about her truly confused me. Every moment leading up to the retreat had told me she'd carried the same feelings for me, but now I wasn't so sure.

MONDAY WAS THE LONGEST DAY OF THE WEEK FOR ME—ESPECIALLY THIS particular Monday since Claire wasn't answering my texts or phone calls. I'd gone to her cottage, but she wasn't there. And Mrs. Omura said she'd called out sick. Did Claire regret what we'd done? I hadn't even considered that it might have meant nothing to her.

My phone buzzed on the wooden desk, the sound jarring in the quiet of the rectory. I glanced down, my heart tightening in my chest as Bishop Valenti's name flashed across the screen. FaceTime. *Fuck me.* There was no hiding from this.

With a sigh, I swiped to answer, bracing myself as the bishop's face filled the screen. His kind dark eyes crinkled in a smile, his white collar stark against his dark cassock. I straightened in my chair, suddenly feeling like I was under a spotlight.

"Father Bellucci! How are you, my son?" Bishop Valenti asked, voice warm, comforting. The weight of his authority settled over me like a heavy cloak.

"Your Excellency," I said, keeping my tone neutral. "Doing well, thank you."

He leaned back in his chair. The background behind him blurred, but I could make out the faint outlines of religious iconography on his office walls. "How'd the retreat go?"

"It went smoothly. The couples were engaged, and I think we helped them start to reconnect."

"Good, good," the bishop said, pleased. "You know, love—especially within marriage—is one of God's greatest gifts. You and Sister Claire have helped these couples understand that."

His words hit me like a one-two combo. Love was a divine gift. I knew that, had preached it countless times. But as he spoke, the dissonance I had been feeling began stirring again, louder and difficult to ignore. How could the very thing God represented, that sacred emotion, be denied to those who had chosen to serve Him? Why was it that real human love was an experience we were forced to turn away from?

"I'm glad we could be of service," I said, trying to focus on the conversation. But my mind kept drifting back to Claire, to the way she had looked at me last night and the way my body had responded to hers. Was that not love too? Was it not a reflection of God's design, of our humanity?

The bishop's voice shifted slightly, his tone more serious now. "But remember, Damian, as priests, we have a different kind of calling. Our love must always be, first and foremost, for God and above any earthly desires or connections. The Church asks for this sacrifice because it believes in the purity of our devotion. Celibacy is a way for us to dedicate ourselves fully to the Lord's work without distraction."

There it was.

The reminder.

The *rule*.

I nodded along, but his words were starting to feel empty. As he spoke about devotion and purity, all I could think about was the contradiction simmering beneath the surface. Love was divine, yet I was supposed to deny it? The same love that brought people closer to God, the same connection we've been told to cherish, was forbidden just because of some vows to the Church? How did that make sense?

"Yes, Your Excellency," I said, though my voice was distant, like it belonged to someone else.

Bishop Valenti continued, unaware of the conflict brewing inside me. "It's not always easy. I know that. But your love for God must remain steadfast. These earthly desires, they come and go. But your service to the Church, to His people—that is eternal."

The knot in my chest tightened. Was it really eternal? Or was it just another way the Church controlled the lives of those who served it? The more the bishop spoke, the more I realized I wasn't just struggling with my feelings for Claire; I was struggling with the entire structure of what I had been taught to believe.

I loved God—that much I knew, and that would never change. But maybe my calling didn't have to mean a life of denial. The type of love I had for Claire didn't stand in opposition to my faith. It was part of it.

As the bishop finished speaking, I nodded, murmuring, "Thank you, Your Excellency."

His words about love being a divine gift clashed with his insistence on celibacy. How could both be true? How could I serve God fully if I was denying such a core part of what it meant to be human?

The bishop had given me the same speech I'd heard a hundred times before, but this time, it didn't sit right. When the line went dead, what lingered wasn't doubt, but clarity. I stared down at the phone in my hand. My place wasn't in the collar anymore.

I glanced up at the crucifix hanging on the wall above my desk, the worn wood casting long shadows in the dim light of the rectory.

I wanted to serve God. I always would. But the desire to live a life that honored both my faith and my love for Claire didn't feel like a betrayal anymore. It felt like an acceptance of who I was—of what God had made me to be.

I spent Monday morning hiding in the parish hall, boxed in—literally—by retreat materials, which seemed to multiply and grow heavier when no one was looking. My hands moved automatically as I sorted feedback forms, but my mind kept drifting to specific moments: Sarah's face when she finally looked Tod in the eyes during the forgiveness exercise, her voice breaking as she said, "I want to try again." The elderly Rodriguezes discovering they could still make each other laugh after forty-three years of marriage. Even Jasmine and Rhea taking those first tentative steps toward healing, Jasmine's hand finally accepting Rhea's touch during the blessing circle.

I was smoothing out one particularly wrinkled feedback form from a couple who'd written *This saved our marriage* in shaky handwriting when the recognizable click of designer heels on linoleum announced my impending doom. My fingers unconsciously found the cross at my throat, tracing its edges.

Mrs. Fontana swept in with the precision of a general surveying a battlefield in her immaculate Chanel skirt suit and with flawless hair. Around her, the parish hall told a different story: folding tables bowed beneath boxes and half-sorted papers, and retreat banners slouched against the wall like they'd given up on standing straight.

"Sister Claire." The greeting was warm as honey, but I caught the underlying chill. "Working early on a Monday morning? Aren't we dedicated."

I straightened, forcing my hands to still on the stack of forms. *Here we go.* "Mrs. Fontana. I was just organizing the retreat materials." I gestured to the scattered papers. "The transformation stories are incredible."

"Oh, I have no doubt it was quite . . . memorable." She approached with the deliberate slowness of someone savoring gossip, her designer purse clutched in perfectly manicured hands. "Though I've been hearing some interesting feedback myself."

My stomach performed an impressive gymnastics routine. "Oh? I hope it's been positive. We worked so hard to create a safe space."

Play optimistic, Claire. Find the silver lining.

"Well, dear, that's the thing." Mrs. Fontana settled herself into a chair across from me with practiced grace. "I'm afraid not everyone felt quite as comfortable as you thought. The Hendersons mentioned they felt the retreat took some unexpected directions. And the Millers, bless their hearts, seemed rather concerned about the atmosphere."

Ah, there it is. I remembered the moment clearly—Mrs. Henderson's sharp intake of breath when I'd welcomed Jasmine and Rhea with the same enthusiasm as the other couples, the whispered conversation by the coffee station, and the quiet departure that had followed. But we'd stayed focused on the twenty-three couples who'd remained. The ones who'd needed us.

"Well, you know how it is," I said, trying to keep my tone light. "When you're working with couples in crisis, sometimes it's hard to accommodate *all* different comfort levels when it comes to healing. But the beautiful thing is how many hearts opened that weekend. The

Rodriguezes told me they haven't felt this connected in years, and Sarah—"

"Yes, dear, I'm sure many found it educational." Mrs. Fontana's smile had all the warmth of a winter morning. "But you know, I've been thinking about your approach to ministry. So passionate and . . . modern. Sometimes I wonder if that enthusiasm might lead you to make choices that, while well-intentioned, could be misunderstood."

We're doing this dance now. My hands smoothed my habit, a gesture that usually brought me comfort. Today, it felt like adjusting armor. "I'm not sure I follow. Could you be more specific?"

She leaned forward with the concern of a devoted grandmother. "Well, I've known you since you were a little thing running around this very hall. I watched you altar serve in that very sanctuary." She paused, letting the personal history settle like emotional manipulation wrapped in nostalgic ribbon. "That's why this conversation is so difficult for me. Because I care about you, sweetheart. I care about this parish. And I certainly care about Father Bellucci."

And there's the real target. I forced myself to stay calm, drawing on every lesson I'd learned when managing classrooms full of hormonal teenagers. "Well, that's wonderful. We all care about each other here. That's what makes Saint Anthony's such a special community."

"Indeed." Mrs. Fontana's eyes held mine with laser focus. "Which is why I felt I should mention some concerns that have been brought to my attention."

Mrs. Fontana arranged herself more comfortably, as if she were settling in for a particularly important story. "I received some phone calls yesterday from parishioners who attended the retreat. They mentioned noticing some very close interactions between our dear father and his cofacilitator."

The blood drained from my face so fast I worried I might actually faint. My hands gripped the edge of the table, knuckles white. *Breathe,*

Claire. Remember what you told Sarah about facing hard truths— sometimes you have to walk through the fire to get to the other side.

"Mrs. Fontana, I think there might be a misunderstanding—"

"Oh, I hope so, dear. I truly do." Her voice carried the patient sadness of someone delivering difficult news. "And then," she continued with the gentle persistence of water wearing down stone, "someone saw Father Damian leaving your hotel room Saturday night."

Holy hell. Think, Claire. There has to be a way to explain this. There's always a way forward.

"Mrs. Fontana," I began, but she held up a gentle hand.

"Oh, sweetheart, please don't feel you need to explain anything to me." Her voice was all maternal concern now. "I'm not here to judge or condemn. God knows we're all human, and the heart can be such a complicated thing."

Right. Because this sounds like understanding and not a setup.

"But, you see, I have a responsibility to this parish. After Father Martin's troubles, we needed someone who could restore faith in our leadership. The congregation simply adores Damian. He's brought new life to Saint Anthony's, and he's carrying on his dear brother's legacy."

Translation: He's valuable, you're replaceable. Message received, loud and clear. My fingers found my cross, and I thought of what I'd taught my students about Joan of Arc: *She followed her convictions even when it led her to the stake.*

I searched for solutions the way I always did when faced with seemingly impossible problems. *Maybe if I talk to the bishop directly and explain the context.*

"What exactly are you suggesting?" I asked, though I was already dreading the answer.

Mrs. Fontana smoothed her skirt. "Well, I've been thinking. You're so talented, so devoted to your calling. And there are parishes all over that could benefit from your gifts. The Midwest has some lovely Catholic communities, I'm told. Fresh starts can be such blessings, don't you think?"

The Midwest. Because nothing said "fresh start" quite like cornfields and the flattest landscape God ever created. I thought of my classroom, decorated with quotes from saints who'd defied convention. Of the trust I'd built with kids who'd been written off by everyone else.

"You're asking me to leave this parish," I concluded, my voice wavering despite my efforts to stay strong. "To abandon my students. Connor Ryan is finally opening up about his father leaving. Calla Santos trusts me enough to talk about her struggles."

"Oh, honey." Mrs. Fontana's voice softened with what sounded like genuine sympathy. "I know how much those children mean to you. But sometimes we have to make difficult choices for the greater good."

Her words sparked that same fierce protectiveness I felt when someone criticized my students. I thought about the couples from the weekend: Sarah and Tod working through infidelity with renewed hope, the elderly pair rediscovering intimacy after years of distance. All of it could be overshadowed by this scandal.

Damn it. She wasn't wrong, and we both knew it.

"How much time are you giving me to consider this?"

"Until Friday, dear. That gives you a few days to pray about it and make arrangements after you choose to submit a transfer request." Mrs. Fontana gathered her purse with the satisfaction of someone who'd successfully navigated a difficult conversation. "I do hope you'll make the choice that's best for everyone."

She paused at the doorway. "You know, Claire, I remember when you and Damian were just teenagers. I always thought you two had such a special connection. It's heartbreaking how life sometimes takes us down paths that separate us from those we care about most."

Special connection. Like it was just some sweet childhood memory instead of a love that had taken part in shaping both our lives.

"But perhaps this is God's way of helping you both find where you truly belong," she said, taking on that philosophical tone people used when they wanted to sound wise.

She traipsed out, her heels clicking against the floor. As soon as the door closed behind her, I sat there in silence, surrounded by the evidence of a weekend that had felt like a miracle but had apparently been nothing more than my own personal apocalypse.

My hands shook as I picked up Sarah and Tod's feedback form, reading their words about finding hope they'd thought was forever lost. But even as I sat there, feeling like the world's most spectacular failure, I couldn't bring myself to regret Saturday night.

My fingers brushed the cross at my throat, grounding me in the decision I'd already made. I just hadn't realized how quickly it would demand its price.

Chapter Thirty-Seven

CLAIRE

Damian had been calling and texting since my conversation with Mrs. Fontana yesterday. Each ring of my phone made my stomach flutter like I was seventeen again, sneaking out to meet him at the Cliff Overlook. But I couldn't answer. Not that I didn't want to talk to him. God knew every fiber of my being ached to hear his voice. It was because I knew myself too well.

One word from him and I'd throw in the white flag. I'd march right back into the school and pretend like I could keep living in this impossible space between loving him and serving God.

Damian could convince me of anything. He'd tell me that staying would be the right choice—that we could somehow make this work. That we could convince Mrs. Fontana that there was nothing happening between us. And I'd be weak enough to believe him.

The waves crashed against the shore in a tranquil rhythm as Jasmine and I walked along the beach, our feet sinking into the cool sand with each step. The sun was setting, painting the sky in deep purples and oranges.

"You're sure about this?" Jasmine asked, her voice gentle against the sound of the surf. "Leaving without talking to him?"

I kicked a small shell, watching it disappear into the foam of an incoming wave. "I have to, Jaz. Mrs. Fontana practically threatened me. And if I try to talk to him . . ." A lump formed in my throat, and my eyes blurred with tears. "He won't let me go. Not again."

Jasmine was quiet for a moment. There was just the sound of our footsteps in the wet sand between us. Then she stopped, turning to face me. "Remember when we were kids, Mom and Dad used to bring us here after Sunday Mass?"

I nodded. "Dad let us run in the waves in our church clothes. Mom would get so mad."

"But Dad always said there was a holiness about the ocean," Jasmine continued, her eyes on the horizon. "Something bigger than the walls of any church."

We walked farther down the beach, past the rocky outcropping where Damian and I used to sit in our high school years, talking about our futures and dreaming about what life would look like. The memories of his smile, his laugh, and the way he stared at me like I was his entire world all came rushing back, making my chest ache.

"I've been sleeping with him," I blurted out, the confession burning on my tongue. "For a while now."

Jasmine didn't look shocked or judgmental. She just nodded.

"I've been trying to convince myself it was just something we needed to get out of our systems. That we could go back to normal, back to our vows, but . . ."

"But?" she prompted gently.

"It wasn't just sex," I whispered. "It was everything. The way he held me after. The way we fit together like no time had passed at all. And I wanted more. I still want more."

We reached a cluster of weathered rocks, and I sank down onto one, the stone cool beneath me. The tide was coming in, each wave reaching a little farther up the beach.

"You know what the worst part is?" I asked. "I don't even feel guilty about what we did. I feel guilty about not feeling guilty. What kind of nun does that make me?"

Jasmine sat beside me, her shoulder pressing against mine. "A human one. One who's finally being honest with herself."

I looked out at the horizon, where the sun was sinking into the ocean, bleeding red and gold across the water. "I used to think I knew exactly what holiness meant. What faith looked like. Now I'm not so sure anymore."

"Maybe that's okay."

"Mrs. Fontana may have threatened me, but I was already thinking about leaving."

She cocked a brow. "Why?"

I sniffled and said, "I don't want to be the reason he leaves the priesthood. I don't want that kind of power over someone else's faith. If he leaves, it has to be his choice."

"And what about your choice?" Jasmine asked. "What about your faith?"

"I love God and my job," I said, tears spilling over. "I do. But I can't keep denying who I am. It's killing me, Jaz. Every time I put on that habit and say those prayers, I feel like I'm lying."

She drew me into a tight hug, and I allowed myself to break a little, letting the tears fall as the waves crashed in front of us.

"Then go," she whispered. "Find your own way to serve—to love."

When we pulled apart, I wiped my eyes, tasting salt on my lips— from tears or sea spray, I couldn't tell. The sun had almost completely set, leaving just a thin line of gold on the horizon.

"You know what Dad would say right now?" Jasmine asked, a small smile playing on her lips.

I couldn't help but let out a soft giggle. "That God is in the ocean, in the sky, and in everything beautiful, wild, and free."

"Exactly." She squeezed my hand. "That's where you need to be right now."

We sat in silence for a while, watching the last light fade from the sky. Stars began scattering across the darkening canvas above us like diamonds on black velvet. I thought about all the nights I'd spent in prayer, searching for answers and peace. But maybe peace wasn't about finding all the answers. Maybe it was about being brave enough to live with the questions.

And then his words echoed in my mind: *By the light that guides us, I promise to always find my way back to you, no matter how lost I get.*

I broke open, sobs tearing out of my chest again until I couldn't breathe. My hands shook as I tried to cover my face, but it was useless—the grief poured out in great heaving waves. Because he had meant every word, and I wanted so desperately to believe them. But the truth was a merciless demon. I couldn't have him. Not now. Not ever.

Jasmine slid closer without a word, wrapping her arms around me once more. She didn't try to hush me, didn't offer empty comfort. She just held on, her presence anchoring me while I fell apart.

When the tears stopped, I stood up, brushing sand from my clothes. The night had settled in fully, the moon casting a silver path across the water. "I'll meet with Mother Superior tomorrow," I said, feeling stronger now—more certain.

Jasmine stood too, understanding in her eyes. "And Damian?"

I took a deep breath. "I'll write him a letter."

Her lips pressed into a thin line. She didn't say anything, but the look she leveled at me was enough—a quiet, pointed, *Really, Claire?*

"It's the only way I can do this without falling apart."

As we walked back to the car, certainty rooted itself inside me—not peace, but an ache that spread through my chest like wildfire. The kind that told me I was doing the right thing, even as it hollowed me out. Because the right choice still meant tearing myself away from the only man I'd ever truly loved.

The ocean would keep rolling, the tides would keep changing, and somewhere in all of it, I would find my way back to myself. Back to a faith that felt real and true. Back to a life that was mine to live, not just a role I was trying to fill.

IN JASMINE'S GUEST ROOM, I KNELT BESIDE THE BED. NO HABIT, NO VEIL. JUST me in borrowed pajamas with salt still clinging to my skin from the beach and the familiar weight of my rosary pressed into my palm.

"I don't even know how to talk to You anymore," I whispered. "I've spent so long trying to be the perfect nun, the perfect Catholic, that I forgot how to just be Your daughter." I traced the cross with my thumb. "I still feel You here. In the quiet. In the doubt. Even in this mess I've made."

The ocean hummed beyond the window. "I'm leaving, but I'm not leaving You. I'm just . . . finding a different way to love You. One that doesn't require me to cut away pieces of myself." My voice cracked. "I'm scared. Terrified, actually. But for the first time, this fear feels honest. Real."

I didn't end with "amen." I just sat there, letting the night wrap around me, listening to the waves until my knees ached against the hardwood floor.

Chapter Thirty-Eight

CLAIRE

The chapel of my convent felt smaller before sunset, shadows pooling in the corners where the flickering votives couldn't quite reach. The worn kneeler pressed against my shins, an ache that usually helped quiet my mind. This morning, every sensation felt sharper—the cool bite of stone against my fingertips, the way my breath seemed too loud in the sacred silence.

My fingers found the silver cross at my throat, the same one I'd worn since my profession. Such a simple thing, really. Two pieces of metal crossed and blessed, meant to remind me of sacrifice and devotion. But as I traced its simple lines, all I could think about was another kind of devotion—the kind that had blazed in Damian's eyes at Cliff Overlook when he'd pulled me against him like I was the answer to every prayer he'd ever whispered.

"I can't stay." The words fell from my lips like stones into still water, each syllable rippling through the empty chapel. "I can't lie anymore."

Eight years . . . I'd built walls around my heart and called it holiness, and here I was, unraveling like a poorly sewn hem with every memory of his hands on my skin.

"This isn't failure. I haven't failed You," I whispered to the crucifix above the altar, where Christ's face remained eternally peaceful despite the nails and thorns.

I stood, my legs unsteady after hours of kneeling, and smoothed down my habit with trembling hands. The fabric that had once felt like armor now seemed thin as tissue paper, insufficient protection against the truth clawing its way up my throat.

Mother Superior's office glowed faintly behind frosted glass, her silhouette bent over paperwork even at this early hour. I didn't think she ever slept, our stalwart leader, as if rest were just another luxury she'd sacrificed for the good of the community.

I raised my hand to knock, then hesitated. Once I spoke these words aloud, there would be no taking them back. No pretending I was just struggling through a rough patch or wrestling with temporary doubts. This would be the beginning of the end.

My knuckles rapped against the door before I could lose my nerve.

"Come in, child."

Mother Superior looked up as I entered, her steel-gray hair framing a face lined with decades of prayer and responsibility. She didn't seem surprised to see me, just gestured to the chair across from her desk with the kind of calm that suggested she'd been expecting this conversation for longer than I cared to think about.

"I can't—" My voice cracked, and I had to start again. "Mother, I need to confess."

She set down her pen and folded her hands, giving me the same patient attention she'd offered since the first day I'd arrived at these doors, lost, broken, searching for my purpose in this too big and too cruel world.

"I'm listening."

The words came in fits and starts, tumbling over one another like water through a broken dam. I told her about the restlessness that had been growing for months, the way my prayers felt increasingly empty, and the growing certainty that I was playacting at a calling I'd never truly received. I couldn't bring myself to mention Damian by name, but somehow, I suspected she heard him in the spaces between my words anyway.

When I finally fell silent, she studied me with those sharp blue eyes that missed nothing. The grandfather clock in the corner ticked away the seconds, each one feeling like a small eternity.

"Sister Claire," she said finally, her voice gentle but unwavering. "How long have you been wrestling with this?"

"Months. Maybe longer." I twisted my hands in my lap. "I keep thinking I can pray my way through it, that if I just try harder—"

"Faith isn't to be forced, child." She leaned back in her chair, looking every one of her seventy-odd years. "Sometimes the Spirit calls us away from one path so we can find the one we're truly meant to walk."

The kindness in her voice nearly undid me. I'd expected anger, disappointment, lectures about commitment and perseverance. Instead, she was looking at me with what looked almost like . . . relief?

"You've seen this before," I reasoned.

A faint smile touched her lips. "More times than I care to count. The religious life isn't for everyone, Claire, no matter how much we might wish otherwise. There's no shame in recognizing that your calling lies elsewhere."

She opened her desk drawer and withdrew a form I recognized— the same one I'd filled out eight years ago, but in reverse. A formal request for release from vows.

"The process will take time," she explained, her fingers trailing over the paper. "Canonical requirements, paperwork, a period of discernment to ensure you're certain. But if this is truly what you feel called to do—"

"It is." The words came out steadier than I felt. "I know it is."

She nodded, pushing the form across the desk toward me. "Then we'll begin." She paused, studying my face with those perceptive eyes. "Given the circumstances—the temptation you mentioned—I think it would be wise for you to vacate the cottage immediately. You can't continue in your position at the parish during this process."

My heart hammered against my ribs. I'd expected it, but hearing it made it all feel suddenly, urgently real.

"I understand," I breathed.

"Do you have somewhere to go? Family? Friends?"

"My sister, Jasmine. She lives about an hour south."

Mother Superior's expression softened. "Good. The separation will be better for everyone involved while we work through the requirements." She stood, moving around the desk to place a gentle hand on my shoulder. "This doesn't have to be goodbye forever, Claire. You'll always be welcome here as a friend."

I stood to leave, then turned back at the door. "Do you think God is disappointed in me?"

For a moment, I saw not the formidable Mother Superior but the woman who'd held my hand through panic attacks and celebrated my small victories with genuine joy.

"My darling girl. God isn't some scorekeeper marking down our failures. He's the father running down the road to welcome the prodigal son home. Whatever path you choose, you carry His love with you."

I walked out of her office with a heavy heart. As I traipsed through the halls to the exit, a pang of sorrow coursed through me. There were so many memories here—so many faces that had become like family. I had been part of this community, and leaving it felt like leaving a piece of myself behind.

As I stepped outside, rain started falling, almost as if the sky were grieving with me. I walked to my car, the drops cold against my skin. Standing there, I let the rain soak into my clothes, mixing with the tears I hadn't realized had begun trailing down my cheeks.

A part of me felt relieved, as if a weight had been lifted from my shoulders. But there was also an emptiness, a hollowness in my chest that ached with the loss of what could have been. I would miss them all—the sisters, the parishioners, the quiet moments of prayer. I would miss the sense of belonging that came from dedicating myself to something greater.

But I couldn't stay.

Chapter Thirty-Nine

CLAIRE

I stumbled into my cottage, tears streaming down my cheeks as I crossed the threshold. Every step felt like betrayal, like leaving pieces of myself scattered across the floor. My hands trembled as I dropped to my knees, dragging the large suitcase out from under the bed. The scrape of it against the wood was deafening, and when I flung it open, the sound shattered me—I folded over it, crying so hard I could barely breathe.

I packed everything I'd brought into this life: The poetry books and dog-eared novels that had kept me company through lonely nights. The purple cardigan Jasmine had given me last Christmas, still smelling faintly of her perfume. The small box of crosses, each one marking a different chapter of my journey.

When I started going through kitchen items, my hands lingered on the fresh herbs I'd been drying—rosemary for remembrance, sage for cleansing, lavender for peace. Here I was again, trying to find healing in small rituals and the quiet magic of growing things. But that was faith: finding the sacred in small moments, in the simple act of nurturing life.

I caught my reflection in the window, pushing up my glasses. The gesture was so familiar that it made me smile despite everything. Some habits stuck, whether I was wrapped in a habit or not.

It struck me how small a life could become—how it could fit into the back of a car. I avoided the last look around the cottage. I didn't want the view of the white walls and the ghost of what had been imprinted in my mind.

With the trunk shut and the engine running, I sat there, fingers white-knuckled around the wheel, listening to the low hum of the car. The vibration rattled straight through me, stirring the hollow ache in my chest. I inhaled a shaky breath, letting the moment settle like lead. This was it. The severing. The air smelled faintly of gasoline and wet leaves, sharp and damp in the cool midmorning, and for some reason, that ordinary scent made my throat burn.

The drive should have been nothing, barely three minutes from the cottage to the school, but every second stretched thin, cruelly slow. The tires hissed over the old roads. Each landmark was a goodbye—the weathered signpost at the corner and the chapel steeple peeking above the trees.

I pulled into the lot and parked in front of the school. Inside, the halls were quieter than usual, the routine bustle tucked away behind classroom doors. The sharp tang of sanitizer clung to the quiet halls while my footsteps struck the tiles loudly.

The door to Laura's office was open; her eyes were focused on the laptop in front of her as she typed. I knocked softly, the sound barely a breath. Her expression brightened—until she saw my puffy face.

"Claire?" she asked, her brow furrowing with concern. "What's going on?"

I stepped inside and closed the door, the sound of it shutting the start of heartbreaking finality. I handed her my resignation letter, my fingers brushing against hers for just a second, and I could feel her worry deepen.

"What's this?" she asked, already knowing the answer.

"I'm sorry for the short notice, Laura, but . . . I'm leaving," I said. "Today."

Laura's face tightened, her fingers clutching the letter as if it might disappear if she didn't hold on tight enough. "I see." Her eyes skimmed the letter. "Is there anything I can do?"

"This isn't something that can be fixed," I said, trying to keep my tears at bay.

Her gaze searched mine. "Is this about what's been going on between you and Damian?"

There it was. The truth out in the open, hanging in the air between us. My throat constricted, and I could no longer hold back the tears. "Please don't tell anyone," I pleaded, my voice breaking. "That's why I have to go."

I didn't have the heart to tell her about Mrs. Fontana's threat or how I'd come to this conclusion.

Laura sighed, setting the letter on her desk. "I don't agree with this. But I understand if you feel like this is what you need to do."

"Thank you," I whispered.

The tattered pieces of my heart gave way, breaking all over again, as if they hadn't already been shattered enough.

I reached into my bag and pulled out an envelope, holding it out to her. "Could you give this to Father Bellucci?" I sniffled.

She hesitated but took it, her fingers wrapping around the edges as if she were holding delicate porcelain. "I'll make sure he gets it."

I couldn't help myself. "Where is he?"

Laura's dark eyes softened. "He's giving last rites at a hospice center."

I nodded, relieved that he was far from here. "Thank you. For everything, Laura."

She stood and rounded the desk. Her arms wrapped around me in a warm embrace. "We'll see each other again, sweetheart." Pulling away, she stared straight into my eyes. "I know everything seems grim now, but I see great things in your future. Don't put limits on yourself, Claire."

There were too many emotions swirling inside me—grief, guilt, fear. We said our goodbyes, and I left her office. Making my way through the halls, I said goodbye to the people who had become part of my daily life: the librarian, the school secretary, a few teachers who had always greeted me with smiles in the mornings.

When I reached my classroom, a substitute was already there, teaching in my place. I stood by the door for a moment, watching my students as they worked, their heads bent over their desks. My chest constricted, but I forced myself to step inside.

"Sister Claire," one of my students called out, his face lighting up. "You're back."

"Just for a moment," I said, fighting to keep my voice steady. I smiled at them, even though it felt like my heart was shattering for the millionth time. "I wanted to say goodbye."

The substitute caught my eye and gave me a kind nod, stepping aside as if to grant me the room. My students looked up one by one, the realization dawning in their expressions. A ripple of voices rose, questions tumbling over one another.

"Where are you going?"

"You can't leave!"

"Who's going to play kickball with us?"

I laughed softly, though it trembled at the edges. "I'll never forget you. Each of you has made me proud in ways you'll never understand."

A hush fell, followed by the scrape of chairs as a few of them rushed forward. Arms wrapped around me, others tugged at my hands.

"Don't go," Emma whispered.

I met their eyes, forcing my tears back. "You're going to do amazing things," I said. "Better things than I could ever teach you. Promise me you'll keep working hard."

"Promise," they chorused, some solemn, some reluctant.

I hugged them, one by one, memorizing the warmth of their trust. Swallowing the lump in my throat, I stepped back, knowing if I stayed a second longer, I'd never leave.

My footsteps echoed against the hallway tiles as I walked away from my classroom for the last time, the children's precious goodbye hugs still lingering on my skin.

My fingers brushed over the old scars on my thigh through my skirt.

Another goodbye.

"Really? You're just going to sneak out like this?"

I stopped, my heart clenching at Jessica's voice behind me. When I turned, she was standing in the middle of the hallway, no longer the polished image of perfection I'd grown used to seeing. Her hair was pulled back in a messy ponytail, and she wore jeans and a tan sweater—a far cry from her usual designer outfits.

"Jess—"

"What's going on?" She stepped closer. "Is everything okay?"

I shifted my weight from one leg to the other. "It's complicated. There are things I can't explain, but I turned in my resignation. I'm leaving."

"Leaving?" Her tone was softer now, less confrontational. "Talk to me, Claire."

I looked away, unable to meet her eyes. Sterile light flooded from above, the same fixtures that had witnessed our conversation months ago when she'd broken down about her marriage.

"I can't explain it right now. Maybe one day," I said, glancing toward the exit.

She studied me for a heartbeat. "I don't know what happened that makes you feel like you have to leave, and I won't pretend to understand it, but this community won't be the same without you. These kids won't be the same. I won't be the same."

In a few hours, the parking lot would fill with students' parents picking up their children. My window for leaving quietly was closing.

"I'm scared," I whispered, the admission slipping out before I could stop it.

"I know." Jessica took my hands just like I had taken hers months ago. "But you taught me authenticity is worth the risk."

I looked at her through tears. This woman who'd learned to be vulnerable in her marriage, who'd found her voice again, who'd become stronger by admitting her weaknesses.

"Whatever's happening," Jessica started, "whatever choice you're making—I trust you. I trust your judgment. You've shown all of us what real compassion looks like. What it means to see people for who they really are."

If she knew the truth—that every step I took away from this place was for him—she might not call it bravery, but it was the only way I knew how to love him, to protect him from ruin. I wasn't leaving because I'd lost my faith; I was leaving because I'd found something even more dangerous: a love I couldn't unchoose.

"You're not broken, Claire. You're one of the most whole people I've ever met. And wherever you go next, whatever you do, that won't change."

I closed my eyes, inhaling a breath before meeting her gaze for one last time. "Thank you. I really should go."

Before she could say goodbye, I turned and walked away. The

heavy doors groaned as I pushed through them, and the noon sun spilled over me, too warm, too kind, like a blessing I hadn't earned. My car waited in the lot, crammed with the pieces of my life I prayed would be enough to start over.

Hey Dames,

I don't know how to start this without breaking, so I'll just say it: I'm leaving. If I tried say it to you face-to-face, I never would have made it out the door.

We crossed a line, and in that moment, I knew the truth I've been trying to bury—my vows were never strong enough to hold against the way I feel about you. I never wanted to be the reason you questioned yours. I never wanted to be the crack in the foundation of your faith. You've given everything to this parish, to God, to the people who look at you and see hope. They need you. And I love you too much to be the one who takes that away.

That's what this is. Love. The kind I can't confess in daylight without losing myself completely. If I stayed, I would keep choosing you until there was nothing left of the life I promised to live. And you would keep choosing me, even when it tore you apart. I can't let us destroy each other in the name of something that feels like salvation but could ruin us both.

Rico told me once that we're more than our mistakes. More than the weight of our regrets. And I believe that's true. So, I'm choosing to step away from this life and find my purpose beyond the walls of the church.

You deserve the space to figure out who you are and what you want without me complicating everything. I know you'll continue to be a source of light for these people whether I'm a part of it or not.

Despite everything, I don't regret the moments we shared or the friendship we built. Those memories will always be a part of me, and I'll treasure them.

I hope when you think of me, you remember me with kindness and not regret. And I pray that whatever decision you make, it'll be one you can live fully and freely.

Take care of yourself, Dames. And don't carry the weight of my choice as a burden in your heart. I made this decision for myself.

With love,
Claire

"No." My voice cracked with the word, barely a whisper. "No, she wouldn't—" I couldn't finish the thought.

The letter slipped from my grasp, fluttering to the ground, even as it carried the full weight of my world crumbling around me. My fingers curled into fists as I bolted out of the church, my heart pounding in time with my frantic steps. I didn't stop to think, didn't lock the door behind me. None of it mattered.

I ran faster than I thought possible, every stride filled with the panic rising in my throat. My breath came in ragged gasps as I reached her house, the place I'd prayed would still hold her inside. But it was too quiet. Too dark. The windows stared back at me, empty and lifeless, reflecting all I feared most.

"Please," I whispered as I took the front steps two at a time, my pulse thundering in my ears. I yanked at the door handle, but it wouldn't budge. Locked.

"Claire!" I shouted, my fist slamming against the wood, the sound ricocheting through the stillness of the night. "Claire, open the door." Desperation spilled into every syllable. "Don't do this! Don't leave me."

I pounded harder, my fists burning with every hit, but the house remained silent. Empty. Abandoned.

"Goddammit, Claire." I stumbled back, my chest heaving. I scanned the windows once more, hoping for a miracle. A flicker of light, a shadow—anything. But there was nothing.

She's really gone.

And just like that, my heart shattered.

I collapsed to my knees on the porch, the weight of my heartache crashing down like a torrential wave, dragging me under. I pressed my hand to my chest, trying to ease my breathing, but I couldn't. It was like the air had been sucked out of my lungs, leaving me with a hollow unbearable ache.

I lost her. Again.

How had I let this happen?

I closed my eyes, the sting of tears burning behind my lids. I forced them away. I wasn't going to cry. Not here, not like this. But the pain, the raw agony tearing through me, was too much to hold inside.

"Claire," I whispered, her name like a prayer, but there was no comfort, no solace. Only the cold realization that I'd let the one person I needed most slip through my fingers.

I was furious—at her, at myself, at God. Especially God. How could He let this happen again? How could He dangle her in front of me, let me feel that connection again, only to rip it away? What kind of cruel joke was this? I had dedicated my life to Him, to His service, and this was what I got?

"Why?" I muttered, my fists clenching against the wooden floor of the porch. "Why did You let her go? Why do You keep taking her away from me?" My chest heaved, the anger surging, burning through the heartbreak like wildfire. "Why can't You just let me have her?"

No answer. Just the empty street, the darkened house, and the gnawing pain of having lost her all over again.

My Claire, my Sparrow, was gone.

A few hours later, I was stumbling in the direction of Father Max's rectory, a bottle of honeyed amber liquid clutched in my hand like it was the only thing grounding me. My head was spinning, my heart a hollow ache I couldn't escape. By the time I reached his door, I didn't bother to knock. I just stood there, my knuckles white against the neck of the bottle, staring blankly at the wood.

Eventually, I knocked, the sound barely more than a tap. The door opened after a few moments, and there stood Father Max, his blue eyes soft with concern as he glanced down at the whiskey in my hand.

He didn't say a word, just stepped aside and let me in.

"Come on," Max said, motioning toward the small sitting room.

I followed him inside, my body moving like it wasn't my own, numb. The warmth of his place hit me, but it didn't thaw the cold gnawing at my insides. He gestured for me to sit, and without a word, I placed the bottle on the table between us.

Max grabbed two glasses, his movements calm and steady. He poured the whiskey, handing me a glass, then took a seat across from me.

We sat in silence for a while, just the two of us, staring at our glasses.

After a few sips, the burn of the alcohol dulled the edges of my anguish just enough to speak. I swirled the whiskey in the glass. "She's left. Claire's gone."

He didn't react right away, just nodded as if he'd already expected that. His silence was heavy, like he knew what I was going to say next but was waiting for me to spill it.

I took a deep breath, the words getting stuck in my throat. "All she left was a measly letter," I lamented, and I quickly downed the rest of the whiskey, welcoming the burn searing down my throat.

Max reached for the bottle and poured another shot for both of us. "What did it say?"

I stared at the glass in front of me, the words replaying in my mind. "She doesn't want to be the reason I leave the priesthood. She doesn't want to be the reason I lose my way."

He leaned back, his eyes filled with that same quiet understanding that had always unnerved me. "Maybe she's right."

My head snapped up, disbelief cutting through the haze of my buzz and grief. "I've lost her again. She's gone. How the fuck am I supposed to be okay with that?"

Max sighed, running a hand over his face before taking a long sip of whiskey. "You've been wrestling with this for a long time. Claire leaving gives you space to think. You need that."

I shook my head, my jaw tightening. "I don't need *space*. I need *her*."

Max set his glass down and leaned forward, his gaze sharp. "You need to finish what you started. Get laicized. Only then can you figure out if this—if she—is what you really want. Until then, you need to stay away from her."

Stay away from her. How could I? How could I stay away from the only person who made me feel like there was more out there?

Max's expression softened, but his words didn't. "If you don't, you're only going to make it worse for both of you. Do you really want to risk dragging her into something neither of you are ready for?"

I wanted to argue. To tell him he was wrong. But deep down, I knew he was right. I knew I couldn't see her—speak to her. Not until I was free of this collar.

"I don't know if I have that kind of strength," I admitted, my voice barely more than a whisper.

"You've already shown more strength than you realize, Damian. Admitting your sins, facing your doubts—that takes courage."

I swallowed hard. The whiskey wasn't doing much to numb the ache anymore. "What if I can't find my way?"

Max's voice was low but steadfast. "I'll be here for you, no matter what decision you make."

I nodded, my mind a whirlpool of emotions—anger, sorrow, fear, love. But Max was right. I needed to see this through. And maybe there would still be a chance for me and Claire on the other side of this hell.

I finished the last of my drink and stood. "Thanks, Max."

He placed his glass on the table. "You'll get through this, Dame. Just take it one day at a time."

That night, I called Mrs. Walker and told her every Mass was canceled until further notice. She pressed me for answers, and I gave her the only one I could manage: That this collar had never truly been mine to wear. That I couldn't keep standing at the altar when my heart was kneeling somewhere else. She said she'd pray for me before hanging up, but I didn't need her prayers. I needed a reason not to burn for the rest of my life.

Chapter Forty-One

DAMIAN

The highway stretched before me like a long run down a slope, propelling me forward rather than back. I was on my way back to Saint Anthony's from the chancery. Bishop Valenti's words still echoed in my mind, his face etched with that mixture of disappointment and understanding I'd come to know so well.

Each signature had felt less like rebellion and more like release. Freedom, scrawled in ink. And still I found myself thinking, *If I'd done this sooner, if I'd had the courage to walk away before she did, maybe Claire would still be here.*

"Are you certain about this, Damian?" the bishop had asked, his weathered hands resting on the stack of forms I'd placed on his desk. "Once you start this process, there's no turning back. No changing your mind six months or a year from now when things get difficult."

I'd met his gaze steadily, even as my heart thrummed. "I'm sure, Your Excellency."

He'd studied me for a long moment. "You know, I've seen many priests wrestle with this over the years. Some were running away from something. Others were running toward something." His eyes had softened then. "What are you doing, Damian?"

"Both," I'd admitted. "And neither. I'm just trying to be honest with myself, with God, with everyone."

He'd pursed his lips before saying, "Bravery isn't clinging to a path that's breaking you. It's having the humility to step away from it."

I pulled into Saint Anthony's empty parking lot and sat there, engine idling as I drank in the sight of the church that had been my sanctuary. The stained glass burned with evening light—Mary's robes and Christ's crown bleeding color into the dusk. A beauty I could see but never touch. The stone walls cast their shadows across the empty lot, stable and familiar, like they were mourning me as much as I was mourning them.

How many times had I walked through those heavy oak doors, my shoes clicking against the worn marble steps, wearing this collar, feeling certain of my calling? How many confessions had I heard? How many Masses celebrated? How many prayers whispered into the quiet of the sanctuary?

My phone buzzed against the console—an email from the diocesan office. More forms. More questions to answer. They wanted a detailed account of my journey to priesthood—every step that had led me here.

Inside the rectory, wrapped in the silence that felt more like peace than emptiness, I opened my laptop and started typing:

Subject: Formal Request for Laicization

To Whom It May Concern,

My path to the priesthood began the night I lost my brother. In my grief, I believed serving God meant denying everything else—love, connection, the fragile humanity that makes us who we are. Over time, I have come to understand that I was mistaken.

Faith is not denial. Faith is truth. And the truth is that I cannot serve God or His people by hiding behind vows I can no longer keep. The collar that once felt like devotion has become a barrier to honesty, both with myself and with those I am called to serve and love.

This is not an end, but a beginning—one where I can serve with greater integrity, every breath a prayer, every step forward an act of faith.

For these reasons, I am formally requesting laicization.

Respectfully,

Rev. Damian Bellucci

Chapter Forty-Two

DAMIAN

It had taken long, agonizing months of paperwork, meetings, and internal battles, but I was finally laicized. No longer Father Bellucci. Just Damian.

The parishioners at Saint Anthony's had been disappointed, of course. Some hadn't spoken to me since the news broke. A few still showed up for morning coffee, offering quiet support or the occasional prayer. But the whispers? The sideways glances? They'd only grown louder as my final days at the rectory approached.

Boxes were stacked high, filled with books, mementos, and the few personal items I had left. I was sealing the last of my books into a cardboard box when the sharp rap of knuckles against the rectory door echoed through the empty hallway. I wasn't expecting Laura and Max for another hour, so I wiped my hands on my jeans and went to answer it.

Mrs. Fontana stood on the doorstep, her silver hair perfectly coiffed despite the morning breeze and her designer purse clutched like a weapon. The disapproval radiating from her could have frozen hell itself.

"Mrs. Fontana." I stepped aside, though every instinct told me to slam the door in her face. "What can I do for you?"

"I think you know exactly why I'm here, Father." She swept past me into the rectory, her heels clicking against the hardwood like a judge's gavel. "Though I suppose I should call you Mr. Bellucci now."

I closed the door and turned to face her, crossing my arms. "If you're here to lecture me about my decision—"

"Your decision?" Her voice rose an octave. "You call abandoning your sacred vows for that woman a decision?"

There it was. The real reason for her visit. Not concern for my soul or the parish—just her obsession with controlling everyone around her.

"Claire had nothing to do with my choice to leave the priesthood," I said, though we both knew it was only partially true.

I could taste the bitterness in Mrs. Fontana's laugh. "Please. Do you think I'm blind? I've been watching you two. The way you looked at her during Mass, the way you found excuses to be near her. I tried to warn you—tried to protect you from yourself—but you wouldn't listen."

Heat tore through me, white-hot. She didn't know a fucking thing about what Claire and I had bled for or the nights I'd begged God to stoke these flames. We'd fought it—Christ, I'd fought it. But Mrs. Fontana didn't want honesty. She wanted control. And I'd be damned before I let her twist Claire into some cheap scandal.

The words exploded from her. "Rico died before he could fulfill his calling. You were supposed to carry it forward. For him. For this parish. For God."

My nostrils flared. "Rico is dead," I said, my voice low and dangerous. "And I am not him."

Her composure cracked, revealing the grief and fear underneath. "This parish needed you. I needed—"

"You needed control." I stepped closer, my hands clenched at my sides. "You needed to groom me into your perfect priest. One who would never ask questions, never want anything for himself, and never love anyone more than the Church."

Her face went pale. "Is *that* what you call this sin you've been wallowing in?"

"Yes. I call it love."

"She's a nun, Damian!"

"Claire left the convent—not that it's any of your business."

Mrs. Fontana staggered back as if I'd struck her. "What?"

"She left because she thought she was saving me. That was her act of mercy. Her cross to bear. Don't you dare twist her sacrifice into sin just to satisfy your need for judgment."

"This is insane," she whispered. "You're both throwing away everything for some teenage infatuation—"

"Stop." My voice sliced through her words. "Just stop. Claire and I were always meant to be. Always. Rico's death, the priesthood, the convent—none of that changed what we felt for each other. And all your meddling—all your watching and judging—didn't change anything either."

Her face crumpled. "Your brother—"

"Would want me to be happy." The certainty in my voice surprised even me. "Rico loved her. And he sure as hell wouldn't want to be the reason I spent my life miserable."

Mrs. Fontana headed to the door with shaking hands, her earlier confidence completely shattered. At the threshold, she turned back one last time.

"I hope she's worth it," she said.

I slipped my hands into my pockets and let her words linger. Mrs. Fontana wanted to pull me back, but that life was already gone. I'd signed it away, piece by piece. Too late for her. Too late for me. All that remained was the truth. My truth.

I watched her walk to her car, her shoulders hunched in defeat. For the first time in years, I felt completely free—not just from the collar, but from the expectations and judgments that had been burdening my shoulders.

When Laura and Max arrived, they found me sitting on the rectory steps, staring at the school building across the parking lot. I hadn't asked for help, but they'd insisted.

The new apartment was just across town. Close in miles. A lifetime away in everything else.

We managed to load all my belongings into my truck and Max's car. Once the last of my possessions was loaded, Laura turned to me, her eyes soft with understanding. She stepped closer, wrapping her arms around me in a tight embrace.

"May God guide your path, Damian," she whispered, her voice thick with sincerity. "We'll see each other again once this all blows over."

I hugged her back, letting her warmth offer me some semblance of comfort. "Thank you," I muttered, pulling away and offering a small grateful smile. "For everything."

She gave me a final nod before stepping back, her eyes shimmering. Laura had always been a reliable figure in this chaos. She'd stayed strong, though I knew this transition was difficult for her.

"Have you heard from her?" I asked; the question had been burning in my chest for weeks now.

Her expression shifted, an emotion I couldn't read flickering across her features before she looked away. "No, I haven't."

My shoulders dropped with disappointment, but then she continued, her voice careful.

"I did see her last week. Walking down Maple . . ." She met my eyes with obvious reluctance. "With Preston."

Claire's ex, Emma's uncle. Fucking Preston Kane. I should've known he'd make his move. My chest tightened, the green-eyed demon coursing through me so fiercely that I had to grip the truck's tailgate to steady myself.

"I see," I muttered.

"They looked friendly," Laura said quickly, her tone reassuring. "Just talking, nothing more."

Friendly could mean anything. Friendly could be the beginning of more I couldn't compete with. My mind immediately conjured images I didn't want to see—Claire laughing at Preston's jokes, accepting comfort from someone who could offer her stability, a future without complications.

I needed to call her. Right now. I needed to hear her voice—

Realization crashed over me: I didn't have her number anymore. Claire had changed it.

"Damian?" Laura's voice seemed to come from far away. "You okay?"

I blinked, realizing I'd been staring at nothing, my hands clenched into fists. "Yeah. I'm . . . fine."

But I wasn't. Nothing about this was fine. Claire was moving on, possibly with someone else, and I was powerless to even reach out to her. I was starting over from nothing—no collar, no way to bridge this gap between us.

Laura studied my face with concern. "Claire's not the type to rush into anything."

I wanted to believe her, but doubt gnawed at my insides. I'd been stupid to think Claire would wait for me to figure out my life. Of course Preston Kane would step in. He had no baggage and could offer her everything I couldn't.

Laura glanced over at Max, who had started wrestling with the boxes, then back at me. "Just don't give up yet, okay?" she whispered before stepping away. "Call me if you need anything."

After saying her goodbyes, Laura got into her car and drove out of Saint Anthony's parking lot.

Max straightened up from his car, apparently satisfied with his rearrangement, and walked back over. His gaze had been intense the entire afternoon, and I knew what was coming before he even opened his mouth.

"So," Max started, his tone more pointed than usual. "What're you going to do?"

My chest squeezed at the question. I'd asked myself the same thing every day since she'd left. Every sleepless night, every quiet moment at Saint Anthony's, her name had been on my mind. But I hadn't dared to reach out. I couldn't. "I don't know, Max. What if she doesn't . . . What if she doesn't want me anymore?"

He studied me, his eyes narrowing like he was searching for some deeper meaning in my answer. "There's only one way to find out."

"I've lost her more than once. I don't think I can do it again."

He inhaled a deep breath, his gaze softening as he rested a hand on my shoulder. "You've shown more courage than most priests ever will. But God doesn't ask us to let go of love—He asks us to fight for it. If she's your future, if she's the one He's placed in your path, then go. Find her."

I swallowed hard. Max always had a way of cutting straight to the heart of things. I nodded, my voice caught somewhere in my chest.

He gave me a final pat on the shoulder before stepping away, his hands sliding into his pockets. "Come on. Let's get this stuff to your place. And I'm going to need a beer after this."

"Not used to physical labor?" I teased. "What were all those hours in the gym for?"

He smirked, shrugging. "The gym's for looking good, not moving your sorry ass across town."

I said over my shoulder, "Vanity's a sin, you know. Not that I'm in the business of handing out absolution anymore."

Max smirked and got into his car. "Good thing too; otherwise, you'd still be stuck absolving me for cussing at your shitty driving."

Shaking my head, I took one last look at Saint Anthony's, the church standing tall in the distance, its stained glass windows reflecting the late-afternoon sun. This place had been my home, my refuge, for so many years. I'd given my life to it, to God. And now I was walking away.

I'd made my choice, and it'd cost more than I ever thought it would. But this ache was mine to bear, and the uncertain road ahead was still mine to walk.

I closed my eyes, took a deep breath, and then, with one final glance, I climbed into my truck and drove away.

MOVING INTO MY NEW APARTMENT WAS STEPPING INTO A LIFE THAT DIDN'T seem like mine. Small, functional, boxes in the corners, walls stripped bare. Max and I unloaded and shared a beer, and then I unpacked for hours. But when the sun had made its final descent, the place remained foreign—silent, hollow, empty.

That first night, I lay on the unfamiliar bed, staring at the ceiling, my thoughts drifting to Claire more than I wanted them to. It was strange being out of the rectory—out of Saint Anthony's. The structured prayers and rituals that had anchored my days were gone, replaced by something more intimate but harder to define.

I found myself talking to God differently now—not in formal liturgy or prescribed devotions, but in quiet, honest conversations. It felt like I'd severed a piece of myself and left it behind. Yet somehow, God's presence felt closer, more immediate, freed from the constraints of collar and ceremony.

Monday, I'd start at the local YMCA as the new youth and teen director. It was a fresh start. At least I had the weekend to get my bearings. *Relax*, Max had said. But how could I, when everything still felt like it was shifting beneath my feet? Even my prayers were changing, becoming less about performance and more about connection—messy and imperfect but deeply authentic.

I pulled into my parents' driveway on a Sunday afternoon. Without the collar filling my schedule, I'd been able to stop by more—third time this week. Rico's absence was still woven into the silence, but it didn't crush us the way it used to. We were learning to breathe again.

The rich aroma of garlic and herbs hit me before I even opened the front door. Mom's marinara sauce—the real stuff that took hours to simmer properly. I followed the scent into the kitchen, where I found her humming softly while stirring a large pot, her movements no longer mechanical but purposeful. Alive.

"There's my handsome son," she cooed without turning around. "Perfect timing. The sauce is almost ready."

Dad appeared in the doorway, grinning. "Your mother's been cooking since dawn," he said, gesturing toward the counter, where fresh bread was cooling. "She's been plotting this since your last visit."

"Guilty as charged," Mom said, finally turning to kiss my cheek. Her eyes were bright, present in a way they hadn't been for years. "I've missed cooking."

Dad chuckled, leaning against the counter. "Remember when you boys used to time your arrivals right when dinner was ready? Like little vultures circling."

"Rico was the vulture," I protested, settling onto a kitchen stool. "I was just following his lead."

"Oh, please." Mom laughed, the sound filling corners of the house that had been silent too long. "You were worse than he was. At least Rico helped with prep work. You'd just appear with those big green eyes, all innocent, right as everything came together."

Dad started slicing the now-cooled crusty Italian bread, the kind Mom used to make for Sunday dinners when we were kids. "Some things never change. Look at him now—probably hasn't eaten a real meal since Thursday."

"I cook," I said defensively.

"Cup Noodles doesn't count," they said in unison, then looked at each other with surprised laughter.

I watched them move around each other in the kitchen with an ease that had been missing for so long: Dad refilling Mom's wineglass without being asked. Mom automatically handing him the oven mitts. Small gestures of partnership that grief had temporarily stolen but were slowly returning.

"So," Mom said, lowering the heat under the sauce. "Have you spoken to Claire yet?"

I should have known this was coming.

"No."

"Why not?" Dad asked, pulling out a chair at the kitchen table.

I joined them at the old oak table where we'd shared countless meals—where Rico and I had done homework and fought over the last piece of pizza. Mom poured me a glass of wine, and all I could think was, *Claire would love this.*

"What're you afraid of?" Mom tilted her head, studying my face with that maternal intuition that could read me like an open book.

God, that was a loaded question. I was afraid she wouldn't want me. Afraid she'd already closed the door I kept standing in front of.

Afraid she'd started building a life, steadier and freer than anything I could ever give her.

And then there was Preston. I rubbed a hand over my jaw and finally said, "I'm afraid she's moved on. That I waited too long."

Dad leaned forward, his voice gentle. "You've been given a second chance, son. What're you going to do with it?"

Mom squeezed my hand. "I understand it's complicated—there's pain and doubt and history. But the best things in life are never easy. They're the ones you fight hardest for."

I looked between my parents, seeing an emotion in their faces I hadn't noticed before: Hope. Not just for me, but for themselves—for the possibility that their family could be whole again in a different way. That happiness was still attainable after loss.

"Find her," Dad said. "Not just for the possibility of a future together, but for closure. For both of you. You can't keep living in limbo, wondering 'what if.' "

"Then at least you'll know," Mom agreed. "And you can both move forward with a sense of peace."

Dad started plopping servings of pasta into my and Mom's bowls. "Your mother's right. You need to have that conversation."

"But first, you're going to have dinner with your parents. Because this is what we do now—we show up for each other," Mom said, her lips turned up in a warm smile.

We sat around that same table, sharing bowls of pasta with Mom's perfect marinara, fresh bread, and wine that loosened tongues and eased old wounds. Dad told stories about work that actually made us laugh. Mom shared gossip about the neighbors. I found myself talking about my new job, my hopes, and even some of my fears about the future.

It wasn't the family we used to be—Rico's empty chair would always be felt. But it was the family we were becoming. Scarred but healing. Different but whole in our own way. And as the evening light faded outside the kitchen windows, I realized this was what moving forward looked like—not forgetting the past, but creating space for new memories alongside the old.

"I thank God every day for you two," Mom said softly, raising her wineglass. "To new beginnings."

"To family," Dad added.

"To Rico," I said. "And to not being afraid to live."

Chapter Forty-Three

CLAIRE

T he familiar scent of freshly ground coffee beans filled my nose as I sat inside Coastal Grind, the little shop that had somehow become the backdrop for so many of life's important conversations.

Never in a million years had I ever thought I'd be sitting across from Preston Kane, having coffee. Irony thought itself funny as I sat with a man from my past who represented all the pain I'd tried to run away from at the very same table Damian and I used to have glazed donuts and lattes at.

But surprisingly, Preston had turned out to be a dependable friend. The listening ear I needed when the world felt like it was spinning off its axis. I'd told him everything about Damian, including how I'd ended it—how I'd walked away from both the man I loved and the life I'd built because staying would have destroyed us both.

The late-afternoon light caught the steam rising from my mug, creating tiny rainbows that danced and disappeared. I wrapped my hands around the ceramic, letting the heat seep through my palms and chase away the chill that seemed to live permanently in my bones these days.

It had been a few months since I'd officially been released from my vows, but it still felt like yesterday. I'd gone no contact with everyone at Saint Anthony's—a clean break. I could only assume that Damian had stayed and continued to live out his vocation, which was exactly what I wanted for him. He deserved to find peace in his calling —to serve God without the complication of my presence. But knowing that didn't make it hurt any less. If anything, it tore me to shreds inside knowing I'd given up the chance to fight for us because I was too afraid of what loving him might cost.

"Penny for your thoughts," Preston said, sipping his vanilla latte from a to-go cup, the sound of his voice pulling me back from the dangerous territory my mind had wandered into.

Damn, I drifted again. I'd been doing a lot of that lately, losing myself in memories that felt more real than the present moment. With a faint smile that was more muscle memory than genuine emotion, I took a swig of my coffee and said, "Nothing important."

We were cool, but not *that* cool. We'd at least gotten to a place where he didn't ask me out anymore, where I could breathe without feeling like I was disappointing him just by existing in the same space. The easy friendship we'd developed over these months was a small miracle—proof that people really could change and that past mistakes didn't have to define every future interaction.

His blue eyes studied me for a moment, and I could see the wheels turning behind them. Preston had always been observant, able to read the subtle shifts in mood that others missed. It was what had made him such a good study partner in college and what made him dangerous when he wanted something. "I've been wanting to talk to you."

A knot of anxiety twisted in my stomach. I placed my cup on the circular café table, the ceramic making a soft clink against the wood. "Okay. Shoot."

"I know you're probably tired of me asking this, but I have to try at least one last time." He inhaled deeply, as if gathering courage, and

I watched the way his shoulders rose and fell with the breath. "Is there a world where you and I could try this again?"

Preston had been many things in my life—fun, exciting, a distraction from deeper pain—but he'd also been part of a chapter I'd closed for very good reasons. Looking at him now, I could see he was sincere, hopeful in a way that made my heart ache for what I couldn't give him.

The coffee shop buzzed with late-afternoon energy—the hiss of the espresso machine, the gentle murmur of conversations, the scrape of chairs against hardwood floors.

Letting out a long breath, I said gently, "Preston, I don't know if I'll ever be able to give you the love you deserve."

How could I tell him that my heart still belonged to someone who'd chosen God over me? That every time I looked at him, I saw a good man who deserved a woman who could love him without reservation and without the ghost of another love haunting every moment?

Preston's jaw tightened, a muscle jumping near his temple as he processed my words. His fingers began drumming against the table in a familiar rhythm—a habit I remembered from our study sessions when he was working through a particularly difficult problem. The sound was oddly comforting, a bridge between who we'd been and who we were now.

"He's an idiot for letting you go," he said. There was no malice in it, just a resigned understanding.

"No, he's not." I grinned despite the tears threatening to gather, my throat already closing up with the ache that came whenever someone mentioned Damian, even indirectly. "He did what he thought was right. What he believed God was calling him to do."

Preston ran a hand through his dark hair. "So . . . friends, then?"

I nodded. "Friends. Someone's got to keep me humble when I get too preachy."

His smile was rueful but genuine, tinged with a sadness I pretended not to notice. "Friends with the woman who broke my heart not once, but twice," he muttered, but there was humor in it too —the kind that comes from learning to laugh at your own pain.

Letting out a giggle, I said, "You're supposed to move forward, not backward."

He leaned forward, and for a moment, I saw a flash of the charming boy who'd swept me off my feet in college. "Baby, I'd do the moonwalk for you."

We were both laughing now, the sound bright and genuine in the coffee shop's warm atmosphere. It felt good to laugh. The tension that had been coiled in my shoulders started unwinding.

The afternoon light had shifted while we talked, painting everything in shades of gold that reminded me why I'd always loved this place. Preston and I sat in comfortable silence, watching customers come and go, listening to the gentle hum of conversation and the rhythmic hiss of the espresso machine creating its caffeinated magic.

A young couple at a nearby table shared a piece of chocolate cake, feeding each other bites with the kind of unconscious intimacy that made my heart ache. An elderly man sat alone by the window, reading a newspaper with the focused attention of someone who had all the time in the world.

"Speaking as your friend, I think you and him have to settle some things," Preston said, glancing out the big window at the passersby— people hurrying home from work, couples walking hand in hand, a woman pushing a stroller while talking animatedly on her phone.

My heart skipped. "What makes you say that?"

He grinned, and this time, it reached his eyes. "Call it 'male intuition.'"

I chortled and stared into my coffee cup, watching the surface ripple slightly from the vibration of the espresso machine. "Maybe one day . . ."

When I looked up, I found him watching me. This wasn't the cocky college boy I'd known, or even the slightly manipulative man who'd shown up at the school all those months ago. This was someone who'd grown up—who'd learned some hard lessons of his own.

Preston had been hurt too. Maybe not in the same way and maybe not as deeply, but he understood what it meant to love someone who couldn't love him back. That was why he'd been so patient with me.

Preston stood, pulling on his coat with smooth movements that spoke of someone ready to close this chapter with grace. "Come on, I'll take you home."

I shrugged on my own jacket. "Thanks for today, as always."

His lips curved up into that easy smile that had charmed half our economics class. "Anytime. You sure I can't change your mind about me? I'm a pretty amazing boyfriend."

He beckoned another laugh from me. "I'm sure. And thanks for keeping my past where it belongs. When you showed up at the school that first time, I thought you might use it against me."

His gaze softened, and I saw a flicker of what might have been shame cross his features. "I'm sorry it seemed that way. I want you to know I'd never do that."

We stepped out into the late-afternoon air. The ocean breeze carried the scent of salt and possibility, mixing with the lingering aroma of coffee that clung to our clothes. Preston was right about one thing: Damian and I did have unfinished business. The question was whether I had the courage to face him and whether either of us was ready for the truth we might find.

The sun painted the sky in watercolors of pink and orange. *My future holds a beauty I can't see yet.*

Chapter Forty-Four

DAMIAN

I'd burned three weeks chasing scraps of where Claire might be. When I went to the convent, Mother Superior had been kind but unmovable—yes, Claire was with Jasmine, no, she wouldn't hand me an address. The parish directory gave me three old addresses for Jasmine, each one a dead end.

Christ, why did she have to move so damn much?

Just when I was ready to quit, I caught sight of a familiar car outside a weathered oceanfront complex only a few miles from my new apartment. Jasmine's white Honda—the pride flag sticker fading on the bumper, the small dent in the passenger's door, and the wooden cross hanging from the rearview mirror.

My chest clenched, breath catching sharp as the sight pulled me forward and held me back all at once. The blue townhouses faced the water, salt-worn stairs climbing to second-floor balconies where pots of succulents lined the rails.

She's here. She has to be.

I sat in my truck, pulse racing, and stared up at the units. After what felt like an eternity, I'd finally found her. But now that I was here, doubt crept in. Where had she found peace these past months? Had she moved on with Preston?

The longer I sat there, the more I started to feel like some kind of stalker. What was I doing? Sitting outside someone's home, waiting and watching.

I should leave.

The sun cast the parking lot in the dusky golden hue that came just before dark. I was so caught up in my thoughts, sitting in the growing twilight, that I didn't even hear the footsteps until a sharp knock on my window nearly made me jump out of my skin. I jerked, my heart racing. Jasmine and Rhea stood there with matching smirks.

"Jesus," I breathed, rolling down the window. "How the hell did you even see me?"

"Your truck isn't exactly subtle," Jasmine said with a laugh. "Plus, Rhea spotted you from the upstairs window about twenty minutes ago. We've been watching you sit out here like some lovesick teen."

"We were wondering when you'd finally show up," Rhea said, exchanging a knowing look with Jasmine.

Letting out a sigh, I muttered, "Trust me, it was no easy feat." I brushed my fingers through my hair. "How is she?"

Jasmine crossed her arms. "She's been as well as she can be, considering."

I nodded, a lump rising in my throat. "Maybe I should go."

"No," Rhea protested. "You should talk to her. We're heading out for a few hours anyway—"

Her words were cut off as a sleek black car pulled into the complex parking lot. My stomach dropped when I recognized the driver: Preston Kane. And there, in the passenger's seat, was Claire.

"Fuck," I muttered under my breath, sinking lower into my seat.

Jasmine followed my gaze and winced. "Oh. Yeah, that."

I watched, frozen, as Preston parked and walked around to open

Claire's door. She stepped out, looking radiant in jeans that hugged her perfectly and a simple sweater and light jacket that made her look soft and approachable. She was laughing at something Preston had said, her face bright with genuine amusement. The sound carried across the parking lot. When was the last time I'd made her laugh like that?

They walked toward the building together, and I had to grip the steering wheel to keep from getting out and making an absolute idiot of myself. Preston's hand rested lightly on the small of her back as he guided her up the steps, a casual, intimate gesture that made the pathetic organ in my chest twist painfully.

At the door, she hugged him, an easy embrace that spoke of a solid foundation—maybe more than I wanted to admit. When they pulled apart, Preston cupped her face, murmured something I couldn't read, and then headed for his car.

Claire stood there a moment, watching him go, her face unreadable, before slipping inside.

"How long's that been going on?" I asked.

"They're friends," Jasmine said. "He's been good to her. Helped her through some rough patches after she left the convent."

I tracked Preston's car down the coastal road. "Friends." The word scraped my throat raw, acrid as burnt coffee.

"Damian." Jasmine's voice softened. "When Preston showed up, he gave her someone outside the Church. Someone who could see clearly."

I leaned back and shut my eyes—then hissed a curse when a sharp smack caught the side of my head. My eyes flew open to Jasmine's smug look.

"What the hell was that for?" I muttered, rubbing the sting.

She arched a brow. "You going to sit there sulking, or are you going to get off your ass?"

I shoved my door open. "Guess I'm getting off my ass."

She stood a few inches shorter, studying me like she was trying to see if I had any backbone left. Then she nodded once. "Good. She's been through enough bullshit. Don't fuck this up, Bellucci."

I shook my head, jaw tight. "I won't."

As they walked away, heading toward their car, I stood there staring up at the unit Claire had walked into. A light had come on in what I assumed was the living room. She was just a flight of stairs away, probably making tea or settling in with a book like she always used to do in the evenings.

She was alone now. My chance—maybe my last—to say what I should've said before I let her go. My chest hammered as I crossed the lot, every step a fight against myself. But I couldn't keep bleeding her out of my life. She had to know. Even if it ruined me, she had to know.

Chapter Forty-Five

CLAIRE

I settled into the corner of the couch, letting out a contented breath. Tucking my legs beneath me, I opened the book I'd been wanting to read for weeks. The last traces of dusk softened the room, shadows stretching long while the first streetlights flickered on outside. Preston had dropped me off just a few minutes ago, and the comfortable silence that followed our coffee shop conversation still lingered.

"You know I'm not going anywhere, right?" he'd said as we sat in his car outside the townhouse. "Emma needs stability, and honestly, so do you. I know things got complicated between us before, but we're different people now. I just want to be here—as a friend. No pressure, no expectations. Just . . . let me be in your corner for once, instead of the guy who made everything harder."

He'd paused, studying my face in the dashboard light. "You've been carrying so much alone. First the transition out of religious life, now dealing with whatever's going on with Damian. You don't have to figure it all out by yourself. I may not have been the best version of myself in college, but I'd like to think I've learned something about being the kind of person worth counting on."

This wasn't the Preston who'd once made everything about conquest and ego. This felt . . . real. Like maybe we could actually build a genuine friendship from the wreckage of our complicated past.

The breeze rolled in off the water, salt clinging to it, carrying with it the hush of open horizons. These quiet moments had become my new form of prayer—finding peace not in the rigid structure of convent life, but in the simple beauty of existence.

I'd discovered that God wasn't confined to church walls or morning Mass anymore. I'd found Him in unexpected places—in the way dawn painted the ocean gold, in thunderstorms that shook the townhouse windows, in the salt air that clung to my skin. He was in the laughter shared with Jasmine and Rhea over morning coffee and the quiet satisfaction of helping a struggling student finally grasp a concept. In the freedom to question and doubt.

After years of searching for God in ritual and structure, I was discovering Him in life's raw, messy beauty and in the parts of myself I'd once tried to pray away.

I had just opened to the first chapter when a soft knock came at my door. Probably Jasmine forgetting her wallet again. Setting my book aside with a small smile, I padded barefoot across the hardwood floor to the front door.

"Jaz, you really need to remember—" I started as I pulled the door open, but the words died in my throat.

Damian stood on my doorstep, hands shoved into his pockets, and for a heartbeat, I forgot how to breathe. The sheer force of seeing him again—those green eyes, that unshakable intensity—knocked the ground out from under me. My heart jolted painfully in my chest, and the silence between us swelled, thick with all the months we'd been separated.

"Dames," I breathed. "You're here."

We stared at each other. Uncertainty flickered in his green eyes, and his shoulders tensed as if he was preparing for me to slam the door in his face.

"You want to come inside?" I asked softly.

He nodded, following me through the doorway into the living room. The space became smaller somehow with him in it. I turned to face him, my fingers fidgeting with the hem of my sweatshirt, suddenly hyperaware of him—the scent of his cologne mixed with ocean air, the careful distance he was maintaining.

"What're you doing here?" It was a dumb question, but I didn't know how else to fill the silence.

He took a step closer, and I caught the flash of vulnerability in his expression. "You changed your number."

"I needed space." I wrapped my arms around myself. "Time to figure out who I was outside of . . . everything."

His jaw worked. "I saw him drop you off," he said finally, his voice carefully neutral. "Preston. Are you two . . . ?"

"We're just friends."

His shoulders relaxed. "Good. I mean—" He ran a hand through his hair, looking almost embarrassed. "I don't have any right to care, but—"

"You do." I surprised myself with the admission.

Letting out a breath, he asked, "How could you just leave like that?" His voice wavered, and the months of hurt bled through. "A fucking letter, Claire?"

The raw pain in his voice tightened my chest. I had to look away, focusing on the book I'd abandoned on the table, its pages still pristine and waiting. "What was I supposed to do? Stand by while you resented me for making you question every choice you'd built your life on?"

"You didn't even give me a chance to figure it out before fucking disappearing."

"Because I couldn't live with being the reason you left." The words burst out of me, carrying all the guilt and love I'd been holding inside for months. "Your calling—your job—meant the world to you. I couldn't be the person who took that away."

"I'm not a priest anymore."

The words splashed me like cold ocean water. I blinked, trying to process what he'd just said, my mind spinning with the implications. "What?"

"I left." He took another step closer. There was peace in his eyes now, a certainty that hadn't been there before. "Not for you. For me. Because I mistook God's silence for direction and rushed into vows that were never mine to keep. My true calling was still waiting."

"Your true calling?"

"I've been working at the YMCA," he said. "Youth and teen director. It's, well, different. But I feel fulfilled there in a way I never did before."

My breath hitched as I absorbed what he was telling me. The thought of Damian working with kids, using that natural gift he had for reaching people without hiding who he was—it filled me with a fierce kind of pride. Of course it made sense. He wasn't walking away from his calling; he was finally stepping into it.

"That's not all," he said.

I swallowed, my throat dry.

He inhaled deeply before saying, "I love you. I've carried our love through silence, through shame, through every fucked-up decision. It's the only thing that's never wavered. I could live with all the sins I've committed. But I *can't* live without you."

The air between us electrified, heavy with all the emotions that had been bottled up for so long. Tears stung my eyes, and my heart pounded so hard I thought it might break out of my chest. This was all I'd dreamed of hearing. Everything I'd convinced myself I could never have.

"I love you too, Damian." The words slipped out on a trembling breath. They were carved so deep it pained me to say them aloud. "I tried to silence it, bury it beneath vows and obedience, but nothing could touch it. Through the silence, through the distance, through every goodbye . . . I never stopped." My voice faltered, tears spilling hot and unbidden. "Not for a breath. Not for a heartbeat."

Damian closed the distance between us, his hand cupping the side of my face, his thumb brushing my cheek. And before I could even think, his lips were on mine—gentle at first, then deeper, more urgent, like we were making up for all the time we'd lost. I melted into him, my hands finding their way to the back of his neck, pulling him closer.

He pushed me against the wall, the cool surface a stark contrast to the heat of his body. His hands roamed my curves, fingers tracing the dip of my waist, the swell of my hips, drawing out a moan I couldn't hold back. Through his jeans, his hard cock pulsed against my inner thigh, making me ache with need.

That spark ignited low in my belly, a slow burn that spread through my veins like hellfire.

"I missed you," I panted as he trailed kisses down my jawline to the curve of my neck. His breath was hot and ragged against my skin, and his clean woodsy scent filled my nose.

"I missed you too, Sparrow," he rasped, his voice rough, like gravel against silk. The nickname made my heart squeeze and ache all at once, the sound of it sending a jolt of longing through me.

He picked me up as if I weighed nothing, my body sliding against his as he lifted me, and set me on the edge of the kitchen counter. My fingers dug into his shoulders as he popped the button of my jeans and gently pulled the zipper down, the sound of the metal teeth parting impossibly loud in the quiet room. His eyes stayed on me as he slid them off, the denim whispering against my skin.

His fingers glided along the scars on my thighs. "Every part of you is perfect." His emerald eyes darkened with desire, and the muscles in his jaw clenched as he fought for control. "I want to marry you someday," he murmured, the honesty in his words slicing through the haze of lust like a blade.

A giggle escaped me, tinged with disbelief and hope. "Damian Bellucci, are you proposing to me?"

He grinned, leaning closer so our foreheads touched, his breath warm on my lips. "Not yet. Not until I get you a ring."

I shook my head, my fingers threading into his hair, tugging gently. "I don't need one," I said too quickly, the desperation in my voice betraying me. My heart pounded, the sound of it echoing in my ears like a drumbeat.

His eyes bored into mine, his smile softening.

"I don't," I repeated.

He undid his jeans, pushing them to his knees, and stood between my legs, his hands trailing down my thighs. His fingers pushed my underwear aside with deliberate slowness, his touch igniting every nerve ending in my body. His breath hitched as he lined up his cock with the entrance of my already-wet pussy.

"Well, then, will you?" he asked, his voice low and gravelly.

I met his gaze. "Will I what?"

He leaned in, his lips brushing the shell of my ear, sending a shiver down my spine. "Will you marry me, Claire Vergara?"

The raw sincerity in his voice stole the air from my lungs. I cupped his face, my fingers grazing the stubble along his jaw. "Yes," I whispered, the word trembling with all the love I'd buried for him.

His relief was palpable, his grin breaking through the tension in the air as he pushed into me with one hard thrust. My head fell back, a gasp escaping my lips as he filled me completely, each thrust stealing the ground from beneath me. I could feel him everywhere—his hands on my hips, his chest against mine, his breath hot against my neck. The sound of our bodies slapping together was a symphony

of desire, and tension coiled tighter and tighter inside me, like a spring about to snap.

We weren't hiding, weren't holding back. We were raw, vulnerable, and utterly unguarded. This wasn't sacrilege anymore. It was salvation.

All those years of searching for God in silence and ceremony, and here He was in the space between our heartbeats. In the warmth of Damian's hands, in the pure, honest love we'd fought so hard to deny.

This was what faith really meant—not the denial of human connection, but the embrace of it. Not the rejection of love, but the recognition that sometimes, God's greatest gifts came wrapped in the very things people were taught to resist.

Epilogue

DAMIAN

One Year Later

The salty breeze tugged at my jacket as Claire and I approached the old community center. A year of planning, fundraising, and determination had transformed this humble building into everything we'd fought for. Everything we believed in. The freshly painted white exterior bore a simple sign: *The Light House: A Place of Hope and Healing.*

Through the open windows drifted a symphony of life—voices murmuring, papers shuffling, children laughing. Sunlight slanted low, striping the old steps, while the ocean's brine tangled with the rich aroma of coffee seeping from the break room. Sometimes I caught myself marveling at how different this felt from the sterile formality of parish work. Here, faith lived in action, not ceremony.

Claire walked ahead of me, her quiet confidence evident in each step. She paused at the entrance, turning back with that smile that still made my heart skip. Her dark hair caught the breeze, and my breath caught at the sight of her.

The simple gold band on her finger glinted in the sun—a

reminder of the day, six months ago, when we stood on Cliff Overlook, the place where everything had begun. With Jasmine and Rhea at our side and our parents gathered close, we'd said our vows with the ocean spread wide below us. In that moment, I swore I could feel God's presence in the wind, Rico's blessing in the crash of the waves.

She caught me staring and raised an eyebrow. "What're you thinking about?"

"Just grateful," I said, closing the distance between us. "And maybe a little proud. You've got Mrs. Rodriguez's grandson actually excited about reading."

"That's because I bribed him with skateboard lessons." She laughed, that bright sound that had become the soundtrack to my happiness. "Not exactly traditional teaching methods."

I wrapped an arm around her waist, drawing her close. The steady crash of waves filled our comfortable silence. Claire relaxed against me, her warmth anchoring me to this moment—this life we'd built from the ashes of our old calling.

I spotted Preston's car in the parking lot—he'd started volunteering with our teen mentorship program, and his friendship with Claire had grown into something genuine and uncomplicated. It had taken me a while to get used to him being around, but watching him work with the kids, I understood why Claire valued his presence.

"Sometimes I can't believe we get to do this together," she murmured, watching a flock of seagulls wheel overhead.

I pressed a kiss to her temple, breathing in the familiar scent of jasmine shampoo mixed with the salt air. "Me too."

The center's doors burst open as kids spilled out into the courtyard, their laughter echoing off the walls. Among them, I spotted Emma—Preston's niece—chattering excitedly about the art project she'd finished in Claire's after-school program. Laura emerged behind them, tablet in hand and pride in her smile.

"Full house today!" She crossed to us, gesturing at her tablet's screen. "Tutoring sessions maxed out, three new families joining support groups, and the teen art program needs more supplies. Oh, and that reporter from the *Coast Weekly* wants to do a feature on the center."

"I'll order more art supplies tomorrow," I said. "And set up the interview for next week."

She nodded, jotting down notes with the stylus. "Got it."

"We wouldn't have been able to do this without you, Laura. Thank you so much for doing this." I placed a hand on Laura's shoulder and gently squeezed.

She waved off the praise, but I could see how much this work meant to her. After leaving her position as principal to help us launch the center, she'd found a new lease on life. "This place changes lives. You two made that possible. Though I have to say, watching you both find your happiness has been just as rewarding."

Claire had drifted to chat with a volunteer, her hands moving animatedly as she explained the new family counseling protocols we'd implemented. The calm in her voice, the light in her eyes when she spoke of healing grief—this was her calling. Here, rolling up our sleeves to counsel troubled teens or sitting with struggling families, we'd found what true ministry meant: walking alongside people in their darkest moments.

I watched as she knelt down to tie a little girl's shoelaces, the simple gesture filled with the same care she'd once brought to her classes at Saint Anthony's. The difference was that now she could be fully herself.

By the time the shadows reached the far wall, the last family had gone, and Preston had taken his leave. Claire and I stood together in the empty room, the silence folding in close. Through the open windows came the salt-washed air, the surf's rhythm calm as breath —our nightly litany.

"Do you miss it?" I asked, adjusting the framed photo on my desk —our wedding picture, taken as the sun set behind us on the cliff.

She turned to study my face in that careful way she had of reading my moods. "What?"

"The life we had before."

Claire was quiet for a moment, considering. "Parts of it," she admitted. "The ritual, the tradition. The way morning prayers used to make everything feel possible. But not the guilt. Not having to choose."

I nodded. We'd both struggled with the transition. With people who questioned our choices, with former colleagues who saw our departure as betrayal rather than evolution. "We found our way."

She laced her fingers through mine, her wedding ring clicking softly against mine, a sound that still made me smile. "We're still serving," she said. "Just with more . . . authenticity."

Through the window, I could see the last volunteer locking up the community garden we'd started behind the center. Tomorrow, Claire would be here at sunrise, working with the kids to tend the vegetables they'd planted. Next week, we'd have three new support groups starting. The following month, we'd be launching a program for adults reentering society after incarceration.

I pulled her into my arms, her heart beating against my chest, steady and sure. "I love you, Sparrow," I whispered into her hair. "You and everything we've built. Every messy, imperfect, beautiful piece."

"I love you too." She lifted her face to mine, and her eyes held the same wonder I felt every day—that we got to love each other openly, completely, without shame or secrecy. "More than I ever thought possible. More than I thought God would allow."

Somewhere in the distance, the evening bells of Saint Anthony's began to chime, and instead of old longing or regret, only gratitude remained. Our old life had led us here—to this work, to each other, to a faith that was broader and deeper than anything we'd known before.

We'd found our truth not within church walls, but here—in service, in love, and in each other's arms. And maybe that had been God's plan all along.

Sign up for my newsletter to stay informed on upcoming releases!

BONUS CHAPTER

Bonus Chapter

CLAIRE

"Absolutely not." Damian stared at the small device in my hands like I'd just suggested we burn down the Vatican.

"It's for the kids, Dames."

"I'm not doing it. That's a torture device with a USB cord."

I dangled the menstrual cramp simulator between us like a carrot. "The youth group raised three hundred dollars specifically for this challenge. Are you really going to disappoint Madison and her color-coded fundraising spreadsheets?"

His eye twitched. We both knew Madison Douglas's organizational skills were legendary and slightly terrifying.

"Besides," I continued, "it's educational. You'll finally understand what half your parishioners go through."

We were alone in the church hall, surrounded by the aftermath of teenage chaos—overturned chairs, candy wrappers, and a whiteboard covered in Monique Ochoa's aggressive reminder about tonight's video deadline, complete with three exclamation points and a frowny face.

Damian dragged a hand through his hair. "This is ridiculous," he muttered, eyeing the machine the way most people eyed a dentist's chair.

My eyes narrowed. "Scared, Father?"

"I've given last rites in gang territory. I'm not intimidated by a pink gadget."

"It's coral, actually." I held out the electrodes. "Ten levels, fifteen seconds each. Loser cleans the church kitchen for a month."

"That's hardly fair. You've actually—"

"Had cramps?" I grinned. "This thing is like period pain's yoga-practicing little cousin. Trust me, you'll survive."

He stared at me for a long moment, and I could practically hear his internal debate.

"Fine. But when I meet Saint Peter, I'm blaming you entirely."

"Fair enough."

"Now, where do we attach these?" Damian went red reading the manual. "It says lower abdomen. Just above the—" He cleared his throat.

I sighed. "For the love of God, spit it out. We're adults."

"Reproductive area," he finished, looking like he'd rather discuss literally anything else.

"Jesus, Mary, and Joseph." I grabbed the manual with a huff. "It goes above your pelvis."

Twenty minutes later, we sat across from each other, both wired into medical-grade torture equipment, my phone perched and ready to record.

"I look like I'm part of some sci-fi experiment," Damian muttered, giving the electrodes a tug.

"Please. You'd never survive the first ten minutes of a sci-fi experiment."

"Careful, Sparrow. You sound like you're volunteering to run the experiment."

I tilted my head, lips curving slow. "Why? Worried you wouldn't survive what I'd put you through?"

He leaned in, voice rough. "Survive? Hell, I'd beg you not to stop."

I needed to stop this before we passed the point of no return. Ignoring the heat in his voice, I asked, "Are you done? We have work to do." I wiggled my fingers over the control dial like a cartoon villain. "Ready to meet your maker?"

"I already know Him. We have coffee every morning during prayer."

"Well, you're about to get a lot more intimate. Level one, here we go!" I hit record on my phones camera.

The first few levels were basically a gentle massage from a very polite robot.

"This is it?" he asked at level three, looking genuinely offended. "This is why you stuff your face with chocolate?"

"Oh, sweet summer priest. Just wait."

Level four made him blink like he'd walked into a spiderweb. Level five straightened his spine so fast I thought he might salute.

"Still planning to lecture women about pain tolerance?" I asked sweetly as we moved to level six.

The machine pulsed, and Damian made a sound like someone had just told him the Pope was retiring to become a backup dancer.

"What in the name of—" He caught himself. "What the heck is this?"

"Language, Father. We're recording."

Level seven hit, and Damian started doing breathing exercises they taught pregnant women to do during labor. "Sweet Lord," he wheezed. "How do you function like this?"

"Coffee, spite, and the knowledge that complaining makes men deeply uncomfortable." I was definitely feeling it now—that demon trying to redesign my internal organs—but years of practice had taught me to suffer gracefully. "Also, heating pads and pretending chocolate counts as medicine."

"This is actual torture."

"No, torture would be more efficient."

Level eight folded him in half, hands pressed to his stomach like he was trying to keep his organs from staging a prison break.

"Claire," he gasped, "I think my insides are having a revolution."

"Welcome to menstruating, my friend."

"How long does this usually last?"

"Three to seven days. Sometimes longer if you've somehow offended the period gods."

His face went through the five stages of grief in fast-forward before crash-landing on pure horror. "Days? Multiple days?"

"Multiple days. While you're expected to work, smile at people, and not commit any felonies."

"I formally retract every complaint I've ever made."

Level nine arrived like the Four Horsemen of the Apocalypse. Damian made a noise that was part groan, part prayer, part existential crisis.

"I formally apologize," he announced to the ceiling, "to every woman who has ever existed."

"Write that down. I want it notarized."

Level ten clicked on, and Damian crumbled.

"I'm done! For the love of all things holy," he practically shrieked, lunging for the off switch with the desperation of a man trying to stop a nuclear meltdown. "You win! You win everything! The kitchen, my dignity, possibly my soul!"

I let the machine run for another few seconds, partly for the victory and partly because watching a grown man discover the reality of menstruation was oddly therapeutic.

"So," I said, finally switching off the device. "What did we learn today?"

Damian was still hunched over, staring at his hands like they'd just signed a peace treaty with Satan. "I've learned that God has a very dark sense of humor."

"Just wait until you hear about childbirth."

"Please don't. I'm having enough of a religious crisis as it is. I owe every woman in my parish an apology," he mumbled. "And possibly sainthood."

"Just monthly chocolate offerings will suffice."

He finally looked up at me with the thousand-yard stare of someone who'd just discovered everything they thought they knew about the universe was wrong.

"Done. Whatever you want. I'll take out a loan if necessary."

I reached over and turned off the phone, then studied his shell-shocked face. It was endearing seeing him so thoroughly humbled by an electronic device smaller than a smartphone.

"You know," I said, "you're going to be a much better priest after this. Nothing builds empathy faster than having your organs feel like they're being twisted by an angry poltergeist."

"I'm going to rewrite half my sermons about suffering." He sat up straighter, wincing. "And possibly donate my entire salary to women's health research."

I giggled. "Now you're talking."

<u>Fantasy Romance</u>

Half Blood: The Tale of Samara

Of Flesh and Steel

Of Blood and Onyx

Of Wrath and Chaos

<u>Contemporary Romance</u>

Sunshine and Madness

Sweetness and Madness

Passion and Madness

Acknowledgments

This story is a piece of my own journey through the slow unraveling of doctrine, tradition, and the weight of expectations that were never truly mine to carry. Writing it has been part of a long, sometimes painful road to understanding that faith doesn't have to be bound by rigid rules. I've come to believe, deeply and honestly, that you can hold onto your faith in God while living life on your own terms. This story is for anyone who's found themselves in that same space—between devotion and freedom, between belief and becoming.

To my girls; Brittany, Lana, and Kasey, cheers to another one! Thank you for keeping me accountable and for pushing me to be better.

As always, my love and gratitude to my husband, Bobby. You hold me steady through the highs and lows. Thank you for supporting me every step of the way, for being my sounding board, and for always believing in me.

To my family—Mom, Dad, Amber, Alex, Annamarie, Angelica, and Aliyah—you are my heart and my foundation. Your love fills everything I write, and I am endlessly grateful for each of you.

Alyssa is a US Navy veteran with a degree in psychology. She's a multifaceted person who enjoys a variety of activities. When she's not writing or reading, she can be found editing for clients, traveling the United States with her husband and dog, Fiona, or hiking and exploring the outdoors.

www.authoralyssagreen.com/links

www.ingramcontent.com/pod-product-compliance
Lightning Source LLC
Chambersburg PA
CBHW070308310726
48976CB00005B/1624